MEMNON

SCOTT ODEN

Platinum Imprint
Medallion Press, Inc.
Printed in USA

DEDICATION

To SLM: Siren, Muse . . . and friend.

Published 2006 by Medallion Press, Inc.

The MEDALLION PRESS LOGO
is a registered tradmark of Medallion Press, Inc.

Cover Illustration by Adam Mock

Printed in the United States of America

Library of Congress Cataloging-in-Publication Data

Oden, Scott.
Memnon / Scott Oden.
p. cm.
"Platinum imprint."
ISBN 1-932815-39-2 (hard)
1. Greek mercenaries--Fiction. 2. Greece--History--Macedonian Expansion, 359-323 B.C.--Fiction. 3. Macedonia--History--To 168 B.C.--Fiction. 4. Iran--History--Macedonian Conquest, 334-325 B.C.--Fiction. 5. Alexander, the Great, 356-323 B.C.--Fiction. 6. Darius III, King of Persia, d. 330 B.C--Fiction. I. Title.
PS3615.D465M46 2006
813'.6--dc22

2006012343

10 9 8 7 6 5 4 3 2 1
First Edition

ACKNOWLEDGEMENTS:

To reach our dreams, writers of historical fiction must stand on the shoulders of giants — authors of the past and present, scholars, archaeologists, and antiquarians of every stripe. We trail them like eager camp followers, scavenging through the scraps of their genius to give our own work verisimilitude. I've said this before but it bears repeating: without the sweat, blood, and tears of academia, the field of historical fiction would be a barren place.

I would like to thank Dr. Jeanne Reames-Zimmerman, who shared with me her insight on Macedonian culture and politics, and fellow author and philhellene Ruth Kozak, whose travel photos and journals transported me across the landscape of Memnon's world. I owe a debt of gratitude to Dutch scholar Jona Lendering. His vast and reliable database of antiquity, Livius (www.livius.org) has become an indispensable tool for research. I would also like to recognize the members of Alexander the Great's Forum at Pothos (www.pothos.org/forum), who courteously answered some of my most basic questions. Any mistakes found herein are mine, alone.

As always, I am grateful to Helen, Leslie, and the staff at Medallion Press, my agent Rebecca Pratt, and the Usual Suspects: Darren, Sarah, Wayne, Tanja, Kris, Kristie, Josh, Edna, Adam, and Laura.

"The most brilliant exploits often tell us nothing of the virtues or vices of the men who performed them."

—Plutarch

Prologue

The summons delivered to Ariston that damp winter morning was written on the finest vellum, in an elegant hand that suggested a discriminating intellect tempered with the manners only good breeding could engender. Certainly not the handwriting of a mercenary captain or a middling merchant, his two most recent patrons. Nor was the note suggestive of a Hellene; though brief, it had nothing of the brusque tenor so fashionable among the arrogant Macedonians who ruled Ephesus. Ariston read it again:

To Ariston of Lindos, son of Thrasyllus, greetings. May the gods bless you, your household, and your endeavors. My mistress begs an audience with you. Come at your earliest convenience to the estate called The Oaks, *on the slopes of Mount Coressus.*

It bore no signature.

Ariston's imagination raced. The note conjured visions of shaded pools and hidden gardens haunted by a woman, an Ephesian Sappho, who kept lonely vigil as her servants scoured the city for men of distinction, men who could entertain her mind rather than her loins. Ariston fancied himself that sort of man. Though not quite twenty-one, his first work, the epic *Chalkosidae*, found some small favor at the City Dionysia. Obviously, the note's author wished to secure a private reading for his employer.

"It must be good news," said Nicanor, the one-legged Macedonian who owned the food stall on the waterfront where Ariston broke his fast. "You've read it three times now."

Ariston looked up and grinned at the old soldier. "The poet says to call no man happy till he is dead. I'm slain by this note, Nicanor, murdered by the promise of patronage." Indeed, an offer of sponsorship could not have come at a more opportune time. His last *obol* had gone to Nicanor for his meager breakfast: a heel of day-old bread slathered with lentil paste and a cup of bitter wine. Without a patron, his next meal would be at the grace of god. "What's the best way to reach the estates on Mount Coressus?"

Rain pattered on the food stall's awning. Nicanor arched an eyebrow. "Coressus, eh? In this weather? You're a braver man than I. Head inland toward the Magnesian Gate. Once you reach the agora, take the Street of the Charites across the valley floor. That'll get you to the mountain's foot easy enough."

"My thanks, Nicanor," Ariston said, dribbling the last of his wine on the ground. "For Apollo and the Muses." He gathered his belongings—reed pens, clay flasks of ink, and scraps of papyrus and parchment, all of it wrapped in an oft-mended *chiton* and stuffed into a sailor's oilcloth bag—and stepped into the street, pulling his cloak tight against the weather.

The persistent rain washed the gutters of Ephesus clean, sluicing the dust and debris accumulated over the long autumn months into the sea. The smells of moist earth, brine, and baking bread filled Ariston's nostrils as he set off, following Nicanor's directions. From the waterfront, the street twisted along the foot of Mount Pion, a serpentine avenue rutted by the tread of countless feet, hooves, and wheels. It wound past the *gymnasion*, where a delegation of Spartans trained naked in spite of the rain. Ariston watched them for a moment, envious of their battle-hardened musculature, and continued past the theater. Colorful wooden broadsides announced the arrival of a troupe from Attica who had gained renown performing the tragedies of Euripides and Aeschylus.

Shivering, Ariston reached the agora and took advantage of the shelter offered by the columned stoa. Knots of men gathered around the communal braziers, listening as a ship captain from Piraeus spoke from atop a makeshift rostrum. Spontaneous applause erupted as he concluded his speech. Ariston turned to the man closest him, a man of means if his robes of cream-colored Milesian wool were any indication.

"What goes?" Ariston asked.

The fellow eyed him, noting his bedraggled appearance, his dripping bag. His lips curled in a moue of distaste as he returned his attention to the envoy. "He bears news from Athens. Demetrios has freed that great city from Kassandros's vile grasp." The man moved away, adding his voice to those who peppered the captain with questions.

Ariston stepped into the now-vacant spot near the brazier and warmed his hands. While ostensibly good news, the liberation of Athens meant four years of peace among the *Diadochi* had ended. Those men, the successors of Alexander, fought to reunite his empire under their own auspices. In the division of spoils, Antigonos, a canny old fox and the father of Athens's current savior, received Asia and Syria—including Ephesus; Ptolemy, said to be Alexander's bastard half-brother, contented himself with Egypt. Alexander's bodyguards, Lysimachus and Seleukos, received Thrace and Babylonia, respectively, while Macedonia and Greece fell into the brutal hands of Kassandros, son of Antipatros. Freed of the burden of peace, the *Diadochi* could marshal their armies once more. Kassandros would doubtless try and retake Athens, while Ptolemy longed to make himself master of Syria and the Aegean. Come the spring, Greek blood would flow like thawed snow.

Ariston listened to the rhetoric of war for close to an hour before restlessness got the better of him. His errand beckoned, a Siren calling out to him from the slopes of the mountain. Ariston quit the agora for the Street of the Charites and crossed the valley floor, using porticoes and trees as shelter until he reached the foot of cloud-wreathed Mount Coressus. There, he ascended a cobbled footpath full of switchbacks and curving steps. Wind and rain cut through his sodden clothing like shears through fleece. He paused once, glancing over his shoulder.

Mount Coressus lay south and east of the waterfront, its rocky summit overlooking the temples and public buildings of the city's center. On a clear day, Ariston could have seen past the tradesmen's shops on smaller Mount Pion, beyond the golden facade of the great temple of Artemis, to the banks of the river Cayster. Today, he could barely see back to the agora. Teeth chattering, Ariston clutched his cloak's edges tight. On the slopes above, amid groves of fragrant cedar and black pine, the affluent citizens of Ephesus—Greek, Macedonian, and Persian—made their homes. Their estates bore evocative names, such as *Hound's Run* or *Pride of Leonidas* or *Blessed of Mithras,* displayed above the gates or on plaques woven into the hedgerows. A few had armed men guarding their entryways. These last looked at Ariston like so much offal left at their master's door.

"*The Oaks*?" he called each time he passed a brace of sullen-faced guards, miserable in their cold bronze breastplates and damp cloaks. "Do you know it?" Each gave the same answer: a jab of the thumb, a gesture, directing him off down the road. Soon, the cobblestones gave way to mud, and the guards gave way to equally dour servants. The responses, though, never varied. Keep going. It's just ahead. Finally, Ariston spotted the denuded boughs of the trees that gave *The Oaks* its name. He quickened his pace, fairly trotting up the road; his heart pounded as his excitement reached its apex . . .

. . . then plummeted, like Icarus from the heavens on wings of melted wax.

Ariston's steps faltered. Even to his unfamiliar eye the estate looked uninhabited, its stone and wood in the early stages of decay. The gate stood askew on its hinges, the hedgerow bounding the property overgrown with every manner of weed and bramble. A boggy path, lined with oaks as tall and straight as a squad of hoplites, ran from the gate to the villa's sagging portico. The young scholar's cheeks burned with equal parts embarrassment and anger as his hopes for reputable patronage dissipated like smoke. This would be the same as the others—a few *drachmas* for a couple of lines, an epitaph for the family patriarch perhaps. He could live another week on his earnings, more if he practiced Spartan economy.

With a sigh, Ariston walked up the path between the oaks, careful of the mud. He mounted the portico and paused before the weather-scarred door. Inside, he could hear the soft strains of a flute playing an unfamiliar tune. He listened for a moment before knocking. Instantly, the fluting stopped. Ariston knocked again, harder.

Wood scraped wood as an unseen hand drew back the bolt; hinges creaked as the door inched open, revealing a dark and careworn face. Eyes the color of mahogany, moist and filmed with cataracts, peered out and looked Ariston up and down. "May I help you?" the old man said, speaking impeccable Greek, though heavy with the fluid accent of Egypt.

Ariston bowed slightly. "I was told the mistress of the house seeks an audience with me."

The fellow's demeanor changed. He eased the door open and stepped out. "Ah, then you would be Ariston of Lindos, on the island of Rhodes?"

Tension drained from Ariston's shoulders, replaced by pride. *At least they know my name.* "The same. You have me at a disadvantage, sir, for I know not who you are."

"I am of no importance," the old man said. "A mere servant. Truly, though, I had not expected to see you today, with the weather as it is. My mistress will be pleased."

"Who is your mistress?"

The old man averted his eyes. "If it pleases you, come, and I will show you to a place where you can dry yourself and take a bit of warm wine."

Ariston, his curiosity piqued, allowed himself to be ushered into the vestibule. Whatever mystery might surround his new patroness did not extend to her villa. Its dismal interior fit hand-in-glove with the exterior. A pebble mosaic underfoot, depicting Herakles slaying the Nemean Lion, showed gaps where stones had broken in the past and never repaired. Patches of mildew mushroomed along the baseboards, doubtless fueled by the humidity of the past summer. Murals decorated the walls, scenes of the hunt, of the hearth, of gods and goddesses frolicking amid the glory of nature, all of it dulled by a patina of grime. At every hand, Ariston saw the telltale signs of fading opulence. It reminded him of those oak trees lining the path, their limbs flensed to reveal skeletal wood beneath.

"If it's all the same," Ariston said, "I'd prefer to be taken to your mistress now."

The Egyptian nodded. "As you wish."

Ariston followed the servant down a darkened hallway and out into the peristyle, its columns pitted from exposure to the elements. Here, aromatic herbs grew in the shade of an evergreen olive tree, its trunk as gnarled and bent as that of the old man. They entered another corridor, this one lit by a narrow window at its end. The old Egyptian stopped at a door, its cedar planks bound in bronze. He knocked lightly, and then opened it to reveal a woman's bedchamber.

Unlike the rest of the villa, this suite of rooms had an aura of cleanliness, of elaborate maintenance. An artist's brush had touched up the wall mural, this one an Arcadian glen where the Muses performed for their father, Zeus; thick rugs and colorful carpets from the heart of Persia strewed the floor. A fire crackled in the hearth. The smell of wood smoke mingled with that of incense. A breeze from the open window ruffled the sheer linen panels circling the bed. The old Egyptian tsked as he shuffled over and drew the shutter closed.

"Mistress, you'll catch a chill."

"I wanted to smell the ocean, Harmouthes." The woman in bed coughed, struggling for breath. "One last time."

"You will have many more opportunities for such pleasures, mistress. For now, though, I've brought you a guest. The young scholar about whom I told you."

She craned her neck, peering at Ariston with eyes darker than a moonless night. "Bring him closer."

Before the old man, Harmouthes, could say anything, Ariston stepped to the edge of the bed and bowed. The gesture brought a wan smile to the woman's lips. Ariston reckoned she had been sick for some time, long enough that he could not fathom her age, though in the flush of health she must have been an incomparable beauty: olive-skinned with lustrous black hair and the delicate features of Persian nobility. Still, her illness-ravaged body bore a measure of its old fire, though muted, as if seen through Death's gossamer veil.

"Your eyes speak too clearly," she said, her flawless Greek tinged with a light Persian accent.

"Pardon?" Ariston blinked, taken aback.

"You're thinking how cruel are the Fates for making the only offer of patronage you've had this winter come from the shriveled breast of a dying woman. You're thinking of how best to preserve your reputation." She glanced at Harmouthes. "Leave us, my old friend."

Harmouthes bowed and left the room.

"Harmouthes swears by your skill," she said, after the door snicked shut. "He attended the City Dionysia and claims he has not seen your equal since Xenophon put ink to paper. Unstinting praise especially from an Egyptian, whose people invented the scholar's art."

Ariston inclined his head. "I am flattered, truly. You seem well informed about my current plight, yet I know nothing of you, or of why I am here. The note your man sent was cryptic, and I had half a mind to dismiss it as a jest."

"But you didn't," she said.

Ariston gave a thin smile. "No, Lady. I didn't. Poverty has a way of making even the noblest man desperate. And, to be honest, the mystery of it appealed to me. Though even mystery wears thin when taken to extremes."

"Fair enough. As for my name, you may call me . . ." She paused, lost in thought. "Melpomene."

Ariston's eyebrows inched upwards. "You are bold, Lady, to call yourself by the name of a Greek goddess when you are obviously Persian. Very well, then. What would you have of me? I have brought my latest work, should you desire to hear it for yourself."

"*Chalkosidae.* No, master Ariston. That is not why I have summoned you. I wish to commission a work, a life recorded for all time."

Ariston said nothing for a long moment, his lips pursed and brow furrowed. "Forgive me, Lady, but my art is not like that of the painter or the sculptor. When I write the subject must move me in some way. It must inspire me to seek the favor of the Muses. I wrote of Phanes of Halicarnassus because his genius, his passion, stirred the feeling in my breast. I sought only to understand him, not to immortalize him. It will be the same for the next man whose life I chronicle."

Melpomene nodded. "Will you listen as I tell you of a man I once knew? Then perhaps the Muses will exert their influence and compel you to record the story of his life for generations to come. If it's a question of payment, do not fret. Despite my surroundings, money is something for which I do not want."

"And if I should deem your subject unworthy of my skill?" Seeing he had touched a nerve, Ariston held up his hand to stave off her outburst. "Do not take offense, Lady. I have studied the character and deeds of some of the finest men of our time. Men who stood shoulder to shoulder with divine Alexander. Perhaps this knowledge has jaded me in some way, blinded me to the plight of lesser men."

The woman's eyes narrowed. "You are a fool, Ariston of Lindos, if you think the men who squabble over Alexander's leavings are fine," she said, her voice hard. "The Lion has died, and his followers fight over the corpse of his empire like dogs! Antigonos? Bah! That *kyklopes* thinks more with his groin than with his head! His bastard, Demetrios, is worse. And Kassandros! Were I a man, I would flay the skin from his body and bathe him in the Asphalt Sea!" She spoke of these men with a familiarity and a rage that gave Ariston pause. "The man I would speak of possessed more grace and nobility in his tiniest finger than all of Alexander's companions combined! Even more than . . . than . . . !" Melpomene coughed, her face purpling as she strangled on the very air that gave her life. She sank back on her pillow.

"Peace, Lady. Peace. Should I fetch your man?" Ariston glanced at the door, concern etched on his brow.

The woman calling herself Melpomene shook her head. She gestured to a sideboard, to a small chest of silver inlaid with mother-of-pearl. Ariston frowned as he picked it up and brought it to her side.

"G-Give it to me," she said, her voice a croaking whisper.

Melpomene's hands trembled as she accepted the chest from Ariston, tracing its curves, caressing its surface with her fingertips. Its proximity acted as a balm; the touch of metal on flesh soothed her breathing.

Ariston looked at her, feeling pangs of pity in his breast. Surely he could spare her a few hours? "Who is this man you would speak of?"

Melpomene closed her eyes and sighed. "He was a countryman of yours, a man whose equal I have not seen since the gods saw fit to take him from me. His name was Memnon, son of Timocrates; his enemies knew him as Memnon of Rhodes."

Ariston nodded. "I've heard the name. He fought with the Persians against Alexander. A mercenary, though some might go so far as to name him a traitor."

"Too often do the victors sully their opponent's name with lies, and those of us who know the truth and say nothing are accomplices in our silence. Well, no more," she said, motioning for him to bring a chair close. "You can't remember the Social War, can you, Ariston? No, of course you can't. You're too young. Doubtless your father or grandfathers were among those who voted for Rhodes to leave the shelter of Athenian hegemony, along with Cos and Chios, all three islands praying that the gods would grant them an empire of their own. Yet, as with all things, Time has given the years of the Social War a gloss, a gleam of patriotism you Rhodians find more palatable than the truth. Your peers have forgotten the infighting between factions that nearly tore their island apart. They've forgotten the famine arising from Athenian piracy that drove their uncles and brothers to forsake their homes and seek their fortunes among the city-states of Ionia. They've forgotten the diaspora of your people so they could tell themselves they stood up to tyranny. Memnon did not forget. He came of age in this world . . ."

Rhodes

Year 4 of the 105th Olympiad

(357 BCE)

"MEMNON!"

The man who bellowed the name looked out of place on the docks of Rhodes-town, as awkward as a sailor would be in the lecture halls of the Academy at Athens. Despite the heat he wore a pleated *himation* of faded blue cloth, pinned at the shoulder with a copper brooch fashioned in the likeness of an owl. His balding head glistened in the sun. The man paused in the shade of a statue of Helios, its surface crusted with gull droppings, and mopped at his brow with the hem of his robe.

"Memnon!" he cried again, waving.

Memnon, son of Timocrates, turned at the sound of his name, the sheaf of javelins balanced on his shoulders and ready to hand to another of *Circe*'s crew. Eyes the color of a storm-wracked sea glittered beneath a mane of curly black hair kept in check by a leather headband. "By the Dog!" he muttered. "Will he never let me go?"

At the railing above, Patron, a Phocaean from the coast of Ionia and captain of *Circe*, scowled. Ten years Memnon's senior, he carried himself with the gravity of a Spartan elder. "Who seeks you this time?"

"Glaucus, my father's secretary. No doubt Timocrates intends to fetch me back to his side." At nineteen, Memnon did not give the impression of a rawboned youth; he had the muscular shoulders and flat abdomen of an Olympian athlete, a man on the cusp of his physical prime. The gods of Sun and Wind left his skin burnished and tough like old leather worn from use. Around him moved a handful of young Greeks, self-styled adventurers, modern day Argonauts—men forever linked by the poetic bond of shared hardship. They were the crew of *Circe*, the aging *pentekonter* that would deliver them to Assos, on the Asian shore, and into the arms of Glory.

"He's still furious, I take it," Patron said.

"Father? When is he not furious?"

"Have you not mended the rift between you?"

Memnon shook his head. "Far from it. It's his opinion that we're betraying Rhodes, abandoning her in her hour of need by running off to Assos and joining Mentor's army. He says we should be soldiers of *demokratia*, not mercenaries in a satrap's war. Great Helios! I feared for my health when I let it slip that I thought Rhodian democracy a dying beast, caught as it is between the spears of Athens and the swords of Caria. If ever you wish to sample true rage, mention that around father."

Patron looked askance at Memnon and shook his head.

"What?"

"I think it wasn't such a slip of the tongue as you let on," Patron said. "If Mentor were here, he'd cuff your ears for goading your father as you do. I've half a mind to do it in his stead."

Memnon grinned. "Allow me what small pleasures I have left, Patron. Father has tightened his leash about my neck as though I were an errant hound. His spies dog my every step; every morsel of food that passes my lips, every cup of wine, is reported to him. Even Thalia—dear, vivacious Thalia—has been pressed into service by his minion, there." The young Rhodian indicated his father's secretary with a jerk of his head. "Zeus Savior! I can't relieve myself in the bushes without feeling a dozen eyes on me! You ask me, it's high time my father realizes I am my own man!"

Patron glanced down, his narrow countenance severe. "It must have been Timocrates who had the harbor master look into my doings. Old Herodas wanted to know when I planned to sail, and if I hoped to return. I thought it an odd question, but now . . ." Patron trailed off.

"Forgive my father for his meddling, Patron. It's not personal."

"You think it's not? In truth, Memnon, you're a smart lad, and handy with a tiller, but I'll not go against Timocrates. He's a powerful man, not the sort I'd like to trifle with. If he has other plans for you I'll not be the one to thwart them. Settle this business with him and get his blessing before we sail or *Circe* will sail without you. Understand?"

Memnon's jaw clenched. He nodded as Glaucus bustled up, the secretary's round face the color of a ripe pomegranate.

"Rejoice, son of Timocrates! Thalia said I might find you here."

"You're a long way from your familiar haunts, Glaucus," Memnon snapped. "Has father sent you to spy on *Circe*'s crew? Or will you join us and seek your fortunes among the Persians?"

"Neither, thank the gods. Timocrates asked that I escort you to the Assembly. He's denouncing the oligarchs today; afterward, he craves a word with you."

Memnon looked up at *Circe*'s master and made a show of deferring to his judgment.

"We can spare you," Patron said. The look on his face did not invite debate. "Attend to your father. Remember what I've said. With or without you."

JOSTLING BODIES THRONGED THE NARROW STREETS OF RHODES: PORTERS bearing baskets and bales to the marketplace; slaves on errands only they and their masters knew; the travelers disembarking from foreign ships were outnumbered by natives seeking passage to far ports of call. An air of desperation clung to the people of Rhodes, a perfume of fear and uncertainty. Memnon knew its cause.

Rhodes stood on the brink. Democrat fought oligarch in the Assembly, an inflammatory war of words that trickled down to real violence on the streets. Memnon had heard stories of whole families slain for speaking out against tyranny, of oligarchs knifed in their sleep, and of innocents abstaining from either side burned out of house and hearth. And his father, noble Timocrates, orator, statesman, a Rhodian Pericles in an age of gilded tyrants, only added to the discord with his pro-Athenian rhetoric.

Glaucus cleared his throat. "What did that fellow mean, 'with or without you'?"

"Stay out of my business, Glaucus," Memnon barked over his shoulder. "You're my father's secretary, not mine. Nor do I count you as a friend. It's bad enough you've charmed Thalia into divulging my dealings . . ."

"A lovely girl, Thalia. You are lucky to have her."

Memnon lengthened his stride, forcing Glaucus into a half-run just to keep up. The secretary huffed and puffed, blowing like a winded horse as they ascended a steep, cobbled road lined with columns, each bearing the names of men lost to Poseidon.

"Have I offended you?"

"You presume too much," Memnon said.

Glaucus shrugged. "I only seek to understand you, young sir. It's all Timocrates desires, as well."

Memnon stopped and rounded on the secretary. "How could either of you understand? Zeus! You're both cut from the same cloth! Bureaucrats to the marrow who have dreamed of nothing else since the womb! How could you understand the attraction of distant shores when all you desire can be found in the soil of Rhodes?"

"Now who is presumptuous?" Glaucus said. "All young men would rather pursue the path of Achilles, the path of glory and immortality. I was no different. But if every man could be Achilles, then the mystique of the son of Peleus would lessen, would it not? Warriors are noble and enviable, but they haven't the sole claim to Glory's rewards. A secretary can carry himself with as much nobility; an orator is no less enviable. The only difference being poets don't compose odes to secretaries and orators."

"I'm not a glory-hound, Glaucus. It's just . . ." Memnon trailed off. He walked to the road's edge and stood between two of the columns. At this height, Rhodes-town seemed small and of little consequence against the vast sea of blue. From the mole-protected Great Harbor, with its crowd of ships, Rhodes crawled up the hillside in steps, like seats in an amphitheater. Whitewashed walls and red-tiled roofs stood cheek-by-jowl with crude timber sheds and old thatch. Up the hillside, on a three-hundred-foot spur of rock, towered the acropolis. The High City. Terraced and unfortified, its temples and public buildings were shaded by groves of sacred olive, knotty sycamores, and dusty green poplars. Red-tinted limestone winked in the noonday sun.

Despite its beauty, Memnon saw in that city of rose-red stone the outlines of a prison, a place where his youth would be snuffed out by endless hours of discourse, where his dreams would wither and rot like fruit left overlong on the vine. "Can you truly see me up there," he gestured to the acropolis, "standing atop the plinth in the Assembly declaiming the ills of society?"

"If that's what the Fates decree, then yes."

Memnon sighed. "If the Three Sisters themselves came to father and told him my destiny lay elsewhere, he would dispute them. I want to join Mentor at Assos, to serve Artabazus in his rebellion against the Great King. What is so distasteful about that? Artabazus is a good man; I've heard father say as much. Good enough to marry my sister, Deidamia. Am I any better than my sister? Than Mentor? Zeus Savior! I cannot understand why . . ."

Glaucus gave a start; in a brief moment of clarity, he glimpsed the inner paths of Memnon's heart. "Truly, you cannot see it, can you? I had thought you were only playing a game with Timocrates, keeping him at loggerheads to satisfy some childish whim, but you honestly have no idea what his motives are."

Memnon frowned. "And you do?"

"Listen to me, young sir. For once, pay heed to my words. It is on *you* that Timocrates has pinned his hopes."

"On me? But, Mentor is the eldest, he—"

Glaucus silenced Memnon was a terse gesture. "Yes, yes! Eldest though he may be, Mentor cuts a rough figure in your father's eye. Timocrates praises his competence as a soldier, while mourning the realization that his eldest son will never amount to anything more than a mercenary in Persia's service. And Deidamia, the very image of her mother, is lusty, loyal, and as fertile as Ephesian Artemis. But she, too, will never rise above her station. It is you he would groom to carry on his legacy. He sees in you another Socrates, another Pericles, another Alcibiades, if only you'd come to your senses and forget these foolish dreams of yours."

"I am not so remarkable," Memnon said, as he felt the invisible noose about his neck tightening.

"I would agree, but I am not Timocrates," Glaucus said. "Come. We are lagging. Your father will be mounting the plinth any moment now."

THE ASSEMBLY MET IN THE SHADOW OF THE TEMPLE OF ATHENA POLIAS, Athena of the City, in hopes that the wisdom of the goddess would guide their dealings. Constructed of the same rose-colored limestone as Athena's shrine, the circular Assembly building boasted a sunken floor and marble seats that rose in tiers around the plinth, a platform of polished stone from whence orators spoke. Instead of walls, Doric columns supported a tiled roof that kept the sun off while allowing the cooling sea breezes to flow unimpeded. Memnon turned and glanced north, shading his eyes. From here, he could see the vibrant blue waters of the Gulf of Marmaris and, beyond, a line of purple hills demarcating the frontiers of Caria and Lycia.

"I should have sent word for Bion to reserve us a place," Glaucus said, glaring at the press of men before him. Latecomers, full citizens of every station leavened with a smattering of curious non-citizens and foreigners, circled the Assembly building, each jockeying for a better position where they could hear the man speaking inside.

Memnon scanned the crowd and did a quick tally in his head. Three thousand citizens had to attend the Assembly in order to pass laws. Easily, Memnon counted a quorum. "Is there to be voting today?"

Glaucus shook his head. "Only debate. They'll put it to a vote next week." The secretary clutched at his cloak and elbowed his way through with cries of "Pardon" and "Make way." Memnon followed, slower, shuffling like a man bound for the gallows. They inched down the stairs of the entryway and found a place to stand beneath a statue of Dorieus, the farseeing statesman of Lindos whose dream of a united Rhodes brought the city into being.

Dusty sunlight slashed through the artificial gloom, falling like divine light on the man atop the plinth. Timocrates of Rhodes stood tall and loose, his gestures exaggerated as though he performed his speech at the theater. A slender line divided the two, actors from orators: where one played to the audience for the sake of entertainment, the other played for higher stakes, for the fate of nations. Today, with his fringe of silver hair and close-cropped beard, with his flowing white robe modestly bordered in Tyrian purple, Timocrates could have outplayed even silver-tongued Hermes. Memnon gave an ear to his speech.

"The oligarchs rule Chios and Cos now, and they threaten Rhodes; they are seducing you into what amounts to slavery. Slavery! It surprises me that none of you have conceived of the danger to our constitution, to our freedom, posed by these braggarts, these men who would suborn your ancestors sacrifice and bring their lives to naught. I urge you to regard them as the common enemies of all who love freedom.

"But indeed, it is not difficult to find fault with these demagogues or reproach the rest of you for your ambivalence, but our real task is to find by what arguments and by what course of action may our democracy be salvaged. Perhaps it does not suit the present occasion to deal with every facet of the question, but mine own view is that we ought to grapple with these problems vigorously, and act as becomes Rhodians. Remember, brothers, how it gladdens your hearts to hear a stranger praising your ancestors, describing their exploits and enumerating their trophies. Reflect, then, that your ancestors set up those trophies, not that you may gaze at them in wonder, but that you may also imitate the virtues of those men who earned them."

And with a small bow, Timocrates concluded his oration. A heartbeat later raucous applause echoed through the Assembly. The delegates from Ialysos and Kamiros clambered to their feet, jostling to be the first to acclaim the orator. The men from Lindos nodded their heads and stroked their beards in graceful approval. Only the oligarchs, the followers of Philolaus, abstained. These glowered at Timocrates with undisguised contempt as he stepped down from the plinth.

Beside him, Memnon could feel Glaucus vibrating with excitement. "Brilliant! Without a doubt, his most persuasive speech!"

"You heard but a fragment and you can judge it thus?" Memnon said. "You're more discerning than I, Glaucus."

"I had the opportunity to listen as he drafted it, as could you if only you spent less time carousing."

Memnon ignored him. Timocrates noticed them and threaded toward where they stood, his face an expressionless mask. Memnon saw movement from the corner of his eye, a swirl of blue cloth and flash of gold. He half-turned as a man thrust his way between him and his father. Short and barrel-chested with a swarthy face accentuated by his Persian-style beard, this newcomer smiled at Timocrates. Memnon could sense no warmth in the gesture. Beside him, Glaucus stiffened.

"Philolaus," he hissed.

This newcomer bowed low before Timocrates, a gesture full of scorn. "You've scored a small victory for your precious democrats, today," he said. "But all you've really done is bandage a dying beast. Your allies are hemorrhaging daily, their strength and the strength of your cause ebbing. How long will it last, Timocrates? How long will democracy be in its death throes?"

"You make assumptions without merit, slave of Mausolus. What you really should ask yourself is how long can the Carians play at empire before their master, the Great King, checks their ambitions? A month? A year? Your master cannot dabble long in the affairs of the Hellenes before the Great King makes an end of him."

"He needs to make an example of your son-in-law Artabazus first," Philolaus said, grinning. "And your eldest, I'm told. By the Hound, Timocrates! For a staunch, Athenian-loving democrat, you've had excellent relations with tyrants of all stripes. Why, you yourself once served old satrap Pharnabazus in his war against the Spartans, even as your son serves his, now! By what right do you condemn tyranny when it's part and parcel of your own kin? Are you a leaf blowing on whatever political wind is fashionable these days?"

Timocrates only smiled, saying, "It's one thing to serve tyrants and oligarchs when it's expedient; it's another thing to live under their thumb. Rhodes is free, and should remain thus. If Mausolus of Caria hungers for more let him take it from the Great King's plate, if he dares."

All around them, democrats and oligarchs began snarling at one another, hurling shouts and curses, and emulating the leaders of their respective movements. The chairman of this Assembly, old Diogenes, rapped his staff on the floor and cried, "Come to order! Who wishes now to speak?"

"Philolaus!" someone called. Shouts of "Aye! Let Philolaus speak!"

warred with the voices of those who wanted his blood. Philolaus acknowledged them with a wave and leaned close to Timocrates.

"We will continue our discourse later. For now, the body politic needs true guidance." With a sinister wink, Philolaus brushed past Timocrates and ascended the plinth. He held up his arms, exhorting the crowd to silence. "Men! Rhodians! Your duty, when debating such weighty matters, is to allow freedom of speech to every one of your counselors, be they fair or foul. Personally, I never thought it a difficult task to point out to you the best policy, since you all seem to me to have discerned it already. No, the difficulty lay in inducing you to put it into operation; for when you have approved and passed a resolution, it is no nearer accomplishment than before you approved it!"

Timocrates turned away, motioning for his son to follow.

"Do you not wish to hear him out?" Memnon said.

"He speaks nothing new."

Memnon nodded and followed his father out into the sunlight.

Down the slope from the Assembly a grove of olive trees afforded shade and solitude to those who wearied of political theatrics. Here, servants of Athena's temple maintained a sliver of paradise, a magnet for poets and lovers seeking the embrace of their particular muses. Wide gravel paths meandered under the boughs. Other, smaller trails branched off, leading to leafy grottoes that offered privacy from prying eyes; bordering the path, the generosity of grateful suppliants provided for a handful of stone benches carved with prayers of thanks to the Goddess. Timocrates sat on one of these and motioned for Memnon to join him. Farther down, at a bend in the trail, a young orator practiced his gestures to an audience of trees.

"You're looking well, son," Timocrates said. "Living with a common prostitute seems to agree with you."

Memnon checked his anger. "Thalia's many things, but common she's not, as I'm sure your sycophant, Glaucus, has told you." He nodded back toward the Assembly. The secretary had lingered there, listening to Philolaus. "If you've only sent for me so you can insult my friends, I'll take my leave."

"No, I sent for you because I have good news," Timocrates said. "My guest-friend, Androtion, has agreed to sponsor you in the Academy at Athens. You will travel back with him, once he has concluded his embassy to the Carians."

Memnon blinked. "Athens? The Academy?"

"A happy compromise, don't you think? It answers your need to see the world while addressing my concerns for your future. I cannot claim the idea as mine, of course. It was Androtion who—"

"No, father." Memnon said, his tone one of a man who wearied of explaining himself over and again. "Thank Androtion for his hospitality, but tell him I cannot accept."

The older man's face went livid. "What? What do you mean you cannot?" His voice carried down the path; the young orator turned in mid-exclamation, frowning.

"*Circe* leaves at week's end. I mean to be on her."

"Why are you so intractable?" Timocrates said, lurching to his feet. "I have arranged an opportunity that would make you the envy of most men, and yet you throw it back in my face!"

"Because it's not what I want! Yes, I want to see something of the world before I settle down, before I take a wife and raise sons of my own. Yes, I want to see the glory of Athens. But all of this I will do on my own terms, not yours! I appreciate all you've offered, but you withhold the one thing I ask of you. Your blessing. It costs nothing; requires nothing of you save a smile and a kind word, yet you refuse. Why?"

Timocrates shook his head. "I'll not bless you as you depart down a road

I know leads to nothing but ruin and death!"

"How do you know this?" Memnon said, frustration driving his voice up an octave. "How? Have the gods suddenly gifted you with the vision?"

Timocrates leaned against the bole of a tree. "All my life I've seen it, Memnon. The same tragedy played out on a thousand different stages. You will go off to war full of tales of glory and return a broken man, or you'll not return at all. 'With your shield or on it' is a fine sentiment for poets and demagogues, but it means nothing in the real world."

Memnon said nothing for a long while, his head bowed in thought. Finally, he looked up. "You admire men such as Alcibiades, Pericles, Socrates? They are great men in your esteem, aren't they? Peerless politicians and statesmen?"

"Yes, and you could be their equal, if only you'd listen to me!"

Memnon stood and caught Timocrates by the shoulders. He wanted to shake him. "These men, father, were all soldiers first! They knew the value of blood spilled in the cause of glory; they knew the horrors of war, which made them, in later life, never enter into it lightly. I cannot hope to rise to be their equal by sitting at the feet of dried out demagogues. I must strike out on my own, see the world for myself and decide my own fate. Surely you understand?"

Timocrates sighed, his resistance crumbling. "I forget sometimes that you are a child no longer. Perhaps my blessing . . ." he trailed off. The sound of sandals crunching on gravel brought a frown to the older man's face. Memnon followed his gaze and saw Glaucus running full out down the path toward them. He skidded, nearly falling.

"Peace, Glaucus. What goes?" Timocrates said.

The secretary, his racking breath flecked with spittle and sweat, pointed back to the Assembly building. "Come quickly! It's Philolaus! He's trying to force a vote!"

"Is it not the hallmark of a democracy to allow the people to decide their own fate?" Philolaus stood atop the plinth, surrounded by a sea of upturned faces. Their voices threatened to drown him out. He gestured to the impassioned crowd. "To deny the people their right to vote, when a quorum is present, is tantamount to dismissing the basic premise of your beloved democracy!"

Diogenes, perched on the highest riser in order to be seen, thrust his staff at Philolaus. "I will not allow you to mock our greatest institution! There are rituals to observe before a vote can be taken! Traditions to follow! We—"

"Ritual and tradition? Fear and sloth, more like! Are you too afraid, Diogenes, or are you simply too lazy to fulfill your obligations to the people?"

"He is neither!" Timocrates thrust his way through the Assembly, Memnon and Glaucus in his wake, and took the plinth beside Philolaus. "Diogenes is wise. He's forgotten more about the inner workings of democracy than you or I will ever know! The law is plain, Philolaus! The Council can vote upon no measure or decree without prior deliberation! To suggest otherwise is to risk exile, or worse!"

Diogenes nodded, vindicated, but Philolaus only laughed.

"This is why it takes the word of Zeus Savior himself to accomplish anything in a democracy! A council of old men fattened on spoils stolen from the people decides what can and cannot be discussed? Tell me, how is that any different from an oligarchy? Drop this pretense of freedom and admit . . ."

Memnon felt the crowd's agitation; he felt the heat, the pressure of their anger. He glanced up at his father. Timocrates and Philolaus stood toe to toe, so caught up in their own feud that they were oblivious to the effect their words had on their followers. Like oxen with blinders, they plowed on, shouting each other down, debating esoteric points of law at the tops of their lungs. Beneath the plinth, scuffles broke out. Men shoved one another, cursed, spat, and struggled like leashed dogs.

"Can they not see what they're doing?" Memnon said, clutching Glaucus's arm. "We've got to separate them before they cause a riot!" Glaucus, though, could only stare, his eyes wide, his fist upraised in defiance of tyranny. Memnon released him, turned . . .

Something whistled past his ear. A rock, smaller than a child's fist, missed Timocrates by a fingerbreadth and struck Philolaus above his right eye. The oligarch reeled, clutching at his forehead.

"No!" Memnon yelled. But, at the sight of the oligarch's blood, the simmering crowd boiled over in a frenzy of rage. All semblance of order fled as men turned on one another, punching, biting, and kicking in an effort to voice with violence what they could not with words. Only the ancient prohibition against weapons at an Assembly kept this from becoming a bloodbath. Memnon watched as partisans of each faction rushed the plinth; both orators vanished under a riptide of grasping hands.

"Father!" Memnon surged forward, riding the crest of a human wave. Some fought for their cause; others fought to get away. Underfoot, a shoal of trampled bodies made each step treacherous. Memnon grabbed two men by the scruff of their necks and flung them aside. A fist grazed his cheek. A heel bruised the meat of his thigh. A walking stick cracked across his shoulders. Memnon snarled at this last, turned, and wrenched the stick from an old man's hand.

Armed now with a truncheon of bronze-capped olive wood, Memnon waded through the flailing mob. Oligarch or democrat, he did not care; he left a path of broken bones, teeth, and heads in his wake. He gained the plinth and found Timocrates on the ground, struggling against a wild-eyed young democrat whose hands were knotted around Philolaus's throat. A callous man might have left the oligarch to his fate—is he who incites rebellion not deserving of death?—but Memnon believed in the rule of law, in justice. A man should face trial before his execution. With a savage blow of his cudgel, Memnon broke the zealot's grip and dragged him, cursing and screaming, off Philolaus. A second blow sent him plummeting into oblivion.

Memnon crouched and helped his father to his feet.

"Have they lost their minds?" Timocrates muttered, disoriented. "Violence only begets violence!"

"Orators beget violence with their loose tongues!" Memnon said. Through the wrack he spotted Glaucus, his face scratched and bloody, his robes torn. "Here, Glaucus!" Seeing Timocrates alive bolstered the secretary's flagging spirits. He rushed to his master's side.

"Thank the gods! I thought—"

Memnon cut him off. "Your people are getting the worst of it! Take Father home and keep watch over him. Keep him safe! I will come when I can."

"As you wish," Glaucus said. Like a Spartan general, the secretary gathered a phalanx of democrats around Timocrates and hustled him from the Assembly building. Memnon watched them leave before turning his attention to Philolaus. The oligarch, on his knees now, clawed at the edge of the plinth as he sought to find his footing. Blood smeared his face, dripping from his beard to stain his blue robes. He coughed and struggled for breath.

"Get up, you damn fool!" Memnon knelt, looped Philolaus's arm around his neck, and pulled him upright. "Get up before someone kills you!"

"They've tried," the oligarch gasped. "I owe you my life. To which faction are you pledged?"

"Neither, and you owe me nothing." Memnon noticed a half-dozen of Philolaus's men nearby, watching as one of their number kicked a fallen democrat in the ribs. Memnon's proximity to their leader, and Philolaus's reliance on him, registered in their minds as the actions of an ally. The young Rhodian gestured to one of them.

Philolaus shook his head. "No. I never forget a debt, or a face. Seek me out when all this is over. I could use a man of your talents."

Memnon dropped his bloody cudgel, shrugged himself free of the oligarch's arm, and entrusted him to the care of his men. "My talents, as you call them, are pledged elsewhere." He turned and walked toward the door. Clumps of men dotted the floor of the Assembly, moaning, crawling. Some of those trampled would never move again.

"Wait!" he heard Philolaus croak. "At least tell me to whom I am indebted!"

Memnon paused at the head of the stairs, under the statue of Dorieus. For a moment, he flirted with the idea of a lie. No. He had no reason to be ashamed of who he was. With a nod, he said, "Memnon, son of Timocrates."

Philolaus's face paled beneath its veneer of blood. "I sense the hand of a god in this," he said. "Very well, son of Timocrates. Go in peace with my thanks. Perhaps someday the gods will allow me to discharge my obligation to you."

Memnon turned and ascended the last few steps. "I said you owe me nothing." But, his voice was lost amid the cries of victory that arose from the Assembly building. They could only claim dominance by the slenderest of margins, but claim it they did.

Memnon imagined word of the battle had already reached the harbor. *The oligarchs have risen! Death to the democrats!* Both factions would arm themselves with spears and javelins, swords and knives, arrows and sling stones. Old soldiers would take their shields down from the hearth; young soldiers would don their bronze panoplies. Merchants would beat a hasty retreat to their country manors, or load their wealth onto ships bound for secluded beachheads on the western shore of the island. The threat of civil war, of *stasis*, would paralyze the city. Memnon glanced back over his shoulder at Philolaus, who held court amid the wounded like a conquering king. *All of this because I spared you.*

Memnon had not reckoned that his act of conscience might cost Rhodes its life.

"Come away from the window," Thalia said, clutching her bedclothes tight. The rooms she rented above a tavern on the Street of Ophioussa, near the temple of Aphrodite, reminded Memnon of the seraglio of a Persian satrap. Paneled and furnished in dark wood, its four lamps, two of polished bronze and two of terracotta, drove away the shadows, their sweetened smoke mingling with a haze of costly frankincense. Colorful carpets and brocades covered the floor and the walls. Wide-eyed, Thalia gestured to Memnon. "Please! Come sit by me. I'm afraid."

Memnon smiled, but stood his ground, peering out into the flame-flecked night through drawn shutters. At dusk, Rhodes had erupted in an orgy of fiery violence. A foreign mob, no doubt purchased with Carian gold, rampaged through the homes and shops of known democrats, torching what they could not kill or carry off. Though he'd hoped otherwise, this descent into *stasis* caught his father's faction off guard; the threat of mob rule swayed any who might have thrown in with them to the oligarch's cause. Disgusted, Memnon turned from the window.

"Please, Memnon!" Tears sparkled on Thalia's lashes.

The young Rhodian sat beside Thalia, pulling her into his embrace.

"Don't worry yourself so," he said, stroking her tawny hair. Thalia came from Cyrene in North Africa; her straw-colored hair, common in her homeland, gave her an exotic cast favored by the jaded sailors of Rhodes. "This will be over soon, and your life will return to normal."

"But what will I do with you gone?" she said. "Who will care for me?"

"I expect you'll find yourself a fat, rich merchant and settle down to a life of luxury. Maybe even see something of the world, yourself." Memnon had no illusions about the young woman in his arms. Men were a flock of sheep to her; some ripe for shearing, others earmarked for the altar of Aphrodite—sacrifices to the patron goddess of the *hetaera*. Among men, Thalia could be as sleek and predatory as any leopard.

"The world holds no allure for me if I'm not at your side," she said, her voice a throaty murmur. She craned her neck, kissing the hard line of his jaw. "Take me with you."

Memnon shook his head. "A mercenary camp is no place for a woman of your tastes. The food is of the roughest sort, inedible by all save the hungriest of foot soldiers. And there are no beds, no sheets. Everyone sleeps on the ground at the mercy of the heat and the cold, exposed to the elements. Can you see yourself carrying my gear over mountains and through valleys? No, Thalia. A life as a mercenary's woman is not one I'd wish on you."

"Forget the mercenary life, then," she said. "We could go to Ephesus or Athens or Corinth . . . Corinth, Memnon! Imagine it! They say even the most common courtesans wear gold and jewels in Corinth. What would they make of me, I wonder?" Thalia tossed her head and preened. Her fingers loosened, and the linen bedclothes slid down her body, bunching about her trim waist. Golden skin glowed in the lamplight; the lush curves of her breasts brought a lump to Memnon's throat. *Like a lamb to the altar.*

"What, indeed," he said, reaching for her.

Thalia stiffened as a sound drifted through the door, the squeak of a floor plank. Memnon frowned. A soft knock brought him to his feet. He drew his knife and crossed to the door. "What do you want?"

"Open the door, you damned pup!"

Though muffled, Memnon recognized the voice. He lifted the bar. Patron stood in the narrow hall, his attitude one of wariness. He wore a mariner's leather cuirass, reinforced with disks of bronze pitted from the sea air and waxy with verdigris. A curved sword hung from a baldric over his left shoulder.

"You risk life and limb going abroad alone on a night like this, Patron," Memnon said, stepping aside to allow *Circe*'s captain entrance. "What goes?"

"Still eager to be gone from Rhodes?" Patron glanced sidewise at Thalia, who stretched catlike.

Memnon followed his gaze. "I am."

"We're leaving at dawn instead of week's end," Patron said, keeping his voice low. He walked to the window and inched the shutter open. Acrid smoke drifted in on the night breeze. "I've seen cities under siege, I've seen them sacked and burnt, I've even seen them decimated by plague, but I've never seen a city tear itself apart. Men who were neighbors at breakfast are sworn enemies at supper. All of this because of what, an ideal?"

"There's a point in time," Memnon said, "when the inhabitants of a region or an island come together as one to form a *polis*. Philosophers call this *synoikismos*. Father likened it to the way embers can be raked into a pile and a fire built from them. These flames of political unity burn in different ways, but they all need fodder—new ideas, new obstacles, new challenges. Without such nourishment, the *polis* will consume itself, destroying the very embers that gave it life. Yet, even then hope is not lost. Consider the bird of Ethiopia, the phoenix, whose young rise from the ashes of its elder. If a *polis* destroys itself, invariably the survivors will band together and a new *polis* will emerge." Memnon gestured out the window. "This looks chaotic to our eyes, but in reality it's part of the life cycle of a city. Rhodes will be reborn, hopefully stronger and wiser."

Patron smiled and clapped Memnon on the shoulder. "You are your father's son, Memnon. It gladdens me to see you well after your adventure in the Assembly."

"You heard?"

"It's on everyone's lips."

Memnon's eyes clouded as he leaned his shoulder against the window frame. "What are they saying? Are the democrats cursing me for saving Philolaus's life? Had I done nothing, perhaps all of this," his gesture encompassed Rhodes, "would not have come to pass. The democrats would still be in control."

"The gods marvel at your arrogance, Memnon," Patron said. "Even if you'd let Philolaus die, civil war would have been inevitable. Rhodes has chafed for years under Athens's thumb. The democrats, your father included, are little more than Athenian puppets even as the oligarchs serve the wishes of Mausolus of Caria. Civil war is the culmination of a long chain of events that has little to do with you."

"Perhaps you're right," Memnon said.

"Of course I am. Come, though, make your farewells brief. Some of the others await me out—" Patron stopped as the sounds of a commotion floated up from below, a babble of voices. He and Memnon glanced at one another, then went to the door. One of *Circe*'s crew had just gained the head of the stairs, his face pale, his brow beaded with sweat. Patron frowned. "What is it, Zaleucas?"

"It's t-the mob! T-They've murdered Diogenes!"

MEMNON'S WEAPONS GLITTERED IN THE LAMPLIGHT—A SWORD, A KNIFE, A pair of javelins—their polished iron edges less cold and unyielding than the eyes watching his preparation. At his back, Patron paced like a caged wolf;

Thalia sat on a divan in icy silence. Despite his inexperience in the arena of war, Memnon handled his weapons like a veteran, checking balance, heft, and haft. Satisfied, he placed them on the bed and lifted an oilskin bag off the floor. From it, he pulled a leather corselet.

"Dammit, Memnon! Use your head!" Patron said. "No man can predict the actions of a mob! They're like a pack of feral hounds, driven mad by the stench of blood. There's no reason to their movements."

"I am using my head! This mob is guided, Patron! The oligarchs are using them to dispose of their enemies! Who do you think they'll go after next?" The supple corselet, reinforced in the chest and abdomen with bronze studs, slid easily over Memnon's head. He tied off the thongs that laced down his left side. "Diogenes was one of my father's staunchest allies. Logic dictates their next victim."

"Say it's true, say they're going after Timocrates, what do you think you're going to do? Storm into his home and drag him down to the harbor? Zeus Savior! His own people will kill you if you try that! Then there's the oligarchs . . . will you hold them off single-handedly? You've fought in one skirmish with pirates! One skirmish! You're not Achilles, boy! Get out there in that mob's way and they'll tear you to shreds!"

"So, help me!" Memnon said through clenched teeth. "Or were all those hours spent listening to you go on about our brotherhood just wasted time?"

Patron looked away, stung. "I've got a ship to think about, a commission to fulfill, and forty-nine other lads who look to me for guidance. I can't abandon them and I can't squander them in a street fight. Not now."

Memnon tucked his knife into his belt, slipped the baldric of his sheathed sword over his head, and took up the pair of javelins. "And I can't leave my father here to die," he said. "I've got to get to him, convince him to come with us. Artabazus will offer him asylum, I'm certain. We—"

Patron caught him by the arm. "Listen to yourself, Memnon! You're a fool if you think you can pry Timocrates from Rhodes in her time of need!

Not the gods, not the Furies, not even the golden hoard of Midas could sway the man! This is what he's been preparing for! This is his Great Battle, and he'll not stop till it's over!"

Memnon wrenched free of Patron's grasp. "I won't leave him to die! How can I face Mentor if I don't at least try? What will he say to me when he asks for news of our father and I answer 'I do not know, brother, for I left him to be slaughtered by a mob'? I have to try, Patron!"

Patron exhaled, recognizing the futility of further argument. "We all have our fates, Memnon. Perhaps this is yours; perhaps it's your father's fate to die here. I cannot say. I promise you this, though: I will keep *Circe* here as long as I can. Grab Timocrates and get him back to the ship, if you can." The two men clasped hands. Patron let himself out, leaving Memnon alone with Thalia.

She sat in silence on the divan, her body wrapped in the bedclothes, her fingers knotted together. Tears wetted her cheeks. When she finally spoke, her voice trembled. "You spoke of logic earlier. Does your logic dictate that you throw your life away to save his?"

"No, but my blood does," Memnon said. "He's my father, Thalia. I have a responsibility to him. I don't expect you would understand, since—"

"Since I'm a woman?" she snarled.

Memnon paused, at a loss for the words to make Thalia comprehend the sense of duty a son possessed for his father. This sacred covenant meant that no matter how bitterly he and Timocrates fought they would stand shoulder to shoulder against a common enemy, unite against a common threat, and lay down their lives if the need arose. Memnon sighed, leaned down, and kissed her hair. In a soft voice, he said, "Remember me with kindness, if not love."

The sound of her sobbing followed him into the street.

THE WALLED VILLA OF TIMOCRATES LAY ON THE NORTHERN SLOPES OF THE acropolis, overlooking the least of Rhodes-town's four harbors. The path Memnon chose carried him through neighborhoods where the violence had come and gone. Shops and homes gutted by the mob were defiled again as scavengers of every stripe picked through the smoldering ruin, oblivious to the survivors who crept from hiding to survey the devastation. Bonfires spewed a pall of smoke into the air, a shroud that could not be seen in the darkness, only felt; the flames added an unclean orange glow to the oppressive atmosphere.

Memnon jogged along. With each step, the impression of the mob being led—focused, rather—strengthened in his mind. The destruction was not wholesale, as one would have expected from a rampaging horde; nor did it radiate out from its flashpoint in concentric waves, as though following the whims of capricious looters. No, this mob kept an even course, unwavering, flowing down the street as water through a sluice. At one point, where the avenue narrowed into a natural bottleneck, the democrats had thrown up a barricade of wagons and carts to dam this rage-swollen river of humanity. It proved too flimsy.

Memnon slowed. Amid the detritus of the splintered barricade, a score of bodies peppered the ground, some slashed and trampled, others pierced by arrow and spear. A man with the dark copper complexion of a sailor sat against the wall of a building, holding glistening loops of intestine in his hands. He looked at Memnon, confusion plain in his glassy eyes, and opened his mouth to speak. Blood gushed down his chin. Memnon turned away, a cold knot forming in his belly as he grew cognizant of the sounds rising around him. Whimpers of fear and pain mixed with keening wails; stammered prayers were lost amid pleas for succor. The stench of blood and bowel tainted the heavy air.

"It's not for the squeamish," he heard his brother's voice resonate in his skull. Years ago, he had asked Mentor what his first battle was like, how it differed from the poesy of Homer. The elder son of Timocrates answered him with unaccustomed gravity. "Forget fancy tactics and *paeans* to the gods. To kill a man, you must face him eye to eye and plant your spear in his guts before he does the same to you. When the blade goes in, you'll see his eyes change—anger, fear, pain, grief—a whole range of emotions that would do Euripides proud. You'll hear him scream, an animal sound like nothing you've ever heard, and you'll feel hot blood spurt out over your hands. Then, as the stink hits you, you realize the worst of it." *What could be worse than that?* Memnon muttered, his face pale. Mentor draped his arm around his young brother's shoulder and gave him a gruff hug. "What's worse is realizing it could have been you."

"What would you do tonight, brother?" Memnon said aloud. He crossed through the breach in the barricade. More bodies lay on the other side, victims of a barrage of rocks and hunting arrows, though only one caught his eye. Memnon stopped. In the lee of an overturned produce cart, a white-haired old man lay supine, his face a mask of blood from where a lead sling bullet had sheared through his forehead. For the span of a heartbeat, the icy talons of Deimos clawed at Memnon's lungs, freezing the very breath in his chest. *Is that you, Father?* Shaken, he stumbled to his knees. With a strip of cloth torn from the old man's robe, Memnon wiped away the blood obscuring the corpse's visage, peered closer, and gave an explosive sigh of relief. The face of an old soldier stared back at him, his oft-broken nose and gaping eye socket the trophies of long-ago campaigns. Memnon closed his eyes, his shoulders bowed as relief turned to sadness, then guilt.

"I'm sorry, old one," he whispered. "Be at peace."

A commotion caught Memnon's attention. He glanced up as a half-dozen men barreled through the now useless barricade. A pair of them held torches aloft; the rest carried makeshift weapons—oar shafts fixed with iron spikes, harpoons, and sickles of hammered bronze. Seeing Memnon crouched over a corpse, they took him to be one of their own. One of them lingered, a toothless jackal stinking of piss and rotten onions.

"Hurry!" he said. "Hurry, before we're too late!"

"Too late for what?" Memnon rose.

"Have you not heard? A bounty's been offered: ten *drachmas* for the right hand of every democrat, a hundred for the head of the man who leads them! Hurry," he said. "They're about to break through!"

Memnon ground his jaw in fury, but followed in their wake. Others, too, joined their cortege as it gained momentum. Excited, they brandished their hammers and cleavers and chattered in low voices. As they crested a final ridge, Memnon saw their destination. He slowed, letting the others jostle past him. *Zeus Savior! Father!*

From this distance, Timocrates' home resembled a besieged fortress rather than a villa. An army of scavengers and riffraff clogged the street, each man hoping to claim the bounty the oligarchs had placed on Timocrates. Torches flared, casting bizarre shadows across the makeshift siege lines. Lining the walls, a handful of loyal democrats sent flight after flight of arrows down into the press of bodies clamoring at the gate. In response, slingers rose from the mob, their lead bullets punching into the heads and chests of the defenders.

Nothing he had read in the past—not Homer or Herodotus or Thucydides—offered even the slightest amount of insight into what his next move should be. Patron was right. This was a fool's errand. Still . . . still . . .

Memnon left the street, crouching just inside the portico of a *nymphaeum*, and watched the chaos swirling around his father's house. He studied the mob, noting how they formed up and charged the gates, how they fell back and regrouped into their ragged platoons, their resolve fueled by the promise of gold. For his theory to be correct, Memnon knew there had to be a rhythm to their actions, a sign that, despite having a hundred heads, this Hydra possessed a single controlling intellect. If he could identify it, he could strike at it. Slay the brain and perhaps the Hydra's heads would turn on each other, providing enough of a respite for his father to be spirited away.

A voice bawled orders; a fresh assault wave hustled toward the gate, this time preceded by men bearing improvised body shields. Memnon traced the voice to its source, spotting a burly figure standing outside the house neighboring his fathers, surrounded by a cadre of his peers. Most were oligarchs, but a few moved with the confidence of trained soldiers. Mercenaries, Carians probably, brought over by Philolaus to enforce the edicts of his new regime. The son of Timocrates proffered a thin, grim smile. There was his target.

He would need to get closer.

Leaving his perch in front of the *nymphaeum*, Memnon used the confusion in the street as camouflage to circle around to his father's house—and to the men overseeing this piecemeal offensive. The villa adjacent to Timocrates' estate belonged to a man called Brygus, a political dilettante, and the youngest son of the renowned shipwright Chaeremon. An amiable man, Brygus nevertheless preferred the company of his roses to that of other people. His trellises, with their satiny red and yellow blooms, dwarfed those of his neighbors and were a constant source of pride for a man otherwise unremarkable. Memnon vaulted the low wall bounding Brygus's property and crept through the labyrinthine garden, past garland-wreathed statues of Demeter and Persephone; a haze of smoke drifted in the air, sweetened with attar of roses. The springy turf muffled Memnon's footsteps.

At the corner of the house, Memnon stopped. He heard voices ahead, harsh grumbles distorted by the thudding of axes on wood. "Shame we can't get in there before the others and claim the bounty ourselves. Are you sure there's no other gate?"

Another voice: "What about it, Brygus?"

Inching to the corner, Memnon peered around. Illuminated by the light of distant fires, two men alternated hacking at the base of an ancient olive tree. Both men paused and turned toward the figure cowering behind them.

Brygus knelt in the grass, a slight man clad in a torn and grimy *chiton*, blood staining his face and beard as he watched the destruction of his property through swollen eyes.

"You've been his neighbor for a dozen years, is there another way in?"

Brygus shook his head. "Only t-the front gate."

One of the men spat. "And we need a battering ram for that. You're a useless bag of shit, Brygus. You know that? We should take one of these axes to your hand and use the money for a skin of wine. How about it, Sacadas? You hold him; I'll whack off his hand."

The man called Sacadas shrugged, scratching at a scabby beard that couldn't hide the scars of a childhood pox. "Do what you will, Dyskolos, but kill him first. I don't want to hear the little shit-bag screaming all night long."

Brygus scrambled away from them. "Y-You can't!"

Dyskolos hefted his axe, grinning as he stalked the smaller man. "Who'll know? I should have thought of this sooner, Sacadas. Could have saved ourselves—" Dyskolos never finished. He saw a flicker of movement seconds before Memnon's javelin tore through the base of his throat, its blade nearly taking his head off. Brygus screamed. As Dyskolos toppled, Memnon stepped out into the light, his arm drawn back, his second javelin poised to throw. To his dismay, Sacadas reacted faster.

Time slowed. His senses sharpened by adrenalin and fear, Memnon watched Sacadas lunge, his arm snapping forward, his axe whirling end over end. The clumsy tool missed him by inches, but its proximity caused Memnon to recoil and, from reflex, to throw his javelin. *Too soon!* He knew the second it left his hand that his cast had gone awry. Memnon stared as it soared off into the darkness; when he returned his gaze to Sacadas, the larger man had wrenched the javelin from Dyskolos's corpse and was in motion.

Memnon fumbled for the hilt of his sword. He'd half-drawn the blade when Sacadas smashed into him, driving the butt of the javelin into his midsection. The young Rhodian's breath *whooshed* from his lungs; his body catapulted into the air. He struck the ground amid flashes of color and slid across the grass, struggling for breath. Sacadas straddled his fallen body. Memnon caught the javelin shaft with one hand as the mercenary drove it lengthwise across his throat.

Sacadas fought in silence, without taunts or curses, his lips fixed in a businesslike snarl. Memnon's free hand flailed about for a weapon—a rock, a branch, anything. His sword lay beneath him, its hilt grinding painfully into his back. Memnon's fingers brushed the handle of his knife. In one motion he dragged it free of its sheath and buried it in Sacadas's side. It had no effect. The mercenary bore down harder on the javelin shaft, forcing Memnon's own knuckles into his windpipe and cutting off his air. Memnon gasped, his eyes bulging. Again and again he plunged his knife into his attacker's flesh. Blood sprayed over his hand.

Mentor's voice thundered through his brain. "To kill a man, you must face him eye to eye and plant your spear in his guts before he does the same to you. When the blade goes in, you'll see his eyes change—anger, fear, pain, grief . . ."

The eyes staring down at him were as cold and dead as a shark's. The pressure at his throat vanished; Memnon felt a warm wetness spreading over his midsection as Sacadas's body voided itself at the moment of death. Memnon thrashed and rolled, toppling the body, vomiting both at the stink filling his nostrils and at the overwhelming sense of mortality. *It could have been me.* He lay for a time, his body shaking, his face pressed to the ground as he inhaled the clean smells of soil and grass.

Memnon heard movement. "Are you d-dead?" Brygus. Memnon had forgotten about him.

"Greetings, Brygus," Memnon croaked. He crawled to his knees, recovered his javelin, and used it to clamber to his feet. "Have you seen my father?"

Brygus's eyes narrowed. "M-Memnon? Is that you?"

"Aye. Have you seen him, Brygus? Do you know if my father's still safe?"

Memnon took a step toward the smaller man. Brygus, though, backed away from him, edging toward the gate leading to the street. He glanced over his shoulder, licked his lips. "Brygus?"

With a squeal of panic, Brygus turned and darted through the open gate. "He's here!"

"Damn you, Brygus! What are you doing?" Memnon followed him only a handful of paces before skidding to a stop. Outside the gate, he saw a throng of men turn toward the commotion. Brygus gestured at him, his voice a feminine shriek.

"Here! He's the son of Timocrates!"

A dozen eyes turned on Memnon, eyes brimming with hatred and lust. Patron called them feral beasts; now Memnon knew why. They stepped toward him. A hastily loosed arrow sliced the air, striking the wooden gatepost with a loud crack. An enraged scream followed in its wake. Triumphant, Brygus capered about.

"How much for the bastard's son? How much—"

With a howl of rage, Memnon's javelin streaked from his hand to transfix the body of his betrayer. He didn't pause to watch Brygus's death throes. Memnon spun on the balls of his feet and sprinted back through the gate.

Baying like the hounds of Atalanta, the mob gave chase.

PANTING, MEMNON PAUSED A MOMENT TO GET HIS BEARINGS. HIS NECK throbbed; his legs were rubbery from the exertion of running through the benighted streets of Rhodes-town. Through alley and garden the mob had followed in relentless pursuit, convinced that the son of Timocrates was a prize worth dying for. Twice, they had almost cornered him; twice, Memnon had escaped by the narrowest of margins, his sword swaying the balance to his favor. Still, his luck couldn't hold out much longer.

Memnon glanced back the way he had come. Farther up the hillside, the light from fires outside his father's house smudged the heavens with angry reds and oranges. He could hear the sough and sigh of the ocean, which meant the harbor was near. Unlike the main harbor, this one was little more than a sandy strand, a perfect beachhead for smaller boats. Memnon knew the area: as a boy he had played among the ship sheds and fishing shacks lining the strand. He stared again at his father's house, a lance of ice piercing his heart. What started as a noble endeavor had degenerated into a race against time. He—

"There!"

A voice split the night. The most persistent of his pursuers, torches held aloft, poured into the street. Leather whirred. Memnon ducked and ran as a sling bullet cracked on stone behind him, peppering his shoulders with fragments of lead. Down the alley and around a corner, he leapt a low retaining wall and nearly fell as sand shifted underfoot. *The strand!* He crouched, his back to the wall, and waited. Moment's later, a body hurtled over, wheezing, a staff of fire-hardened wood clutched in his fists.

He never knew what killed him.

Memnon struck his head from his shoulders, turned, and impaled another man as he vaulted the wall. Wrenching his sword free, Memnon loped along, following the circuit of the wall, his body in a half-crouch. Behind him, he heard the others stumble over the corpses of their companions. If he couldn't lose them, perhaps he could demoralize them, sap their interest in him by killing them one at a time. Memnon stopped. Too late, he heard the crunch of a foot on sand, the whistle of wood swinging through the air. He half-turned . . .

. . . and staggered as thunder and lightning exploded behind his eyes. A groan escaped his lips as his attacker drew back again and cracked a club across his skull. Memnon sank to his knees. His attacker towered over him.

"Ha! Gotcha, you son of a who—" The man stopped and looked down, his eyes bulging. Memnon followed his gaze. A spear blade had erupted from his chest like an obscene vine. He fell beside Memnon. He heard metal clash and ragged screams. The son of Timocrates glanced up, his world dwindling to a pinprick. A score of familiar faces emerged from the gathering dark, one in particular hovering close, edged in shadow. A sense of relief flooded his weary limbs. "P-Patron?"

"I couldn't just leave . . ." Memnon heard him say as he sank into the welcoming arms of oblivion.

He couldn't breathe. The fingers at his throat choked off his air and threatened to crush his windpipe, his vertebrae. Memnon struggled. His hand grasped the hilt of his knife and, with a triumphant snarl, plunged it into his tormentor's flesh. Hot blood spewed. Again and again, Memnon sank the blade into his attacker, until the pressure against his neck loosened and the fellow toppled to the side. Strength flooded Memnon's limbs. Grasping his attacker by the hair, he wrenched his head back, exposing his throat for the killing blow. Memnon looked down. Staring back at him, his eyes glazed with the nearness of death, Timocrates spat blood and struggled to speak. "W-Why?"

Memnon jolted into wakefulness, unsure of his surroundings. His skull throbbed. Bright morning sunlight stung tears from his eyes, while the creak of rope against wood and the murmur of the sea added to his confusion. *Where am I?* Beneath his naked body, the weathered pine planks felt familiar, as did the smells of sweat and salt and sun-warmed pitch. Above him, an elaborate finial, carved in the shape of a woman, watched over him like a guardian spirit. "And I went through the dark to *Circe*'s flawless bed . . ."

Circe.

Memnon groaned as he ran his fingers through his hair, feeling the crust of matted blood, the knot behind his ear. Twinges of pain cut knifelike through the haze. He struggled upright, on his elbows, and saw Patron sitting a few feet away, grinning. Others of the crew—Zaleucas, the Argive brothers Lycus and Sciron, the golden-haired sons of Attalus—looked up from their dice games and whetstones.

"Zeus Almighty, lad! I thought that clout on the head did you in," Patron said, tossing a skin of water to Memnon's side.

Memnon dragged himself into a sitting position, picked up the skin, and uncorked it with trembling fingers. He drank a few swallows before upending the rest over his head. Cool water washed away the blanket of fog that clouded his memory. Memnon wiped his eyes. "I wish it had."

"Get him a clean *chiton*," Patron said to Zaleucas. Turning back to Memnon, he added, "I'd be a hand short, then, wouldn't I? Besides, I rather like having you in my debt. It gives me leverage once we reach Mentor in the Troad."

If he heard, Memnon gave no sign of it. He stared at his hands, at the grime, at the blood caked beneath his nails. "I failed him, Patron. There's no way he and his men could have lasted the night, not with what the oligarchs were throwing against him. I had one chance and I failed." Memnon looked up, his eyebrows cocked. "Why were you on the beach? I thought . . ."

"Conscience." Patron allowed himself a faint smile. "It cannot be a virtue of any use to a mercenary, yet I find myself saddled with it. Nor am I alone." He jabbed a thumb at the rest of the crew. "These malcontents thought you worth saving, too."

The younger man's head sagged. "I thank you, but you should have left me to my fate and rescued Timocrates, instead. He would have been of more use."

Patron stood and accepted a bundle of cloth from Zaleucas. "Stop tormenting yourself. You tried, Memnon, and that's more of an effort than most would have made. If Timocrates indeed died last night, then it was his destiny, woven from birth, regardless of what you or I might have done."

"Tell it to his shade, Patron." Memnon struggled to stand, his footing still unsure. With each movement a fresh barrage of pain lanced through his skull. "Where are we? How long till we make landfall?"

"Landfall?" Patron handed the *chiton* to him. "We've not left Rhodes, yet. We're riding our anchor offshore a ways."

Memnon's brows knitted as he glanced out over the railing. *Circe*, her oars shipped, her stern to the wind, lay just outside the mouth of the smallest harbor, on the seaward side of a headland of surf-scoured rock. Water the color of lapis lazuli, flecked with white spray, faded to turquoise as it neared the shore. Beyond the headland, Memnon could see thin columns of black smoke rising over red-tiled roofs; towering above the city, the glittering temples of the acropolis appeared as distant and aloof as the Olympian gods, themselves. With a shudder, Memnon realized the thickest smoke rose from the neighborhood of his father's house.

Patron came up beside him and sighed. "For some men, Conscience is a balm. For others, it's a brass-winged Fury. That's why I stayed."

"Have you seen anything," Memnon said, "any activity?"

Patron shook his head. "Nothing. The city's been like a tomb most of the morning, almost as though . . ." the captain of *Circe* trailed off, frowning.

"Almost as though they're ashamed of what they've done." Memnon turned to face his captain, his eyes hard as flint, his voice thick with desperation. "I've got to go back. I've got to see for myself what's happened to him. I'll go alone if—"

"I failed you once, my friend," Patron said, clapping the younger man on the shoulder. "I'll not fail you a second time." He spun away and bellowed at the crew. "Look alive, you sons of whores! Armor up and man the oars! This time, Memnon's not going it alone!"

SAND CRUNCHED BENEATH *CIRCE*'S KEEL. SINGLY AND IN PAIRS, TWENTY-five men vaulted the gunwales and splashed ashore, charging through the knee-high surf like Homer's Achaeans. Sunlight blazed from the burnished bronze of their shield facings, shimmered silver and gray from the iron blades of their spears. Four of them bore heavy Persian style bows. They paused a moment while their fellows remaining onboard the ship bent their backs to the oars, forcing the *pentekonter* off the strand and back out into the harbor. Satisfied *Circe* would be safe with only half its crew, Patron gestured for them to move out.

Curious faces watched from the shelter of the ship sheds and fishing shacks as Memnon took the lead, guiding the double column of warriors up the beach and over the retaining wall. Palm fronds rustled in their wake. Around the little harbor, those few who braved the quiet streets, scavengers and honest men alike, fled as the armed party ascended the terraced hillside. Shutters slammed at the sound of jingling harness. A panicky hand stifled an infant's cry. Memnon felt hidden eyes on him, glaring, hot with rage and afraid the least movement on their part would spark a fresh outbreak of violence. He sensed something else, too, lurking beneath the anger, the fear. He sensed despair. Those who had witnessed the savagery firsthand knew they had seen a singular event: fifty-one years of liberty destroyed in a matter of hours. It was almost too much for them to bear.

Ahead, Memnon caught sight of a familiar landmark: the columned portico of the *nymphaeum*, the fountain house, where he had spent a moment's respite the night before. His pace increased. The street dipped into a shallow valley, thick with groves of cypress and olive watered by a gurgling spring sacred to Artemis. Like an Olympian sprinter, the son of Timocrates surged forward. He crested the ridge, his face ashen, and stopped.

"Zeus Savior! No!"

The gates leading to his ancestral home stood open, blasted off their hinges by makeshift battering rams; debris strewed the ground: chunks of masonry and broken roof tiles, splintered wood and scraps of scorched linen. Skeins of black smoke floated up from the detritus of day-old bonfires, thinning to translucent charcoal in the freshening breeze. The crisp smell of ruptured cedar mingled with the stenches of burning tar, seared oil, and cooked flesh. Memnon's legs trembled; he might have fallen to his knees had a reassuring hand on his shoulder not imparted its strength on him. Patron stood by his side.

"He couldn't have survived it. He couldn't have."

"Easy there, lad," Patron said. The others drew up alongside them, muttering curses and admonitions to the gods. "Maybe his people got him out. Whoever built that place had a siege in mind when they raised those walls."

The villa's walls were old—older than the foundation of Rhodes-town—and thick, designed to repel raiders from land or sea. Ivy softened the hard lines of the stone, adding a touch of color to what once amounted to a fortress. "My grandfather's grandfather," Memnon said. "He grubbed each stone from the earth, cut, shaped, and mortared it into place with his own hands. All of this," he gestured behind him, "from the shore to the summit of the acropolis was his."

"How did Dorieus get a hold of it?"

"From my grandfather. He gifted the land to Dorieus in order to make the city of Rhodes a reality, with the proviso he could keep the house and grounds intact as a haven to raise his sons and grandsons. A haven . . ."

Through soot and sear, Memnon could still make out the image of Helios carved into the stone lintel over the gate. He imagined his father standing beneath it, his hair less gray, his face less lined and careworn, smiling as his two young sons ran a footrace up the road, the elder stopping to allow the younger time to catch up. The race would end in a tie, and Timocrates would sweep both sons up, balance them on his shoulders, and parade them through the gate like Olympian conquerors.

"Look," Zaleucas said, pointing. A knot of men, eight in all, stood to the left of the gates. Most were young, Memnon's age, armed with spears, knives, and harpoons, and displaying scraps of blue cloth knotted about their biceps. They stiffened, eyeing *Circe*'s war party with nervous anticipation.

Patron turned to his men. "Constrain yourselves. If it comes to blows I'd prefer not to have to kill the lot of them." The captain of *Circe* didn't bother lowering his voice and his words had an immediate effect on the young men at the gates: they paled; their weapons clattered as they sought reassurance in the touch of wood and iron.

One of them stepped forward. "Memnon?" he said. Sweat beaded his long forehead, plastering his unkempt dark hair to his scalp. A pale scar tugged at the corner of his left eye. "You may not recall who I am. I—"

"I remember you, Eumaeus," Memnon said. "Father often paid you to look after his olive trees. If that blue rag you're wearing marks you as one of Philolaus's toadies, then we have nothing to discuss. Go back to your new master and tell him I will come for him soon enough!"

Eumaeus shuffled from foot to foot, taken aback at the rancor in Memnon's voice. "He knew you'd come, Philolaus did. That's why he put us here and gave us a message for you."

"A message?"

Nodding, Eumaeus said, "Philolaus seeks a parley."

Patron grunted and spat. "That son of a whore has balls the size of gourds if he thinks we'll trust him. Likely it's a trap, Memnon. A ruse to get you alone and cut your throat."

"Likely," Memnon said. "What are his terms?"

"You and he, alone, in the Assembly, at dusk. You may bring an escort of no more than ten men, and he will do likewise. As a gesture of goodwill, he ordered us to keep any looters away till you got here."

"Goodwill?" Memnon snarled. "That's his concept of goodwill? His dogs swarm over my father's house but he'll protect the ruins until I'm able to tour them! Zeus Savior and Helios! Goodwill? Someone shoot this fool! That should send a loud enough answer to Philolaus!"

In a single fluid motion, Sciron of Argos drew an arrow, nocked it, and bent his bow. Three others followed suit. Eumaeus's courage flowed away like water through a sieve. His spear toppled to the ground; Eumaeus held out his hands, imploring, as he backed away. "Wait! Wait! I had no part in your father's death! None!"

Memnon stopped the archers with a gesture. "So he is dead?"

"I . . . I don't know," Eumaeus said. "Not for certain, at least. We were told not to pass the gate, either. Philolaus's orders."

Memnon said nothing for a moment; then jerked his head, dismissing the guards. "Clear out, all of you." Relieved, the other guards scurried away. Eumaeus, though, lagged.

"What do I tell Philolaus?"

Memnon exchanged glances with Patron. "There's no way you can trust him, lad," the older man muttered.

"I know." Memnon's eyes narrowed as he stalked toward his father's home. He passed Eumaeus and said, "Tell him I accept his terms, but if I catch even the slightest whiff of betrayal he'll not live to enjoy it." Eumaeus nodded and withdrew as Memnon crossed the threshold of the gates, Patron and the others in his wake.

Rubble choked the courtyard—shattered stone and brick from where the battering rams had breached the gate; charred timbers, smashed floor and roof tiles, and toppled statuary all covered in a glaze of ash and pulverized plaster. Bodies lay twisted amid the ruins, their limbs crusted with dried blood, their right arms ending in jagged stumps. The faces of men Memnon had known for most his life now looked foreign to him; waxen, like masks carved at the instant of death. Memnon stepped lightly, cursing as his foot nudged a corpse and dislodged a cloud of flies from a gaping belly wound.

"Merciful Zeus!" Memnon felt a tightening in his stomach. "He's here,

I know it. But where to start? The grounds first, then the house? Or should we split up?"

"Wait," Patron said, nodding back toward the gate. Memnon followed his gaze. A woman stood in the shadow of the wall, her *peplos* stained with soot and dust. Loose strands of graying hair escaped from beneath her fringed scarf. In her hands, she clutched a terracotta votive statue, rubbing it as though the gesture would make her wishes reality.

"I know her," Memnon said, picking his way back to her. "Cleia?"

The sound of a voice speaking her name startled the woman. She blinked and glanced about, like an innocent soul awakening before Hades' throne, afraid of what she would see but unable to look away. Memnon said her name again, softly. This time, Cleia focused on him. Tears welled up in her eyes. "Oh, Memnon! Have you seen my husband? They wouldn't let us in to look. Have you seen him? I begged him not to come, but he wouldn't listen. He's fond of your father. Have you seen him, Memnon? Have you seen my Bion?"

"I haven't, Cleia, but I'll help you look," Memnon said, offering his arm for the woman to lean on. Other women, too, crept through the gate. Patron detailed men to help them as they sought familiar faces among the dead: brothers, sons, husbands, and fathers. Wails of grief accompanied each success. The eldest among them, matrons well acquainted with Death, hushed their cries and set about tending to the bodies with quiet dignity.

Memnon found Cleia's husband a dozen feet from the gate. Though three times Memnon's age, Bion had fought with Spartan ferocity until, his shield hacked and broken, a spear thrust had ended his life. Cleia sank down beside him. "Oh, Bion."

Memnon tried to think of something to say that would ease her grief, provide comfort, and give her hope all in the same breath. He could think of nothing, save his own father. Timocrates' body lay amidst the wrack and ruin, waiting with the infinite patience of the dead for someone to uncover him. Memnon could feel it in his marrow. He—

"I've found a survivor!" Patron, near the wall, bellowed. All semblance of thought fled from Memnon's mind as he left Cleia and rushed across to his captain's side.

"Who is it? My father?"

"No," Patron said.

Both men crouched and prized up a charred timber. Memnon saw a familiar swatch of faded blue fabric, part of a *himation*, as he lifted his end. The young Rhodian gagged at the stench of seared tissue, blood, and bowel that rose from the uncovered body. "Glaucus."

A shower of fiery debris, including a timber from the gate, had fallen crosswise over Glaucus's body, its weight pinning him to the ground and roasting his flesh in smoldering increments rather than all at once. One eye, boiled like an egg, had ruptured; fluid wept down his cheek. Night's veil must have hidden him from trophy-seekers, since he still possessed both hands—though the heat left them charred and blackened.

"He's still alive?"

In answer, Glaucus struggled to move. Blood and liquefied fat seeped through cracks in his skin as he fought to form speech. "W-Water . . ."

Memnon knelt and cradled Glaucus's head, careful not to touch the burnt flesh. "We'll get you some water, Glaucus. Rest easy, now."

He clutched at Memnon's arm. "W-we looked for you . . . we h-hoped you would c-come and lead us. T-Timocrates kept asking after y-you . . . w-we hoped . . ."

Memnon bowed his head. "I'm sorry, Glaucus. I tried to fight through. I tried."

"H-Have you s-seen T-Timocrates . . . ?"

"I cannot find him, Glaucus. Where is he?"

Glaucus coughed, bloody foam flecking his lips. The secretary's grip on Memnon's arm loosened. He whispered something, and with a last rattling breath, Glaucus's spirit departed on the long road to Tartarus. Memnon exhaled and stood.

"Where?" Patron said.

Memnon didn't hear him. Turning away, the son of Timocrates strode toward the squat bulk of the house.

AFTER THE MOB'S BATTERING RAMS COMPROMISED THE EXTERIOR GATES, the defenders must have fallen back on the villa itself. The gentle, tree-lined slope where Memnon played as a child was scorched and bloody, littered with the corpses of his father's friends. He stepped over the bodies of men who had bounced him on their knees, men whose sons he had scrabbled with in the dust, and he felt nothing. He saw nothing, save the delicate iron and gold-filigreed gate that should have barred the entrance to the villa. No one had tried to close it; Memnon doubted that it could be closed—its hinges were useless from a generation of neglect and exposure to salty air. He touched the rough iron as he passed.

Through the entry, a short dark tunnel opened on an inner courtyard ringed in a peristyle of timber, black with age, whose tall red-daubed columns supported a roof of baked clay tiles. On either side of the entryway, clumps of damp earth and fragments of terracotta were all that remained of a pair of poplar seedlings, doubtless ripped from their pots to serve as fuel for the fire. At the center of the inner courtyard stood the household altar to Helios, the patron god of all Rhodes, the Charioteer who drives the stallions of the Sun across the heavens to the Isles of the Blessed. Here, Timocrates would have asked the god's blessing for his family, offering in return gifts of bull's blood and wine.

All around the courtyard Memnon saw touches of his father's personality: a high table brimming with empty pots and gardening tools; an overturned couch of sun-faded wood, its legs carved in the likeness of a horse's hooves; niches in the right-hand wall held small statues and busts of men, heroes, and gods. On the left-hand wall, between a pair of doors leading to his father's offices and Glaucus's apartments, the russet-colored wall bore a painted copy of Parrhasius's *Demos*, depicting the goddess instructing Theseus in the ways of *demokratia*. Seeing the painting again brought back a flood of memories: a soft twilight; warm air laced with the smell of hyacinth and wet brick; his father sitting on the couch, weary from unknown struggles, nursing a goblet of watered wine. He would stare into the depths of the painting until the light faded, as though searching the pigments for the answers to his questions. "Always surround yourself with great art, Memnon, for great art is like a mirror that only shows us the best in ourselves."

"Father!" Memnon crossed to the door of Timocrates' offices and peered inside. Empty. He whirled . . . and felt his blood turn to ice. In the sun behind the altar, a body lay like a suppliant abasing himself before the god. Memnon edged forward. Folds of bloody soot-fouled white cloth, edged in Tyrian purple, clung to the corpse's splayed limbs. "Father?"

True to their word, the oligarchs had taken his head. Memnon stared at the whitish vertebrae protruding through the ragged flesh, at the pool of blackening blood, and felt his gorge rise. He spun away, retching.

Memnon staggered to the couch. He righted it, sat heavily, and cradled his head in his hands. Time lost all meaning. How long he sat there, the sun burning his shoulders, he didn't know. His mind kept replaying the arguments of the past few months. Every look of disappointment and caustic remark drove the sharp spike of guilt deeper into his heart.

A shadow fell across Memnon; he felt a hand stroke his hair. "Do not mourn too much, dear boy," Cleia said, her voice a soft hum. "He is with your mother now, beyond the Styx, beyond the grim halls of Tartarus, in the eternal springtime of Elysium. Imagine your father's joy at seeing your mother's face once again."

Memnon said nothing for a long time. The muscles of his jaw clenched and unclenched; his knuckles whitened around the sword hilt. Twice he seemed on the verge of speaking, only to exhale through flared nostrils. When finally found his voice, it emerged as a cracked whisper. "We . . . We did not part on the best of terms. I fear he went to his death believing me to be a disappointment."

"All fathers want what's best for their sons, but few take the time to ask what their sons want because no one asked them," Cleia said. "I believe Timocrates wished only to spare you the hardships he'd endured in his youth. In his heart, I think he knew you could no more follow in his footsteps than he could sprout wings and fly."

Memnon stood. "We'll never know, though."

"What will you do with your father?"

He glanced up at the cloudless azure sky. "A pyre. Father always said he wanted to be placed on a pyre, so that after death his shade could wander the earth on wings of smoke. I'll send Glaucus with him, ever-faithful."

"And Bion?"

"Would he wish it?"

Cleia sighed. "Our sons are dead, our daughter, too. Once I pass on there will be no one left to tend his grave. I think Bion would be honored to mingle his ashes with those of your father." Memnon looked away. Tears welled in the corners of his eyes.

"You do him great acclaim."

Cleia took Memnon's hand. "Come. Let's make them ready for their last journey."

LATE AFTERNOON SUNLIGHT FLOODED THE INNER COURTYARD WITH GOLDEN radiance, illuminating every crack and flaw in the plastered walls. The body of Timocrates lay on the couch with his feet facing the door, covered in a white linen bier cloth. Cleia had gone to look after the other bodies, leaving Memnon alone in the shadow of the peristyle. He sat grim-faced, his chin resting on the pommel of his sheathed sword as he contemplated the corpse of his father. Timocrates had been an elemental force in the young man's life—a god to be appeased; a tempest who thrived on struggle; a taskmaster who demanded excellence from his sons. Though Memnon longed to be free of his influence, Timocrates' passing left a bewildering void, a tainted sense of freedom.

I should have stayed with him instead of running off to Thalia's. After the brawl in the Assembly, his natural inclination had been to seek out a safe place where he could regroup and gather his thoughts. The speed of the oligarchs' response had surprised him, true, but it wasn't unexpected. He should have been prepared; instead, he created a lull in the fighting where none existed and it had cost his father his life. *Is this how I'll act in the Troad? If battle is offered, will I scamper away to hide in my mistress's skirt?*

From beyond the open gate leading to the heart of his father's villa, the sounds of men arming—coarse jokes, muted laughter, the jangle of harness—broke his concentration. He heard footsteps on the paving stones. "Memnon?" Patron called, his voice echoing in the entryway.

"In here."

Circe's captain ambled into the inner courtyard, glancing at the makeshift bier as he walked over to where Memnon sat. "Come, it's getting late. I've picked ten men to go with you to this damnable parley. Zeus! I hope you know what you're doing."

Memnon's eyes hardened. "Philolaus owes me his life. I go to collect."

"A wise man," Patron said, shaking his head, "would knock you senseless and haul your carcass back to the ship. I should be the one going, not you."

"No, Patron. This is something I must handle on my own." Memnon's leather armor creaked as he stood and looped the baldric of his sword over his shoulder. The weapon settled on his left hip; he slid the blade partly from its sheath, loosening it. "As you said, it's likely I go to an ambush. If that's true and I don't return, will you see to my father?"

"If that comes to pass I'll see to the both of you," Patron said. "But, no matter what happens, lad, don't trust anything that comes from Philolaus's mouth. Accept no promises from him, and promise nothing in return. His cause isn't served by bargaining with you." He glanced again at the bier, at the shrouded body, and exhaled. "My father died a few years back. I wasn't there for it."

"I pray he died with more pride in his heart for his son than my father had for me," Memnon said.

"I wouldn't wager coin on that. When I was your age, my father arranged for me to apprentice with a counting house in Phocaea. He thought I should make my fortune selling Chian wine to merchants out of Naucratis."

Memnon raised an eyebrow. "You? A trader's apprentice?"

Patron smiled. "I know, but the old man had a dream. I had a dream, too. So, one night I slipped from my bed, gathered my things, and fled down to the docks. By sunrise I was an oarsman on a galley bound for Taenarum in the Peloponnese. He never forgave me, and he died 'ere he could see me at the tiller of my own ship. I don't doubt his shade wanders the grim landscape of Hades' realm, unable to forget the bitter disappointment I caused him."

Memnon extended his hand. "I swear to you, Patron, on my honor, when I meet your father across the river I will set him right on that score."

Patron took the proffered hand and tugged the younger man into an embrace. "Do nothing foolish, you damnable pup," he said, "or, on my honor, I swear I'll send you across the river myself."

IN THE FADING LIGHT OF DUSK, MEMNON LEFT HIS FATHER'S VILLA AND ascended the hillside. Behind him, the Argive brothers Lycus and Sciron, with eight others of *Circe*'s crew, followed in silence. The road approached the acropolis from the north, its slope gentler than the dramatic cliff face that loomed over the great harbor. Around them, groves of cypress, olive, oak, and poplar provided shade for fields of fragrant violet and narcissus, hyacinth and wild thyme. Amid this *pairidaeza*, on stepped terraces whose retaining walls were of dressed stone and timber, rose the temples and public buildings of the Rhodians.

The architecture bore the stamp of Doric simplicity: baseless columns with wide shallow flutings, plain capitals, and friezes of unadorned marble suffused with the crimson glow of twilight. Memnon led them past the Odeion, the music hall where wealthy *choregoi* prepared their singers for the great festivals of Greece; they skirted the Prytaneion, the symbolic home of Rhodes, where priests tended to the sacred flame of Helios, and cut through the deepening gloom of a columned stoa. Ahead, above the dark boughs of Athena's hallowed olive grove, the red-tiled roof of the Assembly glistened as though drenched in blood.

Sciron caught Memnon's arm. "Wait. Let us scout it out." He gestured to his brother, and the two Argives sprinted off, vanishing under the trees. They returned minutes later, barely winded.

"How many?" Memnon asked.

"Only ten," Sciron said. "Mainlanders; Carians, most likely. I couldn't get close enough to tell if any were hiding inside. The bastard looks to be keeping his word."

"We'll find out soon enough." As a group, they left the shelter of the stoa and plunged into Athena's grove. Fingers of ruddy light pierced the leaf canopy. Under the trees, the cooler air of dusk mingled with the warmth rising from the ground, intensifying the smells of freshly spaded earth and crushed olive husks. Memnon followed the main path, passing the bench where he and Timocrates had spoken the day before, and emerged near the entrance of the Assembly.

Sciron gestured. Light spilled out from between the columns of the Assembly and striped the shadows with bands of pale gold. Opposite the main entrance, seven men in bronze-scaled corselets lounged in the grass, their spears planted upright. Three others stood together, watching the grove. One of them spotted *Circe*'s crew; the others clambered to their feet, their movements deliberate, non-threatening. The spotter acknowledged Memnon's presence with a wave of his hand then withdrew with his mates to the other side of the building.

The son of Timocrates returned the wave. In a low voice, he said, "Wait here in the grove. The trees will give you cover if they have any archers hidden about. Should something happen to me—and I mean anything—get back to Patron. Understood?" Memnon looked at each man in turn; though he was the youngest of *Circe*'s crew, the past few hours had given him gravity beyond his years. Nodding to himself, Memnon turned and strode down the path to the entrance of the Assembly.

Beyond clumps of torn sod and flattened grass, Memnon saw no signs of the past day's violence. Where were the swatches of bloodstained turf? Where were the mounds of severed hands or the makeshift tables where Philolaus's paymasters would have disbursed their coin? He had expected some outward display of the shift in power, but the grounds of the Assembly remained virtually unchanged.

Memnon made his way to the stairs and peered inside. At the center of the sunken chamber Philolaus sat alone, his forehead bandaged, his fleshy legs dangling over the edge of the plinth. A wooden platter of food rested next to him, along with a clay jug of wine and a pair of cups. The oligarch selected the wing of a small fowl from the plate, stripped the flesh from it with his teeth, and tossed the bone into the shadows. With the same relish, he raised a cup of wine and drained it. He caught sight of Memnon standing in the doorway. Grinning, Philolaus wiped his face and hands on a linen napkin and hopped off the plinth.

"Blessed Zeus! You came! Eumaeus made it sound like you'd see me chained to a wheel in Tartarus first. I'm pleased you've agreed to talk. Can I offer you some—" Philolaus's voice trailed off as he noticed the hard line of Memnon's lips, the naked fury in his eyes.

The younger man's hand dropped to the hilt of his sword; metal rang against metal as he tugged the weapon free, stalked down the stairs, and crossed the limestone floor of the Assembly.

"Don't be foolish, Memnon," Philolaus said, frowning. "This is a parley, not a duel."

"This? This is neither. I have a loose end to tie up before I leave Rhodes. I saved your life yesterday because of my own misguided sense of fair play. I see now I was wrong. I've come to set the balance straight." Lamplight glinted on the edge of Memnon's blade.

Philolaus backed away, his hands away from his body, away from the knife belted about his waist. "If you mean to kill me then there's little I can do to stop you, but at least hear me out before you put me to the sword. I called this meeting to offer atonement for your loss. I've brought you your father's slayer."

A grim smile twisted Memnon's lips. "Indeed."

"You have it wrong. I didn't kill Timocrates. For all our differences, he was a worthy adversary and an honorable man. I wished him no harm."

"Liar! I saw what your men did to him!"

Philolaus bristled, matching anger with indignation. "Do you think me a barbarian, that I would order the mutilation of my own countrymen? Faugh! What the mob did last night they did of their own volition, not because of anything I offered them! I ordered my captains to keep a close tally of the dead; I did not realize to a Carian that meant lopping off the right hand. In that, the blame is mine, but the idea of a bounty is fiction, a lie propelled by greed. For myself, I desired a peaceful exchange of power, at most a few scuffles and a cracked head or three, with exile for those who did not share my vision, your father included. Now, I assume a mantle of leadership tainted by slaughter."

Memnon closed the gap between them; his hand snaked out, catching a fistful of Philolaus's tunic. He raised his sword, its tip angled toward the hollow of the oligarch's throat. "Tell it to the Ferryman, you son of a bitch!"

Philolaus's eyes blazed. Recklessly, he seized hold of Memnon's naked blade and pulled it toward his breast. "Strike me down, then! Strike me down and avenge your father! But if you kill me, my Carians will annihilate you 'ere you reach the harbor! Your friends, those not slain outright, will die slowly, their tortured passing an example of what will befall those men who flout Mausolus's will!" The oligarch's voice held a note of cold certainty that gave Memnon pause. "Go ahead! See your vengeance through, consequences be damned!"

Memnon's blade wavered. In a rush to pronounce judgment on his father's slayer, he had not given thought to the effect his actions might have on those closest to him. Philolaus wasn't bluffing. If he chose vengeance,

Patron and the others would die; if he chose mercy, Timocrates' shade would wander Hades' realm unavenged. Caught between hammer and anvil, Memnon ground his teeth in frustration.

"We're not so different, you and I," Philolaus continued, softening his tone in response to the boy's uncertainty. "Neither of us believes in the supremacy of *demokratia*; we're both fiercely loyal to our friends and ruthless to our enemies. But, I have the benefit of years and the meager wisdom their passage imparts. Choose only those battles you can win, Memnon, and if you must lose, do so with grace and dignity. I understand your desire to avenge Timocrates. He was your father and blood calls out for blood. I beg of you, let me ease the burden of your task! I've brought the man who murdered your father. I'll give him to you, along with what he took from Timocrates' body. Afterward, we part ways—you to the service of Artabazus and me to the service of Mausolus. What say you?"

Philolaus's words incited a war between Memnon's logic and his emotion, and its effects were plain to see. Cords of muscle stood out in his arms and neck; the knuckles of the hand holding his sword whitened and cracked. His eyes, though, presaged the war's outcome: they gleamed with tears of resignation. Slowly, Memnon let his blade fall to his side. With great effort he nodded assent.

Philolaus gave a small sigh of relief. "There's a sensible lad. I must signal my men now. Upon your life, make no sudden moves." The oligarch raised two fingers to his lips and whistled. A moment later, a pair of his Carians appeared at the side door to the Assembly. One carried a covered wicker basket in his arms; the other dragged a third man by the scruff of his neck, his arms and legs bound, his tattered clothing smeared with soot and blood. The Carian dropped him at Philolaus's feet as his mate placed the basket on the plinth. Both men stood their ground, glaring at the sword in Memnon's fist, until Philolaus waved them away. "This is the wretch who slew Timocrates, who struck his head from his body."

Memnon scowled at the figure crawling at Philolaus's feet. "Is this true? Did you kill my father?" The man groveled, rolling moist eyes toward the heavens, toward the oligarch, toward Memnon. Dried blood and sputum caked his scraggly beard. Indelicate hands had worked him over, breaking teeth and splitting open his cheek. Fear paralyzed the man's tongue.

"Answer him!" Philolaus barked, to no avail.

Disgusted, Memnon shook his head. "I cannot kill this man. I have only your word that he has done me injury."

Philolaus shrugged. "I have played fair by you. This *is* the man who killed your father, whether you acknowledge it or not. If you agree I've kept my word, then our business is done."

Memnon slammed his sword home in its sheath. "I will take the tale to my brother, along with the details of our arrangement. If Mentor rejects it, I expect he and Artabazus will either petition Mausolus for your head or come for it themselves. Is this still acceptable for you?"

"It's a chance I'm prepared to take," Philolaus said. "What of this wretch?"

"Do with him what you will."

"As you wish." Philolaus turned, lifted the basket off the plinth, and handed it to Memnon. "Take what time you need to set your father's affairs in order. None of my men will molest you so long as you cause no trouble. Farewell, Memnon. I hope you find everything you deserve on distant shores."

The son of Timocrates gave a slight nod; his eyes lost none of their murderous fire. "And I hope the mantle of leadership you covet so becomes your death shroud." And with that, Memnon backed away and slipped from the Assembly. For the second time in as many days, he couldn't help but feel as though he had betrayed Rhodes.

THE MEN OF *CIRCE* DESCENDED FROM THE ACROPOLIS BY THE LIGHT OF THE rising moon. As they neared the walls of Timocrates' villa, a sentry caught sight of them and bellowed a warning. Sciron answered, and at the sound of his voice a ragged cheer went up. Patron walked out to meet them. "So?"

Memnon brushed past him, clutching the basket to his chest like it was wrought of gold. Patron glanced at Sciron; the Argive shrugged. *Circe*'s captain turned and followed Memnon inside. A dozen feet from the gate, on a level stretch of ground leading up to the house, the pyre stood ready.

"It's done," Memnon said, thankful that the torchlight concealed his red-rimmed eyes.

"What happened?"

In a few words, Memnon sketched out his meeting with Philolaus.

Patron shook his head in disbelief. "Zeus! You left him alive?"

Memnon glanced at his captain. "I did what needed to be done, to assure our survival. The final decision of what should befall Philolaus I leave to Mentor. It's his right, as elder brother." He placed the basket on the pyre, near his father's body. Bion and Glaucus rested on either side, their corpses washed, wrapped in linen, and saturated with oil. It would be a quick funeral, without sacrifices. Memnon prayed the gods would understand.

"When you left here, you were adamant about his punishment. What leverage could he have used to sway you? What . . . ?" Patron glanced from Memnon to the others of *Circe*'s crew and found the answer to his question. "He used us against you."

Memnon motioned for Zaleucas to bring him his torch. "Did you not counsel me to embrace wisdom, to do nothing foolish? I said it's done. Let it be, Patron." He accepted Zaleucas's torch and, without preamble, thrust it into the heart of the pyre. Old pitch-soaked wood ignited; the flames, fanned by the gentle sea breeze, crackled and spread, following rivulets of oil seeping from the linen. Gouts of black smoke vanished in the night sky. Cleia hung on the arm of her neighbor's wife, both women sobbing as the flames roared fully to life. Other shapes gathered on the edge of the firelight, men who had known his father in life come to pay their respects in death. *Circe*'s crew stood apart from the rest. Memnon turned from the pyre, a nimbus of light playing over his body.

"My father often sang the praises of his city," Memnon said, his voice carrying, "but it was the courage, the gallantry, of men like Glaucus and Bion, and all the others who fell with them, which made her splendid. No words suffice to do justice to their deeds. Doubtless each of them had their faults—we all do—but whatever harm they did in their private lives has been erased by their courage. They go to the gods clothed in white, and wreathed like victors at Olympia."

Memnon paused and looked back at the flames. In his armor, sword at his hip, the son of Timocrates could have stepped from the poet's verse, a living Achilles—ferocious, touched by the gods, perhaps even a little mad. The eyes of the audience never left him; they waited in rapt silence for him to continue.

"I have no wish to make a long speech; truthfully, I have not the stomach for it. Those men who fell defending my father, defending their belief in democracy, were the best of men. Rhodes will not see their equal for a generation. Does that mean we who survived are of a lesser quality? In many ways, I believe so, yes. But, as we are alive, we can learn, and we have the unique opportunity to remake ourselves, to become better men. I urge you all to embrace the lesson my father taught. Timocrates was a harsh man, but he was fair. Like the Athenians he admired, he did not let his love of the beautiful lead him to extravagance, nor did his love of things of the mind make him soft. He regarded wealth as something to be properly used, rather than as something to boast about, and he befriended all: rich, poor, healthy, infirm, pious, blasphemous, judging them not by the contents of their purse, but by the quality of their character. When the trials of the coming days leave your spirits heavy with sorrow or fear, remember the example set by these men, remember their valor, their sacrifice, and let it inspire you to find the best and bravest in yourselves."

The heart of the pyre collapsed, sending a shower of sparks skyward. Memnon glanced up, watching as each ember blazed like a tiny star. Some vanished a moment after their birth while others endured, drifting high over the fire that spawned them. *Like men.* With a weary smile, Memnon returned his gaze to the people around him.

"I have said enough. With the dawn, I leave Rhodes and my father's bones come with me; this island is our home no longer. But, for tonight, let us gather as kinsmen. Let us speak kindly of the dead and give our grief free expression. Join me, brothers and sisters, raise your voices with mine so Lord Hades will know that men have come unto him this night, and he will know to honor them as we have."

Interlude I

Ariston sat in silence as the woman's voice trailed off and her breathing softened. He glanced out the window, surprised to see night had fallen. The rain must have ceased sometime before dusk; now, a damp chill permeated the room. The young Rhodian rose and added a few logs to the glowing embers on the hearth, stoking it with a poker of blackened iron. The dry wood blazed, sending a shower of sparks up the chimney. *Burning bright, like the souls of men.*

In the renewed light he watched Melpomene as she slept, her face drawn and haggard from the exertion of tale telling. Despite being born some thirty years after the fact, much of what she spoke of was familiar to Ariston. His grandfather and namesake, a ship's carpenter from Lindos, lived through the War of the Allies (as the Athenians called it) and the Carian occupation, though he loathed speaking of either. Only in his last years, when his mind began to fail, would he delve into the past and talk of friends long dead, deeds long forgotten; he would wake from naps trembling in fear, and hoard bread from his evening meal in expectation of some half-remembered famine. In his rare moments of lucidity, he would regale his grandson with tales of Athens, of Demosthenes, and of the Greek world's struggles against that fearsome tyrant, Philip of Macedonia.

Melpomene groaned in her sleep, clutching the small silver casket tight against her side. She wheezed something in Persian. Twice during the day, Harmouthes had brought them possets of honey-sweetened wine, spiced and warmed; doubtless hers contained additional herbs to combat her illness. *Who is she?* Ariston searched his memory for fragments of information, tiny scraps he might have overheard and filed away. Unfortunately, he knew very little about Memnon of Rhodes, save that he contested Alexander's presence on Asian soil. That Melpomene knew the man intimately was a given, but how? She was Persian; Memnon was Greek, which ruled out any blood connection. A wife, perhaps?

Ariston finished tending the fire, straightened. When he turned to collect his belongings, he noticed Melpomene's eyes were open now, moist and shimmering in the firelight.

"I'm sorry," he said. "I did not mean—"

"You remind me of my son." Her voice barely rose above a whisper.

"He should be here at your side, madam, to help care for you. Is he aware of your illness? If you'd like, I can try to get a message to him."

"I wish you could." With some effort, Melpomene rolled onto her side, away from Ariston, and buried her face in the coverlet. Unsure of what to say, or of what he had said, Ariston picked up his bag and crept from the room. He met Harmouthes in the hallway.

"She sleeps?" the old Egyptian said.

Ariston nodded.

"Good. Come. I have taken the liberty of preparing you a light supper. You will stay the night, of course?"

"Yes," Ariston said. "I'll stay." In truth, where would he go?

Harmouthes smiled. "Her story, it is infectious, is it not?"

"More so than I would have imagined."

Ariston followed the old Egyptian to the kitchen. It lay off the peristyle, and like the Lady's room, it too showed signs of repair, with fresh plaster on the walls and new mortar on the hearth. Enough supplies to maintain a much larger household cluttered the corners: sacks of grain, onions, and dried dates, bunches of garlic, pottery jars of honey, and a half-dozen large shipping *amphorae*, the kind used to transport wine and olive oil. A savory incense of stewed vegetables, herbs, and pork filled the air, bubbling from an iron pot hanging over the fire. The smell reminded Ariston he had not eaten in hours; his growling stomach reminded him he had not eaten well for some days. Harmouthes gestured to a table of age-polished oak, directing Ariston to take a seat.

The Egyptian bustled about the kitchen, setting out a platter of cheese, dates, and bread, with a small bowl of oil for dipping. He drew wine from one *amphora*, enough for the both of them, and finally spooned a helping of stew into a bowl for Ariston. The young Rhodian smiled his thanks and attacked the food with gusto. Harmouthes eased himself onto the bench across from him, poured two cups of wine, and selected a date to nibble on.

"Who is she?" Ariston said around a mouthful of bread. "Your mistress, I mean."

Harmouthes shrugged. "She is one who knew Lord Memnon and who believes the Macedonians do a great injustice to his memory."

"That much I gathered. Her knowledge of him is the knowledge of an intimate. Was she his wife?"

"A woman of court," Harmouthes said, averting his eyes. "Nothing more."

Ariston paused to down a gulp of wine. "I may be young, Harmouthes," he said, wiping his mouth with the heel of his hand, "but I'm not stupid. If Melpomene is only a woman of the court, why all this secrecy?"

"Consider it a by-product of our times. The Macedonians do not foster an atmosphere of openness. If my mistress desires to hide her identity for the time being you should honor her wish. Truly, she is not seeking to deceive you, only to protect herself."

"From whom?"

Harmouthes gave the young Rhodian a weak smile. "You are tenacious, I give you that. I am weary, and I must check in on my mistress before bed. I am sorry we cannot offer you more palatable accommodations, but this hearth will have to do. Help yourself to whatever you see—wine, bread, more stew. Is there anything else you require?"

"Answers, but I see those won't be forthcoming tonight."

"Perhaps tomorrow more will be made clear to you," Harmouthes said, rising. "Sleep well, Ariston of Lindos."

The young Rhodian finished his stew and fetched another helping from the pot. As he ate, the tale of Memnon turned over and again in his mind. *No words suffice to do justice to his deeds.* Many such phrases were readily identifiable to Ariston—they belonged to Thucydides or Xenophon—and the emotions invoked hearkened back to Sophocles. Still, something was compelling in the tale. Ariston pushed his bowl aside, moved his bag to the end of the table nearest the fire, and drew out his ink pots and reed pens, his last few sheets of papyrus and parchment. Quickly, he wetted a reed in the ink and put it to the papyrus:

> *In the waning years of Athenian hegemony, there was born to Timocrates of Rhodes two sons, Mentor and Memnon . . .*

Though exhausted, the Muses sang to Ariston, their voices strong and rich. He would not ignore them.

Ariston stirred from the hard bench that served as his bed, his extremities tingling from a lack of circulation. Pale winter sunlight filled the kitchen, slanting through the bare limbs of oak trees on the slope behind the house. He reckoned it to be nearly midday. Ariston knuckled sleep from his eyes. Shivering, he stood and stretched, feeling a familiar ache in his back, arm, and hand—the aftereffects of a night spent in the Muses' embrace.

A light breakfast of bread and honey, dates, and wine waited at the far end of the table, along with a bundle of fresh parchment pages—*pergamene* of the finest quality—and new reeds to serve as pens. Of last night's pages, Ariston saw no sign. The young Rhodian frowned. Of course, Harmouthes must have taken them. Who else? Doubtless the Egyptian did not understand the breach of protocol he had committed by disturbing a work in progress. More than once, Ariston had seen such infringements dissolve into violence. A volatile breed, writers, as proprietary toward their work as the sculptor or the painter.

"He should thank his heathen gods I'm a temperate man," Ariston muttered, pouring a measure of wine. He carried the bowl with him out into the peristyle, to take in the day. A chill breeze rustled the olive branches; the sky was a washed out shade of blue, crisscrossed with skeins of silvery clouds. Soft fluting emanated from the hallway leading to Melpomene's room, interrupted now and again by the Lady's hacking cough. Ariston followed the sounds. He paused to knock lightly on her door before easing it open.

Harmouthes sat on a stool near the window, engrossed in a complex tune of his native land. Melpomene sat upright in bed with pillows stacked high behind her, reading his previous night's pages. "You have an extraordinary memory," she said, after a moment. "I hope you don't mind. When Harmouthes said you had spent much of the night writing, my curiosity got the better of me." Melpomene coughed, her shoulders wracked with spasms. It took her several seconds to catch her breath. The old Egyptian glanced up from his flute, concern in his eyes. Ariston understood; even to him, the mistress of the house seemed paler, frailer. Her hands trembled as she tapped the pages back into a neat pile.

"No, madam, I don't mind," Ariston said. "If you're feeling well enough, shall we continue?"

"I fear I shall never feel well enough, again," she said. "Still, I would feel worse if I left my narrative unfinished. Are you familiar with the inner workings of Persia's monarchy?"

Ariston brought his chair closer to her bedside. "To some degree, yes."

"Through Herodotus, no doubt, or Xenophon. Perhaps Ktesias. Imperfect sources all. Among my people, it is customary for a new monarch to secure his throne upon accession. Civil war, you see, is as abhorrent to the Mede as it is to the Hellene. His uncles, cousins, even his brothers and sons were kept under guard or posted to the edges of the empire, well away from possible intrigues. In extreme circumstances, the new King would guarantee his personal security through execution and assassination. Such was the atmosphere in Persia the year before Memnon quit Rhodes." Melpomene coughed, recovered, and sank down in her pillows.

"The Great King, Artaxerxes the Second, called Arsakes, died in the forty-sixth year of his reign. He had three sons. The eldest, called Darius, conspired against him and was executed; the second, Ariaspes, was a halfwit; that left only one, Ochus—as cruel and bloodthirsty a man as the gods ever created. Upon donning the mantle and peaked tiara, Ochus perceived threats from every quarter, some real, others imagined. He apprehended the need to strike first, and to strike without mercy. His minions decimated whole houses. They slaughtered males of fighting age, as well as grandfathers of four-score summers and newborns still damp from their mothers' wombs. Even those not in his presence were in danger.

"One such was Artabazus, the husband of Memnon's sister and satrap of Hellespontine Phrygia. Since he bore royal blood—his mother was a daughter of old Artaxerxes—Ochus ordered him to relinquish his satrapy and present himself and his sons in Susa. Knowing it to be a death sentence, Artabazus refused . . ."

Dascylium

Year 2 of the 106th Olympiad

(355 BCE)

MUD SPLASHED BENEATH HIS HORSE'S HOOVES AS MEMNON LED HIS cavalry squadron through the rebel encampment, their cloaks flaring out behind them. Torrential spring rains turned the ground around Zeleia into a bog, the precise rows of tents into islands of canvas. Despite countless days of idleness, the soldiers—Persian and Greek—never allowed their discipline to flag. Each day, as if on cue, they put away their dice and turned their attention to their panoplies, inspecting the bronze for corrosion, the iron for rust. They drilled in ankle-deep muck and stood their watches without regard to the weather. These were the men who looked up from their afternoon meal as Memnon's squadron thundered past.

Artabazus's headquarters lay atop a small rise, which it shared with shrines to Mithras and Athena Promachos. Standing alongside Greek battle priests garlanded and in full panoply, white-robed Magi with peaked caps and curled beards sacrificed goats and studied the lowering sky. Other men waited outside the command pavilion. A deputation from the city of Lampsacus chatted amiably with a knot of junior officers and pages; dour-faced commoners stood apart, nursing grievances only Artabazus could resolve.

The squadron's approach scattered them like quail. Memnon curbed his horse and leapt off the frothing animal, tossing the reins to a startled page. The men guarding the pavilion, mailed Persians bearing spears and shields of Greek design, acknowledged him with a smart salute as he rushed past in a flurry of leather and sweat. Inside, he shrugged off the eunuch chamberlain who importuned him to remove his cloak and wait to be announced. Memnon barged into the inner sanctum, where the commanders of the rebel army—Artabazus, Mentor, Chares the Athenian, and Pammenes of Thebes—glanced up from the map table.

"He's taken the bait!" Memnon said, short of breath. "Mithridates has marched from Dascylium!"

The news galvanized the generals. They spoke all at once, a babble of questions fired at Memnon like a volley of arrows. Artabazus silenced them with a gesture. Before this enterprise began he served his grandfather, King Artaxerxes, as governor of Hellespontine Phrygia—the official name for the collection of Greek and Persian states occupying the extreme western tip of Asia, bordered by the Aegean to the south, the Hellespont and Europe to the west, and Propontis to the north. Well past his fiftieth year, Artabazus should have been ensconced in his seaside palace at Assos, enjoying the fruits of long and loyal service to the king. And so he would have, had his kinsman, Ochus, not come to the throne. The new king wanted Artabazus dead, as much for the influence he wielded among the embattled Greeks of the Asian shore as for the royal blood in his veins. When the order came from Susa for Artabazus to surrender himself to Mithridates of Dascylium, he had no choice but to defy it.

The satrap smiled at the young Rhodian, the weathered skin around his eyes crinkling. "So our little ruse worked. Mithridates believes I am bedridden, too ill to move, and that my army is falling apart. Very good." Clear-eyed and vigorous, Artabazus wore a saffron-colored *chiton* beneath a plain Median robe, a combination emblematic of his ability to bridge the disparate cultures of Europe and Asia. He spoke fluent Greek; his cadence and manner reminded Memnon of his father, though Artabazus possessed such a surfeit of warmth that it made Timocrates appear Spartan by comparison. The mercenaries called him *Megapatros*—Great Father. They respected him; what's more, he knew it, and went to great lengths to see it reciprocated. "How long ago did he march?"

"Four days," Memnon said. "We rode as hard as we could."

"Well done, Memnon," Artabazus said.

"What road did Mithridates take?" Mentor asked. A head shorter than his brother, Mentor had the thick shoulders of an Olympian wrestler, with slabs of heavy muscle embroidered by a frieze of old scars. A ruff of black hair encircled his head, thinning over his scalp. Mentor's face may have been handsome once, but years of staring through the eye-slits of a Corinthian helmet had altered its structure, flattening his nose and leaving pads of callus on his cheeks and forehead. He scratched his thick beard.

"The coast road. We shadowed him for a day, to make certain this wasn't a trick. It wasn't. Mithridates is expecting stiff resistance. He's stripped every village within a hundred *stades* of men; he's given them a spear and shield and placed them in his front ranks."

"An act of desperation," Pammenes said. Excepting Memnon, he was the youngest man present; an exile from Thebes, he claimed to belong to the House of Epaminondas, an association he has exploited to the utmost. Still, Pammenes was affable. His round face and quick smile hid ambitions that would shame the most hardened courtier. "He hopes to overwhelm us with numbers."

"He may as well hope to fly," Chares said. Of all the generals, only the Athenian looked the part. With his bronzed limbs and silver-chased armor, Chares could have sprung from a sculptor's imagination, *andreia* given life, masculine virtue clothed in flesh. Memnon, though, knew Chares for what he was—a freebooter masquerading as an upright citizen of Athens, an admiral elected by popular acclaim, but more for his beauty than for his martial skill. "Now that he's marched, Mithridates has squandered his only viable asset—Dascylium's walls. That courtly fool and his peasant army could have held us off till midsummer."

"A lack of respect for your enemy is the quickest path to defeat," Artabazus said, capturing and holding Chares' eyes for a long moment. He circled the table, limping from a spear wound older than the men he addressed. "You assume Mithridates is desperate or a fool because he doesn't think as you do. I assure you, he is neither. But, he is an Achaemenid to his very core. He cannot conceive of losing to a rabble of *Yauna* led by a doddering old man. What does that tell us?"

Memnon frowned. Like a sophist, Artabazus taught war's principles through disputation. "That he's arrogant?"

"Indeed. And as with a spent arrow or a discarded sword, arrogance is a weapon that can be turned against its owner." Artabazus patted Memnon's shoulder.

"If Mithridates has been on the move for four days," Mentor said, "he should be . . . here." He touched a spot on the coast near the island of Arctonnesus and frowned. Artabazus noticed his clouded look.

"What troubles you, my friend?"

The elder Rhodian tapped the map with a black-nailed finger. His eyes narrowed. "Cyzicus. It's a rich port, and from my experience such enclaves of wealth breed hotbeds of dissension. They could easily raise a mercenary force of some consequence. But, their loyalty is an unknown quantity. Could Mithridates have struck a bargain with them?"

"What of it, Memnon?" Artabazus said. "You've been in the vicinity of Cyzicus. Do they seem disposed to help us or hinder us?"

Memnon shook his head. "Neither. I've spoken with Demostratus, who leads their Assembly, and he assures me that the folk of Cyzicus value their independence too highly to interfere, as allies or enemies. They will pledge their allegiance only when a clear-cut victor is decided."

"And if they've played you false?" Chares said. "What then? I mean you no insult, Memnon, but by what measure do you judge this Demostratus? In Athens we have politicians of every stripe, and in listening to the least of them even I have difficulty winnowing truth from tale. Have the gods granted you some special wisdom that allows you to see beyond political motivations and into a man's heart?"

Memnon smiled, though his eyes remained cold and hard. "No, the gods gave me a far greater gift. It's called forethought. If a man thinks I'm a fool, it keeps me from loosing my tongue and proving him right. I trust what I see, Chares. I trust what I hear and what I can feel in the pit of my stomach. Most of all, though, I trust what I know of democracies. In theory, it's a noble endeavor; in practice, it's as useless as racing a hobbled stallion. If Demostratus wanted to join forces with Mithridates, he would first need to present his case to the Council, argue it before the Assembly, secure the required votes, dicker over raising a mercenary force versus a citizen militia . . . Zeus Savior! By then, Mithridates will be dead and Artabazus in control of the whole of the Hellespont." The Athenian's face darkened, but a look from Artabazus silenced the retort forming on his lips.

"I am inclined to trust Memnon's judgment," Artabazus said. "What say you, Mentor?"

Mentor, hunched over the table, glanced from his brother to the map. He chewed his lip; his forefingers beat a staccato rhythm against the table's edge, drumming out a message of war. Beneath his blunt and brutal features, Memnon could see the mechanisms of thought grinding away as Mentor tallied their numbers. Seven thousand Athenian hoplites under Chares formed the core of Artabazus's army, supported by five thousand of Pammenes' Boeotian brothers. The satrap had his own contingent of household troops, called *kardakes*, which numbered twenty-five hundred, and a small force of horsemen. All told, fifteen thousand men compared with what Mithridates could raise: ten thousand Persian spearmen, levies from as far away as

Babylon, provided by the King to see his will be done; another ten thousand local levies, both spearmen and archers, along with upwards of two thousand horsemen from Paphlagonia. Twenty-two thousand versus fifteen thousand. Levies versus professional soldiers. Still, despite their inferior numbers, the odds favored Artabazus.

Finally, Mentor said, "Memnon's right. Cyzicus poses no real threat for the near future. I say we strike camp at dawn and march west toward the Granicus. We swing wide, in a half-circle, with enough outriders deployed to give us warning of Mithridates long before he's aware of us." He gestured to a point on the map, between Zeleia and the island of Arctonnesus, where the road skirted the shores of Lake Manyas. "And we take them here." The other generals nodded.

"Until now," Artabazus said, "your only crime has been by association. For myself, I have no choice but to rebel. But you, my friends, can still depart here and be held blameless. I daresay Ochus would reward you for it. The time to decide this once and for all is at hand. What say you?"

Mentor stood up straight. "I speak for myself, my brother, and my followers: we will stand with you, till death if need be!" Memnon muttered in agreement, his chest swelling with pride.

Pammenes came over to face Artabazus. "You've given me a home when the city of my birth would rather see me dead. I swear by Herakles that my men and I will not fail you!" At this, Pammenes clasped Artabazus's hand and kissed his signet ring.

Lastly, Chares stepped forward, his manner one of unaccustomed humility. "In autumn, after our defeat at Embata, my men and I lacked the will to live. We had failed our city against the rebels of Cos and Chios and slunk away like whipped dogs, our honor lost. When you found us on Imbros, Artabazus, we were starving, unable to repair our ships, and ready to fall on our own swords; we needed succor and a cause, and you gave us both. What could warm an Athenian's heart more than bloodying the nose of a Persian king? If the hour is indeed at hand, the men of Athens will stand with you!"

Artabazus exhaled. He approached each man in turn, embracing him in the Persian fashion and kissing his cheek. As he drew close, Memnon saw tears sparkling in the old satrap's eyes. "The gods have blessed me with sons, with station, and with long life. Now they have blessed me yet again with companions of the highest caliber. If our enterprise succeeds, I'll not forget the loyalty you've all shown me. If we fail," Artabazus shrugged, "well, if we fail nothing we've said or done here will matter. We've much to do in the coming days, and I daresay there will be precious little time for food or rest. After you've seen to your men, I invite you to return here and join me for the evening meal." Artabazus dismissed his generals. He smiled as he took Memnon's elbow and walked with him toward the door. "Except you. You're useless to me exhausted. Go and rest, Memnon. You've earned it."

"I will," Memnon said, his brow furrowing, "after I've seen to my men."

"Your enthusiasm does you great justice. Very well, then. Tend to your men, and pass along to them my gratitude." Artabazus turned and limped back into the heart of the pavilion.

Memnon paused by the entrance for a moment, listening to the faint murmur arising from the camp, to the clash of harness as one of the guards shifted his weight, to the twittering of the chamberlain as he laid out plans for his master's dinner. Memnon could feel a change in air pressure, a tension that presaged motion. Thunder rumbled in the distance. "We won't fail," he said suddenly, his voice low and brimming with a young man's ferocity. "We can't fail!"

The village of Zeleia lay in the thickly wooded valley of the Aisopus River, its dark waters rain-swollen and frigid from the melting snows of Mount Ida. The land had known a variety of masters—from the Trojans, who seeded the woods with game for their hunting pleasure, to the kings of Lydia, who preferred fragrant gardens and exotic birds. The rise of Persia brought little in the way of change. Now, it was the King of Kings in distant Susa who granted estates to his favorites, to the cream of Iranian nobility, who brought their retinues here in the spring and autumn to hunt the uplands and to stroll the ancient parks.

To Memnon's eyes, the town looked small and rustic, wholly unworthy of its noble antecedents. Houses of rough stone and timber, roofed with tiles of reddish clay brought overland from Sardis, lined the road leading up to the castle of the local grandee—a Milesian Greek who owed his position to Artabazus's patronage. By rights, the old satrap could have commandeered the castle for his own use, but its small size would have forced him to billet his men elsewhere. Artabazus preferred to keep company with his soldiers.

Lightning crackled across the sky, followed by the crash of thunder. Thick drops of rain spattered on Memnon's cloak as he trotted past the last house on the road to the castle, careful of the basket he carried. The wind picked up, roaring through the trees on the slopes above Zeleia. Another night of rain meant tomorrow's departure would be a slow and muddy affair. For an instant, Memnon regretted the errand that brought him out of his quarters and up to the castle, but it was unavoidable. It would be bad manners if he didn't pay his respects to the ladies of Artabazus's harem.

Memnon ducked through the open gate of the castle as the sky unleashed its tempest. Just inside, a Persian, one of the *kardakes*, stood guard, his body muffled in a thick cloak. Though traditionally the term *kardakes* applied only to young Persian men in training for war, Artabazus's father, the satrap Pharnabazus, used it to denote a hybrid soldier, a Persian who trained and armed himself in Greek fashion. The *kardakes* carried heavier spears, eight-footers counterbalanced by a butt-spike, and bowl-shaped shields faced with bronze. They wore the typical Median trousers and boots, with a coat of iron scales and a turban-wrapped helmet as their only defensive garb.

Memnon reckoned it was the innate stubbornness of the Persian that kept them from adopting the full panoply, despite witnessing its superiority in battle after battle. Perhaps Artabazus would allow him to experiment with it.

"Peace be with you, Memnon," the guard said, leaning on his spear. "I rejoiced to hear of your return. Have you come to see the girls?"

"Greetings, Arius," Memnon grinned, shaking water from his eyes. "This weather doubtless has them skittish. I thought they would enjoy a bit of company."

"I imagine they would, at that," Arius chuckled. "Is the rumor true? Are we moving out at dawn?"

"It's true."

"Praise Mithras," Arius said. "I am ready to quit this place. The weather is abominable."

"You'll get no argument from me," Memnon said. "If I'm still here when you're relieved, tell your replacement." The young Rhodian, mindful of his wicker basket, left the shelter of the gate at a dead run. He veered away from the entrance to the castle and made for the stables, vaulting the fence around the yard and sprinting inside. The foundations of the structure doubtless dated back to the days of Pandarus, who led the men of Zeleia against the Achaeans in the Great War at Troy. Stone pilasters upheld a roof of heavy timbers and glazed scarlet tiles, while the flat river rocks paving the floor gave off a moist, earthy smell.

"*Chairete*, ladies," Memnon said, panting.

From their spacious stalls, Artabazus's four Nisaean mares—each standing close to fifteen hands high and as black as the folds of Hades' cloak—whinnied and stamped in greeting, recognizing Memnon's voice. Thaleia, Aglaia, Euphrosyne, and Celaeno, they were, three Graces and a Harpy. Memnon sat his basket down and went to each stall, stroking their magnificent heads and allowing them to nuzzle him in return. "I apologize for not visiting you sooner," he said. "But I was off on an errand for your lord." The grooms had done their job well, insuring the stalls were spotless and well provided with water and feed. The mares' coats shimmered, their manes and tails displayed not the slightest knot, and their hooves rang like chimes on the stone floor. Celaeno nudged Memnon, who laughed aloud, sensing what she wanted. "Yes, yes," he said. "I know better than to visit you without a gift." Memnon knelt and retrieved four apples from his basket, the last of the winter stores, wrinkled and sweet. The horses whickered and snorted as he fed them each in turn.

Horses were a rarity on Rhodes; the island's sparse grasses and rocky landscape being better suited to asses or oxen. It wasn't until making landfall at Assos two summers ago that Memnon had a chance to ride. He found himself drawn to the animals, to their beauty, their grandeur; he shadowed Artabazus's Thessalian horse-master for the better part of a year, until he felt confident in his own ability.

"Now, ladies," he said, "if you'll permit me, I'd like to sit and eat my dinner." In response, Celaeno tossed her head. Memnon smiled, picked up his basket, and carried it over to the hayrick. For himself, the young Rhodian had a loaf of flat bread, a covered clay pot of spicy lentil stew, and a hunk of cheese. He dined slowly and washed it down with a flask of Chalybonian wine from Artabazus's own stock. Memnon knew he should head back to camp and check in with Mentor, but the combination of rain and exhaustion made him sluggish. He sank back into the hay. A sense of warmth stole over him. The sound of the rain drumming on the stable roof faded as he grew more relaxed, his eyelids fluttering.

Thunder murmured . . .

A heartbeat later, Memnon bolted upright, his eyes wild. The horses were gone, as were the stables, the rain, and the cool air of Zeleia. He sat in the midst of a dusty road that cut across a barren plain. Overhead, in the gray-white sky, the sun hung motionless in a state of perpetual eclipse, heat and pale light emanating from the blackened disk. Tall grass, like stalks of ash given form, waved to and fro as though buffeted by a freshening breeze. Memnon felt not the slightest stirring in the desiccated air. Behind him, he heard the sound of dust crunching beneath bare feet, accompanied by sobbing and faint invocations to Hades and Persephone. Memnon stood and turned toward the sounds. Up the road, coming toward him, a funeral cortege moved in solemn procession. Memnon stepped aside as they passed.

Women led the way, their black garments whitish with dust, their faces streaked with ash. Their hair writhed like a Gorgon's snaky locks as they beat their breasts and gashed themselves with stone knives. In their wake came a bier borne on the backs of ten gnarled men, their naked flesh scarred from innumerable battles and crusted with filth. The body atop the bier was massive, a giant covered in a shroud of purple and gold. A lone black-robed figure followed the cortege.

"Who died?" Memnon said, his voice hollow. No one answered him. "Who is it?" A sense of despair washed over Memnon. "Please! Tell me who died!"

The last figure in line stopped and looked at Memnon. He drew his hood back, revealing the gaunt face of Timocrates.

"Father!" Tears spilled down Memnon's cheeks and sizzled like acid on his chest. "I tried to save you! I swear it! Who is it you carry down to Tartarus? Who . . . ?"

Timocrates opened his mouth and spoke, though Memnon heard no words. The cortege halted and lowered the bier to the ground. Timocrates beckoned Memnon forward. Weak, overcome with emotion, Memnon staggered to his father's side. He felt an ice-cold hand take him by the elbow. Together, they approached the bier.

Timocrates reached down and flung the cloth back . . .

"No!" Memnon bolted upright, one flailing hand sending the empty wine flask skittering across the stable floor. Gray light filtered through the doors and windows, the air cool and heavy with the scent of a thousand cook fires. A shadow fell across Memnon's prostrate form. He looked up, his eyes wild.

Mentor smiled down at him. "You look like hell," the elder Rhodian said.

Memnon rubbed his eyes. His limbs ached. "What time is it?"

"Nearly dawn," Mentor said.

"Dawn? Zeus Savior! No wonder I feel like I've been thrashed." Memnon clambered to his feet and staggered over to a water barrel. He thrust his head into the chilly water, came up spluttering. Afterimages of his dream flashed in his mind. He glanced back at his brother. "How did you find me?"

"Arius found you asleep and passed the word to me should I need you for anything." Mentor's armor creaked as he approached Celaeno's stall and cooed at the mare. The horse eyed him with apprehension before submitting to his touch. "You've taken to these creatures."

Memnon stretched, working the kinks from his shoulders and back. "They're the noblest of animals. Lord Poseidon did mankind a tremendous boon when he created the horse. He gave us an example."

"An example?" Mentor looked askance at him. "Never forget, little brother, that for all their nobility, horses are slaves of man."

"Are they? Is it not man who serves their food, cleans their stalls, and cares for them when they're injured or sick? Who serves the other more, I wonder?"

Mentor chuckled. He backed away from the animal and walked to the door. "I wanted to talk with you last night, but I guessed rightly that you needed the sleep. You know I appreciate your skills, little brother, but yesterday you almost crossed the line when you insulted Chares."

Memnon snorted. "Insulted him? That Athenian whoreson is a dense as a stump. I'll never understand why you show deference to him. He's—"

"Why?" Mentor rounded on him, his voice the sharp crack of a general dressing down his subordinate. "Because he has troops we need, that's why!

Dammit, Memnon! This enterprise hangs by a thread as it is! I don't need you dancing around it with your sharp tongue! If you have to swallow every ounce of pride you possess just to deal with Chares, then swallow it you will, and with a smile! If you can't, I'll send you back to Patron and you can pull an oar for a few months. Do you understand?"

"Perfectly," Memnon said, his nostrils flaring with barely suppressed anger.

"Good." Mentor nodded. "Artabazus likes your mettle. He thinks you're ready for something more, so he's ordered me to reassign you to his staff."

Memnon blinked. "What . . . ?"

His brother grinned. "You're his lieutenant now. You'll be responsible for his maps and intelligence, among other duties. This is your chance, little brother. Don't make Artabazus regret his decision. Stop your gawking and let's go. We've a long day ahead of us."

Silent, Memnon fell in beside his brother.

Pale orange light breeched the eastern horizon, lancing through the haze of smoke and fog cloaking the valley floor. Like some great Titan stretched out full upon the earth, the army of Artabazus roused itself and made ready to move.

The rebels curved slowly through the hills north and west of Zeleia, a screen of cavalry flung out far ahead of the main body. Tramping feet churned up mud during the first few days of their advance, then dust as the clouds and rain gave way to brilliant spring sunshine. On the fifth day, this parti-colored river of burnished bronze and iron turned east and marched straight into the rising sun. Two days later, spies brought welcome news: a bloody flux had deprived the loyalist cavalry of most of their horses; that night, the Greeks sacrificed a bull to Zeus. Finally, at noon on the tenth day since leaving Zeleia, scarcely three miles from Lake Manyas, Artabazus called a halt. His scouts had spotted the enemy.

They were right where Mentor said they would be.

A faint breeze stirred Memnon's hair. He stood atop a spur of rock, its carpet of flowering moss jeweled with dew, and looked to the eastern horizon. The chariot of Helios fired the azure sky with orange and gold. Behind him, the priests of the battle train prepared their morning sacrifice. A she-goat bawled as an attendant shaved its throat, while another bound its legs, anticipating its placement on the flat slab of rock that served as their altar.

This spot, chosen for its height and purity, overlooked a lush green plain that sloped to the reed-choked shore of Lake Manyas. On Memnon's left, obscured by a haze of cookfires, he could barely make out the tents of the loyalist Persian army. To his right and back lay Artabazus's camp, protected from the remnants of Mithridates' cavalry by the land itself. The armies had faced one another for four days now, each waiting for the other to make its opening maneuver. Twice a day, Mithridates' herald would approach amid a fanfare of trumpets and demand Artabazus's surrender; twice a day, Artabazus would send scathing replies that brought Mithridates' manhood into question. Every hour of inaction cinched tighter the ropes of anxiety around the soldiers' necks; soon, they would fight, if only to be free of the noose.

Memnon turned back to watch the sacrifice. The Magi, led by their chief, Gaumata, performed the morning rites; the Greeks did the honors at dusk. Tall and thin, the white-robed Gaumata bore the most spectacular of beards. It reached well down below his sternum, a grizzled black pectoral, curled and oiled in the fashion of Babylonian society.

Gaumata gestured. A lesser priest handed him the sacrificial knife, its edge thin and sharp. Chanting in the sibilant tongue of Persia, the Magi offered the blade up to the rising sun as his attendants placed the she-goat on the altar. At the end of his invocation Gaumata slid the knife through the animal's throat. Blood gushed over the rock. A moment later, Gaumata slit the goat's belly open. The Magi's face screwed up in a look of supreme concentration as he reached into the incision, plucked out the animal's viscera, and studied it in the morning sunlight. At length, he gave a solemn nod.

"Tell Lord Artabazus that the omens are encouraging," Gaumata said, handing the bloody knife off to his attendant.

"He will be pleased." The young Rhodian glanced once more toward the enemy encampment before making his way down the slope, leaving the Magi to mutter amongst themselves.

Memnon crossed through the picket lines and passed the rope corral where early-rising cavalrymen groomed and exercised their mounts. Situated in a broad defile, the rebel camp stretched along the banks of a shallow stream, shaded by stands of oak and poplar. Mentor had laid out the camp to mimic the order of battle: at the mouth of the defile stood the tents of Pammenes and his Boeotians, who would anchor the right flank nearest the shores of Lake Manyas. Next came the tents of the *kardakes*, Artabazus's Persians, trained by Mentor to fight in a Greek-style phalanx; they would form the center of the line. Last, at the head of the defile, came Chares' Athenians. Once the call to arms was sounded, Memnon reckoned the allies could save precious time since each man would already be familiar with his place in line.

The young Rhodian hustled through this city of tents, its rows geometric and precise, as the blare of a *salpinx* roused the soldiers. Fires were kindled and the smell of baking bread drifted on the breeze. At the center of camp, Memnon found Artabazus sitting outside his pavilion, his scarred leg thrust out and swathed in an herb-steeped compress. Clerks and aides whirled around the old satrap as he pored over a sheaf of dispatches.

"Another fine morning," Artabazus said, glancing up as Memnon approached. "The gods must love us."

"Gaumata did say their omens are encouraging."

Artabazus chuckled. "Of course they are. They've been encouraging for the past three days. Our goats have very fortunate innards, I think."

"How's the leg?" The day previous, Artabazus had toured the camp on foot, addressing each soldier by name, stopping now and again to trade jokes or tell stories. By noon, the muscles of his bad leg had seized up; by nightfall, he could barely walk. Still, he never let on. He kept moving, kept smiling, until he had seen every last man. Only after returning to his pavilion did Artabazus allow Memnon to fetch him a physician.

"Feels like it's on fire, but it will bear my weight if need be." Artabazus glanced at the sky; he called to his chamberlain. "Datis! My armor. It's almost time for the herald to show."

"Do you think Mithridates suspects why we've not attacked yet?"

Artabazus shook his head. "He thinks we're reticent due to his superior numbers. Still, if we've received no word from the fleet by dusk, I fear we'll have no choice but to initiate battle. For myself, I would prefer to have Athenian ships sitting off Dascylium beforehand."

Memnon understood. If the rebels carried the field here, at Lake Manyas, the Persian survivors would flee back to Dascylium. By having Chares' ships blockading that city's harbor, and Athenian marines drawn up on shore, Artabazus could force Mithridates to surrender without resorting to a costly siege.

The chamberlain, Datis, scurried from the pavilion followed by a slave staggering under the weight of his master's panoply. Artabazus was already wearing his linen tunic, called a *spolas*; now, he stood as Datis brought him his trousers. Memnon offered him an arm to lean on.

Artabazus cocked an eyebrow at the young Rhodian. "You're not planning on wearing that sailor's cuirass into battle, are you?"

Memnon glanced down at his armor. "It's all I have. Why?"

"It won't do. Find something heavier, either from Mentor's armory, or from one of the *kardakes*. A shield and a helmet, too."

Memnon nodded. "I'll see to it today."

Artabazus stepped into his trousers, wincing as Datis tugged the purple fabric over the scarred flesh of his thigh and cinched it about his waist. Next, the chamberlain motioned the slave closer. From the bundle, Datis selected a knife belt of Egyptian leather, worked with plaques of ivory and silver, and buckled it around his master's middle. The corselet itself came next, its iron scales plated with gold. By Greek standards, the satrap's panoply reeked of *hybris*, of arrogance and vanity. More often than not such extravagances called down upon their practitioner the wrath of the gods. It made them a target. Still, for Artabazus this display of excess served to remind his enemies they faced a man of royal lineage; a man whose blood entitled him to the Peacock Throne, yet whose ambitions extended no farther than the borders of his ancestral lands. To the soldiers under Mithridates, it would be a powerful message.

"What kind of man is he?" Memnon said, his brows furrowed.

"Who?"

"Mithridates. Is he as inconsequential as Chares makes him out to be, or is there more to him?"

Artabazus pursed his lips. "In the field there's nothing extraordinary about him. He's competent within reason, and a good judge of officers. That's where the true danger lies. Those serving with him will be as shrewd as a Chares or a Pammenes, though not quite as capable as a Mentor. Mithridates' strength lay in his political ambitions. He was your age when he first entered the King's service, but his rite of passage came a year or so later when he denounced his father, Ariobarzanes, as a traitor."

"Was he?"

"A traitor? Of course. You see when the King summoned my father, Pharnabazus, to Susa to marry my mother, Ariobarzanes received Dascylium to hold in regency. When I came of age, the King ordered me to resume my father's satrapy. Ariobarzanes refused to surrender it. Instead, he and his cronies went into open revolt. I rooted them out one by one, fighting for every yard of my father's land, until only Dascylium remained. But, before I could move against Ariobarzanes, his son betrayed him to the King. In return, the King gave him Dascylium." Artabazus's eyes darkened. "Gave it to him! That land has been in my family since the time of Great Darius. To give it to a man such as Mithridates is the blackest of insults. In a way, I'm grateful to Ochus for ordering my execution. It's given me pretense to recover what's mine."

"That means you've waited—what?—nearly forty years to reclaim it?" Memnon said. "Zeus Savior, Artabazus! I thought only Greeks carried grudges to such lengths?"

Artabazus grinned. "Thirty-eight years, to be exact, and what you Greeks know of vendetta we Persians authored." Artabazus accepted his gold-chased helmet from Datis, the chamberlain fussing over its purple plumes to the very last.

A frantic horn sounded on the edge of camp, its drawn-out note echoing through the hills. Memnon's smile faded. "That doesn't sound like the herald's trumpet."

The old satrap frowned. "It's not." Another horn blared, this one closer. From the mouth of the defile a commotion caught Memnon's eye. A horseman galloped up the streambed, his mount's hooves sending plumes of water skyward. Droplets sparkled in the sun. Wild-eyed, the rider hauled on the reins as he came abreast of Artabazus's pavilion and leapt off, falling once before scrambling up the bank. Memnon caught his arm.

"What goes?" the young Rhodian said.

"The . . . the loyalists!" the rider gasped. "They are t-taking the field!"

Memnon spun toward Artabazus.

"To arms! Sound the call to arms!" the satrap cried, thumping Memnon's leather-clad chest. "Get heavier armor and meet me on the line!"

THE CALL TO ARM AND ASSEMBLE, BORNE FROM THE BRAZEN THROATS OF A dozen trumpets, came as no great shock to the rebel soldiers. If anything, the men felt a sense of relief as they doused their small cookfires and strapped on armor. The sentries who had drawn the night watch groaned as they rolled out of their cloaks and staggered to the rally point, joined by armed squires and a corps of pipers, trumpeters, and runners. Above the jangle of harness, veteran rankers cursed as they chivvied their younger companions into formation. Memnon waded through it as he made for his brother's tent.

Mentor's pavilion lay between the Persians and the Athenians, sharing the crest of a grassy knoll with the spreading boughs of an ancient oak. Its canvas walls reminded all of their general's past—they were sewn from lengths of bleached scarlet sailcloth taken from the wreck of a Rhodian trireme. Memnon could still make out the outline of a great sunburst, the mark of Helios, its golden thread long since plucked out. Persian officers stood at rigid attention outside the pavilion as Mentor dispensed his final orders; he dismissed them as Memnon approached.

"What is it?" Mentor said. He wore a cuirass of polished bronze, inlaid with silver and lapis lazuli, a leather kilt, and greaves etched with the images of the Dioscuri, Castor on the left leg and Polydeuces on the right.

"I need a heavier breastplate," Memnon said. Mentor eyed the stamped leather cuirass his brother wore. He turned to his squire, Diokles.

"Fetch my old panoply."

The squire brought out a muscled cuirass of unadorned bronze, functional and polished to a low sheen, greaves, and an uncrested Corinthian helmet. "This looks familiar. Is it . . . ?"

Mentor smiled. "It's the armor Father gave me when I left Rhodes. You've a good memory." He rapped the chest piece, listening to its solid ring. "Still, it's serviceable and it should fit you well enough, for now. I was smaller back then."

Memnon stripped off his leather and, with the squire's aid, shrugged into the heavier bronze carapace. Mentor helped him with the buckles while Diokles knelt and fitted the greaves over Memnon's shins.

"Keep your wits about you," Mentor said. "Keep your shield centered and balanced, and make sure you don't extend yourself too far beyond the allied line."

"I've been in battle before, brother."

Mentor snagged the neck of Memnon's cuirass and hauled him close. "You've never been in a battle like this, so shut up and listen! When your helmet's seated your peripheral vision's going to be poor. Understand? You won't be able to see from side to side, so keep friends on your flanks! Also, it'll be damn near impossible to hear with any certainty. But, listen . . . when the *salpinx* blares, you can feel its vibrations along your scalp and down your spine. Persian trumpets don't have the same effect."

Memnon swallowed, nodded. He looped his baldric over his shoulder and adjusted his sword, then caught up his helmet and a pair of javelins. Mentor frowned.

"Lose those pig-stickers and get yourself a proper spear." To Diokles, he said, "Bring him my spare shield." The bowl-shaped *aspis,* with its oak chassis and bronze facing, added another twenty pounds to Memnon's kit. He slipped his left arm into the sleeve and wrapped his hand around the grip-cord. Along its inner rim, the shield-maker had carved a hymn to Athena:

Sing, O Muse, of Athena Promachos,

Shield-bearer, defender of men.

O goddess, give me courage to escape

The enemy's charge and a violent death.

Memnon read the inscription again, and with each syllable the icy talons of *phobos* constricted about his throat. Could this be his last day under heaven? His last hour? The young Rhodian's eyes wandered toward the mouth of the defile and the gently sloping plain beyond. By nightfall the ground would be a ruin, its soil churned up, harrowed by thousands of feet and enriched by the blood of the slain. Would he . . . ?

Mentor clapped a hand on his shoulder, forestalling his thoughts. "Do your best, fight with heart and with honor, and leave the rest to the Fates." He gestured to Diokles, who handed him a small leather flask. Mentor uncorked it, dribbled a libation of wine on the ground between them, then took a swallow and passed the flask to Memnon. "For Zeus Savior and Victory."

Memnon exhaled and followed his brother's lead, surprised at the steadiness in his own voice. "Zeus Savior and Victory."

IT TOOK THE REBELS LESS THAN AN HOUR TO MARSHAL ON THE PLAIN, WHOLE divisions moving into place with the quiet efficiency of men bred to war. The genius of Artabazus's strategy became apparent to Memnon as he watched the battalions dress ranks—the old satrap sought to emulate the success of the Athenians at Marathon. On the right wing, Pammenes and his Boeotians presented a front five hundred shields across and ten deep; facing them, if Mithridates clung to Persian tradition, would be light troops, levied spearmen and javelineers. The *kardakes* occupied the center of Artabazus's line, their formation as close and tight as a Greek phalanx. Despite their numbers, Mentor aligned them on a front five hundred shields across, equal to the Boeotians, but only five men deep. They would need every scrap of courage they could cobble together if they hoped to survive against the cream of Mithridates' army, his household troops and the spearmen of Babylon. Chares and his Athenians anchored the left, their formation mirroring the others. The Athenians, though, loaded each file with fourteen men. The light troops and unhorsed cavalry facing them, though numerous, stood little chance against such a mass of muscle, bronze, and iron. If all went as planned, the Persians would concentrate on the rebel center even as the Athenians and Boeotians decimated the wings and rolled up Mithridates' flanks.

Shuffling feet sent clouds of dust into the air and with every breath Memnon tasted grit. The young Rhodian swiped his forearm across his sweat-dampened brow. He stood on the frontline, a *promachos*; his position one hundred thirty stations right of where the *kardakes* joined with the Athenians. Mentor would fight in the same position on the Boeotian side; Artabazus, with his bodyguard and standard-bearers, trumpeters and flute-players, took the middle, over Mentor's protestations. A mile separated rebel from loyalist, a mile of rolling grassland split by the ruddy scar of the Zeleian road, by scrubby trees and rocky streamlets. At two hundred yards they would become targets for the Persian archers; at fifty yards the *salpinx* would sound the order to charge. "Your leg won't bear you through that hell!" Mentor had said.

Artabazus's eyes had flashed in anger, the sole occasion Memnon had seen that emotion turned against the satrap's own kinsman. "Do not presume to tell me what I may or may not do! I've not come this far only to sit back and let others do my fighting for me!"

Tension knotted Memnon's gut. He knew he should say something to the men around him—a word or two of encouragement, perhaps a fitting quote—but his eloquence deserted him, the first casualty of *phobia*. Instead, he contented himself with looking up and down the line. Each man developed his own ritual before battle, some small thing he could do to restore a measure of control over his emotions. For the veterans, something practical—a buckle readjusted, a sword loosened in its sheath, a handful of dirt abraded along the grip of a spear. Those less experienced preferred the spiritual observances—a talisman kissed and tucked away, a prayer chanted under breath, a dialogue with the gods responsible for winnowing spirits from the battlefield. As always, one or two of the soldiers possessed irrepressible humor; their jokes and the attendant laughter calmed even the most terrified among them.

Three stations to his right, in the second rank, Memnon caught sight of a familiar face: Arius, the guard from Zeleia. He had his spear propped in the crook of his shield arm as he busily patted his scaled cuirass, looking for something.

"What have you lost, Arius?" Memnon said.

"His mind," someone from the third rank muttered. "Careful underfoot!" The Persians chuckled. Arius shook his head, smiling.

"No, my mind is less precious to me. Ah, here it is." From the hem of his armor, Arius withdrew a talisman on a broken leather thong. Memnon, his interest piqued, leaned forward. It was a coin. Arius offered it to Memnon for a closer look. "It has been in my family for generations, passed from father to son, since my ancestor earned it in the employ of Cyrus the Great. It is Lydian, from the hoard of King Croesus." The coin, a flat, irregular disc of worn silver, bore the faint image of a lion on one side, a punch mark on the reverse. Memnon handed it back to Arius, who tucked it inside his armor.

"May it hold the luck of Cyrus," the young Rhodian said.

Arius nodded. "For us all."

Memnon faced front. A breeze whispered through the grass, rustling pennons and cooling his sweat-soaked forehead. Near the center of the formation, Artabazus stepped out in front of the mass of soldiers, his panoply glittering brighter than the ripples on the surface of Lake Manyas. Memnon tensed. The aging satrap raised his spear aloft, paused for effect, then bellowed. "Forward to victory!"

A chorus of trumpets blared the order to advance, holding the note for the span of a dozen heartbeats. Memnon's hand trembled as he grasped the bottom edge of his helmet's cheek guard and tugged it down, muffling the pipers' wail as it cut through the din of the *salpinx*. In unison, the phalanx stepped off their mark, shields interleaved, spears held at the vertical. Partially robbed of sight, Memnon kept his attention riveted straight ahead, on the enemy lines. A pall of dust hid any details.

Memnon checked his right and left, sweat dripping from the inside of his helmet's cheek guards. Unbroken, the rebel line advanced through knee-high grass. Birds exploded from thickets all around, startled at the crash and thunder of armored men marching to the shrill music of the *aulos* flute. The pipers' steady pace carried the army along faster than Memnon imagined. They passed the midway point. A half-mile remained. Elements of the enemy line grew distinct with each step: wicker shields and javelins, bronze-scaled jerkins and helmets of hammered iron, pennons of purple and gold. Above the tramp of thirty thousand feet, the jangle of his harness, and the scrape of his shield rim against another, Memnon heard a distant cacophony of ox-hide drums and brazen horns as the loyalists stoked their courage to a fever pitch.

With a quarter-mile to go, the young Rhodian experienced a sudden rush of panic. As one of the *promachoi*, the frontline fighters, he had no avenue of escape. He couldn't backpedal, nor dodge from side to side. The pressure of the phalanx meant he could only move forward, onto the spears of the enemy, where a wrong move, a misstep, would find him, in the words of the poet Tyrtaeus, "holding in his hands his testicles all bloody."

The tune of the *auloi* quickened; the phalanx broke into a trot. Half a dozen paces later, a haze of missiles lofted skyward, arching over the heads of the enemy's front-rankers. Arrows and javelins, their flight at once graceful and terrifying, reached their apex and descended to earth in a lethal rain of razor-tipped iron. Memnon's bowels seized up.

He thrust his shield high, canting it so it covered his head and the right side of the man beside him. Arrows peppered the ground; they struck his shield face with the crack of a mallet on wood. Heavier javelins caromed off his bowl-shaped *aspis* and clattered into the grove of upraised spears behind him. Memnon heard the voices of those nearest him, mindless screams and prayers, mantras of names—fathers, mothers, wives, children, ancestors, heroes—chanted over and again at the tops of their lungs. He added his own shouts to the din as another fusillade buffeted their lines, then a third. Through it, the phalanx advanced at the double-quick, their ranks unbroken. Before the Persians loosed a fourth volley, the *salpinx* wailed the order to charge.

A dull roar rose from the throats of the rebels. As they surged forward, sprinting the last fifty yards or so, Memnon and the other frontline fighters leveled their spears to full horizontal. Soldiers of the next two ranks followed suit, thrusting their weapons over the shoulders of the *promachoi* to create a murderous hedge of ash and iron.

Forty yards, now. Thirty. Adrenalin sharpened Memnon's perceptions. He singled out one man, straight ahead of him, a Babylonian in a bronze-scaled tunic and gold-embroidered pantaloons. Bright sunlight shone on the razored edge of his spear. The fellow stood his ground, his face grim and resolute. Twenty yards. Ten. Every muscle in Memnon's body tensed; he angled his torso, placing his shoulder in the hollow of his shield. Iron fingers gripped the haft of his spear, knuckles cracking. The soldiers' roar grew in volume, becoming the basso scream of a cornered animal. All fear fled as the cathartic wave of sound coalesced into a single word:

"Victory!"

The two armies collided not with a thunderous crash, but with a less climactic noise—the wet crack of bone coupled with the rasp and slither of iron, amplified a thousand times over. Spears shattered like kindling; wicker shields crunched under the impact of bronze-sheathed *aspides*, driven by the mass of an entire phalanx. Memnon felt the pressure of the army behind him as he barreled through his chosen target and into the second rank of Persians, his spear plunging forward. Gore sprayed from torn breasts and throats, the droplets hanging in the air like brilliant rubies cast by the hand of a benevolent tyrant. Men collapsed, writhing in a mixture of churned soil, blood, and bowel.

Caught up in the wrack of war, Memnon lost all concern for himself. Individuality vanished; he became part of a common personality, threatened by a common enemy and driven by a common desire. The soldiers fighting alongside him became precious, his brothers. His shield moved of its own accord, protecting the man to his right, just as another protected him. Memnon struck overhand with his spear, again and again, punching through the flesh and bone of his enemies.

The two fronts ground together like millstones, the sheer mass of the

Persian center stalling the *kardakes*' advance. Heels dug in; toes scrabbled for purchase amid sundered bodies, the ground slick with blood and piss. Memnon's lungs worked like a forge bellows. Sweat and blood stung his eyes, blinding him. Persian blades sought out chinks in his defenses; they grazed his helmet, scraped along his breastplate, shattered on his shield. A red rage gripped the young Rhodian, the furious exasperation of a lion pestered by yapping hyenas. He wanted to reach out and brush his enemies aside like they were nothing more than pieces on a game board.

"Hold them!" Memnon roared, his shield mashed against a wall of flesh. "Hold the line!" The pressure at his back redoubled, driving the air from his lungs. Spears ceased to plunge as men on both sides threw everything into this shoving match. The rebels heaved and shook against the overwhelming crush of bodies, their feet plowing furrows in the blood-dampened earth. Memnon struggled for breath. "Hold!"

Inexorably, the rebel line foundered.

Against the mercurial floods of springtime, a farmer's crude dam of sticks, rocks, and earth can save a field if the structure stays intact, unbroken. But, should one element—a twig, say, or a pebble—become dislodged, roiling water will surge into the breach and assault the cohesion of neighboring elements. Inevitably, the dam will weaken and buckle, washing away the seeds of autumn's harvest. In the dam of rebel fighters, the first breach opened on Memnon's shield side. He heard the man bawl as he lost his footing and collapsed, affording the Persians a toehold. Lances ripped into the rebel file. Instinctively, Memnon edged to his left, shifting his *aspis* to defend his now-exposed flank. The breach widened as the spearmen of Babylon, howling in fury, spiked into the heart of the rebel formation and tore it asunder.

A shoulder rammed Memnon's midsection. He staggered back and lashed out, his spear shattering against a bronze helmet. Through a haze of dust the shape of his attacker loomed, a massive Iranian in bloodied armor, his tunic ripped and gore-blasted. The Iranian's scimitar hammered on

Memnon's shield, driving him to his knees. Successive blows dented and cracked the bronze facing but failed to penetrate it. Desperate, Memnon fumbled with his broken spear. He reversed his grip and rammed the butt-spike up into his attacker's groin, twisting till it grated on bone. The Iranian doubled over, screaming and clutching himself. Memnon lurched to his feet. Snarling, he brought the edge of his shield down on the back of his foeman's neck with such force his vertebrae shattered like pottery.

Memnon backpedaled, ripping his sword from its sheath. Around him, battle lines degenerated into a maelstrom of hand-to-hand fighting. Persians swarmed over the embattled *kardakes*, attacking with broken spears, swords, or knives. Even the wounded fought tooth and nail. Hands grasped at Memnon's legs; he hacked at them as a farmer hacks at clinging brambles, oblivious of the thorns. Time and again his borrowed panoply saved his life. The wide bowl of his shield intercepted enemy lances thrusting for his heart, his head. "Re-form!" he shouted. "Re-form!"

Clouds of yellowish dust rolled across the field to create a nightmare landscape of grotesque silhouettes, half-glimpsed maenads of war cavorting in Dionysian abandon. Solitary figures pierced the veil in a swirl of blood and iron before falling back into the pandemonium. Memnon saw Arius stumble from the dust, gore-splashed, his shield and helmet lost to the fray, his arms outstretched in a gesture of succor. The young Rhodian screamed his name just as a bearded Chaldean emerged from the haze and drove his spear through Arius's body, bearing him to the ground. With a shriek of homicidal rage, Memnon leapt, slashing his blade across the Chaldean's face. The enemy cried in horror and reeled away. Memnon followed, bracing for a fresh Persian onslaught. What he saw through the murk, though, gave him pause.

The Persians ceased to advance. They milled about, confused. Something unseen sent ripples of alarm through their ranks. Memnon motioned to the *kardakes*. "Form a new line! Quickly, brothers!" In pairs and clusters, the rebels regrouped, lapping shields to create a tenuous wall.

From his left, Memnon heard the skirl of flutes. To his numbed ears, Persian cries of triumph became screams of terror. Veteran soldiers recoiled; their courage ebbed as, above the din of battle, a clear voice rang out:

"*Athena Promachos kai Nike!*"

The Athenians.

Memnon snarled, thrusting his sword at the mass of men across the blood-soaked interval. "For Artabazus and Victory!" Like a madman, Memnon led the *kardakes* pell-mell over the corpse-littered field toward the scrambled enemy ranks. Panic took root among the spearmen of Babylon, doubtless fed by enduring memories of the disaster at Marathon, the slaughter at Thermopylae, the ravages at Cunaxa. By the hundreds, the loyalist Persians cast their weapons aside and turned to flee, their retreat hampered by the compacted ranks behind them. Men who had been so hot for rebel blood only moments before now bellowed like stampeded cattle, trampling their own in haste to escape the pale hand of Death. As one, the *kardakes* and their Greek allies smashed into the Persians like an axe blade into rotted wood.

Then, the true slaughter began.

Morning gave way to midday before the trumpeters sounded the call to disengage. Memnon, spattered with gore from head to toe, heard the strident order and obeyed without thinking, so dazed was he from exhaustion and thirst. His sword slipped from his cramped fingers; his arms trembled and his legs felt unstrung, the muscles and tendons burning with pain. With effort, he pried his helmet off, his hair a tangled mass. Memnon spat blood, his back teeth splintered from the grinding of his jaw. A breath of wind caressed his face.

Off to the east, the noontime sun struck golden fire from the surface of Lake Manyas; high grasses swayed, and slender trees bearing leaves of translucent green rustled, idyllic in the breeze. Gulping air, Memnon forced himself to turn and look back at the plain.

The floor of hell greeted his blank stare.

A swath of destruction stretched a mile in width and continued on for two, the field of Ares. The War God disdained oxen, preferring to let the yoked power of contending armies harrow his demesne. Into this flayed earth poured the fluids of war, the sweat and blood, the bile and bowel, the coward's piss and the dying man's tears, mingling to form a sludge that clung to the ankles of those men left standing. The ground itself heaved and shook with the convulsions of the wounded. Slashed torsos and severed limbs lay on carpets of spilled entrails; hands stained black with blood protruded from the mass, splintered weapons yet clutched in immobile fists. Spear shafts projected at angles, some upright, resembling stakes awaiting a transplanted vine. In places, the bright flash of gold embroidery or the shimmer of rich fabric appeared unreal against the devastation, a mirage borne of dehydration.

Memnon's legs gave out; he collapsed into a bier of gore-slick limbs, his shattered body cradled by the corpses of friend and foe alike. Overcome, the young Rhodian closed his eyes . . .

RETRIEVAL PARTIES WORKED WELL INTO THE NIGHT, SCOURING THE FIELD for wounded allies, dispatching those with no hope of survival, and securing the bodies of the slain. A deputation of Persian captives, drawn from those who had not fled with Mithridates, was allowed to do likewise for their countrymen. Others were put to work preparing mass graves.

Memnon sat atop the spur of rock where the Magi conducted their morning sacrifice and watched torches bobbing on the plain below. He still wore his borrowed cuirass, the bronze scraped and dented, crusted with blood. Grimy bandages swathed his right arm and leg. Memnon hunched forward, his elbows on his knees and his chin propped on his fists, and stared at the field, lost in thought. His lips moved as he silently talked himself through the battle, disassembling every minute of every hour to examine content, context, and resolution. Gaps developed, long, hazy sections of memory bereft of detail save for a flash of metal, a scream, a spatter of blood. The end result proved as frustrating as trying to rebuild a shattered mosaic without all its tiles.

A sandal crunched on stone. Memnon half-turned and saw his brother's thick silhouette limned in the light of the distant fires. Mentor bore only scanty wounds from the day's carnage; bathed, clad in an old russet-colored *chiton*, the elder Rhodian's features were flush with wine and triumph. More wine sloshed over the rim of the antique golden *skyphos* Mentor carried, the cup and its contents plundered from Mithridates' own tent. He staggered to the edge of the rocks, peered over, then came back and plopped down beside Memnon.

"You're drunk," Memnon said.

Mentor belched. "Damn right I'm drunk, and you would be, too, if you had any sense. Zeus! We snatch a victory and here you sit, brooding over the dead like dark Hades, himself. What bothers you, brother? Is war not the glorious enterprise you imagined it to be?" Mentor took a deep draft of wine before nudging Memnon's shoulder and offering it to him.

Memnon waved it away, frowning. "I don't know if it was glorious or not. I can't remember. My last clear memory is of hearing the call to charge, after that it becomes a jumble—a shape here, a scene there—like something I may have read about or watched at the theater. It's as though another took control of my body and guided me through the battle."

"Your *daimon*," Mentor said. Memnon looked askance at his brother. "It is the guardian spirit every man is born with. It guides our actions, for good or ill. Your *daimon* took over in a time of extreme dislocation, as a way of protecting you from the ravages of war."

"I never imagined *you* to be a follower of Socrates."

"Why, little brother, did you not know? I am a man of many parts."

Mentor belched, again.

"Indeed. How's Artabazus?"

"His leg's useless, for now," Mentor said, "and he has a couple of nasty cuts, but he's in good spirits. He keeps asking after you, afraid your first battle might have left you irreparably scarred." The elder Rhodian grinned.

"I'll see him before I turn in." Memnon listened as the sounds of revelry drifted up from the rebel camp, harsh laughter and music masking the screams of the surgeon's precinct. "How many dead?"

"The estimate is rough," Mentor said, flexing the muscles of his spear-arm. "It looks as though we lost perhaps two hundred Greeks and over a thousand *kardakes*. Mithridates placed fewer men on his flanks so he could increase the power of his center. Chares claims he nearly had the bastard . . ."

"Where did Mithridates go?"

Mentor shrugged. "Sardis, most likely. He lost ten times our casualties, so if he survives Ochus's wrath I doubt he'll trouble us further. Dascylium is ours. We'll use this respite wisely and prepare for a counterattack. Artabazus is sending me back to Assos. I'll be escorting the family to Dascylium, and raising a new force of mercenaries, provided I can get old Eubulus to keep his hands off his catamites long enough to spread the word into the Aegean. Chares is going up the coast to Lampsacus to make use of its shipwrights. Pammenes is being redeployed into the Macestus Valley, to watch the Royal Road."

"What about me?"

"You'll stay with Artabazus. Protect him, Memnon. He's our best hope for a future." Mentor draped a hand on Memnon's shoulder and pulled him closer. "Listen, brother. You acquitted yourself well, today. You may not remember it, but—by the gods!—you stood your ground despite adversity, and you did what was needed of you. No more can be asked of any man. You and I are in an enviable place. Artabazus will need trustworthy men to administer his holdings in the Troad, Aeolus, Mysia, perhaps even into Ionia."

"And who is more trustworthy than family?"

"Exactly."

Memnon nodded. He said nothing for a moment; his brow furrowed. "Why . . ." he started before again lapsing into silence. His eyes flickered to his brother's face.

"What?" Mentor sipped his wine.

"It's nothing," Memnon sighed. "I am reminded of Rhodes."

"Rhodes, eh? You were going to ask me why, if family is of such importance, did we not avenge Timocrates." Mentor grunted and swirled the dregs of his wine around in his cup before emptying it. "Zeus! You know how to sober a man up."

"Am I that transparent?"

"Like sheer linen, brother. Perhaps you're right. Perhaps we should have raised an army of our own and used it to restore democracy to Rhodes, maybe Cos and Chios, too. But, would we have fared any better on that score than the Athenians? Perhaps we should have returned home, you and I, to reorganize the democrats against the oligarchs, to drive Philolaus back to the man who bought him, Mausolus of Caria. But, would we have fared any better on that score than Timocrates? Perhaps I should have just sailed into Rhodes-town, hunted Philolaus down, and murdered him. Simple. Clean. A death for a death. But, would I have fared any better on that score than you?"

"Now you mock me!" Memnon snarled.

"No," Mentor said. "I ask you in all honesty, what would you have had me do? Father died in battle, in a war of his own choosing. Philolaus may have been his enemy, but I cannot condemn him for something I, too, would have done had I been in his place. Look at it from another perspective, Memnon: Arius died in battle, in a war of his own choosing, if not his own making. Should Arius's father and his brothers now blame Mithridates for leading his killer into battle? Or should they mourn their fallen kinsman and leave the fate of his killer in the hands of the gods?"

Memnon's shoulders sagged; he glanced at Mentor, his eyes haunted, rimmed in fatigue. "I believe I'm beginning to understand."

"Good," Mentor said. "Come, let's get you cleaned up. There's much to do tomorrow." Mentor stood, reached down, and hauled Memnon to his feet. The young Rhodian's legs could barely hold him erect, so crippled were they from the day's exertions. He grimaced.

"Is it always like this?"

Mentor chuckled. "As with virgins, the next time comes easier." Arm in arm, the sons of Timocrates made their way down to the rebel camp.

CELAENO, ARTABAZUS'S BLACK NISAEAN MARE, THUNDERED DOWN the straightaway of Dascylium's *hippodromos*, its hooves raising plumes of dust in the still afternoon air. Naked to the waist, Memnon hunched over the animal's broad neck, the reins held loosely in his left hand, a javelin in his right. Ahead, near the sculptured column that served as a turning post, stood a straw bale bearing the silhouette of a man daubed in charcoal, a circle of red at its center. Horse and rider moved in cadence. As they neared the column, with its hairpin turn beyond, Memnon rose up and let fly his javelin. The target flashed past the horse's left flank. Memnon craned his head to look. His javelin had struck wide of its mark, burying itself in the straw at the edge of silhouette. Impact sent the target skittering on its side.

"Son of a bitch!" Through the turn, Memnon slowed the horse to a canter. Sweat drenched the young Rhodian's muscular upper body, soaking his short linen kilt and the fringed saddlecloth under him. This was his fourth run and still he had gotten no closer to the target's center. He patted Celaeno's damp neck. "Do you have a fifth try in you, girl?" The horse tossed its head and whinnied. Memnon circled back to the starting point.

A small crowd gathered to watch his exercise: Pharnabazus, the satrap's eldest son, a lad of twelve, stood with his pedagogue, a sullen Greek of Ionia; near them were a trio of Thessalian horse-breeders and four of Artabazus's grooms. Patron waited off to one side, his face shaded by a broad-brimmed hat, a sea-bag slung over his shoulder. *Circe*'s captain flashed a wide grin. Memnon raised a hand in greeting. He glanced at his nephew.

"Pharnabazus! Fetch me another javelin!"

"Yes, Uncle." To his pedagogue's chagrin, the Persian lad rushed to the weapons rack, selected a cornel-wood javelin, and trotted over to where Celaeno pawed the ground, restless. A pair of slaves hurried out and righted the straw dummy.

"Why do I keep missing?" Memnon said, taking the weapon. He readjusted his grip on the reins. "Have you any idea?"

Pharnabazus pursed his lips. He had the finely chiseled cheekbones and nose of his mother—a Persian lady who died giving birth to his younger sister, Barsine—and his father's piercing eyes. His wild shock of chestnut hair defied grooming. As did all in the satrap's family, Pharnabazus spoke flawless Greek. "You're waiting too late to cast, I think."

Memnon smiled. "I think so, too. Where, then? Four lengths from the target?"

"Four or five." Pharnabazus nodded.

"I trust your judgment. You wouldn't lead me astray, would you?"

"Never, Uncle."

Memnon winked, touching his heels to Celaeno's flanks. The mare sprang forward, its muscles bunching beneath its glossy coat as it achieved a full gallop in a matter of seconds. Memnon sat easily, gripping with his thighs, his legs relaxed below the knee. He kept his upper body as loose as possible. Horse and rider barreled toward the target. At twice the distance than before, Memnon rose up on his thighs and hurled the javelin. Iron flashed; this time, it struck center mass. A man would have died on the spot with his heart split in two. A cheer arose from the onlookers.

Memnon wheeled and rode back to where Pharnabazus stood. "By the gods, you were right!"

The Persian lad beamed.

Memnon dismounted, throwing his right leg over Celaeno's neck and dropping to the ground. The horse whickered and shook its head, rattling the silver disks accenting its bridle and headstall. The young Rhodian motioned for the grooms to take the reins, then draped an arm over Pharnabazus's shoulder and walked with him to where his pedagogue waited, impatience written across his wrinkled forehead.

"Are you late for something again?"

"Rhetoric," Pharnabazus said, his brows knitting in distaste. "That dried-up old bag Nikeratos hates me as he hates all *barbaroi*. Father should send him back to Paros in a box. Can I try casting a few tomorrow, Uncle?"

Memnon looked sidelong at the lad. "You think you can handle Celaeno?"

Pharnabazus nodded. "I believe I am ready."

"I have no objections, but only if your father approves. We will ask him this evening, after supper." Memnon gave the boy's shoulder a squeeze. "Go on, now, and learn whatever Nikeratos teaches, even if it's only the meaning of patience."

Pharnabazus smiled and waved as his pedagogue shooed him toward the hillside palace.

"That one's the image of his sire," Patron said, joining Memnon.

"He'll make a fine satrap, someday." The young Rhodian turned. "I'm sorry Artabazus has asked you to sail so late in the season, but he didn't want winter to pass before sending an envoy back to Macedonia, to formalize his guest-friendship with their king."

"No need to apologize, Memnon. Artabazus is right. This Philip seems dead-set on wearing the robes of Agamemnon. Four years on the throne and already he's shattered the Illyrians, laid Amphipolis low, double-crossed the Athenians, captured Potidaea and Pydna, and snatched a victory in the horserace at Olympia. What's next for him? Asia?"

"All the more reason to make him a friend rather than an enemy," Memnon said. "When do you plan to leave?"

"As soon as I get to the ship," Patron said. "If we sail with the full moon tonight, *Circe* can put in at Cyzicus before dawn. I want to be clear of the Hellespont by week's end. Come, walk with me down to the harbor."

Memnon issued orders to the grooms, entrusting Celaeno to their care. He followed Patron from the *hippodromos*. A dusty path, shaded at times by groves of sycamore, followed the high banks of the Little Macestus River, chuckling in its rocky bed as it wound down to Lake Dascylitis and the harbor. The chirr of cicadas abated as the two men passed. Through the trees, off to the right and away up the hill, Memnon could see stone terraces and earthworks rising to meet the walls of the palace-fortress of the Pharnacids, Artabazus's ancestral keep. Limestone glimmered in the sun, and flashes of gold marked the position of sentries.

Patron followed his gaze. "This whole rebellion would have been for nothing had Mithridates simply stayed put."

"We're lucky he didn't, then."

"But, when the time comes, will Artabazus?"

Memnon frowned. "What do you mean?"

"Ochus hasn't forgotten his western satraps," Patron said. "Another army will come, larger, led by someone with far more experience than Mithridates. What will Artabazus do? Will he stay and defend Dascylium, or will he ride out and meet them?"

Memnon weighed his answer. In the five months since the battle at Lake Manyas, Artabazus's sole concern had been the rebuilding of a satrapy left barren from years of misrule. While he dealt with the affairs of state—from foreign envoys seeking favor to Iranian nobles bent on brokering peace with the Great King to commoners nursing grievances stretching back to his father's day—Artabazus left the execution of the war to Mentor and his mercenary generals. "The fighting's ground to a halt," Memnon said, at length. "The probes down the Macestus Valley from Sardis have ceased. Pammenes sends us word that the Royal Road is clear, save for the usual dispatch riders. Chares' scout ships have encountered nothing out of the ordinary in the Propontis or the Euxine Sea. I don't doubt what you say, that another army will come, but likely not this season. Artabazus has until late spring, at least, to decide his course of action." After a moment, he added, "I wish I were going with you. At sea, a man knows his place. He knows who his friends are, his enemies. There are no politics to pulling an oar."

"I'd take you along," Patron said, "if I thought you'd be content. You must face facts, lad. You've found your true calling. You're a soldier, a cavalry officer, and a leader of men. The anonymity of the rower's bench is no longer yours for the asking."

Their path widened and joined with the main road running from the hilltop fortress to the harbor. Dascylium lay on the southern shore of Lake Dascylitis, in a cove that created an ideal shelter for ships against the ferocious spring and winter storms. North, across the lake, the Macestus River continued on, deep and slow, completing the twelve-mile journey to the Propontis.

The road cut through the heart of Dascylium, past buildings of stone and timber whose foundations were set in the days of Darius the Great. Those of newer construction bore the stamp of Greek influence. Memnon and Patron dodged ox-drawn wains, loaded with grain and oil and bound for the storage magazines inside the fortress. Men from the outlying villages led strings of horses to the livestock market west of town. "Not the best breed," Memnon said, noting the thinness of their withers and the dull *clop* of their hooves, "but serviceable. They'll make good post horses."

"What about men to ride them?"

"Recruits come from all over," Memnon said. "Artabazus has a good name among fighting men, both Persian and Greek. A far better name than Ochus. You're a mercenary—would you rather side with a foul-tempered despot or a kindly old grandfather who is free with his coin?"

Patron smiled. "That's why I'm in Dascylium and not Susa."

The road debouched at the harbor, where a stone-paved quay ran along the water's edge; parallel to this, and set back from the shore, a colonnaded *emporion* housed local merchants conducting their business. Awnings of brightly colored cloth provided welcome shade as men haggled over a bewildering array of goods: olive oil and wine from the Aegean, fish sauce from Cyzicus, baskets of figs from Phrygia, crocks of honey from the Sangarius Valley, wool from the slopes of Mount Ida. Despite the vigor of Dascylium's market, the absence of luxury goods, of precious metals and jewelry, fine cloth and furniture, stood as a stark reminder of the ongoing war.

"There's an impressive sight," Patron said, nodding out into the harbor. A trireme, its sail reefed, approached the quay at quarter-speed. Its polished bronze ram reflected the sun so brightly that Memnon could barely see that its sternpost bore the carved likeness of Athena. An officer occupied a perch high in the bow, signaling aft with his hand as the ship hove close to the moorage, while sailors stood atop the outrigger with boat poles at the ready. Rope men waited in the catheads; along the quay, their counterparts manned the cleats.

"Is that one of Chares' ships?" Memnon said.

"It's Athenian, but . . ." Patron peered closer, grunted in surprise. "That's the *Salaminia*, one of their state galleys. I saw her once before, rounding Cape Sunium on her way back to Athens. Zeus only knows what business brings her here, but it can't be good. She's not sent forth as a deliverer of glad tidings."

"I'd better go and see. If it's bad news Artabazus will want to hear about it. Farewell, my friend," Memnon said, embracing Patron, "I will sacrifice to Poseidon for your safe return."

Patron smiled and clapped the younger man on the back. "And I to Ares, that he might grant you victory." The men parted. Memnon watched as Patron continued down to the water's edge, no doubt his mind already intent on currents and winds. Ill-timed as his mission to Macedonia might be, that Artabazus would entrust it to him at all was a sign of the satrap's favor. He appreciated Patron's candor; so would the Macedonians, who prized honesty and valor above all things. The young Rhodian could think of no better emissary.

Memnon returned his attention to the Athenian trireme. With ropes and boat poles, the vessel managed to warp into a slip quayside, where reed bundles kept the stone edge from damaging its hull. Sailors swarmed ashore, checking the cleats and ropes, ignoring the protests of the stevedores who tied them. The captain barked orders in Attic Greek, the tongue of orators, rarely heard in this part of Asia.

A gangplank swung out from the stern. A squad of hoplites, their helmets, breastplates, shields, and spear points polished to mirror brightness, disembarked and assumed stations along the quay, facing outward. A single man followed in their wake, his bronze-shod staff clacking against wood and stone. It bore the symbol of an Athenian envoy—a golden owl clutching a wreath of olive. He wore a simple white tunic and a matching *himation*, pinned at the left shoulder by a brooch of enameled gold fashioned in the shape of Medusa's head. The man paused at the edge of the quay and regarded the shifting crowd. His hair and beard—both more silver than black—were close-cropped, and his age-worn face gave away nothing of his mission. "I seek an officer!" he said, in a voice at once cultured and powerful. "An officer of the watch! Is there one to be found?"

Memnon shouldered through the dockworkers. "Greetings. I am Memnon, son of Timocrates of Rhodes, adjutant and kinsman to Lord Artabazus. What business brings such a noble ship to Dascylium?" The Athenian turned. Memnon shuddered at the force of his gaze, so like that of his father. Here was a man accustomed to dealing with all sorts, from politicians and orators to beggars and thieves; he judged Memnon by that same measure, without thought to his wind-blown hair or his sweat-stained kilt. Finally, the Athenian gave an all but imperceptible nod.

"Well met, Memnon. I am Aristophon of Athens, and I seek the admiral Chares. His lieutenant at Lampsacus said he would be here."

"He is. Chares sits in audience with the Lord Artabazus."

"I must speak with him, and your satrap, too. It is a matter of the utmost gravity."

"I expected as much. Come, I will lead you to him." Memnon paused as Aristophon bade his soldiers to remain vigilant, then added, "It's a long walk from your ship to the satrap's fortress. Shall I summon you a palanquin?"

"It is not my habit to let others carry me on their backs," the envoy said, a sneer curling his lip.

"As you wish." Memnon gestured and, side by side, the two men set out for the fortress of Artabazus. Beyond the harbor district the air grew still and hot, thick with the reek of cooking oil, seared meat, and rotting vegetables. Foot traffic thinned as men sought relief indoors from the relentless sun. Unseen, a dog snarled and yelped—doubtless booted from its patch of shade by an unkind foot. It took nearly an hour to walk from the harbor to the foot of the hill; at the end of that hour, both men were drenched in sweat and parched.

Memnon guided the Athenian envoy to a small fountain in the shade of a sycamore grove where water splashed from a bronze spout into a stone tank. They sat on the fountain's curb and drank their fill. Aristophon soaked a corner of his *himation* and used it to sponge the back of his neck.

"Has Chares served your cause well?"

"He has," Memnon said, hastening to add, "while still pursuing the enemies of Athens, of course."

"Of course," Aristophon nodded. "I am not here to judge him. His letter to the people of Athens painted a glorious picture of your satrap's war with Persia. Did Chares truly win a second Marathon against the Mede?"

Memnon sipped water from his palm. "On paper, perhaps, Lake Manyas could be comparable to Marathon, but in reality all battles differ. This need you politicians have to hammer each engagement into the mold of past glories does a disservice to those brave men who died. Lake Manyas was its own battle, and its success belongs to Artabazus, not to Chares. He did as he was told, no more."

"You dislike Chares, don't you?" Aristophon said, after a moment.

"I dislike arrogance."

Both men lapsed into silence. The hillside loomed above them, crowned by the limestone walls of the satrap's fortress. The road widened and split into three, two prongs circling the hill to the left and right, leading to the storage magazines and the army encampment; the center road ascended the hill by way of a series of steps cut into the ashlar retaining walls of each terrace. Trees lined the stair, and landings offered places of respite. Sparrows chittered, wheeling in the faded blue sky.

"I can still summon a palanquin if you choose," Memnon said, eyeing the old Athenian.

Aristophon sniffed in disdain, stood, and marched toward the stairs. The young Rhodian smiled and followed.

Three flights of stairs passed quickly; they paused on the landing of the fourth to give Aristophon a moment to catch his breath. "Revel in your youth, Memnon," he said. "It is the gods' greatest gift."

"My father said much the same thing."

Aristophon sat on a bench, shaded by the boughs of a plane tree. "I knew your father. A difficult man, but a good man. All of Athens grieved when Androtion informed us of his passing."

"He was that well-known in Athens, my father?"

"Does that surprise you?" Aristophon said. "Timocrates was well-known in many quarters. Years ago—he couldn't have been much older than you are now—he made himself a thorn in the side of King Agesilaus of Sparta by using the wealth of old Pharnabazus to put swords in the fists of angry helots. The Spartans had no choice but to recall Agesilaus or face destruction." A troubled look passed across the envoy's face. He stood. "Come, we've tarried here long enough. Conduct me to Chares."

They ascended the last flight of steps. "How fares Androtion?" Memnon said offhandedly. "I pray all goes well for him?"

Aristophon scowled. "All would be well, save for that upstart, Demosthenes. Ere I left, there was talk of leveling charges against Androtion for misconduct. Some nonsense about an Egyptian vessel he seized illegally."

"So the fighting between the two parties continues?"

"Indeed. The War Party has cost Athens her empire, and I fear the Peace Party will drive the price higher still," Aristophon said.

They gained the summit of the hill. Ahead, a pair of statues flanked the gate to Artabazus's fortress, seated figures thrice the height of a tall man and carved in the rigid Egyptian mode. "Images of the kings Proteus and Rhampsinitus," Memnon said, answering the envoy's curiosity. "Gifted to the elder Pharnabazus from the grateful citizens of Naucratis. I find them too inflexible, though they fascinate my brother, Mentor. He means to sample the wonders of Egypt for himself, someday."

"I have seen many of those wonders," Aristophon said. "It would take three lifetimes to sample them all."

The gate itself—age-blackened cedar banded in bronze—stood open, guarded by soldiers of the household troop who saluted Memnon as he passed. Inside, a courtyard paved in reddish stone and bounded by colonnaded porticoes blended Greek and Persian influences: Ionic columns topped by horse-headed capitals of dark polished limestone. Potted trees and shrubs, chosen for their fullness and fragrance, flourished under the expert hands of Artabazus's gardener, Gryllus. Niches in the walls held a collection of foreign treasures—sculptures of mottled stone from Greece, masks of gold and lapis lazuli from Egypt, and figurines of carved ivory from Phoenicia. Memnon led Aristophon across the courtyard and through the far portico.

A little boy hurtled from the shadows and crashed into the young Rhodian's knees. He mock-staggered, smiling as the toddler tried to climb his body. Memnon scooped him up. "Peace, Cophen! Peace! I surrender!" A girl followed on Cophen's heels, nine years old and already in possession of an adult's sobriety. "Your charge escaped again, Barsine."

"He is wily, Uncle," Barsine said, taking Cophen from him before the toddler could latch on to Aristophon's staff. "I foresee great deeds in his future . . . unless he kills himself first."

"Take this little Herakles to his nurse and tell Deidamia I'm back," Memnon said. Barsine nodded and withdrew, Cophen squirming on her hip.

"Deidamia is your wife?"

"My sister, Artabazus's wife. Those are his children. Come, Artabazus and Chares should be here, in the great hall." Memnon ushered the envoy through an arched doorway.

The room they entered was long, with two dozen columns similar to those in the courtyard supporting the high ceiling. Clerestory windows filled the hall with light. At the far end, on a raised platform, the throne of Artabazus—his satrapal seat, where he ruled the surrounding land as a king—stood empty. Instead, Artabazus, Mentor, and Chares sat off to one side, at a small table used by the scribes to record the issuance's of court—Artabazus and Mentor in high-backed chairs, Chares atop the table, itself. With knives, they dug into the juicy heart of a split-open melon. Mentor gestured with his blade.

"There I am, in Eubulus's bedchamber, buried up to the hilt in Eubulus's wife. She's screaming, 'Take me, O Zeus! Take me! I am your Io, your Europa!' So that's what I do." Mentor made an obscene gesture with his fist. "Plow her like there's no tomorrow. I'm two thrusts away from spilling my seed when I hear a groan behind me. Guess who's standing in the door?"

"Who?" Chares said, wiping his chin on the shoulder of his tunic.

"Eubulus, with his robe open and his dog in his fist, smiling at my bare ass as a man in the desert gazes upon a sweet oasis."

Artabazus chuckled, shaking his head. "I've tried to teach you that every pleasure comes with a price."

"Price? Prices can be haggled over, whittled down," Mentor said. "Not Eubulus. For all his softness, that man has a singularity of purpose—"

"Artabazus!" Memnon called, interrupting Mentor's story. The three men looked up from their melon. "I bring a guest. An emissary from the city of the Athenians."

Chares bolted to his feet.

"By all the gods! Aristophon! What do you here?" The admiral came forward and embraced the older Athenian. Memnon moved past them to stand at the satrap's side. Chares gestured to the newcomer. "Artabazus, this is my dear friend Aristophon, an orator and politician without equal."

"You flatter me, Chares." Aristophon turned and inclined his head to the satrap. "Lord Artabazus. Your fame precedes you."

"As does yours, noble Aristophon. Come, sit and join us. We're having a bite to eat. I have often heard Chares speak of you in glowing terms. You are as a father to him, I imagine."

"And he is as a son to me. Though a wayward son, of late, and one who has brought only grief to the city that gave him life. Why have you been away so long, Chares? Athens has pined for you, as Hero for Leander. Every night we kindled the fires on Mount Hymettus and prayed their light would guide you home, and every morning we despaired of finding your lifeless body in the surf. Have you lost your way in the howling darkness of Asia?"

Chares laughed and hugged the old man again. "You are too much the poet to be a man of politics, Aristophon. My letter came to you, did it not?"

"Indeed, but a scrap of paper pales beside the man himself. Come back to Athens with me, Chares. Your people desire it."

Memnon stiffened. Something in Aristophon's tone, a serious edge hidden beneath the playful banter, gave him pause. Hearing it, as well, Mentor glanced up; Artabazus's eyes slid from brother to brother. Chares, though, pressed on, oblivious.

"I have missed you, Aristophon. Here, sit and tell me what goes in the city of Athena. Fetch wine!"

The older Athenian remained motionless, a cool smile on his face.

"You idiot," Memnon said to Chares, his voice cracking. "He's not making sport with you, are you Aristophon?"

The envoy inclined his head. "No, indeed, son of Timocrates. What I said was not spoken lightly or in jest. The Assembly has voted, Chares. I am here to bring you home. You and your fleet."

"What?"

Memnon glanced toward Artabazus; the old satrap sank back in his chair, his brow furrowed. Mentor struck the table with a balled fist, upsetting a wine goblet, and lurched to his feet. "Damn you! That will leave us virtually defenseless!"

"Your defense is no longer our concern," Aristophon said. He turned and met Artabazus's gaze unflinching. "Your Great King, Ochus, has put the people of Athens on notice. If Chares persists in aiding you in your rebellion the Great King will have no recourse but to aid, in turn, the enemies of Athens. Aid them with ships, with men, and with gold. We have no choice, Artabazus. Chares must come with me. I've already ordered his lieutenant at Lampsacus to make ready to sail."

Chares sat heavily, his eyes unfocused. He blinked, looking at Mentor and Artabazus. "Tell the . . . tell the Assembly I cannot do what they ask. It's a matter of honor. I gave my . . . my word."

"You gave your word to Athens first, did you not?"

"He did," Artabazus said. "Chares, my friend, your part in my scheme has come to an end. You are pledged to a higher purpose, guided by the wisdom of Athena, and bound by the laws of your home. I have no claim over you; no oath binds you to my fate. Go with noble Aristophon and carry back to Athens my words of thanks for the loan of so many fine men and my regrets for the loss of those who died in my service."

"Artabazus, I . . ." Chares reached across the table and grasped the old satrap's hand. "I am sorry."

Aristophon nodded. "We are all sorry, Lord Artabazus. Athens bears you no ill will."

"Nor I for the Athenians," he said. "Come, though, you must be weary. I insist you dine with me this evening and take your leave at first light."

"He can have my place," Mentor said, plunging his knife through the melon's half-eaten heart and into the wood beneath. "I have no appetite." The elder Rhodian spun and stalked from the hall.

"Regretfully, we must return to Lampsacus," Aristophon said.

"Of course. I will have a meal prepared and sent to your ship. Memnon, will you see to it?" Though his voice betrayed no anger, Artabazus's knuckles whitened and cracked against the arms of his chair.

"You are most gracious," the envoy bowed, looped his arm in Chares', and retraced his steps from the palace, virtually dragging the stunned admiral.

"Memnon," Artabazus hissed. The young Rhodian leaned close. "Send a rider to Pammenes. He must fall back down the Macestus Valley to Dascylium with the utmost haste. Tell him Ochus has struck from an unexpected quarter."

"I'll go. I—"

"No. I need you here."

"This is too important to trust to a messenger, Artabazus. Send me, and Pammenes will know it's not a trifling decision."

The old satrap pursed his lips, unable to find fault with Memnon's logic. He nodded. "Fine. Take one of my horses and ride like the lash of the gods lay across your back!"

Memnon left before dusk. He traveled light, a goatskin bag holding a clay flask of water, a few hard biscuits, and a coin pouch draped over one shoulder, his sheathed sword over the other. What he needed in the way of food the villages of the Macestus Valley could provide. He left his helmet behind in Dascylium, as well as his heavy bronze breastplate. For this trip Memnon made do with his old cuirass of stamped leather.

The young Rhodian rode through the night, the river on his right hand reflecting silver and black in the light of the full moon. Patron's words haunted him. *What will he do? When another army comes, what will Artabazus do?* Without the Athenians, Memnon doubted the rebels could hold Dascylium, much less field enough troops to win a pitched battle against the King's forces. Chares' recall emasculated their war effort. Now the main concern would be survival. *What will Artabazus do?*

Celaeno's long stride ate up the miles so that, by dawn, the first village lay just ahead. To the unencumbered man, Sardis was a week's ride from Dascylium. A road—often little more than a goat trail—led up the Macestus Valley and into the high country before descending onto a fertile plain watered by the Hermus, Pactolus, and Hyllus Rivers. Seven villages lined the way, each roughly twenty miles apart. Since the reign of the first Darius, who established this road as a spur of the Great Royal Road from Sardis to Susa, the villages were responsible for the maintenance of way-houses, *stathmi*, where travelers could obtain food, water, lodging, fodder for their horses, and fresh mounts. To the King's servants, such amenities were free; to others, they could be had for a reasonable price. The Boeotians, under a writ from Artabazus, confiscated as their camp the lands around the fifth *stathmos*, near the headwaters of the Macestus, in the shadow of the Phrygian plateau.

The first village lay on a bluff overlooking the river's turbulent waters. The way-house stood apart from the huts of timber and thatch. Its architecture was Iranian: a stone foundation with walls of plastered mudbrick and a flat roof supporting a wood-and-thatch loggia; a stable, also of dun-colored brick, abutted the main building. A door creaked open and a man, still rubbing sleep from his eyes, stepped out into the hazy morning sun.

"Welcome," he said, in badly accented Greek.

"See to my horse," Memnon said. "Wake me in two hours." The young Rhodian snatched what rest he could and was back on the road in the third hour past dawn. He followed the same routine at the second, third, and fourth *stathmos*. At this last, four days since the Athenians' recall, the village headman took Memnon aside.

"The Great Road is not empty," he said.

"We've heard. Couriers are riding to and fro, bearing messages from the King, no doubt."

The headman gave Memnon a strange look. His hairless skull glimmered in the morning sun, and his stiff brown beard brushed the rough homespun fabric covering his chest as he shook his head. "My sister's husband and his sons often take their flocks up into the high country, where the grass is still green. For days on end they graze, and the boys have little to do but explore. One track brought them to a point overlooking the Great Road. They sent for their father, and he sent for me. I have seen a host moving through Phrygia, bound for Sardis. Many thousands of men."

Memnon's eyes narrowed. "Are the Greeks at the fifth way-house aware of them?" The headman couldn't say. Memnon gave him a fistful of silver *drachmas*. "Have you a horse? Good. Ride to Dascylium and tell General Mentor what you've told me. If any question you, tell them you're on the satrap's business."

The headman chewed his lip, eyeing the coins in his hand, before he nodded assent and hurried off to find his wife. The young Rhodian leapt atop Celaeno and touched his heels to the horse's flanks. He had to warn Pammenes. Eighteen miles separated him from the Boeotian camp, a day's ride through rough hill country and thick forests where the late summer heat lay heavy on the ground.

Memnon pushed himself and Celaeno mercilessly. The road shadowed the river, at times coming in such close proximity as to dampen the mare's fetlocks. They traversed broken ground beneath looming cliff-faces, skirted boulders larger than a Cyclops's head, and ascended level upon level of rocky shelves where the river ran fast and shallow, collecting in foaming pools that overflowed into waterfalls. Here, an hour after midday, Memnon paused.

No wind stirred; beneath the earthy smell of damp rock, Memnon caught the scent of corruption, of meat left too long in the sun. Likely offal left behind by some nocturnal predator. Flies buzzed. The heat left even the birds torpid, their song muted. Memnon sat at the edge of a mossy lagoon as Celaeno wandered over to a tussock of grass growing at the base of the ledge. The young Rhodian spat dust and washed down a small round loaf of bread with drafts of chill water scooped from the pool.

"Maybe nine more miles," he said to the horse, his voice profaning the afternoon stillness. "Give me nine more miles and I promise you a good long rest. What do you say to that, girl?"

Celaeno's ears flattened against her skull. The horse whickered and tossed her head. Memnon frowned. "What is it, girl?" Suddenly, the horse shied away as a bloody arm erupted from the grassy shelf above them.

"By all the gods!" Memnon rolled to his feet; his sword rang from its sheath. A man, clad in blood-and-sweat-soaked rags, pulled himself to the edge of the shelf and tumbled over, landing at Memnon's feet with a weak grunt of pain. The Rhodian stood still, alert, scanning the road ahead for any sign of assailants. Nothing. Only then did he allow himself to glance down.

The man crumpled at his feet had the look of a villager about him, the remnants of his clothing woven of the same unbleached wool Memnon had seen at the other way-houses. Blood matted his dark hair; it crusted his face and limbs, obscuring his features, even the color of his skin. His injuries looked superficial—cuts and gouges, for the most part—save for a terrible wound at the base of his spine, the likes of which Memnon had seen before. A spear thrust into flesh, twisted, and withdrawn. Cracked lips moved as the man talked, either to himself or to the gods.

"*Yauna . . .*"

"Don't try to speak. Here." Memnon got his flask, poured water into his cupped hand, and held it to the man's lips. He sucked it up, greedy for more. Memnon obliged him. Where had this fellow come from? How did he make it this far? More to the point, Memnon wondered, was who did this to him and why?

"*Y-Yauna . . .*" The fellow spoke Persian, his accent that of the Lydian frontier. "*Wa . . . Wahauka . . . hazarapatish! Wahauka hazarapatish! Hazara—*" Spasms wracked the man's body. He shuddered, gave a last, wet sigh, and would move no more.

"Zeus Savior!" Memnon rocked back on his haunches. The dead man's last words cut the young Rhodian to the bone. *Wahauka hazarapatish.* It meant 'Ochus's chiliarch,' the Commander of the King's Hosts. Memnon knew the title belonged to a jackal of a man called Tithraustes, and that knowledge left a cold knot of apprehension in his belly. "Ochus's chiliarch," Memnon said aloud. The words rang with the finality of a death sentence.

His patience at an end, had the King unleashed the whole of Persia's armies against Artabazus?

Memnon stood, recovered his sword, his flask. The dead man at his feet, likely one of Artabazus's agents, deserved a rich funeral, eternal payment for his sacrifice. For the time being, his shade would have to persevere. Memnon fished an *obol* from his coin pouch, knelt, and slipped it under the corpse's tongue. Next, he scooped a handful of earth from the ledge above him and sprinkled it over the body.

"O mighty Earth, mother of all," Memnon said, "you are the source of fair children and goodly fruit, and on you it depends to give life to, or take it away from, mortal men. Blessed is the man you favor, for he will have everything in abundance." With a nod, the Rhodian turned and dashed to Celaeno's side.

He had to reach Pammenes.

Afternoon turned to evening, and still Memnon rode. The sky above became a cauldron of fire, the oranges and reds cooling to purple, thence to the diamond-studded lapis of night. Beneath the trees, darkness reigned supreme. Memnon sat slumped in the saddle. The song of the crickets lulled him to restfulness; his body would convulse, causing the Rhodian to jerk erect. Fireflies sparkled in the underbrush. He watched them, rubbed his eyes, blinked. The insects' illuminations never dimmed. On the contrary, the glow quickened as Celaeno bore him closer. Memnon rubbed his eyes again.

Zeus! Those aren't insects. They're fires. Hundreds of them, filling the valley ahead with a greasy orange glow. Memnon dismounted and walked Celaeno past telltale signs of habitation: stumps of felled trees, middens of refuse, and geometric patches of tilled earth where vegetables once grew. Skeins of smoke curled from watch and cook fires, hanging over the encampment like a shroud of pale yellow linen.

Memnon heard sharp laughter off to his left, the rattle of dice. "Cheating bastard," a voice muttered in Greek. Coins clinked as they changed hands.

Looping Celaeno's reins over a branch, Memnon inched closer. He stopped just outside the ring of light. A pair of men, hoplites if their breastplates and doffed helmets were any indication, sat on a log, the stub of a candle between them. By its flickering light the men played a game of chance.

"Boeotians?" Memnon called.

The swipe of a hand extinguished the candle; weapons clattered. For a moment, impenetrable darkness descended. By increments, though, the light of the rising moon filtered through the boughs, infusing everything with a silver-gray glow. "Who goes? Show yourself!"

Memnon stepped forward, his arms away from his sides, palms out, to show he carried no weapons. "Peace, brothers. I'm from Dascylium. I bear a message for Pammenes."

"From where? Dascylium?"

"I'm weary, brothers. Take me to Pammenes and all will be explained," Memnon said. He could not see their faces clearly, but it seemed to the Rhodian that the hoplites nodded to one another. The man on his left started to turn.

Without warning, the man on Memnon's right leveled his spear and lunged.

"Zeus!" Memnon twisted his upper body. The iron blade grazed his biceps; he caught the shaft and shoved the unbalanced soldier to the ground. "Damn you! Did you not hear me? I'm from Dascylium! Conduct me to—"

The second hoplite's spear punched through the armor, flesh, and bone of Memnon's right shoulder. The Rhodian gasped. He fell backward, the spearman bearing his body to the ground. Sheets of white-hot pain exploded from the wound; he felt blood cascading over his skin, soaking his tunic and the ground beneath. Overhead, the stars flared, throbbing with the pulse-beat of his heart.

"Finish him, Xeno!" the first hoplite hissed, scrambling to his feet. "He might not be alone."

"Wait. Fetch a light, Tauros. Let's see who this fool is."

Memnon writhed. Pressure on the spear shaft kept him from rising. Bile seared the back of his throat. "W-What are y-you doing?" The candle flared to life. The hoplite called Tauros held it near Memnon's upturned face.

"Great Herakles! Great fucking Herakles! Help me with this, Tauros!" A foot pressed against Memnon's shoulder; a fresh wave of agony broke over him as Xeno gently withdrew his spear. The stars, so cold and distant, faded toward oblivion.

"What is it?"

"You know who this bastard is? It's the Rhodian!

"Hera's tits! Are you sure?" Memnon tried to focus on the speaker, on Tauros. The candle in his hand shed an exquisite heat that bathed his shivering body in warmth. The ground beneath cradled him, like a bier of fleece. He could sleep . . . he needed sleep . . .

"Damn you!" Xeno said, slapping Memnon's cheek. "Stay with me, Rhodian! Give me your cloak, Tauros! Hurry! Go back to camp and fetch the general, but quietly! Whisper it to him, so the Persians won't hear! He'll want to know . . ."

Memnon closed his eyes.

I'm coming, father.

Darkness, stygian and absolute. Through it, Memnon floated like a man adrift at sea, too exhausted to struggle but too stubborn to admit defeat. Silent. Still. How long had it been since the spear penetrated his flesh? A matter of minutes? Hours? Days? Time had no meaning here, on this threshold between life and death. Death? Can the dead feel pain? Can they feel the loss of separation that so plagues those left behind? Can the dead mourn for the living?

Though buffeted by eddies and currents of the void, Memnon found he could not drift off into the heart of oblivion. Something tethered him. A single strand, a dark filament spun from hematite, anchored him to the world of the living. Memnon touched it, felt a yearning in his heart unlike anything he had ever known. *I want to live!*

Light, pale and sickly, pierced the veil of darkness. Overhead—the specificity of direction absurd in a place of such utter nothingness—a sun flared to life, motionless, its disk blackened in a state of perpetual eclipse. Memnon swam toward it, fighting the undertow of oblivion. Each movement produced pain. Not sharp, but growing, the pinpricks of circulation restored. He was writhing in agony as he breached the grey-white aura of light.

Awareness returned. Faint sounds assaulted him: the clatter of pottery, the pop and hiss of a brazier, the scrape of metal on metal. Whispers, too, bled through into the void.

Hold him! Hold him down!

Lower your voice! The Persians . . .

He's going to bleed out unless I can cauterize this! Now hold him, damn you!

When Eileithyia, goddess of childbirth, expels a babe from its mother's womb, its first instinct is to draw a raging breath, to scream at this first injustice marking the journey from cradle to grave. For Memnon, that same instinct asserted itself . . .

He bellowed and thrashed, unable to move as the red-hot tip of an iron descended into the mangled flesh of his shoulder. Pammenes lay across him, both men on the rough boards of a trestle table, its top slick with blood and piss. Meat sizzled. Memnon rolled his eyes; a middle-aged Boeotian in the smock of a surgeon, his bald pate greasy with sweat, stood at his shoulder, holding the iron in his wound until it ceased to glow. The aroma of charred flesh filled the tent, overpowering the scented oils burning in the dozen lamps scattered about.

Memnon blinked. The surgeon nodded to Pammenes, who stood and placed a hand on the Rhodian's forehead.

"Will he live, Heraclides?" Pammenes asked, glancing over his shoulder at the surgeon. Heraclides propped open the tent flap. A draft of cool air caressed the Rhodian's feverish brow.

The surgeon sighed, ran a hand over his hairless scalp. "He's young, but he's lost much blood. Too much. Truly, I know not. I fear he's in the hands of the gods now."

"I must change and attend to Bardiya. Let me know if his condition worsens." Pammenes glanced down at Memnon, concern etched on his brow.

The surgeon nodded. "I'll have Khafre prepare a poultice and fetch some fresh linen for a bandage. What about Xeno and Tauros? They're good men, General."

Pammenes stalked out of Memnon's field of vision. "They're fools," he heard the Theban say, "but they were only obeying orders. Never would I have expected Artabazus to send *him* to us. Fetch your medicines, Heraclides, and get him cleaned up." With that, they left him alone. The Rhodian's eyes fluttered. Despite the lamps, he felt darkness encroaching, drawing him back to oblivion's bosom. The thudding of his heart slowed. Around him, the tent soughed and sighed.

I want to live!

"You will," a voice purred in Memnon's ear. He opened his eyes and glanced around, craning his head to locate the speaker. A man in a short Doric tunic, a silver-gray *khlamys* thrown over his left shoulder, stood unnoticed beside the table. Shoulder length golden hair, shot through with silver, framed a face that displayed equal part's beauty, wisdom, and age. With difficulty, Memnon met his gaze. "You are not yet ready to make the journey, child of Rhodes. It is not your time."

"How . . . how do you k-know . . . ?"

His long fingers plucked at his silver-gold beard. "The *Moirai*, Fates you call them, ration human existence. Clotho, youngest of the daughters of Themis, weaves the stuff of your lives from thread of infinite variety. She passes it to Lachesis, who apportions it however she sees fit. Last, the third sister, Atropos, cuts the thread, handling her shears as deftly for a slave as she does for a king. Her blade is ever poised, Memnon, awaiting the final measure of each life, but yours is not yet ready to be cut."

"W-Who are you?" Memnon croaked.

"Does it matter?" The fellow shrugged, his sky-blue eyes twinkling. "A messenger, some call me. A traveler. A seer on occasion, though not as skilled in the art of divining as others. A musician I have been, and a fighter. A scoundrel, if you ask my father, and a healer. I have worn many robes, Memnon, and likely I will wear many more 'ere this world ends."

Memnon blinked and struggled for breath, fear robbing him of his courage.

The fellow placed his hand over Memnon's wound, his touch searing hot. Pleasure suffused the pain. The touch of a parent, a lover, a killer, and a healer all mingling into one. Memnon gasped. "Listen to me, child. Listen, and do not be afraid. The Fates may dictate the length of your life, but it is the gods who author its content . . . and the gods look askance at those who ignore their work. It is time you forget your melancholy, your predilection toward guilt, and make your mark on the world. Do you understand?"

"I . . . I understand," Memnon muttered. The fellow caught his glance and held it, nodding finally.

"Excellent. Sleep now, and remember what I have said."

Memnon's vision blurred, fading as he sank back on the table; his last waking sight—surely a mirage borne of trauma—was of the strange man turning away from him, his body dissolving in a golden mist.

When next Memnon woke, he did so quietly, from a dreamless slumber. He lay on a cot in the surgeon's pavilion. Across from him, on a table of dark polished oak, he could see the tools of the physician's trade: knives and bone saws hanging between cubbyholes stuffed with papyrus scrolls and terracotta pots. A water barrel stood nearby, along with a brazier of cauterizing irons and a wedge-shaped *amphora* on its stand. Bundles of dried herbs hung from the pavilion's center pole, their aroma competing with that of incense, old blood, and sweat. A breeze rustled through an open side flap; Memnon heard the clash of soldiers' harness, the mutter of voices, and the splash of water on rock, doubtless from one of the springs that fed the headwaters of the Macestus.

The Rhodian touched the thick linen wrappings that kept his injured shoulder immobile. He flexed that hand, making a fist several times; he moved his arm from the elbow down, hissing at the pain that knifed through his muscles. Memnon clenched his teeth as he swung his legs off the cot and levered himself first into a sitting position, then to his feet. His vision blurred; waves of nausea left him weak and sweating. He staggered the handful of steps to the pavilion's center and sagged against the pole.

"Zeus Savior," he muttered, blinking, shaking his head to clear it. His tongue felt dry and coarse, like a hank of sand-scoured leather, and his shoulder throbbed in cadence with his heart. From his vantage, Memnon could see out the side flap and into the camp beyond. The pavilion lay in a grove of shady oaks, on a slight rise that afforded it better ventilation. Nearby, Boeotian soldiers drilled in full panoply, marching and wheeling in phalanx formation, as a troop of cavalry clattered by on their periphery. These caught Memnon's attention as much for their Median trousers and scaled corselets as for the recollection that Pammenes' force possessed no cavalry. They were Hyrkanians, he reckoned, descendants of the military settlers brought west to the Caicus Valley by the first Cyrus some two hundred years previous.

Memnon's eyes narrowed to slits. *Whisper it to him, so the Persians won't hear*, the man who stabbed him had said. A name surfaced in his mind. *Bardiya*. A name spoken by Pammenes himself; a Persian name. Suddenly it made perfect sense. *The Persians*.

"Pammenes," he snarled, "you treacherous bastard!"

Behind him, another flap in the pavilion rustled open. The surgeon, Heraclides, backed in, his hands full with a tray of bread, cheese, olives, and half a roasted fowl. His eyes fell on the empty cot. "What in the name of Hades?" Heraclides put the tray on his table and turned toward Memnon's trembling form. "Dammit, boy! You shouldn't be standing! You'll open the stitches!"

"I shouldn't be alive, surgeon, yet here I am. Have you any wine?"

Heraclides gestured to the cot. "Sit. I'll fetch you a flagon. Is the pain bearable? I can mix you a *pharmakon*, something to take with your wine."

"Just wine," Memnon said. He heaved himself off the center pole and shuffled back to the cot, collapsing at its foot. Heraclides searched through the niches at his table until he found an empty clay cup. From the *amphora*, he dipped out a measure of wine.

"You take it with water?"

"Not today," Memnon replied. Heraclides handed the cup to him. Memnon's hands shook as he drained it. "Another." Heraclides frowned, but dipped out another cup full. This one Memnon drank more slowly. "Where is Pammenes? I need to speak with him."

"The general will attend you when he can," Heraclides said.

"And when will that be?"

"When he can! Great gods, Rhodian, but you're an impatient one!"

"Fetch him!" Memnon said through gritted teeth. "Now! Tell him I know what he's done!"

Heraclides scrubbed a hand across his jaw. Slowly, he nodded. "I'll do it, so long as you lie still." Memnon assented and the surgeon rushed out to find Pammenes.

It did not take him long. A quarter of an hour later, Heraclides escorted the Theban general into the pavilion. Though less than five years Memnon's senior, Pammenes could have passed for a man of two-score years. His curly black hair showed flecks of gray, as did his trimmed beard; wrinkles creased his blue eyes, furrowed his brow, mixing with the scars of a lifetime spent in the worship of Ares. Pammenes wore a black *chiton* edged in gold thread and sandals of stamped leather.

The Theban smiled and gave a low whistle. "By all the gods, Heraclides. You were right. He looks strong enough to wrestle a bear. How are you feeling, Memnon? Thanks to you, my surgeon has become insufferable. He thinks he's Asclepius reborn. What . . ."

"I know what you've done, you son of a whore!" Memnon growled.

Pammenes motioned to the surgeon. "Give us a moment." Heraclides collected his tray and excused himself. The Theban's smile vanished. "What is it you think I've done, Memnon?"

"You've turned. Your guards had orders to kill any messenger coming from Artabazus; they were worried about calling you from a council with the Persians. When you left, you said you had to change clothes in order to attend a man called Bardiya, surely a Persian by his name. I'm no fool and you're a poor liar, so do not try to dissemble with me. I know what you're about. How much did they offer you to betray Artabazus?"

Pammenes sighed. "I'm the fool, Memnon. I forgot how clever you are. Yes, my Boeotians and I have transferred our allegiance to Ochus, but not for gold."

"For what, then? Land? Station?"

"Survival," Pammenes replied. "Artabazus was kind to me, he took me in when I needed succor, but things have changed. Without the Athenians he's no match for Ochus. Yes, I know of their recall. With a letter, the King of Kings demolished Artabazus's army. A letter, Memnon! Now, he's loosed his dogs on his western satraps with orders to return them to their proper place."

Memnon's lips curled in distaste. "You're faithless, Pammenes."

"Faith is a fine thing, Rhodian, but when an axe is aimed at my neck faith makes for a poor shield. These men are my family, my brothers, my children. I'm obligated to do what's best for them. To continue our part in the resistance against Ochus was to invite folly. Surely you understand?"

The logic of Pammenes' argument lanced Memnon's anger like a boil. "I understand your motives, but I do not agree with the manner in which you chose to carry them out. You should have thought out the consequences of your actions long before you gave Artabazus your word. It is a man who will stand by his convictions despite the odds; it is a dog who changes to accommodate the whims of the pack," he said, hunching to his left in an effort to relieve the pressure on his shoulder. "What will you do now? Hand me over to the Persians? Sell me into slavery like a spoil of war? Kill me out of hand?"

"Save your scorn." Pammenes leaned against the surgeon's table, his arms folded across his chest. "If I truly wished you dead, you'd be waking up in Tartarus now. No, I'm sending you back to Dascylium. Tithraustes would have your head if he knew you were here, mine if he knew what I planned. So, you see, I'm placing my life in your hands, as well. Return to Artabazus and convince him to flee. If he values his life, the lives of his children, he'll quit Asia and not look back."

The Rhodian gave a short bark of laughter. "Little chance of that! Asia's his home. He'll not leave. He'll go to ground someplace safe, like Assos, and hire more mercenaries to continue his fight. Yes, he'll make for Assos. Those walls have resisted better men than Tithraustes."

"Assos is closed to him," Pammenes said. "His man, Eubulus, is dead, slain in a coup by his pet philosopher-eunuch, that creature Hermeias. He—*it!*—has already sent tokens of submission to Tithraustes in gratitude for having been named governor."

"You lie!"

"Do I?" Pammenes shrugged. "You yourself said I have no skill at it. No, Memnon, Assos belongs to the King again. You must convince Artabazus to leave Asia before it's too late. Tithraustes is no Mithridates. He'll not stop until he has Artabazus in chains—or his head on a pike—and he has the blessings of the King to use whatever means necessary. I beg of you, Memnon, persuade Artabazus to make for Greece, for Sicily, for Egypt—anywhere, but do not let him remain here, in Asia! I bear him no malice, nor you, but if I am ordered to move against him, I will have no choice.

"I wish we had the luxury of time, so you would have a chance to recover some of your strength before I cut you loose, but time is our enemy. I will have a wagon prepared, with servants to accompany you. You must leave soon."

"Gladly," Memnon said, "but keep your wagon and your men. My horse is all I require."

Pammenes grimaced. "While you are no spoil of war, I cannot say the same for your mare. I placed her in my corral for safekeeping. Unfortunately, Lord Bardiya caught sight of her. He demanded I make a gift of her to the King. It is unseemly, he said, for a mere soldier to possess such a fine specimen of the Nisaean breed. I had no choice . . ."

Memnon's eyes narrowed to slits; he snarled at the Theban general. "That's your pat little excuse in all things, is it not, Pammenes? It would seem slaves have more freedom than you. Have a care, slave! When your new masters tire of you, you may have no choice but to fall on your sword!"

"Watch your tongue, Rhodian!" Pammenes turned and walked to the pavilion's entrance.

"Or what? You'll have no choice but to silence me? Go prepare my wagon. The sooner I am gone from your sight, the better. The very air here sickens me."

"Faugh! So be it. Tell Artabazus what I've said. If he remains in Asia, he will die. As will you." With that, Pammenes swept aside the flap and marched out into the sunlight. Memnon watched him, a slow smile—humorless and cold—forming on his lips.

"Do you not know, Pammenes?" he said softly. "Everyone dies."

A WAGON LEFT THE BOEOTIAN CAMP THE NEXT MORNING, AN UNREMARKable four-wheeled wain drawn by a pair of oxen. It crossed the turbulent headwaters of the Macestus and descended the river's broad and gently sloping right bank. One man, a squat fellow with a brushy black beard, sat atop the driver's bench, snapping the harness traces and clicking his teeth at the plodding oxen; another man, younger than the first—tall and reed-thin—walked beside them, using the butt of his short spear as a goad. Both men wore the boots, woolen tunics and floppy caps of Phrygian highlanders.

A canopy kept the sun off the bed of the wagon, off Memnon's prostrate form. He lay on a straw mattress with a riot of cushions insulating him from the jarring ride. Despite this padding, he felt every rock and rut; the road's imperfections translated into pain, from slight twinges to knives of blinding agony. Memnon fluttered on the edge of consciousness.

A third man rode in the wagon with him, his stubbled brown hair gray-streaked and his hawkish face worn with the cares of a lifetime. At first, Memnon assumed his beardless chin meant he was a eunuch. When he spoke, though, the Rhodian recognized his error.

The man's Greek bore the accent of Egypt.

"I can give you something to ease your pain," he said.

"Later, perhaps." Memnon winced as he scooted his body into a sitting position, leaning left to put his weight on that side. The effort brought beads of sweat to his brow.

"Heraclides said you would be a stubborn man and unwilling to follow sensible advice," the Egyptian said.

"Such as lie down and keep still? What else did he say?"

"That I should guard my impudent tongue and do as I am told."

"Wise man, that Heraclides," Memnon said. "Do you have a name?"

"I am called Khafre." The Egyptian drew a goatskin bag and a copper mug from among his supplies; despite the rattle and sway of the wagon, Khafre poured Memnon a measure of wine without spilling a drop.

"Thank you," Memnon said, accepting the proffered cup and draining it. "Are you one of Heraclides' servants, or are you a fellow physician?"

"Neither," Khafre said. He corked the skin and tucked it away. "I am a slave. Your slave, for the time being. The Theban wretch said if you asked to tell you I am remuneration for a horse. He said, too, that you would understand."

Memnon's eyes clouded. "That son of a bitch."

"I echo your sentiment." Khafre sniffed. "I am worth far more than a horse."

"Not this horse," Memnon said. Carefully, he rolled flat again, his tongue thick, his head swimming. Khafre took the cup from him. "What . . . was the wine tainted?"

"Yes. With something to ease your pain," the Egyptian replied.

"I told you—"

"Yes, yes, yes. You Greeks prefer to suffer silently and without complaint. In the interest of healing, though, it behooves you to keep still and take your medicine. Flesh mends more quickly when the body sleeps. Did you not know that?"

Memnon closed his eyes. "I see now why Pammenes rid himself of you," he muttered.

More than a willful slave, Khafre proved a voluble traveling companion, a stark contrast to the Phrygians, who rarely spoke save to one another. As the days progressed, Memnon spent his waking hours listening to the Egyptian recount the tale of his life—from his birth in Bubastis, the City of Cats, to his ventures at sea, to the storm that wrecked his ship on the Lycian coast and his enslavement by Chian pirates.

"They assumed, as you did, that my Egyptian blood made me privy to the age-old wisdom of the priest-physicians and put me to work caring for their injured. I did not correct them, since their assumptions saved me from hard labor in the mines at Laurium or Pangaeus."

"How did you end up with Pammenes?"

"It was the will of the Seven Hathors," Khafre said. Seeing Memnon's blank look, he continued. "They are akin to your Fates. When a child is born, the Seven Hathors decide the moment and manner of its death, and all things leading up to that death. Thus, it was the work of the Hathors that brought me to Ephesus, with the penurious Chians, at the exact instant Heraclides arrived seeking a new slave."

"The Fates make us who—and what—we are," Memnon murmured, more to himself than to Khafre. He lapsed into silence, and his forehead creased in concentration as he brooded over the words of the stranger in Heraclides' tent. Was it a hallucination born of his injury or had a servant of the gods truly visited him? He touched his bandaged shoulder. Mirage or no, *something* hauled him back from the brink, something mysterious and sacred, Homeric in its implications, akin to the visions and visitations spoken of in the Poet's verse.

That night, after a meal of beans and hard bread, the Phrygians rolled up in their cloaks and slept, their snores louder than the lowing of the hobbled oxen, leaving Khafre to clean up after them. Memnon moved some distance from the fire and sat with his back against a fallen log, staring up at the star-flecked sky. Orion rose from the eastern horizon and marched across the vault of heaven, in endless pursuit of the beautiful daughters of Atlas, the Pleiades.

Khafre's approach drew his eyes back to earth. The Egyptian carried a cup of warmed wine in his hands. "Are you well?" he said, crouching and offering the wine to Memnon. "You have been remarkably quiet most of the day. Are you in pain?"

Memnon shook his head and looked askance at the cup. "What's in it?" he said, sniffing the steaming brew. Heat brought the wine's fragrance out, sharp and savory.

"Just wine."

"Are you sure?"

Khafre sipped it himself before again offering it to Memnon. "Satisfied?"

The Rhodian accepted it as though it were an asp. "Not really. You would drug yourself just to make your point."

Khafre placed his hand over his heart. "I swear to you, by the severed phallus of Osiris, I have added nothing to your wine."

Memnon eyed him carefully as he raised the cup to his lips. He drank and returned his attention to the jeweled sky. Khafre sat on the log and followed Memnon's gaze.

"Sopdu has risen," he said, pointing to a bright star on the horizon, barely visible through the trees. "Your people call it Sirius, the Dog Star. In Egypt, it marks the beginning of Akhet, the season of inundation."

Memnon made no indication he heard Khafre; he sat in silence for a long time, watching the stars as though he were an oracle seeking a sign. Finally, he said, "In your land, Khafre, do the gods mingle with mortals?"

Khafre hunched forward, his elbows on his knees. "It depends on what you mean by mingle. Is it not Amun-Ra who brings the sun back from the watery abyss each morning, or Hapi who governs the rise and fall of the Nile? Is it not Anubis who leads the dead through the vast realm of Osiris, or Ma'at who maintains the scales of Justice for all?"

"But, do they walk the earth as men and women, talking with their suppliants as I talk to you?"

"Once, perhaps, but that was long ago, even as we Egyptians reckon time. Instead, they influence us through wisdom, through dreams, through omens."

"How do you know they're not among you?"

Khafre glanced at the young Rhodian and frowned. "Our priests tell us. They have kept immaculate records for three hundred forty-three generations, and by their reckoning no god has taken mortal guise since Horus, son of Osiris, handed his throne over to Pharaoh and joined his father in the West."

Memnon finished off his wine, feeling its warmth spread through his body. "I wonder *how* they know; the priests, I mean. Say your Horus chose to assume the form of a fisherman. Would the priests know Horus by sight if the god did not wish it? Among my people, the gods of Olympus often walk among mortals, unnoticed for what they are."

"Yes," Khafre grunted, "and it is your Olympians who littered all of Hellas with their half-divine bastards. I have read much of what your people have written—Hecateus, Herodotus, Anaxagoras—and I must tell you, applying the names and attributes of Greece's gods to those of Khem is misguided. *Horu-Sema-Tawy* is no more your Apollo than *Asar-Wen-Nefer* is Dionysus; they differ physically, morally, even spiritually. What you Greeks expect from your gods would be profane to an Egyptian. Our gods are not profligate; they simply do not debase themselves by mixing with mortals."

"Interesting," Memnon said. "I wonder—"

Khafre slipped off the log and prostrated himself under the stars. "Mother of Osiris! Spare me from the curiosity of the Hellene!"

The Rhodian laughed. "Point taken. It's getting late. We can take this up in greater depth tomorrow."

Khafre rose and helped Memnon to his feet. Together, they walked back to the dying fire. Snores ripped from the Phrygians, competing in volume. Khafre sighed. "How much farther to Dascylium?"

"We could be there tomorrow, if we were mounted. It will be another two days, at least, with this cursed wagon. We might ford the river, you and I, and see about finding a pair of horses. I'd like to warn Artabazus and Mentor of Pammenes' treachery *before* the Persians attack. I'm curious about the Hyrkanians, though. I should like to have spied upon them, to learn their numbers and disposition."

"They are two thousand in number," Khafre said. "Lancers for the most part, leavened with five hundred archers—not as skilled with the bow as Scythians, or the men of Crete, but worthy shots nonetheless. Bardiya, their commander, is a nephew of Tithraustes. Both men are Medes, from the region of Ecbatana, and though Tithraustes fancies himself a great wit, I found him boorish and a dullard."

Memnon stopped and stared. "How do you know all this?"

The Egyptian smiled. "Though I am a slave in fact, I possess eyes and ears. If they are kept open, and the mouth shut, wondrous things may be learned."

"Indeed," Memnon said. "Perhaps you are worth more than a horse."

Two days later, in the dark hours after midnight, Memnon prodded the Phrygians from their blankets, Khafre, too. "Get up," he growled. "We'll be at Dascylium's gates by midmorning if we leave now. Up, you laggards!" Patchy fog had crept in, filling the low places with a clammy mist that reeked of river mud and damp rock. Khafre changed Memnon's dressings while the Phrygians hitched up the oxen; together, the four men broke their fast in silence, sharing bread, dried fruit, and cool water, before setting out.

Hours ticked by. The mist burned off with the rising of the sun; the day turned bright and uncomfortably warm with hardly a cloud visible in the wide blue bowl of sky. Memnon fretted; he alternated walking and riding, drifting away from the wagon on occasion to follow the bank or to crest a hill, always keeping an eye on the widening shores of the Macestus.

"We're close," he said to Khafre, who followed him on one of his jaunts.

The Egyptian walked along the bank, pushing aside the low-hanging branches of a willow. "It is quiet," he said, "like the land is holding its breath."

Memnon sensed it, as well. Even after they forded the river, after the track they followed became a proper road, rutted and worn from decades of use, they passed no traffic. Where were the villagers returning to their upland homes, the itinerant merchants, and the wanderers? Had word reached Dascylium ahead of him?

"Memnon," Khafre said, nodding away up the road. The Rhodian followed his gaze.

From the direction of Dascylium, a skein of gray smoke drifted into the sky.

The Hyrkanians.

A CURSE CAUGHT IN MEMNON'S THROAT AS HE SHIELDED HIS EYES from a curtain of drifting embers. They had beaten him to Dascylium; more properly, they had beaten him to the town's outskirts. Flames raged through the mercenaries' camp, south and east of Artabazus's fortress, consuming barracks, armories and stables, gnawing at sun-dried timbers and cracking glazed tiles. Gouts of black smoke rolled across the drill field, obscuring arrow-riddled corpses. The stench of charred flesh burned Memnon's nostrils, a smell he remembered well from his father's villa—like pork left too long on the spit.

"How," Khafre panted, breathless from trying to keep pace with Memnon, who had left the wagon and sprinted the last mile. "How did the Hyrkanians breach their defenses?" A ditch and palisade protected the camp; a single gate faced the stone bridge spanning that shallow creek called the Little Macestus and the road that led up to the satrap's fortress.

"Those sons of whores must have struck before dawn!" Memnon said. "While the men slept! Took out what few sentries were posted and opened the gates! Those bastards fired the barracks and picked off any who tried to escape!"

"Where are they now?" Khafre looked around, suddenly fearful of their exposed position.

"Gone."

Though two hundred years and untold miles separated Bardiya's horsemen from their ancestral lands in Farther Asia, the Hyrkanians of the Troad had forgotten nothing of the steppe-dwellers art of lightning warfare. Strike and retire, that was their way; circle an enemy, shower them with an iron-tipped hail of arrows, and withdraw before they could mount effective resistance.

Memnon and Khafre entered the swath of destruction before the palisade gates. Pandemonium reigned. Bodies littered the ground; through the smoke, men stumbled in search of clean air. Cries of fear and pain mingled with prayers and curses. Survivors milled among the wounded and the dead, seeking friends, companions. A few of the officers tried to organize a bucket line to extinguish the worst of the fires. Scowling, Memnon stood on the verge of shouting orders when, from behind him, Khafre grunted. He glanced back. The Egyptian crouched over a fallen soldier, naked but for the charred scraps of his night tunic, careful of the arrows protruding from his shoulder and his side.

"This one still clings to life, but barely," Khafre said.

"Can you help him?"

Khafre didn't answer; instead, he pried up the soldier's eyelids and pressed an ear to his chest. He straightened, drawing his knife. "The arrow in his side is through and through," Khafre said. "I think it missed his vitals. Hold him."

Memnon did as he was told, watching as Khafre sliced away the bronze arrowhead and tugged the shaft free in a single, smooth motion. The fellow twitched, raising his head slightly. Khafre paused to inspect the second arrow. It stood out from his right shoulder, two fingers below the collarbone; unlike the first, the head of this one remained buried in the soldier's body.

Memnon glanced down at his own bandaged shoulder. *Do you drift on the void, my friend? Do you hear the voice of the god?*

"This will be more difficult," Khafre said. He cut away the fletching, paring the shaft down to a nub the length of his palm. "The head likely broke the blade of his shoulder. Now, I must force it the rest of the way through. When I do, be ready to pack the wound . . . here, use this." The Egyptian dragged his bag close, rummaged in it, and handed Memnon an old linen tunic. "Hold tight to him. Ready?"

Memnon nodded.

Without hesitation, the Egyptian threw his weight against the shortened shaft. The injured man lunged in agony, pounding the side of his skull against the hard-packed earth. Memnon heard the unmistakable grate of metal against bone, the sickening rip of flesh, ending with a wet *pop* as the head burst through the skin. Quickly, Khafre slid the blood-smeared shaft out and tossed it aside as Memnon wadded the linen against both sides of the wound.

"Keep pressure on it," Khafre said, mopping his face with the sleeve of his tunic.

Memnon hunched over the injured man, using his body to shield him from embers and ash, and bellowed commands to the men on the embankment. "Get those men out of the ditch! Move, damn you! You, there, and you! Gather spears and cloaks! Use them to make litters! Do you hear me? I said move! Worry less about the fire and more about your injured brothers! Zeus Savior and Helios! Must I show you how to make a litter?" Slowly, some semblance of order emerged among the survivors. To Khafre, Memnon said, "Come, let's carry him to yonder trees." The Rhodian pointed across the field, to a band of sycamores lining the banks of the Little Macestus River. Beyond it, he could see the stone foundations of the *hippodromos* shimmering in the sunlight. Khafre nodded.

The soldier groaned as they hoisted him up, his head rolling forward and back as he mumbled a prayer. Memnon beckoned others to follow, to bring the wounded to the shade of the sycamores, as they quickly crossed the field. Their charge they laid against a tree bole.

"What do you need, Khafre? What do you need to help these men?"

The Egyptian pursed his lips. "A water-bearer, vinegar to cleanse the wounds, linen for bandages, perhaps wine to ease their pain. And a conveyance, something to carry those with the most grievous injuries to the fortress."

"You will have all that, and more," Memnon said. He turned and began issuing orders. Uninjured soldiers and men from the city he sent scurrying, some to scour the harbor emporium for linens, others to fetch vinegar and wine from the fortress. The nimblest he sent down the treacherous bank the Little Macestus to scoop water—in old jars, their helmets, whatever they could find—and pass it up to their mates. This done, the Rhodian went back to helping the wounded, surveying their injuries and placing them in Khafre's path according to need. A hive of activity formed around Memnon as men assailed him with their questions, their doubts, their fears; he handled each with a reserve of patience he never knew he possessed. To each, too, he asked, "Have you seen Artabazus? What of Mentor?"

His answer came from one of the officers, called Omares. "They led the cavalry out," he said, pressing a scrap of filthy cloth to the gash in his forehead. Of medium height, Omares had the broad shoulders and thickly muscled arms of a brawler. "Told us to rescue who and what we could and make for the fortress."

"Both of them?" Memnon frowned. That both would go off in pursuit of the Hyrkanians troubled Memnon. It smacked of foolishness. They did not know what they faced, nor were they aware of Pammenes' treachery. What would they do if they came across the Boeotians? Hail them as friends? He doubted Artabazus would receive the same gift of clemency from Pammenes as he had. "Artabazus should have stayed behind."

Omares nodded, wincing at the pain it caused. A hairsbreadth to the left and the arrow that had ripped across his forehead would have punched through his temple, instead. Gingerly, Memnon pulled the cloth away and inspected the bone-deep laceration. Khafre peered over his shoulder.

"That's going to need stitching," the Egyptian said, wiping his blood-smeared palms on his tunic.

"This attack," Omares said, "it knocked the wind out of us."

Memnon patted the man on the arm. "Not to worry, Omares. Our second wind will be furious to behold." The officer smiled, but Memnon could tell the man did not believe him. In truth, why should he? Their forces were in ruins, their rebellion throttled by the manicured hands of a despot some sixteen hundred miles distant. All they could do was wait for the final blow.

Memnon stitched Omares' wound himself, using a curved needle of gold and a length of catgut thread while one of the younger soldiers held the officer's head immobile in his lap. A veteran, Omares was no stranger to the surgeon's art. "I have seven wounds," he said as Memnon sluiced vinegar over the bloody furrow. "Each a token of battle, some remind me of my victories, others of my defeats. This will be my eighth."

"And what will this one remind you of?" Memnon pinched the edges of the gash together and drew his needle through it. He felt Omares' body grow tense, heard the knuckles of his clenched fists crack.

"My helmet," the officer gasped.

Khafre passed by, glancing down at his newfound apprentice's handiwork. "Yes, yes . . . you are doing fine, Memnon. If you can mend a sail, you can stitch flesh."

Memnon remained silent, concentrating on the task at hand. Finally, he tied off the ends and cut the thread with his knife. The man holding Omares' head daubed away the blood with a wet cloth. The officer opened his eyes; he was pale, shaking.

Memnon rocked back on his haunches and stood, motioning for a water bearer. "Rest a bit," he told Omares, "then head up to the fortress."

As the Rhodian turned away, a cry of alarm erupted from the edge of the makeshift surgery. Men pointed off to the south, to where a tower of dust rose into the sky. Those still able snatched up their weapons. Even Omares clambered to his feet.

"What is it?" Khafre asked.

Memnon reached for a spear propped against the trunk of a sycamore, its owner unconscious or dead. "Horsemen," he said.

"Ours?"

"Can't tell. Stand ready, Khafre."

Outside the shelter of the trees, Memnon formed the survivors into a crescent, a defensive hedge of spears and javelins around the wounded. He walked the perimeter, shuffling men to fill thin spots and letting his sense of calm infect them.

"Probably our own," he said, his voice carrying. "But, if it's the Hyrkanians, they caught us at unawares once . . . they'll not catch us a second time!"

Through the cloud of dust—a by-product of the driest Boedromion any could remember—a line of riders cantered into view, led by the familiar figure of Artabazus, his armor's gleam muted by a veneer of grime; even the purple plumes of his helmet were matted with filth. Still, the men let out a ragged cheer when they saw him. Artabazus raised his hand in greeting.

"Memnon!"

The Rhodian came forward and held Artabazus's reins as he dismounted. "I tried to get back in time to warn you," he said. "I'm sorry."

"Thank Mithras! You're alive! I feared those savages had waylaid you!" Artabazus slid off his horse and quickly caught the younger man in a rib-splintering hug. Memnon hissed in pain. "What happened to you?"

Touching his bandaged shoulder, Memnon acquiesced as Artabazus placed a hand on his arm and guided him away from prying ears. They walked toward the burning camp. "One of Pammenes' Boeotians speared me."

"An accident?"

Memnon shook his head. "The Theban has betrayed us. This attack was the work of his new allies, the King's Hyrkanians. But, that's not the worst of it, Artabazus. An army—"

"I know." The old satrap held up his hand, prompting Memnon to silence. "We caught up with their rear guard a few miles from here and Mentor captured one of their lancers in the skirmish. Ere he died, he told us of Tithraustes. I did not know about Pammenes, though such perfidy from him is not unexpected."

"Where is Mentor now?" Memnon said, concerned for his brother's safety.

"Leading a scouting party with what cavalry we have left. Barring disaster, they should return before nightfall." Artabazus coughed. Flames had spread to the palisade itself, cracking the pine logs and sending whole sections toppling into the ditch. Any bodies left under those walls would be immolated, denied a proper Persian burial. Artabazus bowed his head. "I am done, Memnon," he said. "If Ochus wants Dascylium, he may have it. For myself, I will withdraw to the Troad, to Assos, and await the inevitable."

"Artabazus," Memnon said, gently. "Assos, too, has been taken from you. Eubulus is dead; his eunuch, Hermeias, rules and he has cast his lot with Tithraustes."

But for Memnon at his side to support him, Artabazus might have collapsed. As it was, the immensity of their situation left the old satrap pale as death. Memnon had not given much thought to their predicament while on the road, so consumed was he with simply reaching Dascylium. Now he could not ignore its gravity. *Merciful Zeus!* With fair Assos denied them, they had no guarantee of a safe haven on Asian soil. Not to Lampsacus, not to Sigeum, not even to thrice-hallowed Troy could the rebels flee and hope to withstand the Great King's wrath. *To Hellas, then.* But no. Ochus had proven, first with the embattled Athenians and then with the cautious Boeotians, that his wealth and influence reached even across the wine-dark sea. *If not to Hellas, where?*

To his credit, Artabazus mastered himself before any of his men took notice. He stood up straight, his hands clasped behind his back to hide their trembling, and turned from the ruined camp. "This is grave news. Grave, indeed. We . . . We have weathered reversals before. I predict, with Mithras's blessing, we will weather this one, as well."

"What are your orders?"

"We wait for Mentor," Artabazus said. "Yes, wait for Mentor. Once he returns, I . . . I will decide a course of action. Until then, let us look after the men. They've suffered a terrible blow. Terrible." Shaking his head, Artabazus retraced his steps to where two of his cavalrymen tended to his horse. At a gesture, one of the soldiers knelt and offered his satrap a leg up; the other held the horse's headstall until Artabazus collected the reins.

Artabazus's horse, a chestnut mare, whinnied and tossed its head. An enemy spear had gouged a furrow through the heavy muscle of its neck; the movement dislodged a horde of flies. Memnon moved closer and patted the animal's cheek. "That son-of-a-bitch Pammenes kept Celaeno," he said. "I am sorry for that, Artabazus, and I am sorry I did not return in time."

"Ah, my dear boy." Artabazus looked down at the young Rhodian. "You have done nothing to warrant an apology. Celaeno followed you willingly, and I do not begrudge you her loss. I know that even among the Boeotians she will be well cared for. But, I ask you this: do you not agree that, as the Poet says, the gods assign a proper time for all things under heaven? If so, then you returned at the precise moment appointed by the gods. If you cannot believe such a thing, at least realize that you returned squarely when you were needed most." Artabazus smiled and glanced around them. "Yes, I recognize your handiwork here. Beyond the smoke and fire and ruin, I see the stamp of shrewd organization, of natural leadership. I have but to ask any one of those men under yonder trees and they will confirm what I know to be true: that though they pledge themselves to my cause, after today, their hearts are sworn to follow you. For the rest of their days, they will remember your actions, they will remember who it was who helped them in their time of need, and their gratitude will never falter. Nor will mine." And with that, Artabazus touched his heels to his horse's flanks and cantered off, followed by a pair of cavalrymen. The rest stayed behind, their eyes fixed on the Rhodian as they waited for their orders.

Memnon gathered himself up. He nodded, accepting his new role and the implicit trust these men tendered, many of them twice his age. "Wagons," he said, his voice cracking with emotion. "We need more wagons . . ."

MIDMORNING STRETCHED TO MIDAFTERNOON, AND THENCE TO EVENING as Memnon oversaw the transport of the wounded and dead from camp to fortress. At his direction, pavilions sprang up at the base of the stairs leading to the palace; iron cressets were driven into the ground, ready to provide light once the sun finished its descent beyond the western horizon. Memnon, though, did not toil alone. Khafre helped those men he could and made comfortable those beyond his skill. No one asked how he came to be there. They simply accepted his aid with prayers of thanks. Artabazus, too, went among the injured with words of praise, making much of each wound and hearing each man's tale. For those near death, the old satrap simply sat at their side, holding their hand and whispering.

"I never know what to say them," Memnon said as he brought Artabazus a flask of water. Datis, his chamberlain, hovered nearby, ready with a fresh poultice should his master's leg buckle. "Truly, what words bring comfort to a dying man?"

"Put yourself in their place," Artabazus said. "What words would bring you comfort?"

Memnon thought about it for a moment, his brows furrowed. Finally, he said, "I would like reassurance that I'm not alone, that I won't be forgotten. Most of all, though, I think I would want to know my sacrifice wasn't in vain."

"It is no different for each of them." The old satrap patted Memnon's shoulder and returned to his ministrations.

Alone for a moment, the Rhodian watched the swirl of activity. Children darted between the pavilions, though not in play. Pharnabazus, with Barsine, had organized them into brigades of runners, bearers, water carriers, and bandage makers; they fetched blankets and food, tended to the cavalrymen's tired mounts, and ran errands throughout the afternoon. Even the women were pressed into service. As wife to the satrap, his sister Deidamia bore the unenviable task of consoling the forgotten victims of the war: the widows and mothers, sisters and daughters of the slain soldiers. She dispensed with the formalities of court and met them on their level, in dusty tents and under awnings; her maids brought water and olive oil for washing and anointing the bodies. A touch, a soft-spoken word, an embrace, and Deidamia was on to the next, circulating between families with faultless grace.

As she stepped from the pavilion nearest him, the sight of her reminded Memnon of something Glaucus—may his shade rest in peace—had said: *She is the very image of her mother.* And she was. The same raven hair, the same sharp features, the same wide eyes. Only in height and carriage did she differ; in both none could mistake her lineage as the eldest child of Timocrates. Deidamia inherited their father's confidence, and she wore it as easily as she wore her long black *chiton*.

She came abreast of Memnon and stopped, words of greeting forgotten, her finely drawn eyebrows wrinkling. "You're bleeding," she said, indicating his shoulder. "Sit. Let me change your bandages."

"It's nothing. I'll have Khafre—"

"Sit." Her tone brooked no refusal. Memnon propped himself against a wagon.

Securing bandages from a passing child, Deidamia directed her maids to cut away the soot-and-blood-encrusted material swathing Memnon's right side, revealing pale skin and an angry red wound. "Has Mentor returned?" she asked, probing his flesh none too gently; satisfied it showed no signs of suppuration, she motioned for the women to begin rewrapping it with clean linen strips.

"Not yet." Memnon winced as he raised and flexed his shoulder. "It's starting to worry me."

"Why? Mentor is imminently capable of taking care of himself. More so than you or I. Though"—she let the pause hang in the air as she considered her words—"you're not the same man who left here. I've kept my eye on you today. You have an aura about you, as though you're now privy to some divine secret denied to the rest of us. The men sense it; they respond by holding you in esteem, as one might a priest or an oracle. Artabazus senses it, as well. Have you been visited by a god, Memnon?"

He looked askance at his sister. Though said half in jest, Memnon could see in her eyes that she was deadly serious. Even eager. Tales of gods taking physical form fascinated her; she pursued such Mysteries with the same rapacity as their father displayed toward politics. Memnon never understood the genesis of her mania, but he knew better than to encourage her. Like Timocrates with his *demokratia*, Deidamia knew nothing of restraint in matters of religion. Still, what occurred in Heraclides' tent—be it manifestation or delusion—was for his benefit, alone. "Visited by a god? Don't be absurd. War is a pitiless teacher, Deidamia; to survive its lessons, a man must become equally pitiless. It took the head of a spear to drive that maxim home for me. As for what you see, this aura, I cannot say. Oft-times, trauma inspires change in a man. Perhaps that is what the men sense." He glanced down at his shoulder as the maids tied off the last bandage, moved his arm back and forth. "Excellent work," he said to them, smiling his thanks.

Deidamia shooed the younger women away. Her voice sank to a whisper.

"Has Artabazus said aught to you of his plans? If the Loyalists drive us from Dascylium, where will we go? Back to Assos?" When he didn't reply, Deidamia calculated his answer by the grim look in his eyes. "Where, then?"

Memnon exhaled and straightened. "I don't know. It is still too early to tell. Wait for Mentor. Once he's returned, Artabazus will be better able to make his decision. You should steel yourself, though. We may be forced to look beyond Asia's shores for refuge."

"Beyond . . . ? Zeus Savior!" Her hand flew up and clutched her throat; tears rimmed her eyes. "What is to become of us?"

Memnon drew her into a brief embrace, kissed her forehead. "Whatever becomes of us, you and the children will be well cared for. You have my word on that. Come, now. Cease this display. Put tomorrow out of your mind, Deidamia. We have enough to occupy us for today."

She swallowed hard and held herself erect. They were of equal height; Deidamia touched Memnon's cheek in a gesture achingly reminiscent of their mother. "Will you not tell me what mystery the gods revealed to you?"

"My own," he said, smiling. He was spared further questioning by the clatter of horses' hooves and the jingle of harness.

Mentor had returned.

"THEY COVER THE EARTH LIKE FUCKING VERMIN!" MENTOR PACED the perimeter of the open-sided pavilion, still in his armor, his dusty cloak flaring out behind him as he turned. "And that goat-fucker Pammenes is right in there with them, as tight as lice on a Thracian's balls!"

Night had fallen and a copper lamp hung from the pavilion's ridge pole, its carved cedar polished from years of use; Artabazus stood under it, his hands clasped behind his back, his head bowed in thought. Soldiers ringed the rug-strewn pavilion, listening to their general's tirade and waiting for the old satrap to speak. Memnon, too, stood off to one side. Beside him, one of Mentor's cavalrymen fairly vibrated with rage.

"A fighting chance!" he choked. "All we ask for is a fighting chance!"

Artabazus looked up at the sound of the man's voice. Memnon could see the resignation in his eyes. "You would fight?" he said. "Even in the face of impossible odds?" A roar went up from the encircling soldiers. Weapons rattled, spears rang against shield rims in resounding acclamation. Artabazus held his hands up, gesturing for silence. "My companions! My brave companions, you have served me well, with all your heart and soul, but now the time has come to see to your own safety, and the safety of your families! Our rebellion is at an end!"

Cries of "No!" and "Lead us, *Megapatros*!" drowned out the old satrap's voice.

"Lead you? Lead you where? No, my noble warriors! I am done! Where would I lead you? The whole of Persia stands against us! Our allies are gone, scared off by the might of the Great King! I ask you, my companions, what choice do we have?"

Even Mentor was swept up in the fury of the moment. His sword flashed from its sheath. "I say we stand! Zeus Savior and Helios! All men die! What does it matter if it's today, tomorrow, or a year from tomorrow?" The soldiers erupted at this display of bravado; behind them, in the shadows, their women and children shrank back in fear.

Memnon took everything in with a glance. Mentor's chest swelled with the acclaim of his men; his face flushed, like a man drunk on the wine of battle. Beside him, Artabazus looked small and bent. His heart wasn't in this fight, and Memnon could tell it. Something needed to be said. Something . . .

As the crowd's mingled voices paused to draw breath Memnon stepped forward. He circled Artabazus, reassuring the old satrap with a steady hand on his shoulder, and passed close to Mentor. He gestured for his brother's sword. Frowning, Mentor passed it to him, hilt first. Memnon studied his reflection in the blade while he waited for the clamor to die down. It seemed the eyes of Timocrates stared back at him. *You have an aura about you.*

"Your loyalty does you great credit, my friends!" Memnon said, elevating his voice. "Such is the quality of your courage, of your convictions, that even Leonidas of the renowned Three Hundred would be proud to call you his men! But, we are not at Thermopylae, and this is not a time for blind heroics"—he drove the sword point-first into the ground at his feet—"no matter how pleasing they may be to the gods! Put aside this eagerness to die for a moment and ask yourselves what would vex the Great King more: crushing his enemies in a one-sided massacre, or the knowledge that his enemies escaped his wrath altogether?" At this, the soldiers murmured; some nodded their assent. "Without our bodies to crucify, without our heads to decorate his pikes, what will the Great King have to show for his time? Let me answer that for you! He will have nothing, my friends, save for the acrimonious sting of a hollow victory!"

"A hollow victory is still a victory," Mentor growled. "And I am not fond of losing!"

"Nor am I, my brother. Nor is any man. But was it not Artabazus who taught us to celebrate our victories with humility so that our defeats will not reek of fallen pride?" Memnon turned and acknowledged Artabazus as a pupil might his teacher. "The gods have decreed that we must lose this war, my friends! There is no way around it! But must we become martyrs, as well? Must your wives suffer indignities at the hands of Tithraustes' men? Must your children grow up tasting the bitter dregs of slavery? Every man here knows what consequences his loved ones will face after his death! Are we prepared to condemn them alongside us?"

The soldiers glanced over their shoulders at their families, suddenly ashamed at their previous outburst. How could they have been so thoughtless? Mentor, too, retrieved his sword and sheathed it, chastened by his brother's words. For the span of a dozen heartbeats no one spoke, no one moved. Finally, Artabazus broke the silence. "It is no easy thing to put the needs of family above our own glory, but Memnon is right. We bear the burden of others on our shoulders. We must think of them, first. Even as I released Chares and his Athenians from my service without blame or recrimination, so now do I release all of you, as well. I beg you, get yourselves and your families to safety!"

Still, the men made no move to disperse. They looked at one another, shuffling from foot to foot, each waiting for the other to speak. Finally, the front ranks shifted, allowing Omares entrance to the pavilion. Scarred and grizzled, Omares' cheeks were wet with tears as he knelt before Artabazus.

"*Megapatros*, I speak for each man here when I say no matter how well we may have served you, you have served us beyond reckoning, as have your kinsmen. I lost a cousin and two nephews today, and my brother stands already among the shades since Lake Manyas. Though you free us from your service, the dead do not. When the time comes, when I join my ancestors, how will I face them as a man of my word if I abandon you today? I cannot leave your service until I know you and yours are beyond the Great King's reach!" A chorus of *hurrah*'s punctuated Omares' words. He grasped the old satrap's hand. "There are ships yet in the harbor, Lord Artabazus! Let us put you on one and get you to safety! Only then will we be free to pursue the same for ourselves!"

Artabazus caught Omares' hand in both of his and urged the soldier to his feet. "Rise, my loyal Omares," he said. "It is I who should be kneeling before you. Kneeling in thanks for your sound counsel and generous offer. And generous though it may be, I cannot accept it. Truly, what kind of leader would I be if I scurried off and left you to face the King's wrath alone?"

"A prudent one," Omares replied. "You are of no use to us dead, my lord."

"Bless you, my friends, but it seems we have a dilemma! I could no more leave you in the lurch than you could me. But, perhaps we can strike a compromise. What say we prepare together? Leave together? That way, I can be guaranteed of your safety, and you of mine. What say you?"

Omares looked back at his comrades. As one, every man, woman, and child voiced their thunderous approval. Artabazus embraced Omares, kissed his cheek, and followed him out among the men. Memnon started in their wake, but Mentor's hand on his shoulder brought him up short. Brother turned to face brother.

"Zeus, boy!" Mentor said, his brow furrowed. "You spoke well. Patron said you had a gift for oration, but I never believed him."

"I only spoke what was in my heart, to remind them what was in *their* hearts."

"Well, not that it matters but—by god!—Father would have been proud!" Mentor nodded and moved off to look after his men. Memnon watched him go. A knot thickened in the young Rhodian's throat.

"It matters," he whispered. "It matters."

THREE SHIPS REMAINED IN DASCYLIUM'S HARBOR, STRIPPED DOWN FOR A winter refit. Two were merchant vessels of the type called *strongyla ploia*, round ships, wide in the beam and deep, with tall prows and masts of aged cedar. The last was an ancient trireme, patched and re-patched, its hull doubtless laid down in the days when Athens fought Sparta. All three would serve Artabazus's purposes.

Commanding a small army of volunteers culled from among the soldiers who had some experience at sea, and leavened with a handful of professional chandlers and shipwrights who called the harbor *emporion* home, Memnon worked through the night to make the ships ready to sail. Crews square-rigged new canvas and rope to the masts while the ships' bellies received fresh coats of molten pitch. The Rhodian knew they would be crossing dangerous waters, so he inspected each joint, crevice, sheet, and lanyard himself, calling on the knowledge of gray-bearded ship-masters when his own stock failed him. At dawn, he sent word to the fortress. Loading could begin at the satrap's pleasure.

"An inauspicious navy," Khafre said, handing Memnon a cloth-covered bowl. Its contents steamed in the chill morning air.

"It will be sufficient for our needs." Memnon sat under one of the *emporion*'s awnings and sniffed at his breakfast of barley porridge, laced with chopped dates and honey. Khafre dipped a cup of wine from an *amphora* perched on the back of a low wagon and handed it to the Rhodian. Other servants of the fortress were distributing similar fare to Memnon's men.

"And what of its destination, this navy?" the Egyptian asked. Memnon shrugged.

"Thrace, perhaps, or one of the independent towns of the Chalcidice. Artabazus hasn't said. How are the wounded?"

"Seven more joined Osiris during the night," Khafre said. "The others resist the call of the god, though I do not think it is for themselves that they fight. Your satrap's affection for them strengthens their resolve to live. This Lord Artabazus, he is an extraordinary man, more so than any other I have met."

"Yes, he is."

"I wonder, though, is he as clement as he appears?"

Memnon nodded. "Why do you ask?"

The Egyptian did not respond at first, his attention drawn by something across from the *emporion*. Memnon followed his gaze. A soldier, his woman, and their child sat in the sun, their backs to the wall of a ship shed, enjoying their meager breakfast and each other's company. The woman laughed as their young son tried to lift his father's mallet, to drive a sliver of wood into the ground. The boy fell backward into the soldier's lap, his own mirth echoing.

Beside him, Memnon heard Khafre's tortured sigh. "I have a wife and a son at home, in Bubastis, and I have been gone from them for nigh on ten years," he said. "Like your Odysseus, I long to return to them, though until now I could see no clear way to accomplish this. Your lord's mercy is the key." He looked over at the Rhodian, his moist eyes pleading. "I am not without means, Memnon. Were I to raise a ransom, would Lord Artabazus consider accepting it in lieu of continued servitude?"

It was Memnon's turn to pause; he sat his empty bowl aside, wiped his fingers on the cloth, and drained his wine. Khafre's fate was something he had already mulled over, something he had already decided. How should he break it to him? "I've known Artabazus for many years," Memnon began slowly, his forehead wrinkled in thought. "So I speak with a measure of authority when I say I don't think he'll take your money, Khafre."

Stricken, the Egyptian slumped back against the wall and drew his knees to his chest. "I see." His voice cracked. "Well, silence gains nothing, and Lord Artabazus is a more laudable master than Heraclides, I suspect. Reassure him, if you please, that I will not seek to escape. He—"

"You misunderstand me, Khafre," Memnon said, smiling. "He'll not take money for something he can give as a gift."

Khafre blinked. "What?"

"You have done us an incalculable service, my friend. Without your skill, many more of our comrades would have gone to the gods. No ready price can be placed on their lives, or on Artabazus's gratitude. I have only to ask and I am sure he will grant you your freedom—though even that is poor recompense for the aid you have provided."

The Egyptian stuttered for a moment before finding his voice. "This is no cruel jest, is it?"

"No, Khafre," Memnon said gently. "Nor is it a hollow promise. Indeed, I am so confident of Artabazus's response that I give you my word on this: as we sit here, my friend, you are a free man."

"A free man . . ." the Egyptian whispered before burying his face in his hands. Sobs wracked his body as he wept; one hand flailed out and caught Memnon's, clutching at it as a drowning man clutches at a bundle of reeds. For his part, Memnon sat quietly, patting Khafre's shoulder and listening to the sound of wagons rumbling toward the harbor. "I am s-sorry," Khafre said at length. His eyes were red and swollen as he looked up; tears glistened on his cheeks. "I thought I was prepared for the . . . for the magnitude of this moment."

"Will you continue to care for our wounded, as a free man, until such a time as we can speed you on your way?" Memnon asked, rising to his feet and looping his sword baldric over his shoulder. Khafre followed suit.

"You need not even ask. Of course I will."

"Good." Memnon gave an encouraging nod. Both men stepped out into the sun as a line of ox-drawn wagons rolled past the *emporion*, escorted by a score of cavalry. Mentor led them, looking uncomfortable astride his horse. He gestured for Memnon to attend him. The young Rhodian leaned toward Khafre. "You and I, we can talk more later."

"Memnon, I . . . I have no words . . ."

Memnon smiled. "None are needed, Khafre. Were our situations reversed, I know you'd do the same for me." Waving to the Egyptian, Memnon crossed to where Mentor waited. He passed wagons piled high with bales and bags, slender-necked *amphorae* and fat pottery jars. Porters assigned to each ship descended on the goods like flies, jostling and shouting in their haste to get each wagon unloaded. Their clamor made Mentor's horse skittish. "Calm down!" the elder Rhodian growled, sawing back on the reins.

"Stop, stop! You'll dislocate his jaw. You have to be patient with them," Memnon said. He reached up and caught the animal's headstall, loosening the bit and stroking its nose. The horse huffed and whinnied. "These wagons are from the supply magazines?"

"Yes," Mentor said. "Personal effects will come later. Artabazus told Deidamia to be frugal in her packing, to leave behind anything too large to fit in a good-sized chest. I think we should burn the excess, but Artabazus balks at that."

Memnon let the horse nuzzle his neck. "Would you expect otherwise? Much of what will remain has been in his family for generations; he'll not destroy it, but leave it in trust for the new masters of Dascylium."

"Nostalgic foolishness. He should raze the palace; deny Tithraustes the benefit of Dascylium's walls." Mentor dismounted, tossing his reins to an adjutant. "Walk with me, brother."

Patting the horse farewell, Memnon fell in beside Mentor. The elder Rhodian moved down to the harbor's edge and away from the moored ships. Water lapped against old stonework. "I'm staying behind, along with some of the younger men, those with no families, to screen Artabazus's withdrawal."

"I'll stay, too," Memnon said.

"No. Artabazus needs one of us with him, and since you're wounded . . ."

"By Hades!" Memnon snarled. "Would you stop trying to protect me?"

Mentor stopped suddenly, caught Memnon's arm and spun him round. "Idiot! You think this is about my sheltering you from harm? I'm not sending you with Artabazus to spare you! If the Hyrkanians trample over my rear guard and reach the mouth of the Macestus, Artabazus's ship will be overwhelmed 'ere it reaches Propontis! That's why you'll be onboard!"

Memnon cocked his head to one side, his expression quizzical.

In answer, Mentor drew his knife and pressed its bone hilt into his brother's palm. "If I fail," he said, "you cannot let them take Artabazus alive!"

Memnon stared at the knife like Mentor had handed him a deadly asp and bid him press it to his bosom. A cold, hard knot formed in the pit of his stomach. "Zeus! I'm no murderer!"

"Consider what the King will do to him if he's taken. He'll be sent to Susa in chains, tortured, and only executed after Ochus has wrung the last bit of sport from him. Tell me you would not spare him that fate!"

Memnon could not argue otherwise. "Are we to abandon you to Ochus, instead?"

"Don't worry about me, brother. I've taken care of myself for nearly as many years as you've had under heaven. In two weeks time, Zeus willing, I'll meet you at the headland of Sigeum, overlooking the entrance to the Hellespont. You remember the place? The shrine to Poseidon, on the cliffs above the shingle called Priam's Harbor?"

Memnon nodded. The brothers had ridden there from Assos the previous autumn, to propitiate the vengeful Lord of the Deep. "You're sure you can get there in two weeks?"

"With days to spare," Mentor assured him. "For now, though, we've little time. I've deployed men to guard the bridge over the Little Macestus.

Unless the Hyrkanians ride east for half a day, that's the only way cavalry can get across. I leave it to you to get the ships loaded."

"They'll be ready before nightfall."

Mentor started to turn, to make his way back to his horse, but paused. His features clouded; he looked as close to tears as Memnon had ever seen him. "What happened, little brother? Five months ago we were masters of our world. We were victors, wreathed and garlanded. Now look at us—reduced to mere shadows, forced to slink away with tails tucked just to ensure our survival. Did we offend the gods somehow?"

"No more than we're wont to do as men," Memnon said. "Life is a great wheel, Mentor. We rose to ascendancy as much from our own strengths as from Mithridates' weaknesses. Now, through no fault of our own, we find ourselves on the wane. Such is the nature of the wheel. No matter how bad things might get, we have only to be patient and our fortunes will be on the rise once more."

"A capricious philosophy," the older Rhodian said, shaking his head. "Come, there is much yet to do."

Memnon, though, stood his ground for a moment, staring off through the trees. Not a hundred yards from his position, the Little Macestus drained into Lake Dascylitis, pouring over a rocky cataract and into the marshiest portion of the lake. Beyond lay open fields. These stretched along the lakeshore, following its curve to the delta of Macestus proper, broken now and again by stands of oak and sycamore and scrubby pine. Metal flashed in those distant trees. Dust rose.

"Mentor!" His brother turned back toward him, frowning. Using the knife, Memnon gestured off across the fields. "The Hyrkanians are on the move!" Mentor's face darkened.

"Get them out of the palace! Now!"

THE TWIN FORCES OF CHAOS AND FEAR SWEPT LIKE VENGEFUL FURIES through Dascylium. What should have been an orderly evacuation to the harbor became, instead, a rout, fueled by the sounds of brazen horns, clashing iron and the screams of dying men arising from the vicinity of the bridge. Memnon waded through the torrent of men and women bearing the balance of their lives in hastily tied bales and wicker panniers, their children driving geese and goats before them. He passed knots of townspeople—carpenters and smiths, potters and painters—who were trying their best to secure their properties against the tide of refugees. These last were the folk who would stay behind, the *emporoi*, the scions of mercantile families; some had pedigrees reaching back to the time of great Cyrus or beyond, to the days when the Trojan King Priam claimed these lands as part of his realm. No doubt they would praise the King's Men as saviors and throw garlands at their feet, even as they had done for Artabazus.

Even at a fast jog, it took Memnon the better part of an hour to reach the fortress. But, unlike the rest of Dascylium, here he found good order had reigned. The palace had resisted the grip of Phobos, herald of Ares, though its walls stood closest to the War God's domain. At the foot of the stairs, three horse-drawn wagons waited, each loaded with trunks and chests containing the whole of Artabazus's treasury, Deidamia's personal effects, and the children's belongings; a fourth wagon remained empty.

Guards ringed the wagons, weapons drawn, pacing like caged lions and eager to join in the fighting or be away. Among them, he saw Omares.

"Where are they?" he asked, breathless.

"On the way out, or so I have been told," Omares said. Blood spotted the bandages encircling his head. "How are our lads doing?"

"I don't know." Memnon grimaced, glancing toward the bridge spanning the Little Macestus. A spur of the hill on which the fortress sat, girded with trees, screened the bridge from view, but the sounds coming from that direction were appalling. "Send a scout, if you must, but be ready. We have no time." Omares detailed a man as Memnon headed up the stairs to the palace gates.

As he crested the final flight of steps, he nearly collided with a cortege of women and children—the maids of his sister's *gynaikeion* and her wet nurses, who carried the twins, Artacama and Ariobarzanes, swaddled to their breasts; behind them came Barsine with Cophen in tow, all of them herded along by Deidamia, her mantle black as cerecloth. Datis trailed the women, and last of all came Pharnabazus, clad in a leather cuirass and armed with a pair of javelins. Memnon did not see Artabazus.

"Where's your father?" he asked.

Pharnabazus jerked his head back toward the palace. "I saw him last in the great hall. Where do you want me, Uncle?" Despite his brave demeanor, Memnon could tell the boy was scared. His lips trembled; he flinched at the sounds of battle coming from the distant bridge.

"Report to Omares," Memnon said. "Ask him to put you where you'll be the most use." He caught and held Pharnabazus's eyes, his hand resting on his shoulder. "Don't be afraid. Your mind inflates what it cannot see. Courage, son of Artabazus, is not fearlessness, but action in spite of fear."

"Y-Yes, Uncle."

Memnon tousled the boy's hair. Before he could go, Deidamia caught his arm.

"Where is Mentor?" she whispered.

Memnon nodded off toward the bridge. "He has volunteered to lead the rear guard." At this, Deidamia paled. Memnon took her hand and gave it a gentle squeeze. "Remember your words to me, sister. He, more than all of us, is capable of making his own way. We'll see him again. I promise. Hurry, now, get to the wagons." Not waiting to see if she obeyed, Memnon turned and swept through the palace gates.

His footsteps echoed through the deserted courtyard, its walls and niches stripped of anything of value, ready for its new masters. Even the potted trees and shrubs were gone, taken to a place of safety by the gardener. Devoid of life, the palace reminded him of a crypt. Memnon passed through the colonnade and entered the great hall.

At its far end, wreathed in light, Artabazus sat on his throne.

"It's time to go," Memnon said. Nothing. "Artabazus?" The old satrap wore the leather-reinforced trousers of a cavalryman, a saffron tunic, and a long emerald coat stitched with gold thread. His sword, a curved saber in a silver-chased sheath, rested across his thighs. At the sound of his name, Artabazus stirred.

"Do you remember my father, Memnon?"

"No. He died 'ere I took my first steps. Timocrates always spoke of him with reverence, though, even years later. Come, Artabazus. We've not much time. The ships . . ."

"They were a pair, your father and mine. How two men of such different perspectives could become fast friends is a mystery worthy of the gods. I was younger than you are now when Timocrates entered my father's service." Artabazus chuckled. "My first foray to Hellas was at your father's side, to distribute the wealth of Persia to the enemies of that Spartan jackal, Agesilaus, who was ravaging the Asian shore. It worked. Our gold roused Corinth and her allies to war. What the King's myriads could not achieve in years, Timocrates achieved in a single season. He forced Agesilaus to leave our lands and defend his own. Oh, the Spartan's rage was epic, like something from the Poet's verse." The old satrap's smile faded. "Afterwards, my father disliked keeping himself in any one place for too long—Agesilaus had instilled in him a terrible fear of being surrounded or besieged—so he stayed on the move, a nomad in his own lands. 'A man in a fortress is a target,' he would say, 'while a man on horseback is a threat.' But he had one weakness." Artabazus raised his head and looked around the great hall, his eyes distant, as though staring at something Memnon could not apprehend.

"Artabazus, please . . . we must go."

"He called this the dwelling place of his soul, and he bid me never again to let it pass into the enemy's hands. I have failed him in this, not once but twice."

"Your father's wishes cannot supersede the will of the gods, Artabazus. You've fought an honorable war, and you've made Dascylium a place of pride. Men will remember your legacy as they toil under Ochus's lash."

"They'll remember an old fool who thought himself better than the rightful King."

Memnon bristled. "They'll remember a just man who defied a despot!"

Artabazus sighed. "Perhaps. Perhaps not. You are right about one thing, though. The will of the gods hold sway, and I can no more change that than I can change the sun's course across the heavens." The old satrap stood and limped down the dais.

"I wish it could be otherwise," Memnon said. Artabazus smiled.

"Even ill fortunes can be reversed. It is all one, Memnon. It is all one."

"My lords!" a familiar voice rang from the courtyard.

"Here, Omares!"

The officer appeared at the door to the great hall, out of breath. "General Mentor sends word, my lords! He bids us hurry and get away! He cannot hold the Hyrkanians back much longer! I dispatched the wagons on to the harbor with a dozen men guarding them! Horses await us! Come, my lords! Hurry!"

"Yes," Artabazus said, frowning, "I've tarried too long." And without a backward glance, he quit the great hall, crossed the courtyard, and passed between the cyclopean statues flanking the gate. "It is Mentor's belief that I should burn the palace, surely an affront to my ancestors. What is your counsel, Memnon?"

Memnon, though, paid him no heed. Something else had captured his attention. The young Rhodian took a step forward, shading his eyes with the palm of his hand.

"What is it?" Artabazus mimicked the gesture.

From their vantage at the head of the stairs, all three men could see the wagons trundling toward the harbor, sunlight striking fire from the helmets and corselets of the guards. But, the brilliant sun betrayed something else, as well: a detachment of Hyrkanians, on foot, crossing the bed of the Little Macestus and scaling the near bank. Unchecked, they would emerge in the wagons' path.

"The guards, they can't see them!" Omares said.

"Sons of whores!" Memnon snarled, flying down to where the grooms tethered their horses. He snatched a spear from one of the *kardakes* and used the tough cornel-wood shaft to vault onto a horse's back. The animal pranced, its nostrils flaring, as Memnon tore the reins free of the startled groom's grasp and lashed them across its neck, spurring the horse to a full gallop.

Memnon's world shrank; everything that had been important, everything that had been a cause for concern, vanished. He saw only the road, the wagons, and the handful of Hyrkanians massing in the shadows, intent on robbing him of his precious family. Instinctively, he readied his purloined spear for a cast.

Time slowed. Hooves thudded on hard-packed earth. A guard at the rear of the cortege paused, looked back at Memnon, a frown creasing his forehead. He gestured to the others with his javelin. More faces turned toward him . . .

Memnon raised himself on his thighs and let fly with his spear. It flashed past the guards, who turned to follow its track, and thudded into the chest of the first Hyrkanian to break from the cover of the underbrush, a black-bearded brute in trousers and an iron-scaled Median jacket. The man pin-wheeled and fell back.

"Protect the wagons!" Memnon roared, ripping his sword from its sheath. Even as he did, a dozen Hyrkanians exploded from the tree line, moving with the rolling gait of lifelong horsemen. They were lancers, armed with slender spears, axes, and long curved knives; they carried shields shaped like half-moons, made of wicker and reinforced with leather.

The rebel guards met them a score of paces from the wagons. Metal crashed on metal, crunched into the Hyrkanians' shields or clanged on the bronze rims of rebel *aspides*. Spears shattered; men screamed as their bodies were riven and thrust aside. Around the edges of the fray, Memnon's horse danced, balking at the stench of fresh blood. He hauled on the reins, trying to control the animal, only to have it rear up on its hind legs, hooves flailing. Seizing the opportunity, a Hyrkanian charged in and drove his lance into the horse's belly. The beast remained erect, screaming and thrashing. Memnon slid off its rump and circled left; too late did the Hyrkanian see him. The Rhodian sprang. His fist, stiffened by the sword hilt, shattered the Hyrkanian's jaw. His riposte sheared through the man's ribcage, lodging in his spine. Grunting, he kicked his blade free of the corpse.

Suddenly, a high-pitched scream sent a chill through Memnon's body. He spun in time to see one of the Hyrkanians hurl his axe. It flashed, striking the chamberlain, Datis, in the chest. The eunuch drove the wagon holding the women and children; it slowed, affording the enemy a chance to clamber up the side, his blade bared, his teeth drawn back in a snarl of triumph. Deidamia covered the smaller children with her body as she fumbled for a weapon. Closest to the edge of the wagon, Barsine kicked at him, her voice shrill with panic. As the Hyrkanian's hand latched onto her foot, Pharnabazus struggled up from the unsteady wagon bed. Memnon watched as the boy, with all his strength, rammed one of his javelins into the Hyrkanian's face. The point entered under the man's cheek, snapping his head back as it plowed through flesh, bone and brain. Blood sprayed, drenching Pharnabazus and Barsine. The boy let go and stared, wide-eyed, as the Hyrkanian crashed to the ground, the javelin sprouting from his face like a gruesome sapling.

Memnon reached the wagon even as Artabazus and Omares rode up alongside. Pharnabazus sat in shock as Barsine crawled into his lap, hugging his waist. Mechanically, he stroked her hair. Cophen and the two infants howled, unhurt but terrified. Deidamia and her maids tried to quiet them. Memnon climbed up onto the driver's bench where Datis sat, still clinging to life, and took the traces. Artabazus joined him, cradling the eunuch's body. Bright blood drooled down Datis's chin as he tried to speak. Pitifully, he rolled his eyes.

"Forgive me, dear Datis," Artabazus said, his hands reluctant to touch the haft of the axe protruding from his chamberlain's chest. "I should have sent you home."

"N-not . . . g-go . . ." Datis croaked.

"Hold on to him, Artabazus! Hold on, all of you!" Memnon said, lashing the leather traces against the horses' flanks. The wagon jerked and lurched as it gained momentum, those behind it following suit; Memnon did not slacken their pace until he reached the harbor precincts.

Their cortege reined in near the *emporion*. "Khafre!" Memnon yelled as he helped Artabazus lower Datis to the ground. The Egyptian hurried to their side. "Do what you can for him!" Memnon was lifting the children from the wagon when Khafre caught his arm.

"He has already gone to Osiris," the Egyptian said. Memnon glanced down. Datis's eyes were fixed and glazing. Artabazus laid the eunuch's head down and rose to his feet. For a moment, none of them spoke. Finally, Artabazus stirred.

"Let us make sure his death is not for naught. Memnon, get the family on the trireme. The wounded?"

"Aboard the larger of the two ships," Khafre said.

Artabazus nodded. "We need to get word to Mentor that we are on the verge of departing." At this, Omares stepped forward. Artabazus turned to him. "You would volunteer for such duty, my friend?"

"With you safe, my lord, I can now turn my attention to slitting a few Hyrkanian throats."

Artabazus embraced the grizzled soldier and kissed his cheeks. "May the gods grant you long life and prosperity, Omares."

"And you, my lord."

Artabazus released him and gestured to the wagon. "Come, Deidamia, bring the children. Pharnabazus?" He lifted the boy off the end of the wagon and hugged him tight. "You are a man now in the eyes of the gods, and let none dispute it. Come, my son. Help your sister." One by one, father and son assisted the women while Memnon and Khafre hustled them to the trireme. Those followers of Artabazus looking to escape by sea filed aboard one of the two round ships; sailors manned their posts. Men from all walks enlisted to pull an oar aboard the satrap's trireme. Artabazus thanked each one as he walked the raised spine between the oar-banks.

The last aboard, Memnon paused at the foot of the gangplank. He scanned the nearly deserted *emporion*, catching sight of Omares organizing a troop of soldiers. He called to him.

"Give my brother a message for me! Tell him two weeks! He'll understand!"

Omares acknowledged Memnon's request with a wave of his hand and went back to preparing his squadron. Inland, the fighting grew closer. Mentor's men were being forced back.

With a heavy heart, Memnon hurried up the gangplank.

From the stern of the trireme, Artabazus gave the order to stand away; mooring lines were hauled aboard, and men with boat-poles thrust them against the quays. Slowly, ponderously, the round ships backed water and made for the center of Lake Dascylitis, where the current from the Macestus River would carry them down the channel to Propontis. The trireme left last; without drum or flute, the sailors kept time for their fledgling rowers by striking two broken spear shafts together. *Clack! Clack! Clack!*

Memnon clambered up through the superstructure and mounted the harbor-side outrigger. From here, he watched as the fighting onshore spilled from street to street. Houses burned, set alight by the torches of the Hyrkanians, the smoke providing excellent cover for the remaining rebels. Memnon saw his brother for a brief moment as he spun his horse about to face the harbor.

"Mentor!" he cried, thrusting both arms aloft. The elder Rhodian spotted him and raised his sword in salute before the wrack of fighting swallowed him up again. Slowly, Memnon dropped his arms. "Merciful Zeus," he whispered, "keep him safe."

Rain lashed the headland at Sigeum, making it treacherous to ascend the winding flight of rock-cut steps leading from the rugged beach called Priam's Shingle to the crest of the promontory where Poseidon's temple stood, overlooking the turbulent waters of the Hellespont. Built on the Ionic order, the temple bore an elaborate frieze of sea creatures—dolphins cavorting with the Nereids—done in Naxian marble, weatherworn and pitted from centuries of exposure to the salt air. Four columns fronted the temple, providing a measure of protection from the elements; between them, a door of bronze-bound pine stood ajar.

Inside, on a pedestal of carved stone, Poseidon held court in the darkened *cella*. Crafted in marble and gold and wearing a crown of pearl, the bearded Lord of the Deep clutched his trident in one hand and a wreath of sacred pine in the other. Generous and cruel was this, the God of the Sea. Brother of Zeus and Hades, Earth-Shaker and Lord of Tempests, in his presence Memnon could not help but feel powerless, inconsequential. He did not relish the feeling.

Ill at ease, the Rhodian paced at the foot of the god, his cloak wrapped tight against the chill wind spilling through the open door. Artabazus stood off to one side, likewise bundled, warming his hands over the coals of a small brazier.

"He will come," the old satrap said.

"It's been two weeks, and more, since we left Dascylium!"

"Mentor gave his word. He will come."

"But dare we wait any longer, Artabazus? Once this rain abates, Nereus assures me a favorable wind will blow, but only for a matter of days. Even then, we will be testing the Sea King's patience. These are mercurial waters. Let me seek Mentor out! When I find him, we can catch up to you in Thrace, or the Chalcidice!"

"You have asked before!" Artabazus snapped. "Still, my answer is no! We await him here!"

"Waiting!" Memnon snarled. "Waiting is for old women! I should . . ." His voice faded as something outside the temple caught his eye. He crossed to the door and shoved it wider, beckoning Artabazus over with a jerk of his head. "Perhaps our wait is at an end."

A figure struggled up the hillside toward the temple, from Sigeum.

"It's not Mentor," Memnon said, crestfallen.

"A messenger, perhaps."

"Or an escaped slave, come to seek Lord Poseidon's protection." Tradition made the Sea God's temples places of asylum for runaways. Memnon backed away from the door, allowing the fellow entrance.

Exhaustion rather than piety put the man on his knees as he crossed the threshold. "I seek," he gasped, "a Rhodian, called Memnon! I was told he would be here!"

Memnon and Artabazus exchanged glances. "I am he. Do you bring a message from Mentor? He is my brother!"

The runner sat, pushing his dripping hair out of his eyes. He was young, a few years Memnon's junior, and clad in sandals and a woolen *khlamys*. "Have you any wine?" he said. Memnon nodded and fetched him a cup from their meager stores. Greedily, the runner accepted it and sucked it down.

"What of it, man? Does my brother yet live?" Memnon said.

"He does. Word came to Assos, from my father, bidding me get a message to Memnon at Sigeum. I am to say to him that Mentor could not fight through to the Hellespont, and that you and your lord should seek shelter on a far shore. My father said Mentor would seek you out when he could."

"Who is your father?" Artabazus asked, frowning.

"Omares, my lord. A captain of the *kardakes*."

"What else did he say?" Memnon grasped the boy by the shoulders, fairly shaking him. The Rhodian's face screwed up in a look of rage, as though he interrogated one of the king's spies. "Damn you! What else did he say?"

"Nothing else, lord! Nothing else! I swear it!"

Artabazus caught Memnon by the arm. "Come. Let him go, Memnon. He is Omares' son, and he has told us all he knows. We must make ready so that when the rain subsides we can get underway."

Memnon nodded.

Omares' son piped up. "Should they send to me, asking where you've gone, what should I tell them?"

"Tell Mentor . . ." Artabazus paused, exhaling. "Tell him to seek us in Macedonia." He laid a hand on Memnon's shoulder. "We will test the limits of King Philip's friendship, eh?"

Interlude II

"Macedonia," Melpomene said, her voice ragged. "Have you ever seen it, Ariston? In the spring, the lowland plains are thick with iris and mallow and green shoots of barley, all of it watered by streams without number. The land rises in rills and folds, past lakes as blue as the sky and groves of willow and poplar and white-flowered acacia, sweeping up through forests of pine to meet the snow-clad peaks of the Bermion Mountains. It is truly the Garden of Midas."

"I have not ventured so far north, Lady, though by your description I am much the poorer for it."

Melpomene arched an eyebrow. "Curious. I would have thought such a staunch follower of divine Alexander would have made the pilgrimage to the Emathian Plain, to holy Pella, to view the place of his birth."

Ariston shrugged. "Alexander might have been born in Macedonia, but his body resides in Egypt, and to Egypt I will make my pilgrimage, when the time is right. Macedonia holds no interest for me."

"It should," she said, "for without Macedonia, there could have never been an Alexander. The land was the crucible wherein his character was forged. His muscle and sinew, his flesh and blood were the raw materials, and the passions of Philip and Olympias provided the flames. When that crucible was broken open, when its contents stepped forth to take its spear-won prize, none could be prouder than the land itself, for Macedonia had given the world a demigod."

"They remain proud, today," Ariston agreed.

"You confuse pride with arrogance. So long were they steeped in his divine light that Alexander's generals have come to believe themselves his equal. He made them, make no mistake, and in dying he unleashed a plague upon the world—a plague of warmongers, bereft of their master's grace. In his day, Xerxes should have obliterated the Macedonians on his march to Greece, even if it meant depriving the world of Alexander. Now, we must endure those he left behind." She coughed; flecks of blood spotted her lips. Silently, Harmouthes rose and handed her a fresh linen cloth. She whispered something to him; the Egyptian nodded, excusing himself. Ariston stood and stretched.

Beyond the window, the morning's chill gave way to a mild afternoon, the faint breeze warmed by brilliant sunshine. At Melpomene's urging Ariston opened the shutters, allowing air to circulate through the room. He could imagine such a day drawing swarms of Ephesians to the agora, where merchants and tradesmen seeking to supplement their lean winter incomes would offer their meager wares to aristocrats, soldiers, and commoners weary of the rain and cold. Oddly, Ariston did not feel tempted to quit *The Oaks* and partake in the carnival atmosphere.

Instead, the young Rhodian turned from the window, frowning. "Why did they flee to Macedonia? Did Philip not have designs on Persia?"

Melpomene shook her head. "This was many years before Isocrates penned his missive to Philip urging him to unite the states of Hellas against the *barbaroi* threat. The exiles—such was their name in the Macedonian court—reached Pella in the wake of Philip's defeat in Thessaly, at the hands of Onomarchus the Phokian. Persia was the least of his worries. As for why," she shrugged. "Athens and Sparta owned but a slender portion of their former glory, and Thebes had lost its supremacy a decade earlier, when

Epaminondas died defeating the Spartans at Mantinea. Only in Macedonia could Artabazus find a ruler whose ambitions rivaled the Great King's, and that ambition virtually guaranteed Philip and Ochus would never unite."

"Neither would be a vassal to the other," Ariston said, nodding. "A shrewd man, Artabazus."

Harmouthes returned bearing a tray of bread and cheese, a relish of olive oil and garlic, two pottery bowls, and a single-handled *oinochoe* of wine. For Melpomene, a separate mug of warmed wine mixed with herbs. Beneath the tray, Ariston noticed the Egyptian carried a flat wooden box, its sides decorated with faded paintings of men crouching at the feet of an ibis-headed figure—doubtless one of the myriad gods of his native land.

Ariston helped him with the tray. The box Harmouthes handed to his mistress. She held it carefully, like something made of fragile alabaster; her fingers caressed its surface, feeling every nick, every gouge in the wood.

Ariston leaned closer. The flat surface of the box bore a painted image similar to those on its sides—a man sitting at the base of a throne, a roll of papyrus on his lap, writing down the words spoken by his lord, the whole encircled by a ring of hieroglyphs. "What is it?"

"A *mestha*," Harmouthes said. "A case used by scribes to hold the instruments of their craft." At one end, the likeness of a beetle was carved into the wood and worn smooth from innumerable handlings. Melpomene pressed her index finger into the beetle's hollowed-out body and slid the case's cover back. The odor of old ink, papyrus, and palm wood rose from the heart of the box. She closed her eyes and inhaled.

"Memnon's letters," she said, her voice barely a whisper. "To my father, to Mentor . . ."

Ariston's face remained neutral, though he marked well her slip of the tongue. *My father*. This meant Melpomene was a daughter of whom . . . of Artabazus? And if so, which daughter? Which . . .

With effort, Ariston returned his attention to the case as Melpomene carefully removed a sheaf of letters; most were written in a firm, spidery hand, on a mixture of papyrus and parchment.

"Memnon wrote often to Mentor, though his brother was miserly with his replies," she said. She handed Ariston examples:

Mentor from Memnon, greetings. Campaign season has come again, my brother—the second since our flight from Asia—and I have yet to receive a summons from you. Do you seek to hoard all the glory for yourself? If so, tell me, and I will find new avenues in which to excel; if not, then send for me! I will gladly serve under you in your expedition against the Great King.

Another, dated the following year:

What news is there to report? Demosthenes of Paeania, the orator, is agitating the Athenians against Philip. This is the same Demosthenes who argued for liberating Rhodes two years past, in the wake of Mausolus's death, and he had as much success in that endeavor as he has had against Philip. For himself, Philip is unconcerned. He has marched out again, this time against the Illyrians and the Epirotes. Truly, I now believe in Patron's assessment: Philip styles himself an Agamemnon, and I think he will not stop until all of the Greeks are under his heel.

Ariston lingered over a third:

Not long past, we were introduced to the Crown Prince, young Alexander. It was an auspicious meeting. We arrived at the palace early, as Artabazus wanted to speak with Philip in private, before the King secluded himself with his regent, Antipatros, and his general, Parmenion. The King had not yet returned from the drill field so we were escorted to one of his ancillary halls to await his arrival. Young Alexander showed up a few minutes later, the self-appointed spokesman of his father. He apologized for his sire's delay and proceeded to sit with us, questioning Artabazus about the inner workings of the Great King's court. Not childish or trivial questions, either! He wanted to know about roads and distances, if the tales of Herodotus were true or exaggerations; most of all, he probed the character of the Great King—his military strength, his prowess. Artabazus found him endearing. I, less so. The boy is only in his sixth year, but already I fear his ambitions. If his promise bears fruit even Philip's celebrated astuteness, his deeds, will pale in comparison . . .

"Alexander's genius was visible so young?" Ariston asked, handing the letter back to Melpomene and reclaiming his chair. She reread it, her brows furrowed.

"Indeed, but Memnon left much unsaid in his letters concerning Philip's court, a precaution in the event his courier was waylaid by those seeking to do him harm. Many branded him a traitor for his allegiance to Artabazus, despite their bonds of kinship. No, what was at the root of Memnon's concern was an assertion championed by Queen Olympias that Alexander was not the son of Philip at all, but of Zeus. Worse, it was an assertion Alexander himself believed."

"Faugh!" Ariston said. "Athenian fiction! Alexander never claimed to be a god!"

Melpomene and Harmouthes exchanged wry smiles. "So his flatterers would have you believe," she said. "His modesty was the true fiction, disseminated for all the world by Callisthenes of Olynthus, that kinsman of Aristotle chosen by Alexander to be his 'official historian,' but make no mistake, Ariston—Alexander perpetuated the notion of his own divinity. Oh, he was careful about it, careful never to let the claim escape his own lips outside his circle of friends, but it was something he, and they, believed strongly. And why not? Olympias had instilled it in him at an early age—and *she* would know if she coupled with a god, he would say."

Ariston said nothing for a moment, his eyes narrowing. "You speak of Alexander with surprising candor, almost as if you knew him."

At this, Harmouthes, who was pouring wine into the two bowls, glanced sharply from his mistress to Ariston. Pottery clattered as he set the pitcher aside. The Egyptian straightened and would have said something had she not stilled him with an almost imperceptible shake of her head.

Ariston interpreted this gesture, as well as her silence, as affirmation. "Great Helios! You did know him!" The young Rhodian found himself unable to keep the superstitious awe from his voice. He slid forward in his chair, his hands knotted in anticipation. "Where? How?"

Melpomene sighed and gathered up the letters, returning them to their case. She withheld a ragged scrap of papyrus. "I was captured at Damascus, along with Queen Stateira and Queen-Mother Sisygambis, in the wake of the tragedy at Issus. We were treated well, our honor inviolate, and Alexander visited us when he could, though never in the manner of a harem. He took to Darius's mother, and she to him. As I speak fluent Greek, it often fell upon me to translate between the two."

Ariston sank back in his chair, unconsciously stroking his beardless chin. *A daughter of Artabazus*, he reckoned, *who was an intimate of both Memnon and Alexander, who was taken with Darius's family at Damascus, and who lived for a time in Pergamum . . . I should know your name, Lady.* He resolved to slip away later today or tomorrow and put the question to Nicanor. The old

Macedonian would know. "You should commit your memories of Alexander to the page, as well."

"Our children's children will remember him well enough without my contributions," she said, placing her hand on the letter-case. "Memnon, though . . . Memnon's legacy is another matter. I fear without my intercession his deeds will be lost in the shadow of *Alexandros Basileus*."

Ariston found he could not disagree. Accepting a bowl of wine from Harmouthes, the young Rhodian said, "How long was Memnon in Macedonia?"

"Not long," Melpomene said, passing the scrap of papyrus to him. Its previous owner salvaged it from an Egyptian source, as its obverse still bore traces in black and red ink of that land's peculiar style of writing. On its face, the scrawl of blocky Greek letters read more like a military dispatch than a note from brother to brother:

> *Memnon from Mentor: Egypt is a scorpion's nest. Take ship at your earliest convenience. I need a man I can trust at my back.*

"Memnon left at the end of their fourth year in exile," she said, settling back into bed. "He joined Mentor in service to Pharaoh Nectanebo the Second, whose people had stood in open rebellion against the Great King for close to sixty years. The brothers, though, saw the whole episode as just another precarious situation, another opportunity to sample the bitter lees of defeat. After another four years of fighting—in Egypt and up the coast in Phoenicia—Mentor finally sent Memnon back to Macedonia with news of an extraordinary plan . . ."

Macedonia
Year 4 of the 108th Olympiad
(345 BCE)

"PELLA," MEMNON SAID, STROKING HIS SHORT BEARD. HE STOOD IN the bow of *Briseis*, a round-bellied merchant vessel out of Miletus, watching the far shore as the ship crossed the muddy expanse of Lake Loudias. "Ever think you'd see it again, Khafre?"

Beside him, the Egyptian's sharp features screwed up in a look of distaste, as though he had taken a bite of a bad pomegranate. "No, nor did I wish to see it again. It is a wretched place, Memnon, full of unclean men who willingly—joyously—eat the flesh of swine and then have the gall to call my people barbarous. I weep for the years Lord Artabazus has had to spend in such rustic surroundings."

"Look at it. Four years gone and I barely recognize the place. Dislike the people as you will, but give Philip his due and don't insult his capital by calling it rustic." Memnon knew he was right. From their vantage on the water, they could see practically the whole of Pella. He pointed out landmarks, both old and new, that would not have looked out of place at Athens.

Guarding the mouth of the harbor, the island of Phakos squatted like a craggy Titan surrounded by reeds, its flanks clothed in dusty fir and chestnut. A small and unlovely citadel of dark local stone crowned the island, Philip's treasury and his jail. Bronze glinted from those ramparts. Memnon reckoned they were under observation; it would only be a matter of time before the King's sharks gathered.

From the harbor, wide streets and cross-streets, forming Hippodamian blocks of uniform size, ascended by degrees to the north, to the rocky hill that served as the city's acropolis. Here, in the reign of old King Archelaos, artisans had flocked up from the south—painters, sculptors, architects, and builders—their influence evident in the public buildings of brilliant-hued marble, stoas and colonnades, theaters and *gymnasions*, abutting large shops and townhouses of limestone, timber, and glazed clay tiles. To Pella, too, had come men of letters, philosophers and poets such as Agathon and Timotheus, Choerilus of Samos, even the renowned Euripides, drawn by the promise of royal favor and the wealth it implied. Fifty years later, Philip reaped the benefits of his ancestor's tradition of patronage. "What did he call it?" Memnon said. "The Jewel of Emathia?"

"Jewel?" Khafre sniffed in disdain. "It is a sheep-pen compared to Memphis."

Memnon smiled. Though he would never admit it to his proud Egyptian companion, he found the Nile Valley to be dusty and monotonous, a place of flies, filth, and oppressive heat. He was glad to be away from there, though the nature of his exodus left a foul taste in his mouth. His smile faded. Mentor and his cursed plan! He—

"Look there," Khafre said, gesturing with a tilt of his head. Memnon roused himself and followed the Egyptian's gaze. From Phakos, a pair of longboats of a type called *pristoi*, rowed toward *Briseis*. The first bore an official of Philip's exchequer, who would assay the Milesians' cargo of Aeolian carpets, bales of wool, and wine from the vineyards of Naxos, and levy an appropriate tax. The second boat ferried an agent of the harbormaster, who sought advance payment for the use of Pella's docks, warehouses, and slaves. A man in the bow of the lead craft bellowed for them to heave to; in response, the Milesian captain ordered the single square sail reefed. *Briseis* drifted, kept on course by a pair of tillers in her stern.

"Time for Philip's sharks to take their bite," Memnon said as the two boats snugged up against the ship. Ropes were lowered; rather than allowing others to haul them up like excess baggage, both officials scaled the side of *Briseis* like seasoned mountaineers. Indeed, Memnon reflected, they likely were.

As they gained the deck, these two ruddy Macedonians, both scarred and grizzled, glanced around, plainly in their element. They wore short *chitons* of blue-dyed linen, heavily embroidered and cinched at the waist with belts of stamped leather. Long knives hung in easy reach. Gold rings glittered on their fingers—doubtless part of the spoils of war—and the man of the treasury sported a thick medallion bearing the symbol of the royal house, a sixteen-pointed star.

The Milesian captain laughed and embraced both men like long lost kinsmen. "Machatas! Amyntor! By the dog of Hades! It is good to see you!"

"Greetings, Eumelus," the treasury agent, Machatas, said. "What wonders of Ionia do you bring on this trip, eh?" He spoke southern Greek with a harsh accent.

"Come and see for yourself," the captain replied, grinning. The two Macedonians followed him to the hold.

The rank and file of Philip's bureaucracy hailed from every corner of Macedonia, from the districts of Pelagonia and Lynkestis, Orestis and Tymphaea. From Elimaea and Eordaea came clansmen who only a generation before would have been at one another's throats, but now shared a common goal—service to a king they respected. Philip instilled a national pride in them that transcended the ancient bonds of clan and kin. "He will make them more Greek than the Athenians," Mentor had said, upon hearing of Philip's triumph in the Chalcidice, "and they'll love him for it." Now, watching the officials as they went about their business, Memnon could see his brother spoke true.

No stranger to the operation of a harbor, the transactions Memnon witnessed unfolded with a remarkable lack of histrionics. The three men haggled good-naturedly, without invoking the gods as witnesses to an act of robbery, without threats. A fair tax was levied and a fair price quoted for the use of the docks. The Milesian, Eumelus, paid both without so much as raising his voice. A quarter of an hour later, *Briseis* was underway, passing beneath looming Phakos as it wallowed toward the lakeside quays.

"The Athenians should send their harbor master to Pella for lessons in proper management," Khafre said, grudgingly, as they gathered their things together in anticipation of disembarking. At Piraeus, the harbor of Athens, Memnon reckoned the selfsame transaction would have taken thrice as long.

"I told you. This place has changed."

Khafre harrumphed. "Still, it is no jewel."

Memnon only smiled and shook his head, saying nothing.

Briseis docked without fanfare; bundles of dried reeds crunched, absorbing the shock as the ship's hull bumped the wharf. Sailors dropped from bow and stern, hauling mooring ropes behind them. These they made fast to wooden bollards on the dock as others of the crew wrestled a boarding plank into place. Harbor slaves, their services bought and paid for, congregated near the ship, their overseers watching them closely. Most of the slaves were big-boned Thracians, their faces and bodies decorated in blue tribal tattoos; a handful of dour, whip-scarred Illyrians leavened their ranks.

Memnon shouldered his gear and raised his hand in farewell to the captain, who mimicked the gesture. Khafre descended to the quay; Memnon paused at the head of the plank. "When do you expect to return to Miletus?"

Eumelus chewed his lip. Though late in the season, there were still merchants desperate to have their goods transported south. Along with Poseidon's Ballast—the pine pitch and timber that were staples of Macedonian trade—he could depend on filling his hold with Thracian furs, sacks of summer wheat, and casks of barley wine. He would need time to make arrangements. "Ten days hence," he said, after a moment. "Weather and the gods permitting."

"Good." Memnon nodded. "Keep a berth open for my Egyptian companion. He will accompany you."

"As you wish. Fair winds to you, Rhodian."

"And to you, Eumelus." With that, Memnon left *Briseis* and joined Khafre at the foot of the boarding plank. Red-haired children in rough homespun darted around them, chasing a hide ball into the forest of Thracian slaves. An overseer sent them scurrying with a crack of his whip. "Your passage back to Miletus is arranged," Memnon said over the din. "Can you stomach Pella for ten days?"

"I have little choice, it seems," Khafre replied, his lip curling.

Memnon smiled and clapped the Egyptian on the shoulder. "Come. Let's see if I can remember the way to Artabazus's villa."

ON THE EASTERN SIDE OF PELLA'S ACROPOLIS, IN THE SHADOW OF PHILIP'S palace, stood the rambling estate the King had gifted to Artabazus and his kin. A low stone wall bounded the property; inside, nestled in a grove of birch and willow, skilled gardeners had transformed the grounds into a lush approximation of a Persian *pairidaeza*. Cool spring water chuckled over moss-covered stones, splashing into leaf-shaded pools and fountains edged in hyacinth and lavender. Fanciful Dryads dotted the path, the sheen of marble complimentary to the brilliant azaleas and rhododendrons and snow-white lilies lacing the greensward. From delicate wicker cages clasped in the Dryads' hands a symphony of birdsong erupted, while peals of silvery laughter echoed deep inside the estate.

Beside him, Memnon heard the Egyptian sigh. He felt it, too—that undeniable sense of being home. Weariness and worry sloughed away as he stepped through the gates, though the gravity of the mission entrusted to him was never far from the surface.

The house itself stood at the center of the estate. It was a mansion by Macedonian standards, but to a man accustomed to the dwelling places of Asian royalty the villa was on par with the fine hunting lodges of the Lydian highlands. Still, it had warmth, and touches of Eastern elegance, such as fretted screens and linen sheers and musical chimes that captured the breeze, made its unassuming plainness extraordinary.

Memnon and Khafre met no one on the path until near the main house, when an elderly gardener looked up from tending a bed of asphodel, squinted at the pair, and whooped for joy once he recognized the Rhodian. "Memnon!"

"Peace to you, Gryllus!" he said with a wave. The old man rose and ambled over, laughing as he embraced both men. "You're looking well," Memnon said. "And your wife, how is she?"

"Ianthe? Oh, she's as fat as a sow and thrice as stubborn!" Gryllus said. He patted Khafre's arm. "She'll be pleased to see you, Egyptian. Her woman troubles have returned and she swears you possess the only cure."

"Sweet Hathor! Take me to her, good Gryllus," Khafre said. "I would not have you endure another day of mercurial moods when succor is so near at hand. Memnon?"

The Rhodian nodded toward the villa. "You go on ahead. I'm going to visit the stables, first."

"I'll tell the Lady you've returned," the old gardener said, meaning Deidamia. Gryllus took Memnon's gear, shouldered it, and shuffled up the path, arm in arm with Khafre. Memnon circled the house.

Though much about Pella had changed during his four-year absence, the stables of Artabazus had not. They were everything one could expect from an Achaemenid, scion of a steppe-dwelling clan accustomed to lavishing princely attention on their horses. Spacious and well-found, the stables were mansions in their own right, with stone-paved stalls canted slightly to provide drainage and two yards ringed by fences of wood and iron—one of hard-packed rock, the other softer, of raked sand and soil. The same spring that fed the estate here gurgled into a trio of stone troughs, their marble spouts carved to resemble the magnificent, and mythical, horses of the Thracian king, Rhesus.

Of equal magnificence were the three horses gamboling about the sand yard—matched Nisaean mares, fifteen hands high, with glossy coats blacker than a moonless night. Memnon recognized them instantly: Thaleia, Aglaia, and Euphrosyne.

"*Chairete*, ladies," Memnon said as he reached the fence. Their ears perked at the sound of his voice; nostrils flared with curiosity, though they balked at coming closer. "Have you forgotten me so soon?" He extended a hand. Boldly, Thaleia approached, nuzzling the proffered hand in hopes of finding a treat. "No apples today." Thaleia snorted and tossed her head, submitting instead to his touch. Soon, all three crowded around the Rhodian, huffing and whinnying, impatient for head rubs or ear scratches. "No," Memnon said, smiling, "you've not forgotten, have you? No . . ."

"They have longer memories than most men," said a voice behind him. Memnon glanced over his shoulder as Pharnabazus walked up, grinning; his arms were weighted down with saddlecloths and bridles. Gone was the smooth-faced teen Memnon remembered; in his place stood a muscular twenty-two-year-old man, his sun-browned skin just beginning to collect the whitish scars of a soldier. In keeping with his environment, Pharnabazus had long since adopted the Greek fashion of sandals and a short tunic, saffron hued, which he pinned at the left shoulder with a simple brooch. He kept his chestnut hair long, after the custom of the Persians, while his beard showed signs of immaculate attention. Beyond that, the gods could have molded his hawkish face and dark eyes from Artabazus's own.

"Longer memories and they're more trustworthy," Memnon said, turning to face the young Persian, his hands on his hips. "Zeus Savior! Haven't you stopped growing yet?"

Pharnabazus laughed and put his burden aside. He caught Memnon in a rib-splintering hug. "It is good to see you again, Uncle!"

"And you, boy, and you! What is this?" Memnon tugged a tuft of Pharnabazus's beard. "Are you trying to be a perfumed courtier, now?"

"A man needs some small vanity so as not to anger the gods with his perfection," he said, making a show of smoothing his beard with his fingertips.

Memnon laughed. "Humility would better assuage their anger." He nodded to the riding tack. "Which were you planning on taking out?"

"All of them, with Father and Cophen. Come, they are in the stables. Father will be pleased to see you again." Pharnabazus eyed the Rhodian critically. "You have collected a few more scars since last you were home. How fares the war in Egypt?"

Together, they walked into the cool shade of the stables. "It fares poorly," Memnon said, frowning. "For the last two years Mentor's been in command of the garrison at Sidon, on the Phoenician coast, in collusion with Sidon's king—part of Pharaoh's plan to create a buffer between Egypt and Persia. Most of Phoenicia has joined Pharaoh's rebellion but the Great King's forces still outnumber us, and Ochus is loath to abandon his ports in that region."

Pharnabazus nodded. "I would think so. We have heard very little news from the south, and what we do hear gets filtered through Philip's eyes and ears. The truth will be a refreshing change." He smiled and gestured to the far end of the stables, to where Artabazus sat with Cophen, instructing him how best to repair a loose chain on a horse's headstall. The old satrap looked more weathered since last Memnon saw him, his hair thinner and consumed with gray. "Father! Look who the gods dropped on our doorstep!"

Artabazus looked up, eyes still sharp and unclouded. A broad smile creased his face; he put the headstall aside and, with Cophen's help, rose to his feet. "I thought I recognized your voice, Memnon. Praise Mithras!" He shuffled forward, his limp pronounced, and clasped the Rhodian's shoulders. "On my soul, with each passing year you look more like your father. It does my heart good to see you again, dear boy."

"You're looking well," Memnon said. "How's the leg?"

"It serves to keep me upright. Beyond that . . ." Artabazus waved. Like his sons, he too wore sandals and a Greek-style tunic, bone-colored and heavily embroidered, cut to allow him to sit astride a horse. Its brevity also revealed the puckered traces of ancient wounds—badges of honor to the warlike Macedonians.

Memnon was poised to reply when Cophen stepped up, his head cocked, and stared at him with all the undisguised inquisitiveness of a twelve-year-old. "Greetings, Uncle. Do you remember me?"

"Indeed, Lord Cophen. One is hard-pressed to forget you." Memnon smiled and would have ruffled the lad's hair had he not shied away.

"Have you a gift for me, from Egypt?"

Quick as a snake, Pharnabazus's arm shot out and caught the scruff of his brother's neck, hauling him close. "Manners, Cophen. It is enough that Memnon has returned home. Forgive him, Uncle. He has learned impudence from the son of Philip, himself."

"Alexander is my friend!" Cophen said, straining under his brother's grip.

Before Artabazus could intervene, Memnon knelt, his eyes level with Cophen's. The boy ceased struggling; Pharnabazus relaxed his fingers. "The son of a king is a good friend to have, and if he is a true friend then the gods have blessed you both. But, in answer to your question: one cannot visit Egypt without bringing back a trove of trinkets. Find Khafre. He will know which is yours."

"Khafre returned with you?" Wide-eyed, Cophen shrugged off Pharnabazus's hand. "Does he still tell tales and weave stories?"

Memnon stood and smiled. "He does. Seek him out, but ask your father's leave, first."

"Father?" Cophen turned, as rigid as a soldier facing his commander. "May I beg off riding today?"

Artabazus nodded. "You have my permission." As soon as the words left his father's lips Cophen took off, sprinting through the stables in a flurry of dust and loose straw. "That one is his mother made over," Artabazus said, shaking his head.

"He is foolish," Pharnabazus said.

"No." Artabazus corrected him. "He's young. As were you. Go ready the horses, my son. Memnon will take Cophen's place, or have the months at sea rusted your skill in the saddle?"

The Rhodian grinned. "Let's find out."

ALONG THE MARSHY VERGE OF LAKE LOUDIAS, MILES FROM THE OUTSKIRTS of Pella, the three Nisaeans stretched their legs into a full gallop, their riders' wishes a trifling annoyance. Thundering hooves tore into the sun-baked earth, sending clods of dirt and pulverized reed into the air to cake the horses' steaming flanks. A half-mile passed, and still they did not slacken. Herons exploded from clumps of sedge; wings beat the shallows as mallards, startled by the crash and clamor, lofted into the cloud-strewn sky. After a mile and more, Memnon, astride Euphrosyne, drew the animal back under control, slowing to a canter, then to a trot, giving it a chance to catch its breath. Artabazus and Pharnabazus followed suit.

All three men were flushed and panting, frosted with dust. Pharnabazus whooped; his father chuckled to himself, no doubt lost in a memory of distant Asia, of a cavalry charge from one of his myriad wars.

"Zeus Savior and Helios!" Memnon exhaled. "There's nothing at sea to rival that! It's as though you're flying on the wings of a god!" He stroked the animal's damp neck. Ahead, a stream, its rocky banks edged with willows, fed into Lake Loudias. Memnon led them upstream about a hundred yards, where all three men dismounted and walked their horses. Once they had cooled, man and beast drank their fill. While the mares nibbled on soft grass, the men sat in the late afternoon shade of a willow tree. Flies buzzed; plovers whirled overhead, hunting insects.

Pharnabazus dozed on a bier of grass and willow leaves; opposite him, his back to the willow-bole, Memnon sat with his legs out-thrust, one arm pillowing his head. Artabazus rested on a half-buried boulder, massaging his scarred thigh. He glanced sidelong at the Rhodian, whose face bore the gravest of frowns. Twice Memnon looked to be on the verge of speaking, only to lapse back into himself.

"There are times," Artabazus said, "when silence speaks more eloquently than the most silver-tongued orator. Your tortured silence tells me this is no mere visit. A task has fallen to you that does not sit well with your conscience. Mentor has set this errand upon you, has he not? Be at ease, then, Memnon. Put aside your concerns and discharge your burden so that you may fully enjoy your homecoming."

Memnon smiled. "You could ever read me as though I were an open scroll." But his smile faded as quickly as it appeared. He hunched forward, elbows on knees, his tone becoming conspiratorial. "Suppose someone could broker a reconciliation between you and the Great King—a full pardon of all your supposed crimes and the chance to be welcomed back to court with a glad heart—what would such a thing be worth to you?"

"It would have as much worth as a palace made of smoke, Memnon. Many of my brother satraps tried to broker just such a compromise in years past. My royal cousin is implacable. Only one resolution will suit him—my head delivered to Susa on a silver platter."

"Say he could be made to relent . . ."

"Memnon, I—"

"Just consider it, Artabazus! What price?"

The old satrap sighed. Pharnabazus, now awake and listening, watched his father with great interest, his brows meeting to form a 'V' over glittering dark eyes. Finally, Artabazus said, "Could it truly be done, it would be worth a great deal. As much as I admire the Greeks, they are not my people. I am a curiosity to them, a well-placed outsider, but an outsider, nonetheless. Yes, there is very little I would not pay for such a reconciliation to take place—as much for me as for my children, who should know their Persian heritage as well as their Greek."

Memnon nodded. "Would it be worth Barsine's hand?"

The old Persian's eyes narrowed. Pharnabazus sat upright, his face a mirror of his father's. "I will say no more," Artabazus said, "until I have heard the whole story. Why does Mentor want to know what price I would pay? Has he a scheme?"

Memnon sagged back against the willow-bole. "Mentor has changed, Artabazus. You would no longer know him, were you to pass him in the agora. He's lost weight and gray streaks his hair like a man twice his years. I noticed it more each time I'd return from the sea. This last time—I'd been away scouting Persian movements from the Gulf of Issus—it was more pronounced . . ."

"What news?"

Memnon marked well his brother's long face, his sullen eyes. "You look as though you know it already," he said.

"Perhaps. Confirm what I know, then, brother." A pitcher of wine stood at Mentor's elbow; his stained tunic and beard betokened a night of hard drinking.

Memnon looked out the window. A warm breeze ruffled his sweat-heavy hair. Sidon's fortress overlooked the mole-protected North Harbor; though war loomed, the Phoenician merchants carried on with their business as usual. Lean ships, their hulls daubed red, hove close to the quays, offloading gold dust and ivory from Africa, tin and amber from Hyperborea, ironwork from Sinope, and wine from the Aegean. In exchange, they filled their holds with dyed textiles, cedar from the Lebanon Mountains, and jars of dried fruit: raisins from Berytus, prunes from Damascus, and dates from Jericho. Memnon could hear merchants' voices buzzing up from dockside, mingling with the cries of gulls and the laughter of women and children.

"Dammit, what news?"

Memnon scowled as he turned back to face his brother. "Ochus is assembling an enormous force at Sardis. He's summoned his satraps to him—Belesys of Syria, Mazaeus of Cilicia, Spithridates of Lydia—and he's secured pledges of troops from Thebes, Argos, and Ionia. I think he plans on reducing Phoenicia to rubble, then marching to the very gates of Memphis. We should warn Pharaoh."

Mentor gave a derisive bark. "Warn him? He wouldn't listen! The pretentious ass believes he's the son of a god, thus infallible." The elder Rhodian hefted his wine pitcher and drained it.

Memnon frowned at the dangerous gleam in his brother's eyes. "What do we do, then?"

"Another precarious situation," Mentor muttered. "Another hopeless cause."

"Perhaps we are always fated to play the underdog. Perhaps . . ."

The pitcher shattered against the far wall, peppering Memnon with wine lees and fragments of pottery, as the elder Rhodian snarled, "I'm done with it! That Sidonian whoreson thinks he can betray me? By Hades and the cursed Styx! I'll show him what true betrayal is!"

". . . Though it took some time, I finally got a full accounting from him. Mentor had intercepted an agent of King Tennes of Sidon bound for Sardis with an offer to betray the Phoenicians in exchange for clemency," Memnon said, his voice full of contempt. "But, instead of arresting both men and packing them off to Pharaoh for execution, Mentor sent Ochus a counteroffer: not only would he give His Majesty Sidon and the Phoenician littoral, but he would hand over the keys to Egypt, as well. The Great King's answer was brief. 'Do so,' he said, 'and your heart's desire will be my reward.' That's his scheme, Artabazus, and that's why he sent me here instead of keeping me at his side! I tried to dissuade him from betraying Pharaoh—let Sidon rot for the perfidy of its king, but not Egypt! He would have none of it, though." Memnon stared at the ground, shaking his head. "It shames me that my own brother no longer feels obliged to honor his word to an ally."

"Ah, my dear boy," Artabazus said, "life is not often as simple as you would have it to be. Hard, even distasteful, decisions are part and parcel of our existence. And we must make them, all honor aside, for the good of our families. Mentor's intent is not to shame any of us, but to restore us to our former glory."

"Where does Barsine fit into all of this?" Pharnabazus asked.

Artabazus slid off his rock and straightened his tunic. "Is it not obvious? If Mentor succeeds, the Great King will do more than grant his wish. Ochus will give him land to rule, either in Ionia or the Troad—both regions where Pharnacid blood carries great weight. A union with the daughter of a Pharnacid will transfer much of that weight onto him." He motioned for his son to rise. "Fetch our horses. It is growing late."

Memnon stood while Pharnabazus did as his father asked. The Rhodian brushed dust from his tunic with savage swipes of his hands. "And if he fails?" he snarled. "What if this lunatic plan of his gets him skinned alive and boiled in oil? What then?"

Artabazus shrugged. "There can be no gains without risks. Mentor understands this, just as I understand that he will do this thing regardless of whether or not I tender my blessing. Do I wish he would reconsider his actions? Of course. But you know as well as I that once Mentor sets his mind upon something he becomes as inflexible as granite. All I can do is reinforce his morale by entering into a compact with him—if he succeeds he will have Barsine as his wife, with my joyous blessing; if he fails, I will mourn him as one of my own sons. His stubbornness leaves me little choice in the matter."

Memnon exhaled a drawn-out sigh full of frustration and impotent rage. "I am glad this burden is mine no longer. I pass it to you, Artabazus, without regret," Memnon said, clapping the old satrap on the shoulder. "In ten days Khafre will take ship back to Miletus, thence to Sidon. Mentor is expecting your answer, be it good or ill. For my part, I stand by whatever you decide." The Rhodian made to turn away, but stopped. "I've not known a season of peace in four years. With winter coming on, I would like nothing better than to spend my days hunting and my nights by the fire."

Artabazus smiled. "Both can be easily arranged. Come, let us ride like the wind. If we get in too long after dusk your sister is liable to set the dogs on us."

Memnon laughed as Pharnabazus led their horses up. "My dear sister," he said, offering the old satrap a leg up into the saddle. "The Macedonian winters haven't chilled her temper, I gather?"

Artabazus shivered in mock horror. "An enraged Deidamia would melt the snows of Hyperborea."

Memnon vaulted astride Euphrosyne and gathered up the reins, touching his heels to the mare's flanks. "Zeus Savior! We'd best hurry!"

DEIDAMIA'S ANGER, IF IT EVER MANIFESTED ITSELF, SOON DISSIPATED IN A flurry of activity. She used the hours afforded by their romp in the countryside to oversee preparations for a feast honoring Memnon's return. Under her meticulous eye, slaves transformed the villa's courtyard into an open-air banquet hall, replete with garlanded columns and braziers smoldering with a delicate blend of aromatic woods and incense. Iron cressets cast hazy light over six supper couches, arranged in a semicircle around the sparkling fountain. Three low tables, carved of pearwood and inlaid with ivory, held communal dishes of food: loaves of bread, shallow bowls of olive oil for dipping, wheels of cheese and mounds of boiled eggs, pots of lentil stew flavored with onions and garlic, and chunks of tuna cooked in an herb sauce.

Memnon, freshly bathed and clad in a scarlet tunic, sat to the right of Artabazus and Deidamia; Pharnabazus sat to their left. Beside Memnon, Khafre shared his couch with Cophen, who listened, enthralled, to every word the Egyptian said. Gryllus and his wife, Ianthe, occupied the last couch on the right, an honor Artabazus afforded them in recognition of their long service to the household. With them sat the satrap's two youngest children: seven-year-old Hydarnes and little Arsames, only five, whose angelic face showed utter concentration as he struggled to untie a knotted cord Gryllus had given him.

On the couch next to Pharnabazus, Barsine sat with nine-year-old twins Artacama and Ariobarzanes. Time and again as the night wore on, Memnon found his attention drawn to the nineteen-year-old daughter of Artabazus, his own brother's prospective wife, who had matured into a dark-haired beauty with eyes the color of the night sky. Beneath her quick smile and quicker wit, Memnon sensed Barsine retained the same gravity she had displayed as a child, bolstered by the words of poets and philosophers she had devoured in her studies. "Ignorance has no place under my roof," Artabazus was fond of saying; son or daughter, all his children received instruction. What would Mentor value more, he wondered, the educated woman or the dynasty she represented?

Finally, Memnon stirred and, almost frowning, reached for his goblet. Though the vintage was an expensive Thasian, apple-scented and sublime, he drained it as if it were some *obol*-per-liter table wine.

"Brooding again?" Deidamia asked. Artabazus lay on his stomach, dozing as she massaged the kinks from his shoulders, oblivious to the children's laughter. They clapped and yipped as Khafre regaled them with tale after tale of his native Egypt, some familiar from Herodotus, others culled from his years as a temple scribe. Even Pharnabazus and Barsine joined in.

"I have become adept at brooding," Memnon said. He poured himself another glass. "Has there been any word of Patron? I would like to see that old scoundrel again."

"He passed through Pella around midsummer," Deidamia said, "bound for Sicily to take part in Timoleon's war against Carthage."

"Sicily? Zeus! If he were that desperate for gold and glory, he should have followed us to Egypt. He would have found both in excess." Memnon sipped wine. "What about Philip? Where does he campaign so late in the season?"

"Illyria," Artabazus murmured, his eyes still closed.

Deidamia smiled. "Another midsummer departure, this one to quell an uprising along the Illyrian frontier with Epirus. Originally, the King had meant to make for Thrace, to reinforce his general, Parmenion. I've heard you men debate Philip's qualities until you're as red-faced as Socrates in the agora, but never have you mentioned his flexibility."

"That's because the poets praise a man for his ferocity or his honor, never for his logistical prowess," Memnon said. He stared into the depths of his wine, hoping to see prophecies and portents, insights into the future; he was disappointed to discover nothing but his own reflection. He sighed and rubbed his eyes. "I'm tired. I think I'll say goodnight before good Dionysus captures me in a Thasian snare."

"I've had the guesthouse prepared for you and Khafre. It's quieter and affords you more privacy, should a strapping Macedonian lass catch your fancy," Deidamia said, her eyes twinkling.

Memnon rose. "You are the soul of preparedness," he said, kissing the crown of her head. He patted Artabazus's shoulder; the old satrap muttered something in response. Memnon said his goodnights briskly, bid Khafre to stay and entertain the children as long as their mother allowed, and submitted to an unsteady hug from Ianthe. She and her husband both wore tipplers' masks—their smiling faces flushed and shining, their eyes glazed from too much wine.

"Gryllus," Deidamia said to the gardener. "Will you show Memnon to the guesthouse?"

Before Gryllus could struggle upright, though, Barsine stood and gestured for the old man to keep his seat. "Allow me," she said. "I am soon to bed, as well, and I could use a breath of air before sleep."

Deidamia assented, and Barsine led Memnon from the courtyard and out into the garden. A sliver of moon hung low in the sky; bats whirred above their heads while crickets and frogs raised a clamor. The guesthouse, little more than a slate-roofed cabin, lay about a hundred yards from the main house, in a grassy hollow surrounded by birches and sycamores. A night lamp hung over the door, a beacon for insects.

Memnon glanced at Barsine as they walked. Near equal in height and slender, she wore a sleeved *chiton* of deep Egyptian blue, girdled at the waist with a gold-embroidered sash, and fastened by four gilded ivory brooches. Unbound, her long black hair fell over her shoulder; she toyed with the ends of it, her delicate brows drawn together in thought.

"I am to be Mentor's bride, it seems," she said without preamble.

Memnon sighed. That she knew meant Artabazus had made his decision. "Yes. It seems so."

She nodded slowly. "I always knew my marriage would be for politics rather than love, but I never imagined it would involve my own uncle."

"It's not set in stone," Memnon said, a bitter edge to his voice. "My brother—that damn fool!—still has to cast his honor to the dogs and avoid getting himself killed in the process."

Barsine cocked her head to one side. "I do not remember Mentor well, but what I do remember is a man of uncomplicated logic. Could he not believe in what he is doing as fervently as you condemn it?"

"I don't care what he believes! He gave his oath, and an oath, once given, cannot be withdrawn simply because a man winds up on the losing side. If this faithlessness only involved the Sidonian king I would support him wholeheartedly, but he's turned against Pharaoh, as well, and he has done nothing deserving of our betrayal! It contradicts everything Artabazus taught us! You remember Pammenes? The Theban your father hired to soldier for him? He renounced his allegiance to Artabazus out of self-concern and we cursed him for it. Am I now to think my brother glorious for following Pammenes' lead?"

It was Barsine's turn to sigh. "Was it not Father's renunciation of his oath to the Great King that drove him to hire Pammenes in the first place? Remove the Theban from the equation and tell me how Mentor's actions are any different from my father's, a man you admire? I love my father with all my heart, but I am not blind to the fact that he will alter his allegiances to suit his needs. Men in positions of power have not the luxury of honor. This, I think, Mentor learned very well."

Stunned to silence, Memnon turned slowly and stared at her, his eyes narrowing. Barsine's face flushed; she blinked and looked away. Suddenly, she looked nineteen, again.

"I apologize, Uncle," she stammered. "Father encourages us to learn by disputation. I fear I have overstepped my bounds and trespassed into places where I have no business. I—"

"Zeus Savior! I know men who cannot command such eloquence! I sense, though, that you've learned the Socratic art at the foot of two masters—Artabazus and my sister, for I hear them both in your speech and your arguments. Don't apologize, Barsine. There's truth in these things you say, and were I not weary and thick-headed with wine I would refute your every point." The Rhodian smiled. They stood now in the circle of light cast by the night lamp, in front of the guesthouse.

Barsine exhaled and said, in mock seriousness, "Then perhaps we should continue this on a day when you are well-rested and free of the grape's influence?"

"Indeed we will, and when that day comes you'd best wear your philosopher's mantle, for I intend to wear mine."

Barsine laughed, clapping her hands together like a child anticipating an afternoon of play. "Good night, Uncle," she said, turning to retrace her steps to the main house. "Sleep well."

"And you." Memnon paused on the threshold and watched her vanish into the night, the muted glitter of gold embroidery marking her progress. No longer the quiet, reserved girl from Dascylium, Memnon wondered how Artabazus had kept his estate free of would-be Macedonian suitors. But, even as the thought flashed through his mind, an answer presented itself: *because she's Persian*. Likely the sons of their Macedonian hosts thought foreign women beneath them. For an instant, the opening of a door wreathed Barsine's slender profile in a nimbus of light, and then she was gone. Memnon smiled.

"What fools, these Macedonians," he muttered as he turned and went inside.

SUMMER'S HEAT FADED, AND THE BIRCHES SURROUNDING THE ESTATE blazed with autumnal splendor, a canopy of fiery reds, oranges, and golds as beautiful as it was fleeting. The end of harvest brought the first frosts of the season; in no time, winter roared down from the mountains, a cold north wind that rattled the brown reeds fringing Lake Loudias and brought snow and ice to the Emathian Plain.

True to his word, Memnon cleaved to the fire save for the occasional foray into the foothills to hunt boar and stag. By the hearth in the great hall, he and Artabazus whiled away the hours debating politics and its practitioners—from Isocrates and his call for Philip to initiate a Hellenic crusade against Persia, to the vituperation of Macedonia by the Athenian demagogue, Demosthenes. Under the eaves of the guesthouse, Memnon reread Herodotus by the light of the pale winter sun, Homer by the glow of firelight.

"Menelaus or Paris?" Barsine said, noticing the scroll on one of her frequent visits. The threat of a spring thaw gave them an excellent reason to take the horses out for a little exercise. "Whose place would you rather take?"

Memnon tugged on his cavalry boots, stood, and slipped a heavy woolen cloak over his shoulders. "Neither. Menelaus was a man who couldn't hold on to what was his; Paris was a man who took what didn't belong to him."

"Who, then?"

Memnon thought for a moment, tapping the scroll basket with his finger. "Odysseus," he said. "Here is a man who goes to war, endures the wrath of Poseidon, and is away a score of years. What does he find when he returns to Ithaca? A wretched pack of suitors held at bay by a cunning wife who refused to believe he was dead. If I am to be cast from a Homeric mold, let it be in the mold of Odysseus."

"Not Achilles?"

Memnon smiled and held the door open for her. A chilly blast of air ruffled the scrolls. "My father's secretary, Glaucus, used to accuse me of wanting to emulate mighty Achilles, of thirsting after glory for its own sake. He never understood, though."

"Understood?" Barsine tugged her cowl up over her braided hair. She, too, wore a woolen mantle, dyed black and lined with sheepskin. Outside the guesthouse, a thin crust of snow clung to the low places where the sun couldn't reach, to the lee of the stream bank and the bases of statues. The thawing ground squelched with each step as they walked toward the stables.

"That Achilles may have been a matchless warrior, but he was forever at the mercy of Odysseus's wits," Memnon said, his breath steaming. "Nor did Achilles outstrip the King of Ithaca in the arena of Glory. They were equals, but Odysseus didn't have to sacrifice his life to achieve lasting fame. No, let others revere Achilles and seek to fashion their sword arms after his. I will style myself after Odysseus and guide their sword arms to victory."

"And return home to your faithful Penelope, little Telemachus on her hip?"

"Should ever I be so blessed, yes."

Barsine's eyebrow arched.

"What?" Memnon said. "You think I'm deceiving myself? Or am I not deserving of such things?"

"No, you deserve it—more so than most—I just . . . I . . ." She paused. Memnon could not tell if the cold or embarrassment heightened her color, but when she spoke again, her voice barely rose above a whisper. "I do not remember you as a homesick Odysseus, but as a dashing Hector, on a great black horse with your armor gleaming in the sun as you hurled back a horde of foul Hyrkanians—ferocious and indestructible. To hear you now speak of home and hearth as your ultimate goal is . . . surprising."

"Inside every man of war is a man of peace, a man who needs to know he has somewhere to go once the wars cease. Crops and herds are prosaic to the young, but these are the things that sustain the veteran through the worst of the campaign season, through defeat and privation. A man facing death needs to know there's someone at home waiting for him. He needs a reason beyond glory to fight."

"Like Odysseus," Barsine said, as though a mystery had been made clear. Often, as the day wore on, Memnon caught her staring; she'd glance away quickly, but with each instance he had the impression she was seeing him in a different light.

Winter held on, but soon enough Persephone left the frigid confines of Hades' realm and returned to the world of the living. To celebrate her arrival, Nature garlanded itself with blossoms of pink and white, violet and yellow, intertwined with leaf-buds of the palest green. Snow thawed on the mountainsides, swelling every stream and watercourse out of its banks; even Lake Loudias, its dark waters ruffled by a south wind, crept up over the stone quays.

Memnon's morning regimen now included a trip to the *gymnasion*, followed by a turn or two about the agora, listening to merchants who had come overland from the south, eager for news. Soon, the sea-lanes would reopen and ships would again call at Pella. Only then, he reckoned, would tidings from Asia reach this far north. The Rhodian contented himself with the usual range of gossip, most of it local—a litany of feuds and marriages, cuckolds and vendettas that mirrored the conduct of the royal house.

"Theirs is not a tranquil union," one merchant said, nodding up toward the palace on the acropolis. Of course, Deidamia kept Memnon apprized on what went on between the King and Queen, but not even she heard it all. She heard even less now that she was pregnant again, and bed-ridden. "Not tranquil at all, what with poor Alexander wedged between them, and now this whole affair with Pausanias." The merchant clucked.

Memnon bought a handful of dried figs from the man. "Who?"

"Pausanias." The merchant lowered his voice, as if he spilled state secrets rather than the latest bit of scandal. "An old lover of King Philip's—he's fancied both since his days as a hostage in Thebes. Anyway, Pausanias was put aside and another, more handsome boy took his place in the King's bed. Being a hot-tempered Orestid, Pausanias insulted the boy at a drinking party, told everyone he would fuck a dead man, if he could get an *obol* or two out of it."

"Brave man, to insult the King like that," Memnon said, munching a fig.

The merchant, a native Macedonian, made a dismissive gesture. "Philip took it in stride, knowing it for the last gasp of love gone awry. The boy, though . . . he took it hard, this slight to his honor. Kept it bottled up inside. Finally, last season, on the Epirote border, the boy tried to redeem his good name. He charged ahead of the King and got himself impaled on an Illyrian spear."

"All because a jilted rival called him names?" Memnon grunted, shaking his head. "What did Philip do to Pausanias?"

The merchant shrugged. "Depends upon whom you ask. Pausanias is an Orestid, as I said, and they are as quarrelsome a pack of curs as ever crawled from the womb. Publicly, the King could do little. Privately, though, I'm told he set the boy's friends on Pausanias. These fellows lured him to the house of Attalus, got him dead drunk, and gave him over to the slaves and the stable hands, telling them he would bend over for anyone, and freely."

Memnon whistled softly.

"Nor were they gentle about it," the merchant said. "Were I Pausanias, I'd rather they just killed me and been done with it." Before Memnon could press him further, another customer drew the merchant's attention; the Rhodian waved his thanks and moved along.

On the way back to the estate, Memnon saw preparations were well underway for the spring horse fair, set to take place in a few days' time. Like poets to the great Dionysia, the fair drew dealers and buyers from all corners of Macedonia and beyond, from Thessaly, Epirus, Thrace, Ionia, even Scythia. Stalls and tents were going up all over Pella to satisfy the growing influx of visitors. Some would serve as dormitories for this retinue or that, some as impromptu wine shops and brothels, and the rest as extensions of the agora, offering for sale everything from last year's apples to gold jewelry of the finest craftsmanship. Hammers thudded as workmen erected the royal pavilion in a meadow outside Pella; others created corrals of wood and rope to segregate breeders' stock so no common stallion could break free and mount some prize racing mare—surely enough to trigger violence among men whose livelihoods depended on maintaining pure bloodlines.

At the gates to Artabazus's estate, Memnon met a messenger on his way out, a young man wearing the livery of the King. The old satrap stood not too far away, a roll of fine parchment in his hand. It still bore the wax seal of the palace.

Memnon frowned. "What goes?"

"Philip desires our company, you and I, during the horse fair," Artabazus said, nodding after the messenger. He held up the scroll. "And this is for Deidamia, from the Queen."

"Desires our company, eh? A polite way of summoning us to his side. What could he want?"

"Ah, my boy. When did you become so suspicious?" Artabazus said. "Perhaps all Philip wants is the pleasure of our company."

Memnon smiled and fell in beside Artabazus, gently draping an arm around the old satrap's shoulder. "When did *you* become so trusting? Philip never does anything on the principle of pleasure—his or someone else's. His every action, every word, serves his interests in some way. He wants us there for a reason, Artabazus."

"I don't doubt that," the old satrap said, "but his reasons are not necessarily sinister. There are times, my boy, when an honest invitation is just that—an honest invitation. You will drive yourself mad if you always seek to discern the motives behind every word. If Philip has some ulterior purpose, so be it. Wait, though, and let him show his hand before you assume the worst." Artabazus patted Memnon's arm.

"Where Philip is concerned," Memnon said, recalling the tale of Pausanias, "I cannot help but assume the worst."

THE DAY OF THE FAIR DAWNED CLEAR AND BRIGHT, THE CLOUDLESS SKY AN azure canopy over the green meadow where the buying and selling would take place. Memnon and Artabazus rose early and joined the crowds partaking of the common business—soldiers looking for spare mounts or trained chargers, sporting men admiring the racers, hill-chiefs seeking to replenish their strings of ponies. Dealers extolled the virtues of each breed, from tall Iberians renowned for their spirit, to lean Scythians of unparalleled speed, to small and hardy Messaras bearing the axe-brand of Pherae on their flanks. None of them, Memnon reckoned, could approach Artabazus's purebred Nisaeans, their pedigrees hearkening back to antiquity, to the chariot teams of great Nebuchadnezzar. The old satrap knew it, too, though he kept it to himself, never boastful. As each dealer presented his wares, Artabazus smiled gently and made small compliments before moving on to the next.

Philip's arrival on the field, past midday, signaled an end to the common business. Unsold stock was led away and the dealers shouted for their grooms to escort their finest wares to the forefront, the pureblood chargers, highly trained and spirited. The King of Macedonia was not a man who stood on protocol; preceded by his bodyguard, he made a leisurely entrance, limping still from a poorly healed wound gained in last year's Illyrian campaign.

"The gods," Artabazus muttered, in Persian, "use his flesh as a scribe uses a waxed board, their iron stylus recording a hymn to Ares."

Memnon nodded, silent. Stark against his dusty blue *chiton*, an impressive array of scars laced the King's arms and legs, his neck and face—some red and angry, others white with age. Each represented an offering of blood on the War God's altar. An eye, too, had gone to placate the Lords of Olympus, to secure blessings of power for his beloved Macedonia.

The King's black-bearded face swiveled as he acknowledged his Companions and his courtiers, his tribal lords, his soldiers, and certain of the dealers. When his good eye lit on Artabazus, though, Philip gave a broad grin.

"My Persian friend!" the King said. "It pleases me you could join us! Who's that with you? Memnon? Great Herakles, Rhodian! It's good to see you've escaped the clutches of the decadent south! Come, join me under the pavilion. This sun's too fierce to stand around jawing like neighbors at the well."

The pavilion's purple cloth shaded the King's throne, a straight-backed chair of heavy wood with armrests carved to resemble lions, inlaid with silver and covered in sheets of hammered gold. Philip sat with a groan, motioned for one of his pages to bring two stools closer.

"I understand congratulations are in order," Artabazus said, perching himself on the proffered stool.

Philip grunted. "For killing Illyrians? Those bastards try to wriggle out from under my heel with Olympic regularity. Kleitos," he said to the nearest bodyguard, a thickly muscled Macedonian sporting a fierce black beard, "find that lack-witted steward and have him fetch wine." Philip turned back to look at Memnon. "What do you hear of that brother of yours? Is he still humping a shield for the glory of Egypt?"

"I left him in Sidon last summer," Memnon said. "Commanding the garrison against Ochus."

"So it's true, then? Ochus is going to try again to reclaim Egypt?"

"He'll likely succeed this time. Thebes and Argos gave him men, Ionia, too. He'll use those hoplites as a skeleton, fingers of a grasping fist clothed in Persian flesh."

"And Mentor?" Philip said. "Will he stand in the way of this fist?"

Memnon spread his hands and shrugged. "That depends on his mood. If he's tired of fighting a losing war, then I suspect he'll renounce his allegiance to Pharaoh and offer himself to the Great King."

"He's already decided, you mean." Philip grinned. A steward, one ear red from a good cuffing, hustled up with three cups and a pitcher of Chian wine, unwatered, as was the custom in Macedonia. The King took a cup and gestured for his guests to do the same. "There's no need to hide it. Mentor's not betraying my cause. If anything, perhaps he strengthens it."

Memnon let Artabazus select first; he took the remaining cup. "How so?" the Rhodian asked.

"I could always use friends on that side of the Hellespont. Men I can trust to do the right thing, and who can trust me to do the same."

"Have you fallen for the honeyed words of Isocrates?" Artabazus said, his eyebrows arched. "Will you push your borders beyond the Asian shore?"

Wine sloshed as Philip slapped his knee, his laughter booming through the pavilion. "Great Herakles, no! I may push my borders to the Hellespont, but not beyond. I have my hands full with Athens and her endless machinations. I need no more grief." Philip sobered, leaned forward on his throne. "But, with friends in Nearer Asia, I need not fret should an attack be forthcoming from that quarter. Friends who can open the doors of trade, who can exchange information . . . and who can warn each other of threats to their mutual existence."

Artabazus looked down as he swirled the dregs in his cup. "I value your friendship, King Philip, so I will tell you, in all honesty, that if Mentor succeeds it is my hope that we will be summoned home to share in his glory. It is my desire to make peace with my cousin, the Great King, so that my sons might claim their birthright as Pharnacids. Does this mean I will set aside my friendship with you, once I am gone from your court? Of course not. You and your family will forever be welcome at my hearth."

Philip drained his wine and held his cup out for a refill. "But what if, in a dozen years, on a day much like this, Ochus comes to you and orders you or your sons to make war on me? What will become of our friendship then?"

"The same question could be posed to you, sire," Memnon said. "Your son is not without ambition. Would he honor your friendships?"

"Ambition?" Philip gave a short, barking laugh. "Alexander already begrudges my every success, telling his friends I will forestall him in all things great and spectacular. Yes, the boy's ambitious, but he understands honor. What friendships I forge he will . . ."

A discreet cough interrupted the King; a man approached the throne without waiting for permission. The newcomer, Antipatros, had no need of it. A King's Man from the early days, he served as Philip's chief statesman, his blunt features, thinning hair, and russet-and-gray beard hiding the sharp intellect of a born diplomat.

"My apologies," Antipatros rumbled, his ice-blue gaze sliding from Artabazus to Memnon. He leaned in close to Philip's ear, whispered something, and glanced back the way he had come. Philip—and Memnon—followed his gaze, seeing a man in a splendid Ionian *chiton* standing at the edge of the pavilion, his hair a golden fringe, his face displaying the smooth agelessness of a eunuch. He looked familiar, though Memnon could not recall where he had seen him before.

Philip nodded to the eunuch and grasped Antipatros's shoulder. "Tell him we will speak later."

"As you wish," Antipatros muttered. Straightening, he withdrew and escorted the eunuch to a different part of the field. Memnon watched them depart. He turned back to find the King staring at him, his dark eye inscrutable.

"State business," Philip said, rising. "It does not stop, even for festival days. Come, my friends, we'd better act like men at a horse fair before they brand us as pedants." Philip waved his guard off as Artabazus and Memnon accompanied him out among the dealers. Thessaly was well represented by nearly a dozen brands, from the axe-heads of Pherae to the centaur-brands of Larissa to the magnificent ox-heads of Pharsalus, the *boukephaloi*. These last consumed the King's attention. He stroked withers and checked teeth, lifted their hooves to inspect the frogs.

"Have you bred those Nisaeans yet, Artabazus?"

"And pollute their pedigree?" the old satrap said. "I would sooner pluck out my own eyes."

"Would it be that distasteful? Think of it, a horse of Nisaean-Pharsalus stock—strength, speed, and incomparable beauty. I can't imagine how much such a mount would be worth to a discerning buyer." The next dealer the King greeted warmly, embracing him as he would a close friend. "Ah, Philonikos! I trust you brought the finest animals ever to tread the sacred soil of Thessaly under hoof?"

The dealer, Philonikos, a squat, bearish man who had the telltale swagger of a born horseman, made an expansive gesture. "My lord King! I bring you horses that would make you the envy of Lord Poseidon, himself!"

"I don't seek to rival the gods, Philonikos, only to replace what I lost to the Illyrians." Philip half-turned to Artabazus. "Philonikos, here, breeds the finest of the *boukephaloi*. He would be the man to talk to, if ever you decide to share your Nisaeans with the rest of us."

"You flatter me, majesty." Philonikos bowed.

Philip motioned. "Show us what you have."

The horses Philonikos directed his grooms to present to the King were fine animals, Memnon was forced to admit, but Philip must have had a particular mount in mind; none of the Thessalian's string measured up to his demands. A crowd formed around the King, watching with interest as his practiced eye noted the tiniest of flaws—some that Memnon couldn't even detect. The onlookers made a sport of it by placing wagers on the remaining horses. To Philonikos, though, this was deadly business. Each rejection pricked the Thessalian's pride. Exasperated, he told his harried grooms, "Bring up Xanthos!"

"Auspicious name," Memnon said.

Philonikos ignored him, his jaw jutting in defiance. The stallion his men led up could very well have sprung from the loins of its legendary namesake, the immortal Xanthos that had once belonged to Achilles. This new Xanthos was large, even among a breed noted for size, and black as soot with a white blaze on its forehead. The animal pranced and fought, tried to rear up. It took two grooms, one on each side of its head, and a wickedly barbed bit to control it, but it was tenuous control, at best.

A buzz of disbelief rose from the assembled men. Philip glanced over at Philonikos. "I'm not buying a horse in need of breaking, so don't waste my time."

"Xanthos *is* broken, sire," Philonikos said. "It responds only to strength. Under the right man, that horse would ride to the gates of Tartarus and back. Absolutely fearless."

"It looks it, I grant you that." The King moved closer, keeping clear of the stamping hooves. "Xanthos," he said. The horse started at the sound of its name, nostrils flaring. "Easy, boy. Easy." As Philip reached for the headstall, though, his shadow fell in front of the horse.

Xanthos exploded. The animal bucked and pawed the air, oblivious of the barbed bit or of the two grooms. One hoof came so close to the King's skull that Philip could feel the breeze off it. He stumbled back, his face darkening.

"Zeus! That bastard can't be ridden and you damn well know it! What manner of fool do you take me for, Philonikos?" Philip roared. "Great gods! I may have one eye, but I'm not blind! That animal's a killer! Get it away from me, you Thessalian whoreson, and thank the gods I don't have you striped for trying to fleece honest men!"

Philonikos paled, plucking at the hem of the King's *chiton* as Philip brushed past him, intent on patronizing one of the Thessalian's rival dealers. "Wait, sire! I—"

Memnon felt a pang of regret for the man. Before Philip could move on, though, a youth's voice crackled above the noise of men settling their bets.

"You're losing a magnificent horse, father, all because you and those men don't know how to handle him, or dare not try!"

A hush fell over the field. Philip swung around, his brow deeply furrowed. Memnon and Artabazus glanced back toward the pavilion. The crowd parted, and Prince Alexander, his face flushed, his thick hair tangled and shining like burnished gold, hurried forward, trailed by an entourage of boys and young men.

Philip, his hands on his hips, growled, "What did you say?"

"That horse!" Alexander gazed covetously at the stallion, his blue-gray eyes wide and gleaming. "You will never again see its like, and yet you dismiss it out of hand!"

"I dismiss it for good reason! A horse like that will get a man killed in battle! It can't be ridden!"

"I can ride him!" Alexander said. The confidence in his voice seemed misplaced on a youth of thirteen summers; Memnon reckoned it part of Alexander's mystery—a mystery the Rhodian was hard-pressed to explain. Already, the Prince had attracted a circle of followers, young men his age or slightly older who professed loyalty unto death for Macedonia's heir apparent. Their fathers, men of Philip's generation, encouraged the notion, thinking them nothing more than children playing a Homeric game. Memnon, though, wasn't so sure. The young faces watching the Prince were rapturous and bright.

Philip's good eye narrowed. "How much is he, Philonikos?"

"It . . ." Like his horse, the Thessalian started at the sound of his name. "Three *talents*, sire."

The King gave a brisk nod. "Done. If you can ride him, Alexander, he's yours. But, if you can't what penalty will you pay for your insolence?"

"Three *talents*, father," Alexander said, without pause.

Philip grinned. "Done, again! You're all witnesses to this wager!" The throng erupted, a cacophony of claps and shouts, of side bets and calls for wine. Philip stepped aside and gestured for Alexander to proceed at his leisure. His lips tensed as he watched the boy advance.

The Prince's face hardened. His eyes flashed as he snarled at Philonikos and his grooms, ordering them to step away. The horse pawed the ground but did not bolt; it let Alexander approach, undaunted perhaps by the Prince's small stature. The boy made soothing sounds but did not use the stallion's given name, calling it instead after its ox-head brand: "*Boukephalos . . . Boukephalos . . .*"

"Are they both mad?" the Rhodian muttered. "Someone should step in and end this before the boy gets himself killed."

Artabazus shrugged. "There is nothing to be done now. Nothing but pray the gods are watching over him."

Alexander reached up and stroked the horse's neck. Slowly, he loosened the bit. The animal huffed and tossed its head. The boy calmed it, took it by the headstall and turned it to face the sun.

"Ah, look there," Artabazus hissed, gripping Memnon's forearm. "The boy does know horses. The shadows were making it skittish . . ."

The Prince spent several minutes soothing the animal, talking in a low voice. He walked with it toward Lake Loudias. Then, without making any sharp motions, Alexander worked his way back and grasped the horse's mane, keeping the reins loose in his left hand.

The crowd held its collective breaths. Artabazus's fingers tightened on Memnon's arm. Even Philip leaned forward, anticipation etched on his face.

Lightly, Alexander vaulted onto the horse's back. Memnon expected the animal to buck and throw the boy. To his surprise, it accepted Alexander's slight weight with a toss of its head and an explosive whinny. Men murmured; coins tinkled like cymbals. The Prince gathered the reins, careful not to pull on the barbed bit, and with a triumphant shout touched his heels to the horse's flanks. Boy and stallion raced away from the field as the crowd loosed a tremendous roar. Soldiers of the Bodyguard clashed their spears against their shields. Members of Alexander's entourage whooped and ran after their Prince.

King Philip threw his arms wide and gathered Philonikos up in a crushing embrace, laughing as he called for someone to fetch three *talents* for the sweat-drenched Thessalian.

"My boy!" Philip said, grinning. "I'm going to have to find a bigger kingdom for him! Macedonia's too small!" The King glanced toward Artabazus. To Memnon, there was no mistaking the menacing glitter in his eye.

ARTABAZUS AND MEMNON BEGGED OFF ATTENDING THE MANY FEASTS associated with the horse fair, knowing full well they would degenerate into the raucous drinking parties the Macedonians were famous for—all-night debaucheries that made even the most notorious Athenian *symposia* appear tame by comparison. As they said their farewells to the King, both men assured him they would give serious consideration to his offer of an alliance.

"He did not seem to care either way," Memnon said. As had become their custom, he sat with Barsine on a wooden bench, one of many scattered around the estate, watching fireflies dart through the deepening twilight as they spoke of the day's events. Memnon could tell Gryllus had been working in this area earlier; he inhaled the smells of freshly cut grass and of soil mixed with crushed tree bark.

"He is a curious man, the King," Barsine said. Her dark hair glistened in the fading light. She wore a saffron *chiton*, sleeveless, its hem thick with embroidery. A shawl of similar material complimented the soft olive complexion of her shoulders and neck. Often, Memnon had to force his eyes elsewhere.

Fool! She's spoken for . . .

The Rhodian cleared his throat. "Oh, there's nothing curious about him. Philip's like Scylla and Charybdis blended into a single ravenous entity, a tentacled Cyclops with an insatiable appetite. Still, for all that, it's Alexander who frightens me more. The father seeks only power; the son seeks power *and* glory. A perilous combination of desires for one man to have."

Barsine's forehead creased. "But, Alexander's not a man—not yet, at least. Let maturity temper his character and his thirst for glory before you pass judgment on him."

"Maturity will temper his body, perhaps, but his character is already fully realized," Memnon said, shaking his head. "You didn't see him today. The look in his eyes was the look of a man, and a capable man at that. Glory is more than a thirst for Alexander. It's a flame, fanned by the hope of great deeds and of greater adulation. He won't be content to stop at the Hellespont, I guarantee you, and any who stand in his way . . ." The Rhodian dusted his palms together, a dismissive gesture.

Barsine shivered. "We are not in any danger, are we, Memnon?"

"No, of course not. The bonds of guest-friendship are sacred, for Greeks as well as Persians. While we are under Philip's protection we are as safe as if we were his kin."

"And when we are no longer under his protection?" Unconsciously, she leaned closer to him until their shoulders touched. "What then?"

The smell of her hair, of roses, drifted up to his nostrils. Memnon resisted the impulse to wrap his arm around her. "We are safe," he murmured, "and safe we will remain so long as Macedonia and Persia are at peace with one another."

Despite deepening shadows, Memnon could see the outline of Barsine's face, inches from his own, as she gazed up at him. Her lips parted. *It would be so easy*, he thought, *so easy just to bend closer . . .*

She, too, fought a battle within herself, decorum versus desire, revealed in the way her brow crinkled and smoothed; restless, her eyes memorized every detail of his features. Barsine shifted. Memnon felt her hand rise, felt the delicate touch of her fingers as she traced the line of his jaw. "I wish . . ." she began, but lapsed into silence.

"Don't." Memnon caught her hand, held it gently. Barsine's eyes closed. Her head dipped and she exhaled.

"I wish," she repeated, this time with more force, "you would not paint poor Alexander with so sinister a brush. He is, after all, only a precocious boy." She sat upright, putting space between them.

Memnon sighed. On the bench, Barsine's hand remained cradled in his. "Achilles was a precocious boy once, too."

"More so than Odysseus?" she replied, her eyebrow raised, a hint of a smile tugging at the corners of her mouth. Together, they stood. "I had best go in and check on Deidamia. Good night, Memnon."

"Good night." He gave her hand a soft squeeze and released it. Then, rather than allow himself to watch her walk away, Memnon turned and withdrew in the opposite direction, a roundabout course that would bring him to the guesthouse door.

By the time he gained his threshold, Memnon's anger at himself had given way to dark melancholy. He opened the door and contemplated the silent, empty guesthouse. A clay lamp burned on his desk, its fresh oil salted to lessen the smoke, and an unopened flask of wine sat beside it. A servant, the same who had lit the lamp and brought the wine, had also turned down the bed clothes in preparation for his slumber.

Sleep, though, was an impossibility.

He sat at the desk. Through the window, past a veil of myrtle leaves, he could see the main house, a few of its lights burning behind fretted screens. He imagined Barsine waiting for him in the doorway, her hair unbound, her linen sleeping gown slipping over her shoulders . . . No! Memnon forced the image aside and reached for the wine flask.

Sunrise found him still sitting at the desk. The oil lamp had burned out, and the wine flask at his elbow lay on its side, drained and forgotten. Memnon's chin rested on his fist; on occasion he shifted, his fingers smoothing his beard.

She's spoken for! Mentor's prize . . .

This litany ran through his head throughout the long night, illuminating one thing with brilliant clarity: to stay would be to risk temptation. Last night proved almost more than he could handle. Better to remove himself from the situation before he lost control and did something he—and she—would regret later. He would leave, but where would he go? The sea-lanes south were open. Perhaps Mentor needed someone he could trust to watch his back? *But, can he trust me? Have I betrayed him by lusting after his bride?* West, then, to Sicily. Surely Patron could use another fair hand . . .

Sound intruded. Memnon glanced up as a hand scratched again at his door. "Memnon?" It was Pharnabazus.

He roused himself. "Yes?"

"You have a visitor."

"Can this wait, nephew?" Memnon barked, in no mood to be civil. He heard muted voices.

"No, Uncle. May we enter?"

The Rhodian sighed. There was nothing for it. "Yes. Enter." Memnon rose as Pharnabazus pushed the door open. The younger man gave him an anxious look.

"Have you slept at all?"

Memnon waved off his concern. Pharnabazus stepped aside, making room for his companion. The fellow was Macedonian, of that Memnon was certain—a powerfully built man in a somber red tunic, broad-shouldered and thick-waisted.

"Memnon," Pharnabazus said. "This is Parmenion, Philip's general."

"Your reputation precedes you, Rhodian," Parmenion said, speaking southern Greek with a harsh accent. Scars seamed his flesh, white and puckered against his burnished hide, some nearly obscured by the coarse hair grizzling his arms, legs, and chest. Gray flecked his beard, his bristling black brows; Memnon guessed him to be in his mid-fifties.

"As does yours, General," Memnon said. Nor was it hollow flattery. In the Macedonian highlands, Parmenion would have been a king himself, a warlord who ruled through iron and fear; under Philip, he wielded a far more subtle power. "How may I be of service?"

"I ran into this Persian pup," he caught Pharnabazus by the scruff of the neck and gave him a good-natured shake, "in the agora. He told me you were in from Egypt, and that you'd been in for most of the year. I thought you might be getting bored with all this soft living and looking for a way back into the field."

Memnon smiled despite his mood. "Why is it when a soldier's in the field, he dreams of nothing but home; when he's home, he dreams of the field?"

"Because home is the field, the place where a soldier feels most like himself. I need a trustworthy man to lead my native light cavalry when I return to Thrace in a few days," Parmenion said. "Short notice, I know, but the bastard who served for me last season got his fool head split in a clan feud yesterday. I'm done relying on hillmen. I need a Greek, and I've heard Artabazus speak highly of you."

Memnon blinked. Silently, he praised the gods for their providence.

He turned back to his desk; through the window, he caught sight of Barsine emerging from the main house and into the morning sun, the younger children in tow. She was taking them to the stables so they could feed tidbits to the horses. For an instant, he imagined their eyes locked.

Mentor's prize . . .

"It'll be a mercenary's work, but you'll be well compensated," Parmenion added, thinking him wavering. Memnon nodded suddenly and turned back to the Macedonian.

"Pharnabazus comes with me, as my lieutenant."

Parmenion assented, thrusting his hand toward the Rhodian.

"I've been casting about for a war I could win," Memnon said, grasping the general's hand. "Thrace seems as good a place to find one as any."

"Quiet!" Memnon hissed.

Surrounded by two-score soldiers, the Rhodian crouched in the high summer grass, javelin in hand, as he strained to pick out sounds arising from the enemy palisade fifty yards off. Carefully, he rose on his haunches and risked a glance at their intended target. His men—a mixture of allied Thracians and coastal Greeks—kept low to the ground; some glared at the young soldier who had cried out when he put his hand down on the back of a harmless grass snake. The boy's face burned with shame.

Memnon held himself upright a second longer, then sank back to the earth. Dawn was not far off; already, the eastern sky was aglow, a veil of high clouds diffusing the golden light of the Sun God's chariot. No one moved along the palisade; from the village beyond came only the typical sounds of a community stirring, making ready for another day of heat and sun. With an exaggerated hand gesture, Memnon let his men know they were as yet undetected. Sighs of relief whispered through the grass. The Rhodian paused to wipe sweat from his eyes. Their enemies on this raid, a village of Thracians of the Odrysae tribe, were legendary for their ability to sniff out an ambush, and infamous for their brutality. "Crush them,"

Memnon told Parmenion a week ago, before leaving Doriscus for the Hebrus Valley, "and you deprive the Thracian king of a valuable ally." Now that they were near their target, Memnon prayed the Odrysians would take the bait, that Pharnabazus and his Greek cavalry could goad the wily Thracians into action. *It is on you, my nephew.*

Memnon surveyed his soldiers by the growing light. Like his men, he, too, wore a *lineothorax*, a cuirass made of layers of linen stiffened with glue and reinforced with plates of dull gray iron on the chest and back. Hours of belly-crawling through the field left behind a patina of dust, stiffening hair and beards, and turning to mud in the sweat-damp creases of eyes, noses, and mouths. Most bore a trio of javelins—two to throw and one to keep for close-in fighting. A few of the Greeks had slings, their plum-shaped bullets cast of lead and wickedly filed, imparting a spin to their flight; on impact, they drilled through flesh like a shipwright's auger.

In range now of the palisade's only gate, Memnon gestured to his left and right, giving the signal for his men to fan out. The young soldier whose inadvertent cry had halted their forward progress made to edge out to the left, in the front ranks, his face transformed into a mask of determination. Memnon had seen that look before—the suicidal look of reckless bravado. He nudged the boy with the butt of his javelin and shook his head.

"No, Callinus." The Rhodian mouthed the words. "You're with me." They would fight as a *dyas*, like Castor and Polydeuces. That way, Memnon reckoned, the boy might live to see this day's end.

Rolling over onto his belly, Memnon inched through the grass, Callinus in his wake. All around, he saw evidence of drought: deep cracks in the soil and yellow tussocks of grass crisped by the relentless sun. Through the still air he could smell the village middens, their stench thick with rotting animal carcasses and soured barley mash, fish-guts and olive husks. This summer—his second in Thrace—Memnon had seen outbreaks of plague spread up from the coast and into the highland villages, a spear-borne pestilence fed by the miasma of war. Given time, the blighted arrows of Apollo might do what Philip's forces so far could not: conquer the Odrysians and their king, Kersobleptes.

Time, though, was an unaffordable luxury.

A horn brayed in the distance. Memnon stiffened; he knew its source. *Merciful Zeus, watch over him!* From inside the palisade came shouts and cries of alarm, a cacophony of voices made all the more chaotic by barking dogs and the screams of women and children.

In his mind's eye, the Rhodian watched the attack unfold. His horsemen, led by Pharnabazus, would attack the palisade wall on the opposite side of the village from the gate, loosing volley after volley of fire arrows from the safety of the tree-line; some of the more nimble riders would venture closer to hurl oil flasks against the desiccated timbers. In the smoke and confusion, the Odrysians would waste little time opening the gate and sending out their own cavalry—a wild wave of red-haired Thracians, their bodies covered in intricate blue tattoos—to circle the village and fall on the foolhardy Greeks like hounds on a wounded stag.

Or so Memnon hoped.

The Rhodian gathered his legs under him and tightened his grip on his javelin. He glanced at Callinus beside him. The boy blinked rapidly, sweat dripped from the end of his nose and he wiped at it with a trembling hand. Memnon wanted to whisper a reassuring word to him, but before he could the explosive creak and pop of hinges consumed his attention.

The gates were opening.

A harsh Thracian voice cracked like a whip, and Memnon heard the clatter of harness as horsemen cantered out the gate. He waited, listening, slowly drawing in a deep breath through flared nostrils. Timing was crucial . . .

In a single smooth motion, Memnon rose up from the grass, his first javelin cocked behind his ear, his eyes searching for a target. Fifty paces distant, dozens of Odrysians rode past in loose formation. They were oblivious to the men on their flanks. *Now!*

"Zeus Savior and Victory!" Memnon bellowed, his javelin leaving his hand even as his soldiers bolted upright and loosed their missiles. Bronze and iron flashed in the hazy morning air; sling bullets hissed, striking flesh with the sound of air bladders popping. Blood sprayed as men twisted, clutching at the ash shafts sprouting from their bodies as if by magic. Horses reared and collapsed. As he readied for a second cast, Memnon saw a sling bullet split apart the head of an enemy Thracian, his startled features blotted out by a curdled mass of blood and brain. Bone snapped as the man's terrified horse staved in the chest of a fallen rider.

Survivors of the first volley milled about, suddenly leaderless. Some reached for their bow cases, others fought to control their mounts. That moment of hesitation proved their undoing as a second flight of javelins tore through their sundered ranks.

A handful of Odrysians at the tail end of the pack managed to wheel and ride for the safety of the gate, screaming for their comrades inside the palisade to cover them. A spate of arrows arched over the walls to land haphazardly among Memnon's men.

The Rhodian grunted as he hurled his last javelin. The iron-headed dart reached the apex of its flight and descended, missing the rider leading the retreat but burying itself in the spine of the man's mount. The horse collapsed like a child's rag doll and snarled the legs of the animals in its wake. A sudden explosion of dust obscured the wreckage of man and beast. Memnon straightened and ripped his sword from its sheath.

"Take the gate!"

The allied Thracians in Memnon's command howled like wolves and threw themselves at the opening with single-minded purpose. The men of this village—Memnon could not even remember its name—had preyed upon them for years, slaying their kin and shaming their women. They relished the chance for vengeance.

The gate was a simple affair: two doors of heavy timber reinforced with bands of pitted bronze. Both valves sat poorly in their hinges, causing their outside edges to churn a furrow in the dirt as the village defenders sought to bar them against Memnon's onslaught. Attacker and defender shoved against one another, each hoping by brute strength to snatch victory. One of Memnon's Thracians, too close to the opening, took a spear in the throat; the man beside him snagged the blood-slimed shaft and hauled the defender into the open, exposing him to a trio of sling bullets. Inch by inch, life by life, the allies gained ground. With a final shove, they threw the gate open and swarmed over the last few defenders, the women and older children, who fought back like feral animals.

A pillar of black smoke rose from the rear of the village, drifting east toward the Hebrus River and obscuring the face of the sun. Memnon, with a handful of his Greeks, hung back, giving his Thracians a free rein over the Odrysians. There would be no quarter.

Memnon found Callinus unscathed and standing over a dead man, one of the first Odrysians slain in the brief fight. Like all his men, the boy marked his javelins with a distinctive symbol—a letter, perhaps, or a tiny image relevant to the wielder's personality—where the head met the shaft or on the butt. Memnon's bore an Egyptian falcon. The boy recognized the javelin standing out from the center of the corpse's chest as his own.

"Your first kill?" Memnon said softly.

Callinus swallowed hard and nodded. "It . . . It must be, but I don't remember throwing it." His fingers curled around the shaft. Iron grated on bone as he tugged the javelin free, stared at the bloodied blade. "I remember your voice. I remember standing, feeling the ground lurch under my feet. The rest . . ."

Memnon laid a hand on his shoulder. "All that matters is that you handled yourself well. You followed orders, did nothing rash or foolhardy, and lived to fight on. This is the moment you should remember, Callinus.

Be proud, but don't forget to give the gods their due."

The young Greek nodded, again. Memnon thumped his shoulder and sent him off to help look after the wounded. As he did, a squadron of cavalry came round from the far side of the village, Pharnabazus in the lead. Dust frosted horse and rider, and Pharnabazus's helmet was gone. Blood dripped from a gash in his forehead to streak the side of his face.

"What happened to you?"

Pharnabazus touched his brow and winced. "One of their brats tried to bounce a rock off my skull. By the great god, Uncle! Your plan worked!"

"Casualties?" Memnon said.

"Cuts and bruises mostly. That fool Pentheus wandered too close to the palisade and had his horse shot out from under him. Went down hard. Snapped his leg like a twig. He should live, provided it does not fester. You?"

Memnon glanced over his shoulder. The fight for the gate had been the worst of it. "Twelve dead, so far. Another dozen wounded. There was the only flaw in the plan," he said. Anger flashed like summer lightning. "I should have thought to bring up shields and a ram crew. Hades! We could have ripped the gate off its hinges with rope and a team of horses!" Memnon turned back and spat in the dust.

Pharnabazus dismounted. "It is done, Uncle, and thanks to you it was done well. Foresight is wisdom; hindsight is but fruitless daydreaming. You recall whose words those are?"

"Yes, yes! They are my own, and had I known I'd be forced to dine on them at every turn perhaps I would have sweetened them with honey." Memnon exhaled. He squinted at the wound in his nephew's forehead. "Get that cleaned and bound, then make sure the horses are rested and watered. I'll see about salvaging a wagon for the wounded before Berisades and his whoreson Thracians burn everything. We can't tarry here. This smoke is going to draw every scavenger in the Hebrus Valley."

"Are we returning to Doriscus?"

Memnon shook his head. "Parmenion should be at Aenus, on the east bank of the river, by now. We'll rejoin him there. For this next offensive, the Macedonians are going to have to throw caution to the winds and strike at the heart of Kersobleptes' kingdom, before Athens decides it's not in its best interests to have Philip so close to the Hellespont."

Pharnabazus chuckled. "Is this a point the Athenians feel they need to debate? Truly, I will never understand how those handwringers defeated Great Darius at Marathon."

"Those were different times, nephew," Memnon said. "Get moving. Tell the men they have one hour." The Rhodian's face hardened into a stern mask as he turned and headed for the village gate. Inside, muffled screams rose and fell, punctuated by peals of raucous laughter.

"Where will you be?" Pharnabazus called after him.

"Bringing the hounds to heel."

WIDE AND SLOW MOVING, THE HEBRUS RIVER WOUND LIKE A GREAT BROWN snake through the foothills of the Rhodope Mountains. Groves of oak, ash, and elm shaded the river's bank from the relentless sun, while errant cypresses stretched forth their roots in an effort to reach the Hebrus's drought-ravaged waterline—so low in places that the river's stony bed lay exposed. Near the banks pools formed, stagnated, and dried out in the oppressive heat, leaving behind the reek of mud and rotting fish. A breeze out of the north ruffled leaves but brought little relief to the column of cavalry that rode along the river's edge.

Memnon drove his men mercilessly over the next few days, stopping only to rest and water their horses, swallow a crust of bread, and perhaps snatch a few hours sleep. Outriders forged ahead, alert for any sign of a potential ambush, while Pharnabazus brought up the rear along with the trundling wagon of wounded Greeks and Thracians. Among them sat Pentheus, who hurled a colorful litany of curses at the driver each time the wagon jarred over rock or root.

On the fifth day, with the sun already below the western horizon, Memnon led his soldiers across the Hebrus, fording the river above where it widened into its marshy delta. He was on the verge of ordering them into camp when one of his outriders brought welcome news: the vanguard of the Macedonian army was barely two hours south of their position. Despite the sky above turning to star-flecked indigo, Memnon decided they would push on. "They'll have better food, at least," he said. He sent the outrider on ahead with orders to make contact and warn the Macedonians of their arrival.

"How far are we from Aenus?" Pharnabazus asked, swatting at a mosquito that flitted too close to his face. Already, it was dark enough that he had trouble making out the trail in front of them.

"A day's ride," Memnon said. "Perhaps less."

"Was it your plan to meet Parmenion on the trail like this?"

Memnon didn't answer. In the back of his mind, he had half expected to find only a token force of Macedonians at Aenus, armed with a message stating this reason or that why Parmenion tarried at Doriscus. King Philip praised his general to the heavens, telling all who would listen that "the Athenians elect ten generals every year, but I have ever only found one." Memnon, however, found Parmenion plodding and over-cautious, though a ferocious adversary once roused to action. What could have roused him this time? He turned the question over again and again in his mind, oblivious to the passage of time. When next Memnon glanced up, he was surprised to see torches flaring ahead.

"Pickets," Pharnabazus said, and over his shoulder, to the men, he added, "Look alive, you sons of whores!"

"Who goes?" a voice bellowed from the darkness.

"Memnon's squadron!" Pharnabazus answered, glancing at his uncle.

Both men hoped the sentry wouldn't demand the watchword, which no doubt had changed since Doriscus.

"Advance and be recognized!"

Memnon took the lead and rode into the circle of torchlight, his hand raised in greeting. A half-dozen Macedonians waited nearby; Foot Companions armed with massive pikes called *sarissas*, twice the length of a hoplite's eight-footer.

"Hades' teeth!" roared the officer on duty, a one-eyed Macedonian in a scarred bronze breastplate. He looked up at Memnon, his head tilted to the right, as the Rhodian drew rein beside him. "Parmenion's going to dance a jig now that you've returned!"

Memnon recognized him. "What goes, Antigonos? You're farther from Aenus than I would have expected."

Antigonos was one of Parmenion's most trusted officers, a man destined for high command in Philip's ever-growing army. An errant sword-stroke in the Illyrian campaign earned him the nickname *Monophthalmos*, One-Eyed. As with his beloved king, Antigonos in no way allowed the infirmity to impede his ambitions. "I'll leave that explanation to the general. Come. I have orders to escort you to Parmenion's headquarters." Antigonos gestured to one of his men, a slender fellow with a thick mane of red hair pulled up to the crown of his head and tied with a leather thong. "Send your lads with Krobylos, here, and he'll find them some food and flop-space."

"Follow him, Pharnabazus," Memnon said. "But make sure the men tend to their horses' bellies before they tend to their own."

The young Persian nodded and signaled for the squadron to move out. Krobylos fell in beside Pharnabazus, holding on to his saddlecloth as they trotted off into the darkness. Antigonos's own horse waited nearby, a roan mare; he vaulted onto its back and gathered up the reins. Clucking, he spurred the mare to a canter, trusting Memnon to follow.

The Macedonian camp sprawled over a low ridge overlooking the river, a temporary *polis* of ill-tanned hides and rough-hewn timbers. To the uninitiated, its precincts appeared identical save for colorful regimental banners fluttering on the sparse breeze. Where a typical city divided itself according to wealth and station, the camp-city drew its societal lines based on combat arms: cavalrymen held themselves aloof from the infantry while missile troops and mercenaries skulked along the edges. In all quarters, around crackling fires, men sang obscene verses to the accompaniment of *aulos* flutes and whetstones. Smells of bread, seared meat, and spilled wine assailed Memnon's nostrils, reminding him of his own growing hunger.

Parmenion's command pavilion stood fly-rigged atop the camp's transitory acropolis—the crest of a low hill crowded with gnarled oaks. Lamplight streamed from the open walls of the pavilion, glittering off the armor of the guards at their posts and striping the surrounding tree trunks with wavering bands of orange and black. Memnon and Antigonos reined in their horses, dismounted, and left the animals in the care of Parmenion's grooms.

As the pair approached, they could hear the general's voice over the din of camp as he laid into one of his officers, berating him for some infraction of Philip's stern rules; even hundreds of miles distant, the King's will held sway. "Let it happen again," Parmenion bellowed, "and I'll scourge the flesh from your back and pack you off to your father! Understood?" The young soldier saluted. A curt nod from the general sent the man scurrying.

Antigonos entered first, made his salute, and jerked his head to one side, indicating Memnon. "The Rhodian, General."

Parmenion dismissed him with a wave, returning his attention to a rough map of Thrace spread over the whole of his campaign table, its corners weighted with a pair of flat stones, a bust of Herakles, and a sheathed knife. Coins marked their position on the map—silver *staters* representing the Macedonian advance and copper *chalkoi* the Thracians. "It's the gateway to Asia," Parmenion said suddenly, striking the map with a balled fist, scattering coins, "and it's guarded by a pack of feral dogs!"

Memnon said nothing for a moment as he paused at a sideboard holding the remains of Parmenion's supper. He poured for himself a beaker of wine, tossed it back, and poured another. "We've made some small inroads," the Rhodian replied, moving to stand beside Parmenion. He retrieved one of the displaced *staters* and used it to mark the position of the Odrysian village his men had decimated.

"Small inroads won't give Philip Thrace!"

"But gold will," Memnon said with the air of a man who has repeated himself too often. "If you want this gateway opened it's going to cost you, Parmenion. It's going to cost the King."

Parmenion grunted and spat. "You Greeks are all alike! You trust gold to solve your problems when you should be trusting iron! Iron is the muscle of war!"

"And gold is its sinew!" Memnon said. "What's more, parsimony breeds failure. We had this discussion at Maroneia and at Abdera before that! I told you this same thing at Doriscus not a fortnight gone and still you balk! Either convince Philip to bring the full might of Macedonia to bear on these Thracians or give me the funds to do it for you! There is no other way!"

Parmenion ground his teeth. "Perhaps you're right," he said, his voice low and tinged with frustration.

Memnon glanced sidelong at the Macedonian. "You've never agreed with me about this before. What's changed your mind?"

"Can a man not succumb to reason and good advice?"

"Any other man, perhaps," Memnon said. "What goes? Is it the Athenians?"

Parmenion grimaced and nodded. "Diopeithes, their stooge in the Chersonese, is agitating for more funds and more soldiers." The Chersonese was a tongue of land between Thrace and the Hellespont, a stronghold of Athenian sympathies. "The King wants these Thracians under heel before Athens can vote to send one of its generals to Diopeithes' aid."

"That's why you left Aenus." Memnon rubbed his chin while gesturing at the map. "Look here. The Hebrus Valley leads right into the heart of Kersobleptes' lands. We've cleared the way up to here." He touched the coin marking the village. "If we make haste we can cross the river while it's low from the drought, swing wide through the hills, and cross back to drive down into Odrysian territory from the north. With any luck we can catch the bastard at unawares in his fortress at Cypsela."

As Memnon spoke, though, Parmenion tugged at his beard and shook his head. "We'll never catch him unaware. We have too many men, too many horses, to make such a reckless gamble. I'd wager my eye-teeth the Thracian has already been warned of our approach."

"Then we move faster . . ."

Parmenion made a derisive sound. "I don't plan to dawdle, but neither will I rush out like a damn fool! Haste breeds failure as easily as does thrift. We'll proceed up the valley at our accustomed pace—which is fast enough to prove ourselves a threat to Kersobleptes. I've dealt with him before. He'll try using ambushes and flank attacks to break up our phalanx battalions. When he thinks he's weakened us sufficiently, he'll strike with his cavalry. What he won't do is wait for us behind Cypsela's walls. The canny bastard's seen the effects of our siege train often enough to dissuade him of that."

Exhaustion weighed on Memnon's shoulders as he studied the map. "Let me rest my men a few days and I'll lead them out in advance of the main body, up the eastern bank of the river. The phalanx might make better time if Kersobleptes is kept too busy with us to spare our battalions a second glance."

Parmenion shook his head again. "No. I want you and your men to take up positions guarding the right flank of the column. The Thessalians under Attalus will take the left flank and Polemocrates and his Paeonian scouts will serve as outriders."

"Zeus Savior!" Memnon snarled. "Putting Polemocrates in the van is worse than being led by a blind man! At least give my men the lead! We—"

"Enough! I've made my plan! You and your men are on the right flank!"

"A flanker?" Memnon's nostrils flared. "I signed on to win a war, Parmenion! Not to escort a pack of inbred ground-pounders! Strike off these fetters and let me win this war for you!"

"*Let* you win it?" Parmenion's face flushed as he turned on Memnon. "Listen to me, you arrogant pup! You signed on to fight, and—by all the gods!—you will fight when and where I say! If I say I want you on my right flank, guarding my kinsmen, then you'd best take that Persian tit out of your mouth and thank the hoary gods of Hellas I trust you enough to give you that honor!" The Macedonian general jerked his head toward the entrance. "We're done here! Dismissed!"

Memnon bit back a scathing torrent of words; his eyes lost none of their fire as he made his salute. "I serve at your pleasure, my lord," he said, turning and stalking from the pavilion.

Outside, a young groom waited with his horse. Memnon snatched the reins from his hand and vaulted onto the animal's back. "The mercenaries!" he snapped. "What pox-ridden corner of the camp were they allotted?" His horse shied at the fury in his voice.

"N-Northeast corner," the groom said. The Rhodian was about to touch his heels to his horse's flanks when one of Parmenion's secretaries stumbled up, driven from his bed by the sound of their arguing.

"Captain! Wait!" He held up his hand; the other struggled with the neck of his tunic.

"What is it?"

"Another messenger from Pella arrived for you while you were in the field. Should I—"

"I'll deal with him tomorrow," Memnon said. The secretary barely had time to scramble out of the way before horse and rider took off at a canter, making for the area of camp where the mercenaries pitched their tents. One thought consumed him as he rode into the fire-studded night: *Those sons of whores better have wine left!*

MEMNON WOKE SLOWLY, THE THROBBING IN HIS HEAD SEEMING TO WORSEN with every breath. His skull felt as though a blacksmith had used it as an anvil. Though his eyes remained closed, the light of day pierced his lids like knives and burned into his wine-fogged brain. The distorted sounds of the Macedonian camp assailed his ears with the raucous thunder of a god; Memnon groaned as he rolled onto his back and pressed his palms to the sides of his head, a futile gesture meant to block out the cacophony—and to keep his skull from splitting open.

"Merciful Zeus," he croaked.

"And so the innocent grape has its revenge," a man's voice said.

"Leave me, Pharnabazus," Memnon said. "Let me die in peace."

The man chuckled. "I am not Pharnabazus, though bless you for thinking me still young and handsome, and you are not going to die. Osiris has a soft spot for fools such as you."

Memnon pried open one eye and winced. "Khafre?" Like an apparition, the Egyptian stood above him, his head freshly shaved and oiled and his thin lips curling in disapproval. Memnon blinked and looked the man up and down. He wore sandals of embossed leather and a sheer, multicolored robe open over a kilt of starched white linen. The golden pectoral on his breast depicted a pair of cats facing one another, a scarab of lapis lazuli between them. Khafre held a clay mug in one hand and a damp cloth in the other. "How . . . ?"

"I am no figment of your drink-addled imagination, so you may as well banish that thought this instant," he said. "Drink this." He knelt and held the mug to Memnon's lips. The Rhodian's stomach heaved as he caught the scent of herb-laced pomegranate juice; he started to protest, but Khafre gave him little choice. He poured the concoction down Memnon's throat. Spluttering and swallowing, Memnon finally gasped.

"What's in that? Damn you! Are you up to your old tricks, again?"

"No. This time it's something to sober you up. You and I have important things to discuss; things that require a clear head," Khafre said. His nose wrinkled. "You camp beside a river and still you cannot find time to bathe? Here." He handed Memnon the cloth, then stood. "Wipe your face, at least."

Memnon did as the Egyptian ordered. The pain in his head subsided, becoming a dull ache behind his eyes. "What are you doing here, Khafre?"

"I am the messenger from Pella whom you swore to deal with, today," the Egyptian said, a faint smile playing at the corners of his mouth. He poked around in one corner of the tent, seeking a fresh *chiton* for Memnon. He found only reeking castoffs and ample evidence of the Rhodian's nocturnal drinking binge in the form of broken wine jars. "Poor Celeus, the secretary you nearly trampled last night, said he despaired of pressing you further about it after the storm of words you shared with Parmenion. A tactical dispute, no doubt."

"Something like that." Memnon grimaced as he struggled to sit upright. "Why were you in Pella, and what message do you bring? It's Mentor, isn't it?" The question came out as a solemn whisper, as if to speak it loudly would make true the gravest answer. "Tell me, Khafre."

The Egyptian left off his search and came back to stand near the tent entrance, where he might enjoy a breath of fresh air. "It is because of Mentor that I am here; though do not mistake me for the bearer of bad tidings. Your brother sends his greetings, Memnon, and it is his most fervent wish for his family to join him at Sardis as quickly as gods and men allow. Though," he added, "if he were to see you in such a sorry state he might change his mind."

"At Sardis?" Memnon frowned. "That would mean . . ."

Khafre nodded. "That Egypt belongs once again to the Great King, and that His Majesty, in his boundless wisdom, has awarded the chief architect of his victory with his heart's desire, and more. The House of Pharnaces is restored and Lord Artabazus with it, absolved of all wrongdoing. The King hopes he will pass many days with him on the long road to Susa, regaling him with tales of Greek courage and heroism. His Majesty also seeks Artabazus's counsel on—" Khafre stopped in mid-sentence and used a flick of his chin to indicate the Macedonian camp around them. Ochus wanted news of Philip, of his intentions and ambitions.

The fires of curiosity burned away the wine haze in Memnon's mind. Clear and bright now, his eyes bored into Khafre's as he hunched forward. "How did it happen, and when? Tell me everything!"

Khafre did, omitting not the least detail—from the attempted perfidy of Tennes and Mentor's intrigues to the punishment of the Sidonians for their part in the revolt. "Adult males and the elderly were put to death while the women and children were enslaved. Mentor tried to beg for leniency on Sidon's behalf, but the King's anger could not be denied. Ochus destroyed the town as an example to the other cities of Phoenicia: support Egypt and share in Sidon's fate. An effective tool, fear."

Memnon said nothing; he only nodded, remembering the bright courtyards filled with date palms and the attar of roses, the liquid laughter of sloe-eyed women. He shook his head. Unperturbed, Khafre launched next into a description of the forces arrayed against Pharaoh. Painting with words like an Egyptian Herodotus, he depicted the Great King's satrapal levies in all their grandeur—from the prancing cavalry of Lydia and Ionia, to the white-robed archers of Syria and the savage spearmen of Cilicia, to the ten thousand Greek hoplites drawn from Thebes, Argos, and the Asian shore. "The King divided his army into three regiments," he said, "pairing a Persian commander with a Greek general. Lacrates and his Thebans served alongside Spithridates, satrap of Ionia and Lydia. Nicostratus of Argos gave his orders with noble Aristazanes, who stands on the right hand of the King. Mentor and his Persian counterpart Bagoas, a eunuch and devilish rogue who had risen to high office, were given the hoplites of Greek Ionia and the Aegean. Ochus himself commanded from the rear."

The actual campaign took Khafre less time to describe; it reminded Memnon that, despite his gruff and simple exterior, Mentor was a genius. Not only did he engineer the bloodless surrender of Khafre's home city of Bubastis, and a dozen other towns besides, but he also spearheaded the siege of Pelusium and the capture of a portion of Pharaoh's river fleet. All the while, Mentor allied himself with the eunuch Bagoas and joined in a campaign of intrigue against their fellow commanders, Greek and Persian, alike. With ruthless cunning, the duo enhanced their rivals' failures while bolstering their own triumphs, all in an effort to elevate their standing in the eyes of the Great King.

"Zeus Savior," Memnon said, shaking his head in grudging respect. "My brother's become the worst predator imaginable: a Greek general with the mind of a Persian nobleman."

"A dichotomy that has served him well. The King's pardon of you and Artabazus was only the smallest portion of Mentor's reward."

Memnon stood, reeling a little, and tugged on the first *chiton* he could find. "He received a grant of land, then?"

"In a manner of speaking, yes," Khafre said. The Egyptian paused, frowning. "It is a difficult thing to describe, but I shall try. His Majesty has divided his kingdom into two halves. As Ochus is revered as the King of Kings, so each of his newly elevated deputies will act as a Satrap of Satraps; the men already in positions of power will be answerable to them, as they are answerable to the King. It is to be Bagoas's lot to administer the East while Mentor governs in the West, from Sardis. If memory serves, your brother now holds the highest position of any foreigner in Persia's long history."

Memnon, his face unreadable, said at length: "And, when you relayed this news to Artabazus, how did he react?"

"Understandably," Khafre said, "he wept. Philip has already given his blessing and wished Artabazus well in his new life. All that is left is to bring you and Pharnabazus home."

The Rhodian shook his head slowly. "And so the wheel turns, again," he muttered. Though the implications of having a brother who was now one of the most powerful men in the West was staggering, Memnon shortened his focus to the problems at hand—he had to find Pharnabazus and secure their passage back to Pella. Only then would he—

"I have another message," Khafre said, shattering his ruminations. From the waistband of his kilt, the Egyptian drew out a wallet of soft leather. He extended it to Memnon. "This one is from Lady Barsine."

Memnon's composure slipped. Lines softened and the shrewd calculations going on behind his eyes abruptly ceased. He glanced at the wallet with a curious mixture of anticipation and fear. "Is she well?"

"She is, though she, too, wept when I told her the news. Later, she came to me and bid me deliver this to you. Will you not take it?"

Memnon accepted the wallet; he stared down at it for a long moment. Finally, with trembling fingers, he untied the thong holding the wallet flap in place, opening it to reveal a folded letter.

"Has this aught to do with her impending marriage?" Khafre asked.

The Rhodian blinked and looked up. "Could I beg a favor of you, Khafre?" he said. "Would you find Pharnabazus? Try the horse paddock, first. Ask outside, if there is a young Greek named Callinus about he will guide you where you need to go."

Khafre pursed his lips and nodded. "As you wish," he said, and ducked from the tent without further comment.

Memnon exhaled. He edged into a shaft of sunlight, drew out the letter and unfolded it with exaggerated care. The words on the fine vellum were unmistakably Barsine's, her calligraphy as graceful as the hand that wielded the pen:

Two years have passed since my eyes last beheld yours, since my ears last enjoyed the soothing timbre of your voice, and not a day goes by that I do not think of you and miss you. Word of your acts has reached us here at Pella and we rejoice in your good fortune. With every dispatch to my father, I held out hope that I might receive a letter from you, a note — some token of forgiveness for my part in the deed which drove you away. Is the rift between us too deep for absolution? I pray that is not the case. If I had known, then, that the cost of a touch would be your friendship and the pleasure of your company, I would have stayed my hand and fled into the night.

Soon, I am off to my marriage bed, to perform the duty of every obedient daughter by exchanging the freedom of youth for the shackles of the harem. I accept this as my fate though I do not go to it willingly. I cannot control my heart, Memnon! I love your brother as my uncle, not as a woman loves a man, not as Penelope loved her Odysseus. I know not how I offended the gods, but whatever my crime they have doubly cursed me, for I can neither love the man I am to marry nor marry the man I hope to love.

Time grows short. Return swiftly to us, dear Memnon. Return to me, so that we may walk one last time under the birches and listen to the song of the cicadas, or lose ourselves in debate over the merits of Homer's children. Even the memory of an hour spent thus in your company will be as a balm to my soul in the years to come.

Take good care, and may the gods bless and keep you.

"She blames herself," Memnon whispered, "when the fault is mine. I am a thrice-cursed fool!" He returned the letter to the wallet and glanced around the cluttered tent with clarity of purpose. Thrace, the army, this campaign, none of it concerned him any longer, and the sooner he was on the road to Pella the better. *We will need to travel light*, he thought, sorting at once through a dozen different scenarios and the obstacles they presented.

Swift action called for swifter preparation . . .

An hour later, when Khafre returned with Pharnabazus, the Egyptian noticed a marked change the moment he entered the tent. Bathed, his hair and beard freshly trimmed, Memnon wore his linen corselet over a tunic of faded blue. Bronze greaves clung to his shins, their knee-guards carved and molded to resemble Medusa's ferocious visage. He sat on a cypress-wood chest, balancing a waxed writing board on his thighs; he paused in his writing and glanced up at his nephew. "Good, you're here."

"What goes, Uncle?" Pharnabazus said, scowling. Runnels of sweat cut through the dust of the drill field. "Khafre said you had news of the gravest sort."

"I thought it best he hear it from you," the Egyptian said.

Memnon nodded. "We're going home, Pharnabazus. Gather only those things you cannot bear to part with. When you're finished, take Khafre and find a pair of horses. I want the two of you to be on the road to Aenus within the hour."

"Do not be absurd, Memnon!" Pharnabazus said. "Going home? We cannot go home! This campaign is not remotely over! If this is because of your words with Parmenion, then swallow your pride, Uncle, and do as he tells you!"

"We're going home," Memnon said, "because Mentor summons us. His plan was successful. Your father is an exile no longer."

Pharnabazus blinked. He glanced at Khafre and the Egyptian smiled, giving his shoulder a reassuring pat. "Uncle, I . . ."

Memnon held up a hand, forestalling him. "You've said nothing that requires an apology, Pharnabazus, but your haste and cooperation are another matter. I need both and I need them now! Pack swiftly; get a pair of horses and some rations, enough for a couple of days. Once you and Khafre reach Aenus, find a ship and secure us passage back to Pella. Understood?"

The young Persian thumped his armor-clad chest. "I have all I need here, but what of you, Uncle? Are you not traveling with us?"

"I will be hot on your heels," Memnon said. He snapped the hinged cover of the writing board shut and stood. "First, though, I must settle our affairs with Parmenion."

THE MACEDONIAN CAMP WAS A HIVE OF ACTIVITY AS THE MEN MADE READY to march the next morning. The last of the supply wagons had come from Aenus, and the quartermasters organized work gangs to help get the last of the rations—the barley and olives, smoked meat and cheese, dried figs, onions and garlic—squared away. No camp followers or slaves traveled with the army; each soldier was responsible for shouldering his own gear and a share of his squad's communal property. Besides weapons and armor and personal items, a man might find himself humping spare *sarissa* shafts or tents and cooking gear, or anything else a file of ten men might require. The few wagons Philip allowed the army were allotted to the quartermasters and the secretariat, the surgeons and the smithy.

Created by Philip and implemented by Parmenion, the Macedonian army ran with a spare and deadly economy unmatched anywhere in the world. It could cover great distances at speed and its diverse arms were trained to fight in unison, under any conditions and in any season. As he walked his horse through its predatory heart in search of Parmenion, Memnon committed its every detail to memory.

Though not in his command pavilion, the Rhodian had little trouble finding the general. He needed only to follow the stream of aides and messengers. Parmenion stood at the edge of the Hebrus River, surrounded by a knot of officers, watching a division of Paeonian cavalry training on the far bank. Plumes of dust rose as the squadrons feigned a withdrawal only to wheel suddenly and fall into the wedge-shaped formation that ended in a thunderous charge.

"Still ragged, Polemocrates," Memnon heard Parmenion say as he dismounted, handing his reins to an aide. "Signal them to do it again." As Polemocrates moved, the general caught sight of Memnon. "By the Thunderer! There's a face I didn't expect to see today! Rhodian! Is it true you wrestled Dionysus during the night?" The other officers chuckled.

Memnon smiled. "Wrestled? No. More like we engaged in pankration, but I was on the losing side and remember little of the beating the God of the Vine gave me." Parmenion grinned at this. Memnon's face, though, took on a serious cast. "I would speak with you, General. Alone."

Parmenion gestured, indicating they should walk. His jocularity faded as they left the circle of his officers. He spoke first, his voice a low growl. "My mind is still set, Memnon. I give you latitude because you're a good officer, but I'll not tolerate further impertinence."

"Last night is forgotten," Memnon replied. "You recall a messenger who arrived from Pella, an Egyptian? He brought word from my brother to Artabazus and from Artabazus to me: our exile has been lifted. We are again free, and Pharnabazus and I have been recalled, with Philip's blessing, to resume our family obligations."

"Recalled?" Parmenion scowled. "The army marches with the dawn."

"It must march two men short, then, for my nephew and I will be on the road to Aenus, and thence to Pella, 'ere this day ends. Give Berisades command of my squadron. He's a good man, even for a Thracian, and the soldiers respect him." Memnon glanced at Parmenion, watching his reaction.

Blood suffused the general's face and turned it the color of a ripe pomegranate. He clenched his hands into fists; his knuckles whitened and cracked. A moment passed before he found his voice again. "Berisades, eh? I'll cut my own heart out before I put a Thracian at the head of one of my squadrons! No, your men will get what they should have had all along: a good Macedonian commander—their respect be damned!" Parmenion spoke loud enough that the other officers turned and stared.

Memnon bristled. “I understand your anger toward me—I would feel it no less, were our places reversed—but don’t take it out on my men!”

“You have no men,” Parmenion said. He motioned for the aide holding Memnon’s horse. “And what you perceive as anger is, in truth, bitter disappointment. I thought you a man of honor, Memnon, a man who would see a thing through to its end. I recognize my error now. I give you my leave! Go! Hurry back to your Persian masters!”

Memnon shook his head as he took the reins of his horse from the aide. In a smooth motion, he vaulted astride the horse, calmed it as it whinnied and pranced. “Your leave? You give me something I neither asked for nor need, unless you believe yourself greater than my host, your King!”

Parmenion shot him a venomous look. “Get out of my camp, Rhodian, before my patience wears thin!”

“Remember my advice to you, General,” he said. “Make haste! You know Kersobleptes’ habits? I would daresay he knows yours, as well. Act contrary to what he expects—”

“Go!” Parmenion roared, spittle flying. His hand dropped to his sword hilt as he took a step forward. “Get out of my camp, you son of a bitch, or—as Zeus is my witness!—I’ll carve your balls off and feed them to my dogs!”

Memnon’s mouth set into a hard line. “So be it, you old fool, but it didn’t have to end this way! Remember *that*!” With a contemptuous snarl, the Rhodian spun his mount and spurred it to a gallop, scattering curious officers in his wake.

THE SHIP THAT FERRIED THEM FROM AENUS TO PELLA WAS CALLED *Eurydike*; its captain, a man of Keos, was stern, humorless, and likely one of the finest sailors Memnon had ever seen. He'd learned deep-water sailing from a Phoenician master, a skill that allowed them to skirt north of Samothrace and drive straight across the Aegean to the triple promontories of the Chalcidice. Stormy Athos they gave a wide berth, took a day's rest on the tip of Sithonia, and rounded Pallene a week after leaving Aenus. *Eurydike* plunged into the Thermaic Gulf, its prow cutting the foam-flecked waters, as the Kean captain, Laertes, guided them with uncanny instinct to the mouth of Lake Loudias.

"Less than two weeks," Memnon said, espying the fortress atop Phakos Island in the distance. "You've more than earned your fee, Captain."

Laertes shrugged. "It was Lord Poseidon's will."

"Where are you bound from Pella?"

The captain shrugged, again. It was his most animated gesture save for when he stood at the tiller of his ship, the wind in his gray-flecked hair and salt spray in his blue eyes. In those instances, Laertes resembled the master of the legendary *Argo*—destined for Colchis, the Golden Fleece, and immortality. "Athens, perhaps," the captain replied. "Then home to Keos."

"I will treble your fee," Memnon said, "if you wait in Pella until my family is ready to depart and see us safely to Ephesus." Ephesus was the closest port to Sardis, and still the Lydian capital lay three days' journey inland. Laertes stroked his beard, his eyes narrowed in thought.

"I am not fond of waiting . . ."

"Quadruple your fee."

At that, the Kean's face lit up. He grinned, his teeth small and white, and extended a calloused hand to Memnon. "Done!"

"Done!" the Rhodian repeated, grasping the proffered hand. With a curt nod, the captain went back to his place at the tiller while Memnon rejoined Pharnabazus and Khafre in the bow. "I've hired him for the outbound journey."

"I expect Father will be grateful," the young Persian said. "I wonder, will Dascylium be returned to us now that all is forgiven?"

Memnon didn't answer; Khafre exhaled, his brows knitted in a frown. "It is doubtful," the Egyptian said. "Your father's old satrapy belongs to one of the Great King's courtiers, a man called Arsites. I cannot see Ochus displacing him for Artabazus' sake."

"Dascylium without a Pharnacid satrap." Pharnabazus shook his head. "It is almost too much to bear. Perhaps Mentor can—"

"Patience, nephew," Memnon snapped. "Let him settle into his new position before you start causing him trouble."

Pharnabazus glanced at Memnon, heat flaring in his eyes. He opened his mouth and would have responded in kind save for the lightest of touches on his arm. He turned to Khafre; the Egyptian gave a barely perceptible shake of his head, a gesture that said, "Let it go." Pharnabazus's nostrils flared but he heeded Khafre's advice. All three men kept silent for the last few miles of their voyage.

The sun had reached its zenith by the time *Eurydike* made landfall, descending into late afternoon as the trio passed the gates of Artabazus's estate. At first glance, Memnon saw little sign that this was a household in flux. Indeed, nothing appeared out of place. A breeze whispered through the birch boughs, and the air itself was heady with the scent of fresh-cut grass and the music of caged birds.

Memnon lengthened his stride. As he neared the house, he could see the main door, of bronze-studded wood with an iron grate, standing ajar; a short passageway led to the courtyard at the heart of the villa. Voices came from within, soft and feminine, followed by the sound of sobbing. "What goes?" he heard Pharnabazus mutter.

"Deidamia?" Memnon called, pushing the door fully open. "Barsine?" He traversed the short passageway and emerged into the sun-drenched courtyard. Chests and bales, the accreted belongings of ten years in exile, stood close at hand beneath the columned peristyle, awaiting the porters that they must soon summon to carry them down to the harbor. Across the way, Deidamia and Barsine sat side by side on a stone bench, their hands laced together. At first, Memnon thought his sister might be consoling the younger woman on her impending marriage, but it was Deidamia sitting with head bowed as in prayer and Barsine who sought to comfort her, stroking her hair with her free hand. She glanced at Memnon, her eyes widening; then, she bent close and whispered something in Deidamia's ear.

His sister sat upright and he could barely recognize the face that stared back at him. Red, swollen eyes blinked; her lips trembled as she cuffed at the tears moistening her cheeks. He'd never seen Deidamia so overwrought. Had something happened to Artabazus? His heart pounding, Memnon crossed to her side and knelt. "What's wrong," he said. But, the strength it had taken for her to raise her head drained away; with a shoulder-wracking sob, she collapsed into his arms. "What is it? Deidamia?"

Barsine answered for her. "It's Cophen. He's run away."

"Zeus Savior." Memnon exhaled, a sigh of relief, and embraced his sister.

"Is that all? Tell me of his haunts and I'll go fetch him back, myself."

"He's gone to Mieza, most likely," Barsine said. Pharnabazus put a hand on her shoulder. She smiled up at him, gave his hand a squeeze.

"Mieza?" Memnon knew of the place, a sanctuary to the Nymphs in the foothills west of Pella. "Why Mieza?"

"To bid farewell to Alexander. The King brought in a philosopher, a former student of Plato's, to tutor the Prince and his retinue. Philip installed them at Mieza, along with a garrison under orders to protect the place from interlopers. Without permission from the King or Queen—"

"They'll kill him," Deidamia said, finding her voice once again. Her arms tightened around Memnon's neck as she hissed in his ear: "Please, brother! Find him! Don't let these Macedonians slaughter my first-born!"

Memnon glanced at Barsine. "Where's Artabazus?"

"Father has gone to the palace, to wrangle a pass from Antipatros. Gryllus is at the stables readying his horse, and Ianthe is upstairs with the children."

Memnon rose, gently prompting Deidamia to her feet, as well. He gestured to Khafre. "Could you see her to bed? Make sure she gets something to help her rest," he said. The Egyptian nodded. Memnon disentangled her arms from around his neck. "Here. Go with Khafre."

"Come, dear Lady. Let's get you out of this heat." Khafre took her hand and together they shuffled into the cool recesses of the house. Memnon watched her go, concern lining his features.

"She's taking this too hard," he said.

Pharnabazus agreed. "You would think Cophen dead already by her reaction. He is simply off on an adventure, a lark all boys his age crave. When he returns, though, he is going to wish the Macedonians had found him first."

"These past two years have been difficult for her," Barsine said. "She lost two infants, a boy and a girl, to fever and clings to the rest, sacrificing daily to Apollo, the Healer, and Mother Hera to keep them safe. She feels abandoned by the gods."

"Then it's our lot to prove otherwise," Memnon said. "Pharnabazus, I need you to supervise the loading of the ship while I'm gone. Get workers from the docks, Laertes' men, whomever you can find."

"I will see it done, Uncle."

Memnon returned his attention to Barsine. She wore a girdled *chiton* of soft blue linen and had her long hair pulled back and fastened with silver pins. Several dark strands escaped, falling over her smoky eyes. "It would be a great boon if Cophen left here on foot."

She shook her head. "A horse is missing. I do not believe he intended to be gone long, though, as all I could discover gone from the kitchen were a couple of apples and a loaf of bread. Do you think you can find him before nightfall?"

"Not with the lead he has. I suspect he'll stop for the night. That's when I'll make up for lost time. I should have him by dawn and be back here by midday."

Barsine glanced over her shoulder. Her brother had moved off, out of earshot, as he double-checked the bindings on their belongings. A loose lid or rope invited pilfering. She lowered her voice. "Could I beg a favor of you?"

"Of course," Memnon said.

"Could you take him on to Mieza? He wants desperately to tell Alexander goodbye. The Prince has had quite an influence on Cophen. He feels . . . obligated as a guest-friend of Alexander's to act no less honorably than Father has with Philip. It would mean the world to him, Memnon."

Memnon scratched the point of his bearded chin. "On to Mieza? That will delay our departure . . ." his voice trailed off. He gave a faint smile. "I will take him, but only as a favor to you."

"Thank you," Barsine said, sharing his smile.

The Rhodian made to turn away, stopped. "I hope," he began, in a small and quiet voice, "you can one day forgive me."

"For what?"

Memnon frowned, dropping his eyes to stare at the pebble mosaics underfoot. "For leaving. I didn't realize, until Khafre brought your letter to me, how my departure had hurt you. I should have written you, to explain my decision, to let you know there was no blame to assign . . . so many times I wanted to, but I couldn't find the courage."

Tears welled at the corners of Barsine's eyes. She reached out and grasped his hand. "You have done nothing that requires my forgiveness, Memnon. We are bound to our own separate fates, you and I, and I have found that no amount of cursing or shaking our fists at the heavens can change it. I am resigned to what I must do. But, promise me this—promise me, in the years to come, that you will make the time to visit me, so that we might sit and talk or read together of the deeds of Odysseus and of his lovely Penelope."

Memnon's throat tightened. He nodded. "I promise."

Barsine smiled through her tears, the gesture as radiant as sunlight glimpsed through the clouds. "Good," she said. "Come, you are going to need provisions for the trip to Mieza, enough for you and my wayward brother." She turned and led him through the house, to the kitchens.

Forgotten in the courtyard, Pharnabazus smiled to himself and wiped away a bit of sweat that must have dripped into his eyes.

THE ROAD TO MIEZA SLASHED LIKE A RAW WOUND ACROSS THE DUSTY GREEN fields of the Emathian Plain. Memnon, astride the Nisaean mare Euphrosyne, followed the road due west, toward where the setting sun struck fire from the peaks of Mount Bermion; he plunged through groves of oak and scrub pine, splashed across streams and skirted tangled thickets of wild rose.

Riding at a steady canter, Memnon divided his attention between the road ahead and the trail below, scarcely more than a rutted ox track, straining his eyes in the deepening twilight to catch the slightest sign of Cophen's passage. A Nisaean had traveled along the road earlier in the day. Memnon had seen an imprint of a hoof, its shape unique among northern horses, in the moist loam of a stream bank not a mile back. He reckoned on the boy stopping for the night, but what if he didn't? If he rode straight through he would reach Mieza long before sunrise. Could he talk his way past the soldiers guarding Alexander? Surely those men had seen the young Persian in the company of their Prince time and again, enough to know he did not pose a threat . . . ?

No, it was a gamble Memnon just could not take.

He put a hand to his chest, reassuring himself that the thick leather wallet he carried had not slipped from beneath his linen cuirass. Its contents—a thrice-folded sheet of heavy parchment inscribed by Philip's Regent, Antipatros, and bearing a wax impression of the Royal Seal of Macedonia—insured their safe conduct to and from the village of Mieza. Reluctantly, Artabazus had given it to him.

"The boy is my concern, Memnon," the old satrap had said, his brow creased with worry. "You should stay and look after your sister."

"She's under Khafre's care. I'd only be underfoot. Besides, Artabazus, I've been cooped up on a ship for these last two weeks. I need to get out, stretch my muscles." He did not need to add what both men knew in their hearts: if it came to blows, Cophen would be safer with him rather than with his father, who had only wielded hunting spears in the past ten years. In the end, Artabazus relented; tears glistened in his eyes as he embraced the Rhodian.

"Bring him back safe, Memnon. For Deidamia's sake."

Euphrosyne whinnied as Memnon reined her in. He leaned out and studied the roadbed. Here, visible even in the gloom, a swath of crushed grass and churned earth marked the spot where a larger body of horsemen entered the road from the north, their passage obliterating Cophen's elusive trail. Memnon couldn't deduce their exact numbers, though he guessed no more than six, nor could he divine their purpose. Hunting party or cavalry patrol, their animals left the same spoor behind. His only certainty was their destination. They, too, were riding hard for Mieza.

"Zeus Savior," he muttered. "Let them be hunters."

Memnon pressed on. A three-quarter moon rose above the trees, tinting the night-time world with silver light, and a faint mist rose from the surrounding fields to drift over the road. Crickets sang in the grass.

Near midnight, Memnon paused at the crest of a rise, startled by the orange glow of a fire coming from the heart of a willow thicket in the hollow below, barely visible from the road. But, who was it, Cophen or some other traveler? Cautious, he circled downwind, walking Euphrosyne close enough that he could hear the clatter of weapons and the chatter of conversation. *Soldiers.* He could tell from their silhouettes and voices that there were five of them, cavalrymen, their horses tied to a makeshift fence created by stretching a rope between two trees. He counted six horses, though. On his second count, he noticed that the sixth was taller than the rest and as black as the surrounding night.

Memnon stiffened. *A Nisaean!*

"I'm telling you," he heard one of the cavalrymen say, pointing back toward the line of mounts. "I recognize that horse. Only three like it in these parts and they all belong to the Persian."

"What about it, lad?" The speaker, a squat Macedonian with a fiery red beard, nudged a shape at his feet. Memnon exhaled in relief. Cophen, a gangling youth of fifteen, his *chiton* in disarray and his arms bound behind him, lay on his side. He snarled up at the cavalryman, his eyes showing more fury than fear. The Rhodian felt a stab of pride.

"The Persian's my father! The horse is his!"

"Father? Lying little bugger! More like you stole it from the Persian! Didn't you? Ha! Keep glaring at me, then! It's all the same punishment, horse thievery or trespassing without the King's blessing! Both warrant a hanging!"

"A bit of sport first, eh, Koinos?" one of the others asked, grabbing his crotch and chuckling. "Prettier than the King's new boy, this one."

Memnon, though, had seen enough.

"Praise Zeus!" he bellowed, spurring Euphrosyne through the trees and into the clearing. "You found him!" Cavalrymen leapt to their feet; iron glittered and rasped as they dragged their swords from their sheaths or snatched at their javelins.

"Uncle!" Cophen shouted, lurching upright. He would have rushed to Memnon's side but a sword point leveled at his belly stopped him cold.

"Don't kill him yet, boys," red-bearded Koinos said, squinting at Memnon in the uncertain light. "Not before we find out his business in these parts. What of it, friend?"

"I mean no harm," Memnon said. He dismounted, careful to keep his hand away from the hilt of his weapon, and looped Euphrosyne's reins around a willow branch. With the same exaggerated care, he tugged the wallet from under his armor, opened it, and held the pass up so Koinos could see the seal. "I'm a guest-friend of King Philip's. Memnon, I'm called. This one's my nephew, the son of Artabazus the Persian. We're on our way to Mieza to pay our respects to Prince Alexander."

"You're an officer of Parmenion's. I've heard of you," Koinos said, relaxing. He nodded and sheathed his blade; the others followed suit. "The lad's telling the truth, I guess. Cut him loose." But Cophen, before they could free him, slipped their grasp and ran to Memnon's side.

"Thank the gods!" he said, his voice rising in pitch. "I am glad you're here, Uncle! Did you see? Did you? These dogs dared lay hands on me! On me! Make sure you get their names, Uncle! I want to see *them* hang!"

Memnon frowned. He placed a heavy hand on his nephew's shoulder. "They were doing the task Philip set them here to do. As far as I can see you're unharmed, save for a bruised pride, so let this serve as a lesson in what can happen when you bolt off without permission."

Cophen, though, shrugged him off. "Am I not descended from the kings of Asia and a sworn ally of their own Prince? Zeus Savior and Herakles! You will all pay, and pay dearly! Alexander will see to it! Loose me, Uncle! Loose—"

Memnon's jaw twitched. The boy was shrieking now, clamoring before god and man to see justice delivered. The pride he had felt earlier at his nephew's stalwart defiance evaporated, and with it his patience. He spun Cophen around to face the Macedonians and kicked his legs out from under him. The lad would have gone sprawling into the dirt had Memnon not caught him—by snatching a fistful of his dark hair. Metal grated as the Rhodian slid his sword from its sheath.

The Macedonians cursed. Koinos motioned for them to hold their ground and not to interfere.

On his knees now, Cophen yelped as his head was jerked back; his eyes brimmed with tears of panic and confusion as Memnon laid the edge of his blade across his throat. "Uncle?"

Memnon stared down at him, making his face pitiless and hard. "How comes this cockiness, this base arrogance? What have you done which entitles you to address your elders as if they were slaves under your heel? Have you led men into battle? Served your family and your king with glory and honor? Or is it simply that you feel a sense of entitlement because you were lucky enough to be born a Pharnacid while these fine fellows were not? You . . . Koinos, isn't it?" Memnon waited for the red-bearded Macedonian to nod in assent. "Tell me, good Koinos, what penalty has Philip decreed for foreigners caught near Mieza without his leave?"

"Death," Koinos said flatly.

"Surely the King makes concessions for pompous young fools too full of their ancestors supposed virtues that it blinds them to the dangers of allowing their tongues free rein?"

"None that I'm aware of, sir," Koinos replied. He kept his features stern.

"We hang them just the same."

"Fetch a rope."

Cophen's eyes widened. He made to speak, stopping as Memnon applied slight pressure to the blade. Koinos glanced from the Rhodian to the boy and snapped his fingers. One of his cavalrymen rummaged through his kit, came up with a length of plaited leather rope and tossed it to the red-bearded Macedonian. Koinos made a show of testing the rope's strength.

Cophen braved the sword's edge. "Uncle, please!"

"Are we supposed to pity you, now? Decide, boy! Either you're man enough to demand vengeance against the King's subjects, thus man enough to accept punishment when you transgress against the King's law, or you're but a callow youth in dire need of instruction! Which is it? Decide, Cophen!"

"Please, don't do it, Uncle! Please! I'm . . . I'm not . . . !" The boy squeezed his eyes shut; tears left their moist tracks through the dust caking his cheeks.

"Koinos," Memnon said, lifting his blade away from his nephew's throat. "I don't think we'll need that rope after all." The Macedonian nodded; a father himself, he could respect a good harrowing. He turned to his cavalrymen.

"What are you whoresons gawking at?" he said. "Your uncles did worse to you and you know it! Get this camp squared away!"

Memnon cut Cophen's bonds; driving his sword point-first into the earth, he knelt beside him and draped his arm around his shoulders. The youth opened his eyes and stared up at the night sky, unable to look down for fear of impaling himself on a phantom blade. He took ragged breaths, choking now and again, snuffling. His face blazed with shame.

"I—I thought you were going to k-kill me," he said, raw-voiced.

"I needed your full attention," Memnon replied. "Listen to me, Cophen. Your blood is unimpeachable—you *are* descended from the kings of Asia—but blood is not the sole measure of a man. Nor are we defined by our associations with other men, be they beggars, princes, or kings. It is our deeds and our words that make us who we are. Now, none will argue that you have bravery to spare, and you're daring. How else could you have stolen your father's horse and made it this far? But, you lack humility. When your bid failed you decided not to accept your failure with dignity, and you compounded that failure by making hollow threats against men innocent of any wrongdoing. That others, men of substance and worldly power, act in this base manner does not give you license to emulate them. Do you understand?"

Cophen nodded. "I do . . . at least, I believe I do."

"Good," Memnon said. He rose and helped the youth to his feet. "Come. Let's get a bit of sup and some rest. I want to be on the road early."

"Back to Pella?" Cophen asked. He had a resignation in his voice that told Memnon he expected further punishment, from his father, his mother, but especially from Pharnabazus. Memnon, though, shook his head.

"To Mieza. Don't you have obligations to discharge to Alexander, as he is your guest-friend?"

The lad brightened. "But . . . But I thought you'd come to fetch me home?"

"To escort you and keep you safe. Deeds and words, Cophen," Memnon replied. "If you've pledged your friendship, then it does you credit to seek out the Prince and bid him farewell. It shows you recognize your duties." They walked toward the fire. Memnon smiled and tousled his nephew's hair. "But running away shows you still have much more to learn. Don't worry, though; the back of your brother's hand will be awaiting you once our business with Alexander is finished."

MIEZA CLUNG TO THE FOOT OF MOUNT BERMION LIKE A SUPPLIANT beseeching a cloud-wreathed lord. In the foothills above the sleepy village stood a sprawling country estate built by legendary King Midas, so he might enjoy his gardens, and renovated by King Philip as an offering to the gods of learning. Whitewashed walls and red glazed tiles gleamed amid stands of maple and birch. Apple orchards, with trees as precise in their ranks as soldiers in a phalanx, shaded the road leading up to the main house. Servants and slaves went about their morning ritual, some fetching water or harvesting apples for the kitchens, others heading out to the fields to tend the olives and prune the vine stocks. Young goatherds tramped along with their bleating charges, bound for pastures higher in the mountains.

Twice Memnon and Cophen were stopped by spear-bearing soldiers—once in the village and once near the house—and made to produce proof that they had the King's permission to be here. "Does Philip fear someone might snatch Alexander away?" Cophen asked.

Memnon shrugged. "Oft times, the best way to strike at a man is through his son. I think, though, the guards are meant more to ensure privacy. He wants his son to learn all this student of Plato has to offer, and without distraction. Which is why . . . ?" Memnon glanced at his nephew, his eyebrows raised.

"Which is why I am to make my farewells brief, but polite, and decline any offer to stay longer than necessary," Cophen said, weary of reciting the same instructions.

"Good."

As they approached the house an older servant in a saffron tunic emerged to greet them, accompanied by a pair of Thracian grooms. Memnon and Cophen dismounted. The man, shading his eyes against the morning sunlight, frowned from one to the other. "You're not couriers from King Philip," he said, his voice dripping suspicion.

"Indeed, we're not," Memnon replied. He brandished his papers for a third time. "We're here with the blessing of the King's Regent, who speaks for the King in his absence. I am Memnon, and this is my nephew, Cophen, son of Artabazus. He is a guest-friend of Prince Alexander's who has come to pay his respects. If you might be so kind as to direct us to the Prince?"

The servant pursed his lips and nodded. He motioned for the grooms to see to their horses. "Come. Alexander is taking instruction from my master, Aristotle, but I shall show you to a place where you may await him." He led them around to the back of the house. A columned portico paved with natural stone offered an excellent view of the wooded eastern face of Mount Bermion, and near at hand Memnon could hear the splash of water that betokened a shallow falls. Paths vanished under oak and rowan boughs. The servant gestured to a bench and excused himself, leaving the pair alone.

"Pleasant fellow," Memnon muttered. Cophen sat as the Rhodian leaned against a column.

"I wonder what sort of lessons this Aristotle teaches?" the youth said.

"Rhetoric, surely," Memnon replied. "Mathematics, literature, and philosophy as well. Remember to ask Alexander when you see him. No doubt he'd be eager to show you the grounds." Movement caught Memnon's eye. From around the far side of the house, opposite from where they sat, a man strolled along the edge of a flowerbed. His hands clasped behind his back, he stopped on occasion to study a particularly vibrant bloom. The fellow wore a long Ionian *chiton*, colored a rich shade of red with a thickly embroidered hem, and allowed his golden hair to drape about his shoulders. As he turned to retrace his steps Memnon was struck by an odd sense of familiarity. He'd seen this man before. His face, ageless and smooth, made the Rhodian think of the many eunuchs who had once been in Artabazus's service.

Recognition dawned. *The eunuch from the horse fair!*

"Who is he, Uncle?" Cophen said, following Memnon's gaze.

"I don't know, though I'm sure I've seen him before." He meant before their exile in Macedonia, though he didn't elaborate. Nor did Cophen press. The young man stood as a flurry of voices echoed from one of the forest paths; presently, a gaggle of youths emerged, shepherded along by a small man impeccably dressed in a bone-colored Ionian tunic, his graying beard well trimmed. Sunlight winked from the rings on his fingers as he spoke with animated gestures to the two young men at his side. The taller one, a handsome boy with dark hair and brooding eyes, Memnon didn't know. The other was Alexander.

"So unlike his father," Memnon said, more to himself than his nephew. Indeed, Alexander shared very little with Philip; so slight was the resemblance, in fact, that it drove the King's detractors to question the boy's paternity. He had his mother's dark eyes, brilliant in their intensity, and a thick mane of fair hair, which he wore long and loose to remind all of the blood he shared with immortal Herakles.

The sight of him put Memnon on edge. He reckoned it akin to watching an adolescent lion—lean and hungry—amid a flock of sheep, trying to apprehend when its rampage would begin.

Of Alexander's retinue, Memnon only knew the three oldest by sight, youths already considered men in their fathers' esteem. Parmenion's eldest, Philotas, walked beside Ptolemy, son of Lagos (rumor, though, painted him Philip's bastard). In their wake came a knot of five boys Cophen's age. These poked good-naturedly at a sixth, a clubfooted lad who smiled and spouted curses with all the creativity of a lifelong soldier. Finally, walking alone, was Antipatros's eldest son, Kassandros, a red-haired youth of seventeen whose sharp blue eyes flickered between Alexander and his tall companion, as though undecided on which one he hated more.

It was the clubfooted lad who spotted them first. "Cophen!" he shouted, breaking ranks and hobbling toward the portico. Cophen stepped down and met him halfway.

"Greetings, Harpalos!" The others, too, swirled around Cophen. Memnon heard a litany of names: Leonnatus, Erigyius, Laomedon, Marsyas, Nearchus. Ptolemy and Philotas held themselves aloof; Kassandros shouldered past them and went to sit under the portico.

"Alexander! Hephaestion!" Harpalos cried. "Look who has decided to pay us a visit!"

The Prince took leave of his tutor and, Hephaestion in tow, rushed over to greet Cophen. Memnon stood off to one side as the pair exchanged pleasantries, watching the tutor, this Aristotle, as he took Cophen's measure, looking the boy up and down as though assessing a slave on the block. No doubt the sophist knew well how to discern Persian blood—and Cophen's heritage was evident in his features. A look of disdain crossed Aristotle's face; as he turned away, his eyes flickered briefly over Memnon. In less time than it takes a heart to beat, the Rhodian sensed he'd been catalogued and pigeonholed as a Median sympathizer, and thus beneath the philosopher's contempt. Memnon dismissed Aristotle with equal ease.

Aristotle finished his turn, spotted the eunuch hovering over a rose bush. He smiled and raised a ring-heavy hand in greeting, his manner at once cordial. *Who is this eunuch? A diplomat, perhaps; or an intermediary between the philosopher and Philip?*

Alexander's voice brought Memnon out of himself. "You must spend a few days here, Cophen!"

"Alas!" Cophen replied. "We cannot. A ship awaits our return to Pella. Father has been recalled to Persia, to be reinstated with full honors. My uncle and I have come to pay our respects to you, as my guest-friend, and to say farewell." Cophen extended his hand.

The gesture touched Alexander, Memnon could plainly see, and he grasped the proffered hand, pulling Cophen into an embrace. "I am pleased for your father," Alexander said, with gravity beyond his years. "Macedonia will always be a place of refuge for you, my friend, should you ever need it."

"As my home will be for you," Cophen said. Smiling, Alexander released him from his embrace and turned to Memnon. The Rhodian inclined his head to the Prince.

"Parmenion is losing his best officer," Alexander said. "Are you sure we can't convince you, at least, to stay, Memnon?"

"You flatter me, Alexander. As much as I would like to remain, the needs of my family are paramount. Besides, where would Artabazus be without me to shepherd his sons to manhood?"

"Do you have time, at least, to see the Sanctuary of the Nymphs?" Alexander said, turning suddenly back to Cophen. "It is a place of great mystery, and not far from here."

"Uncle?"

Memnon nodded. In an explosion of chatter, the younger boys swept Cophen off into the woods, following in Alexander's wake. The older three stayed put.

"Come, Philotas," Ptolemy said. "Let's ride down to the village."

"In a moment." Philotas approached Memnon. "How fares my father?"

"I left Parmenion on the verge of a great victory in Thrace," Memnon replied. "It pains me that I won't be there to take part in it."

Philotas beamed, pride for his father as evident as the sun's light on snow. "I knew he would conquer those blue-skinned *barbaroi*!"

"Are you sure he's victorious, Memnon? I had hoped Kersobleptes might send Parmenion packing," Ptolemy said, smiling. "If only to teach his son the meaning of humility."

Philotas laughed.

Behind them, though, Kassandros cursed and spat. "That's treason."

Ptolemy shook his head. He didn't bother turning to face Kassandros, but directed his words into the air, as if addressing a disembodied nuisance. "No, you dolt, it's a joke. But, I wouldn't expect you to get it since you have the sense of humor of a Spartan."

"Come," Philotas said, walking toward where Aristotle and his guest stood in deep conversation. "The air is cleaner on this end of the house."

Memnon followed them to the end of the portico. "Tell me, if you know, who is that fellow talking with your philosopher? If he's not a eunuch, I'm a Nubian. I swear he is familiar to me though I cannot place his name."

Philotas smiled. "Oh, he's a eunuch, all right. Demokedes of Assos, I think is his name, a guest-friend of Aristotle's and of his former patron, Hermeias."

"Hermeias?" Memnon frowned. "Hermeias was his former patron? But, I thought Aristotle came here from Athens?"

Philotas and Ptolemy exchanged glances. The son of Parmenion lowered his voice to a conspiratorial whisper. "He left Athens after Plato's death and settled in Assos, even marrying Hermeias's adopted daughter, Pythias, though Alexander says he spent much of his time near Mytilene, on Lesbos. I've heard it told that the philosopher was angry over not being made head of the Academy."

"He's sworn to finish what Plato started in Syracuse," Ptolemy added.

Memnon nodded. "Well, Athens's loss is Macedonia's gain, it would seem. Demokedes of Assos . . . I must remember his name." *And his relationship to Hermeias*, Memnon thought. *No doubt Mentor's going to take a keen interest in Assos, especially if its tyrant has become Philip's new Asian ally.* He watched Aristotle and the eunuch for a few moments more and then turned away. "This sanctuary Alexander spoke of, it is truly not far?"

It took Memnon the better part of the morning to gather up his nephew, but still they were on the road before the sun reached its zenith. Their horses were restive and in high spirits; as they cleared the foothills, with the Emathian Plain stretching out before them, Memnon gave them their head. Muscle and sinew surged. Miles flashed by beneath the Nisaeans' hooves. Hour piled upon hour until finally, after sunset, the pair reached the outskirts of Pella.

Lights blazed from the doors and windows of the villa. Memnon dismounted and held the reins as Cophen slid to the ground. The youth was exhausted, his face caked with dust and grime; he stared at the house as though it held his doom.

"Go," Memnon said. "I'll see to the horses." Cophen nodded, swallowed hard, and limped into the villa's courtyard. Leading the horses off, Memnon smiled as he heard one of the younger girls give a squeal of joy.

At the stables, the Rhodian kindled lamps and set about taking care of the horses. The ride had taxed even the Nisaeans' considerable endurance. Euphrosyne's head dipped as Memnon removed her sweat-drenched saddle-cloth, her bridle and headstall. Aglaia's came next. Thaleia, either curious or concerned, looked on as he washed and curried her sisters; she pawed the ground and snorted, doubtless expecting the same treatment.

Memnon turned slightly, hearing footsteps behind him.

"We have grooms for that," Artabazus said. He stood in the stable door, smiling. Young Ariobarzanes followed in his father's wake, balancing a tray with a dish of food, a wine jug, a pair of goblets, and a stone bowl of damp cloths. "Not a drop spilled. A fine lad; now set that down and run along." Artabazus watched the boy off before settling onto a bench by the stable door. "Come, sit. Take some wine with me."

Memnon left off currying the horses and sank down beside the old satrap. His body ached; his wet tunic clung to him, and he stank of sweat and horseflesh. The Rhodian selected a damp cloth, using it to wipe the dust from his face before attacking the food with gusto—grilled fish crusted with garlic and thyme, bread and oil, and a thick honey-cake. "I hope," he said around a mouthful of fish, "Cophen's punishment is not too extreme. I gave him a harrowing on the road he won't soon forget."

"So he told me," Artabazus said, stroking his white beard.

Memnon glanced sidelong at him. "You know I would never actually hurt the boy?"

"Of course not. No, this whole escapade has left me wondering if I am too lax with my other sons. Pharnabazus I kept on a close leash, overseeing his education, his training at arms. But Cophen, Ariobarzanes, even Hydarnes

. . . perhaps I am too old to do justice to their upbringing."

"Too old?" Memnon said. "Never. Perhaps it is simply their Greek blood that makes them headstrong and cantankerous. Truly, were Mentor and I any different?"

Artabazus chuckled. "No, not really."

Memnon polished off the food in silence, then leaned back, stretched his legs, and enjoyed a goblet of wine. He sniffed it, smelling a familiar bouquet. "Thasian."

"None better."

"Everything's set, then? We leave tomorrow?"

"Your man, Laertes, has assured me of favorable weather," Artabazus said. "Pharnabazus has all our possessions loaded, save for the contents of a small wagon. He has also contracted a slower galley to bring the horses over next week or week after. We have made our farewells, offered our sacrifices, and cast our omens. At dawn, we again become Persians."

Memnon sipped his wine. "Will you miss it here?"

Artabazus sighed. "I have asked myself the very same question. I have dwelt here for nigh on ten years but it has never been a home to me, not like Dascylium. With Philip's blessing we have striven to make our surroundings comfortable, even pleasing to the eye, but these touches of Lydia and Phrygia are a mockery of our homeland's beauty. The soil of Macedonia, I've found, is too thin to support the roots of a Pharnacid family tree. Perhaps my children would have been content to live here, but I cannot be content for them. The world is more than Macedonia, more than Greece, and they should experience it in its full glory.

"So should you, Memnon." Artabazus slipped his arm in the Rhodian's and pulled him close, like a man in possession of secret knowledge. "You have served our causes—mine and Mentor's—for much of your adult life and never have I heard a cross word from you."

"You weren't listening," Memnon said, a mischievous gleam in his eye.

Artabazus smiled. "Surely, this is not the pinnacle of your ambitions?"

Memnon's brow furrowed as he stared out through the stable doors, contemplating the fireflies and trying to read their movements as an oracle reads the stars. "When I was younger," he began, "I wanted glory, nothing more. I wanted my name to be sung by poets for a thousand years. But I grew older and, as is the way of things, my desires changed. I became enamored of honor—earned through deeds and words—and the respect it engendered. I admit the quest for each still moves me in its own way, nor shall I ever be wholly rid of their attraction, but a new desire consumes me." He paused, hunching forward with his elbows on his knees. Wine swished as he stirred the lees in his goblet. "Now, I want a place like this, in country of my own choosing, and the wife and family that needs must go with it. A stone house with fretted screens, Artabazus, built on a flat plain by the sea where I can breed horses and still answer Poseidon's call. In the Troad, perhaps, under the shadow of Mount Ida. And with it, a wife who embodies Aphrodite and Athena, who will give me children as bold and bright as infant Hermes." Memnon sighed; slowly, he poured the last of his wine into the sawdust at his feet and stood. "That is the pinnacle of my ambitions."

"An admirable picture you paint," Artabazus said, rising. He caught Memnon by the forearm. "You know, if Barsine had a full sister . . ."

"I know." Memnon exhaled and stared at the stables around them. "I'll leave the rest to the grooms. Come, my old friend, the sun will be rising before we know it."

"Indeed," Artabazus murmured, a slow, satisfied smile spreading across his features. "And when it does we become Persian once again."

THE SUN DID INDEED RISE EARLIER THAN MEMNON WOULD HAVE LIKED, though he chivvied himself out of bed regardless and gathered up the last of his belongings, shoving them into a battered rucksack which Khafre tossed atop the wagon.

"Farewell, Pella," the Egyptian muttered, with not inconsiderable glee, as he clambered up onto the drivers seat and took the traces.

From the villa Pharnabazus herded family members out to the wagon; he allowed no laggards—each child carried their own possessions and stood by like soldiers awaiting a general's inspection. And indeed they were . . . their mother. Deidamia, no longer the frail creature Memnon remembered from days past, swept from the house in a swirl of embroidered fabric and issued orders, not in Greek but rather Persian; the children answered her in the same tongue. Cophen escorted Barsine to the wagon; Pharnabazus passed the smaller children up to his brother. Soon, all were loaded.

Artabazus, leaning his weight on a silver-shod walking stick, left the villa last, making a show of pulling the door shut in his wake. He wore a Median style robe of green brocade, trousers and doeskin boots. Of silver, too, were the accents decorating the sheathed saber at his hip.

Beside him, in a plain blue *chiton*, Memnon felt shabby. "Still time to change your mind," he said.

The old satrap's eyes twinkled. "Home is waiting."

By the time they reached the harbor and loaded the last of their things into *Eurydike*'s hold, the sun stood high in the eastern sky. At a nod from Artabazus, Laertes ordered his men to cast off. Oarsmen backed water while sailors with longboat poles punted them away from the quay. Water slapped the hull; the ship shuddered as the breeze plucked at the reefed canvas of the sail. In the waist, the *auletes* piped a tune, keeping time for the rowers.

The family clustered in the bow, the younger children yipping in glee as a flock of plovers whirled and dashed over the surface of Lake Loudias. Artabazus stood with his arm around Deidamia's waist. Though he couldn't be certain of it, Memnon swore there was a glow about his sister that heralded new life. *Is she with child again?* Surely Barsine would know . . .

Barsine, though, stood in the stern, alone, watching Pella slip away. Memnon drifted to her side. He could feel her sadness as easily as he felt the wind on his face.

"It looks so small and mean from here," she said, tugging her shawl close around her shoulders. "How can it contain so many memories?"

"I know what troubles you," Memnon said. "Mentor is a good man, Barsine, and far more intelligent than he likes to admit. He, too, will enjoy your company, as I do. Imagine the three of us sitting under a massive shade tree in the gardens at Sardis, debating the merits of Herodotus. Imagine the children you will have. I promise you, it's not a death sentence you go to!"

Barsine sighed. "I had a dream last night," she said. "I stood on a promontory overlooking a harbor, its waters flat and lifeless. A ship was hauled up on the strand below. Mentor stood in the bow as his men scoured the beach. I heard them calling my name, faint, like a greater distance divided us, but I had no voice to respond, nor could I divine a way down to join them. I grew frantic as they shrugged their shoulders and set about launching the ship. In despair, I tried to hurl myself over the cliff's edge but even that was denied me—each time, a titanic wind gusted to catch my falling body and return me, light as a feather, to the same spot. I watched them sail away. With each stroke of the oars, Mentor's face grew more gaunt and strained. Finally, as the ship slipped over the rim of the world, the face staring back at me was no longer a face at all, but a bleached skull." Tears filled her eyes. Shivering, she turned to face Memnon, her hand twining with his. "If what you say is true and it's not a death sentence I go to," she whispered, "why does it feel like one?"

Memnon, though, had no answer for her. They stood side by side, hand in hand, watching as Pella dwindled and each stroke of the oars brought Sardis closer . . .

Interlude III

Melpomene's fists knotted in her woolen coverlet; she sobbed, a great wracking exhalation that left her thin body bereft of air. Tears streamed down her cheeks as she fought for each breath, loosening one hand so she might clutch at the silver chest, which Harmouthes had taken to leaving beside her. Again, Ariston witnessed its wonderful curative powers. Touching it calmed her. She closed her eyes and each subsequent breath came just a little easier.

"No more today," she whispered, raw-voiced. "No more."

"As you wish, Lady," Ariston said, rising. "Shall I send your man to you?"

She shook her head, struggling onto her side and curling around the silver chest. Ariston crossed to the hearth and stoked the coals, adding a couple of chunks of wood against the growing chill. Satisfied she would stay warm, the young Rhodian rose and let himself out.

Outside, winter's brief twilight enveloped the world in shadow. In the columned peristyle, Ariston paused and stared up at the star-strewn heavens, seeking answers to the one question spinning in his mind: who is she? *A daughter of Artabazus, by her own admission, who was taken prisoner with Darius's family after the Macedonian victory at Issus . . . would Nicanor know her name?* What little he knew of the one-legged veteran did not foster confidence. The man had been a common ranker in the phalanx battalions, one of the *Pezhetairoi*, not a position to afford a man easy access to the high circles of command. Still, Nicanor represented his best—indeed, his only—hope of identifying his elusive patroness. Nor would he put it off. He would seek out the old Macedonian tonight.

Across the peristyle, Ariston could see light spilling out from beneath the kitchen door. The faint strains of Harmouthes' flute came from within, a slow and mournful tune pitched so low that the young Rhodian had difficulty hearing it. Curious, he eased the door open. Firelight cast the Egyptian's bent frame in silhouette, his head bowed. He wore Median trousers and a heavy, sleeved tunic of fine wool, dyed a deep blue; still, he shivered as his fingers transformed shallow breaths of air into the haunting chords that brought his song to its sad conclusion. Slowly, Harmouthes lowered his flute.

"A beautiful piece," Ariston said, after a moment. "Has it a name?"

At first, the old man gave no indication he had heard, or that he registered Ariston's presence. When he did finally look up, the creases around his eyes were moist with tears. "It is called 'The Lamentations of Isis'."

"It's . . . I've never heard anything like it."

"It is very old." Harmouthes put his flute aside as he roused himself and tried to shake off his melancholy. "Sit, and I shall make you a bite of supper."

"No, that's not necessary," Ariston replied. "I have business I must attend to this evening. I'll be back before the Lady wakes."

"Business," he repeated. "Yes, of course."

From inside his tunic, Harmouthes withdrew a small leather bag that lightly clinked as he handed it to the young Rhodian. Frowning, Ariston tugged the bag open and tapped its content into his palm. Silver. A dozen or so coins spilled out, Ephesian *tetradrachms*—four-*drachma* pieces stamped with symbols sacred to the Mother Goddess of Ephesus, the bee and the stag—

newly minted and gleaming. Ariston cast a sidelong glance at Harmouthes.

"A fair wage for the work you have thus far accomplished," the Egyptian explained. "Should you find yourself unable to return."

Ariston, though, kept only a pair of *tetras*; the rest he returned to Harmouthes. "Consider these a loan," the young Rhodian said, holding up the two coins. "And as I said, I *will* be back before the Lady wakes. Is there anything you need from the city?"

Harmouthes smiled. "Perhaps a fresh draft of manners?" He shook his head, tucking the pouch back into his tunic. "No, young sir. I have no needs, but my thanks for asking."

Ariston patted the old Egyptian on the shoulder as he moved past him and retrieved his cloak from where it lay, neatly folded atop a sealed *amphora*. Harmouthes settled on the bench and took up his flute once more.

"The Lamentations of Isis" followed Ariston into the night.

SOME HOURS LATER, SHIVERING FROM THE COLD, ARISTON PADDED DOWN A scarcely lit street bordering the harbor. The smells of damp wood and brine warred with those of pitch, cooking smoke, and human suffering. It was a neighborhood given over to veterans, bitter survivors of the savage struggle between the *Diadochi* as well as proud, silver-haired relics of Alexander's relentless ambitions. Laughter and song, screams and sobs, and the slaughterhouse music of iron on flesh emanated from alleys and doorways, making Ariston question the wisdom of seeking Nicanor at this hour. Still, he'd come too far to give up now.

The one-legged Macedonian lived in a cramped set of rooms three streets over from his stall, in a block dominated by the reeking piss-vats of a tanners' workshop. Ariston thanked the gods for the small favor of placing Nicanor's door at street level, facing the water, rather than amid the warren of crooked passages that comprised the heart of this particular block. The young Rhodian found his destination; knuckles scraped wood as he knocked on the poorly hung door. Boards creaked. A body moved. Impatient, Ariston knocked again.

"Hades take you!" he heard a bleary voice bellow in reply.

"Nicanor? Open up, if you please! It's Ariston!" More curses greeted him, but Ariston also heard the distinctive scrape and thump of Nicanor's cornel-wood crutch.

"What do you want, boy?" the Macedonian said, flinging his door open. Roused from sleep, the old soldier wore an ill-fitting robe, patched and threadbare, its rich embroidery long since plucked out. He leaned heavily on his crutch as he pawed at his eyes.

"I need to talk to you," Ariston said, "and I promise I'll make it worth your time." He tugged a sealed wine flask out from beneath his cloak. "It's Chian."

Nicanor snatched the flask and motioned Ariston inside with a jerk of his head. "Zeus! A man my age needs wine more than sleep anyway."

The air inside the old Macedonian's quarters was stifling and it stank of sweat and sour wine. A makeshift hearth of flat rocks supported a glowing brazier; near it stood a small table, cluttered with unwashed crockery, and a pair of chairs, one of cheap pine, the other of dark and exotic wood. Nicanor dragged himself to this one and sat heavily. He tore the seal off the flask with his teeth and rooted through the crockery for two clay cups. He poured a measure for Ariston and scooted it toward the other chair. For himself, he filled the cup to the brim.

Ariston sat while his eyes, watering from the brazier's smoke, adjusted to the gloom, allowing him to pick out the small reminders of forgotten triumphs littering the room. Nicanor's armor, his battle-scarred cuirass, greaves, and a Thracian-style helmet with an elaborate faceplate, sat in the corner gathering dust, cobwebs, and corrosion. The chair that creaked under the Macedonian's weight was of Egyptian cypress, stripped of all gilt and glitter, while the upper edge of the smoldering bronze brazier bore a soot-stained declaration:

To NICANOR, SON OF AMYNTAS, FOR BRAVERY

The old soldier noticed Ariston's interest. "Alexander gave me that," he said, "full of gold, after I lost my leg at the Hydaspes. Unfortunately, the King died and I pissed away the gold, but that thing still helps keep my stump warm on cold winter nights. What do you want, boy? I know you didn't come down here just to gander at my trophies."

"Actually, your trophies are a part of why I'm here," Ariston said. "You're the only Macedonian veteran I know, and I need to plumb the depths of your memory for a name, Nicanor. Do you recall a Persian satrap named Artabazus?"

"Aye. He entered Alexander's service in Hyrkania, after Darius died. Brought the last of the Greek mercenaries with him. Aye, I remember Artabazus."

"Excellent." The Rhodian saw a glimmer of hope. "He had a daughter—"

Nicanor gave a short bark of laughter. "The randy old goat had ten daughters."

"Was one of them captured with the baggage at Damascus, after Alexander's victory at Issus?"

Nicanor scratched his neck, his craggy brows drawn together in thought. "The whole gods-be-damned Persian court was captured after Issus, not just the baggage. That bugger, Darius, couldn't take a proper shit without omen-readers, water-carriers, towel-bearers, perfume-sprinklers, and a dozen fat eunuchs to wipe the royal arse."

"But what of the court women?" Ariston said.

"Oh, aye, they were there, too . . . Darius's wives and daughters. For the love of Zeus! The man dragged his gray-haired old mother with him on campaign! Expected his nobles to do the same. After the battle went against them, the men skinned out and left the ladies to our tender mercies. Hades' teeth! Those so-called lords of Asia should have thanked their heathen gods it was Alexander who led us and not Philip. The old King would have taken the best for himself and given the rest to us. Not Alexander. *He* let them alone and made sure we kept our grubby hands off them, too." Nicanor tossed back his wine and poured himself another. "There was one, though. She'd caught Alexander's eye years ago, I heard tell, when her family came to Philip's court seeking asylum."

"Could she have been a daughter of Artabazus?"

Nicanor cocked his head to one side, struggling to remember tiny details fogged by the passage of years. "You know, she *was* one of his girls. I had forgotten that. But she wasn't half-Greek like his other daughters. No, not her. She was all Persian, with hair of midnight silk and a body to shame a Melian Aphrodite. She didn't speak that heathen jibber-jabber, either. Her Greek was flawless, better even than Alexander's. Buggering Zeus!" Nicanor rapped his knuckles against his skull. "What was she called?"

Ariston rocked back in his seat. Could the answer have been plainer, more evident? *A daughter of Artabazus,* he thought, *and an intimate of both Memnon and Alexander!* "It's her," he said, his voice an incredulous whisper. "Barsine."

"Aye, that was her name." Nicanor gave a wet, wine-laced sigh. "You know, she might have been just his concubine, but that woman would have made a better queen than the Sogdian whore he married, that's for certain. I had a tent-mate back then who was sweet on one of the Royal Pages—a chatty lad from Emathia, but a bitch in heat once you got a little wine in him—anyway, he told us that even Hephaestion was fond of Lady Barsine, and that bastard was never one to willingly share Alexander's affections." The old Macedonian drained his cup.

"What became of her?"

Nicanor hiccupped and poured himself another. "Alexander sent her home before he crossed the Indian Caucasus, if memory serves. Last I heard she'd settled in Pergamum with a son she claimed was Alexander's rightful heir. Admiral Nearchus was the only one who believed her, but he was more of a wine-sot than I am." He hiccupped again. "What's got you so curious, boy?"

Ariston shrugged and forced a lopsided smile. "Where the Muses lead, the artist can only follow."

Nicanor chuckled and hoisted his cup. "To the Muses."

"To Melpomene," Ariston replied.

ARISTON RETURNED TO *THE OAKS* IN THE GRAY LIGHT OF DAWN, HIS PURSE depleted and his hair damp from a last-minute detour to the *balaneion*. There, in a terracotta tub filled with warm water, the young Rhodian had scrubbed the stench of the harbor district from his body while one of the bath-man's slaves cleaned his sandals. As he soaked, in the back of his mind he chided himself for not accepting more of Harmouthes' silver. If he had, perhaps he could have done something about his ragged cloak and his faded saffron *chiton. One should not approach the great-granddaughter of a Persian king looking like a vagabond.* Still, he reckoned they would do for now.

He left the *balaneion* and hurried back to the estate, slipping quietly through the door and entering the peristyle. He could hear Harmouthes moving about in the kitchen. Ariston padded down the hall to the Lady's room, gave a brief knock, and let himself in.

She sat in a chair by the hearth, a bundle of cloth in her lap. Outside, light strengthened, though the sun itself stayed wreathed in clouds. At the sound of the door closing, the Lady glanced up from her contemplation of the flames and gave Ariston a weak smile.

"You are early," she said. "I take it your business in Ephesus went smoothly?"

"It did." Ariston came to stand by her chair. "Did you sleep well, Lady?"

Her eyes strayed back down to the cloth in her lap. It was a scarf of some kind, Ariston could see, made from a diaphanous weave of linen, edged in silk and sewn with seed pearls. "I no longer sleep well," she said. "But I slept, yes."

"Madame," he said, his voice trembling with barely suppressed excitement. "It is time we were properly introduced. I am Ariston of Lindos and I am pleased to make your acquaintance, Lady Barsine." He bowed low.

A slow smile crept across her face. She inclined her head, accepting his identification of her. "Memnon always said the men of Rhodes were the shrewdest of Hellenes. Perhaps he was right." Her smile faded. "Sadly, you are only partially correct. I was Barsine, yes, but no longer. Barsine died at Pergamum, poisoned after Herakles," her voice caught in her throat, "after her son by Alexander was executed on the orders of Kassandros. Barsine is a restless spirit in an unmarked grave. I am Melpomene."

Ariston nodded. "The tragic Muse."

"I am glad we understand one another. So, now that you know my secret, what will you do with it?"

"Do?" The young Rhodian frowned.

"I daresay Kassandros would pay well to learn how his murderous henchmen lied to him about my death," she said. A round of wracking coughs reduced her to breathlessness.

"I'm no partisan of Kassandros's," Ariston said, taking a seat opposite Barsine. "Though, if you fear further retribution from him, why not seek asylum inland with Antigonos, or at Alexandria with Ptolemy?"

"To what end?" she croaked. "I have no political currency with any of the *Diadochi*, and they owe me no favors. Why should they trouble themselves over my plight?"

"If for no other reason than to honor Alexander, who held you in esteem."

Barsine made a dismissive sound. "None of them came to Olympias's aid and she was his mother. No, my young friend, such nobility rightly belongs in the sphere of imagination—or in the past. I fear neither Kassandros nor his followers," she said. "So in Ephesus I will remain, though not, my heart tells me, for much longer."

Ariston reached out and took her hand. It seemed so pale, so fragile, and he held it as one might a statuette carved of delicate alabaster. "Then," he said, "it would be my honor to remain with you, for so long as you require my services."

"The honor will be mine," she said, giving his hand a squeeze. Her eyes returned to the scarf in her lap.

"It's beautiful," Ariston said. "A shawl?"

"A veil," Barsine replied. "I wore this the day I married Mentor . . ."

The Troad
Year 3 of the 109th Olympiad
(342 BCE)

THE CITADEL OF SARDIS STOOD ATOP A PRECIPICE, A SPUR OF MOUNT Tmolus that dominated the fertile valley of the Hermus River. Behind triple walls of dark stone and russet mudbrick, palace gardens once belonging to Lydia's last native king, the ill-fated Croesus, were awash in the glow of gold and silver lamps. Carved cedar poles upheld awnings of purple linen, their electrum-crusted tassels faceted to reflect a thousand points of light. Incense and perfume drifted through the cool evening air.

At the center of the garden, beneath a canopy of silk and gold, the Great King of Persia and Media, the King of Kings, His Magnificence Artaxerxes III, called Ochus, held court, surrounded by the lords of Asia and their retinues. From a distance, Memnon eyed with great interest this stranger whom, until recently, had been his sworn enemy, a demigod of his imagination. In person, the Great King was far less impressive. In his sixtieth year or more, if Memnon's eunuch servant could be trusted, Ochus was a paunchy man of average height with a sallow face and a weak chin not even his curled, dye-black beard could hide. His eyes, alone, betrayed his storied viciousness—they were pale, never still, and caught the light of the Magi's sacred flame like razored knife-points.

Crowned in gold and lapis lazuli, clad in richly embroidered robes of Tyrian purple, His Majesty sat stiff-backed, his throne and footstool arrayed upon a high dais of polished porphyry. Four lesser seats rested on the lowest level of the dais; three were occupied. To the Great King's left sat a pair of lords, one robed in crimson, the other in aquamarine. Memnon knew the man in the crimson robes as their host, Spithridates, satrap of Lydia—a saturnine Iranian with a pockmarked face and thin, humorless lips. Spithridates regarded his companion with barely disguised contempt, and with good reason. The man in the aquamarine robes was no man at all, but a beardless, soft-bellied eunuch.

"That is Bagoas," one of the other guests had said, answering Memnon's question as to the dark-haired eunuch's identity. Bagoas ignored Spithridates; the eunuch laughed gaily, muttering something to the Great King that elicited a grin from the monarch. Ochus turned to listen as whatever Bagoas had said was refuted, without rancor, by the man who sat alone on his right-hand side—a man Memnon hardly recognized as his own brother.

Egypt, despite being the land of his celebrated triumphs, had not been kind to Mentor. His face had grown lean, seamed by the desert wind, bronzed by the relentless sun, and scarred by war. He had only a fringe of hair remaining; like his well-trimmed beard it was more salt than pepper. Though clad in Persian-style robes of white and gold brocade befitting a man of his elevated rank, Memnon could tell his brother had lost much of his bulk. *Victorious*, the younger Rhodian thought, *but at what price?*

The final chair, the one beside Mentor, was empty. It would be for his bride. That the Great King chose to remain in Sardis to preside over Mentor's wedding was a mark of great favor. A lion's share of the guests, who numbered close to a thousand, saw nothing amiss in the idea of a princess of the royal house being given in marriage to a Hellene (Barsine's grandmother had been Ochus's eldest sister); they took it in stride and celebrated with unfeigned happiness. A handful, though—among them Spithridates and his brother Rhosaces, satrap of Ionia—viewed the marriage as one of the many mortal insults they'd been forced to endure of late, with the greatest being the elevations of a eunuch and a foreigner into positions of power surpassing even their own. Memnon wondered how long they would bear it, and who would the brothers recruit into their ranks? Arsites of Hellespontine Phrygia, perhaps? What's more, he wondered if Mentor knew of their enmity—

A tug on his sleeve ended the Rhodian's contemplation. He turned to find Khafre standing beside him. The Egyptian wore the traditional dress of his homeland, all swirling linen and heavy gold, with thick cosmetics outlining his eyes. "The Lady would speak to you before the ceremony begins," Khafre said.

"We must be quick about it, then," Memnon said. "The priests will be ready to offer their libations, soon." He gestured toward the altar where a trio of Magi tended the sacred flame of Ahuramazda.

Khafre nodded and retraced his steps. The Rhodian followed him through the garden. Unlike his brother, Memnon decided against Persian raiment—he wore a short white *chiton* hemmed in blue under a silver-chased bronze muscled cuirass, the whole covered by a cobalt-blue cloak, a *khlamys*, embroidered with silver thread.

Khafre led him, as swiftly as the crowd of guests allowed, up a narrow flight of stairs and through a side entrance into the palace. They crossed the many-columned hall known as the Apadana, where by day the satrap would hold his audiences and by night his banquets, and entered a busy side chamber set aside for the bride's family to receive well-wishers prior to the ceremony. Beyond it were a suite of private apartments generally reserved for official visitors to the satrap's court.

Memnon spotted Artabazus, his white hair and beard curled in the current fashion, looking flushed and proud. Soon, flanked by his sons, he would escort Barsine into the King's presence and present her to the bridegroom. The Rhodian smiled and dipped his head in greeting as he and

Khafre passed without comment into the rooms beyond.

Deidamia, swathed in black from crown to foot in emulation of Hades-bound Persephone, met them at the door. She was in a towering rage, her nostrils flaring. "She's intractable! Refuses to come out until she's had a chance to speak with you! With you! Blessed Hera! Has she no sense of propriety? Have you?" Deidamia gestured to the heavens.

Memnon caught her flailing hands. "Lower your voice," he said, cognizant of the noblemen collected in the outer room. "Barsine and I are friends, Deidamia, and friends we will remain, propriety be damned. What's more, I am her uncle and soon to be her brother-in-law. Why should she not wish a few words with me, or I with her?"

"It's not the proper way of things!" she hissed.

"Things change. Go," he said in a tone that brooked no refusal, "take a moment's rest and gather yourself. I will bring her out." Memnon crossed the small antechamber with its tasteful rugs and wall hangings; he ignored the audience of perfumers, hairdressers, and bridesmaids as he scratched once at the inner door, then let himself in.

The room Barsine occupied opened onto a broad balcony that faced west. A russet band of light washed over the dark ridges of the Tmolus range, striking fire from the twisted marble columns. In her white gown, her hair exquisitely braided and held in place with combs of enameled silver, the daughter of Artabazus could have been a creature of divine fire, wreathed as she was in sun's dying light. She stood with her back to the door, turning at the sound of Memnon's approach.

The Rhodian's breath caught in his throat. "By the Goddess!" he said. "I have been too harsh in my past judgments of Priam's son. Were you betrothed to anyone but my brother I would cast aside these bonds of hospitality and steal you away, as Paris stole Helen."

Barsine blushed. "And I would go, willingly, were I betrothed to anyone but your brother. I am glad Khafre found you."

"Is something wrong?"

Her brows drew together. "Flagging nerves, but there is nothing for it." She peered over the balustrade, contemplating the sheer drop. The valley floor was lost to shadows; the onset of night obscured a river whose rocky torrents they could hear even at this height, no doubt a tributary of the wide Hermus. "Does that stream have a name?"

Memnon came abreast of her and leaned out over the railing. "That's the Pactolus."

"Midas's river of gold?"

"The same," he said, straightening. "And the source of Croesus's wealth. It was said in those days that a poor man could ford the Pactolus from bank to muddy bank and when he emerged he would be wealthy from the gold dust stuck between his toes."

"And now?"

"Now, should a poor man wade the river he will emerge in dire straits, for not only will he still be poor," he said, "but he will be soaked, as well."

A ghost of a smile lit Barsine's face. "Did you or Herodotus make that story up?"

Memnon shrugged. "Don't dismiss it out of hand. Croesus *was* fabulously wealthy."

"And unhappy," she said, her smile fading. "Tragically unhappy." Barsine sighed. Her gaze moved from the benighted valley to the ridge to the scarlet-stained sky. "I wish we were back in Pella, Memnon. Just to sit in the garden again, listening to the crickets and the cicadas, watching the fireflies dance through the birch boughs, would be worth a thousand of Croesus's fortunes." She bowed her head; her voice dropped to a whisper. "Is it nearly time?"

Memnon felt a pang of sorrow for her. "The Magi were making ready to offer their libations when Khafre found me," he said. Memnon stepped closer, draping his arm around her shoulder. She welcomed the warmth of his embrace. "I cannot imagine what this must be like for you. A woman's duty to surrender freedom for the benefit of family requires greater courage than most men can comprehend. But, you've nothing to fear. Mentor's not going to make you a prisoner of the harem any more than your father has made Deidamia. My brother's too wise for that."

"Even wise men are shackled by tradition," Barsine said, tears sparkling on her lashes. She dabbed at her eyes. "Look at me. Crying again. You must be growing weary of my constant need for reassurance."

Memnon smiled. Gently, he reached out and wiped away her tears. "Yes, you are a horrible burden," he said with a wink.

"Barbarian." She rapped her knuckles against his bronze-sheathed chest.

"I would be a poor friend, and a wretched kinsman, if I couldn't offer you some manner of comfort," Memnon said, his forehead creasing. "But I will be glad when this spectacle draws to a close. That way, once the dust settles, you will be able to see for yourself that life in Sardis, as Mentor's wife, isn't going to be the nightmarish prospect you imagine."

In the distance, both heard the chortle of silver trumpets. It was the signal for the bridal procession to begin. Barsine sighed, nodding. "You should go. Mentor is going to be wondering where you wandered off to." She embraced him one last time. "Thank you, Memnon, for everything," she whispered, then released him and motioned him to the door. She bustled about the room in last-minute preparation.

Memnon paused on the threshold, looked back. Poise and grace returned as Barsine retrieved her pearl-sewn veil from a divan and settled it over her hair. A sad smile flickered across the Rhodian's visage. "Barsine." She glanced up at the sound of her name. "Mentor is luckier than any man has a right to be," he said. "You are a daughter of kings, and may Zeus protect him if he does not treat you as such." Nodding, Memnon turned and vanished out the door.

THE CEREMONY WAS A WHIRLWIND OF POMP AND SPLENDOR. TRUMPETERS plied their instruments, filling the air with the silvery skirl of horns as the bride, escorted by her family, made her entrance. She descended into the garden by way of a monumental staircase, decorated with carved figures from Lydia's long and storied past. Flower girls scattered a carpet of rose petals for Barsine to walk on, while incense bearers sweetened the air with their censers. The procession wound through the garden; in its wake, men bobbed their heads together as they remarked on the elegant beauty of this daughter of Artabazus.

Memnon took his place at the head of the bridegroom's family, as his nearest living relative. He did not stand alone, though. Mentor had summoned their kinsmen from across the Aegean. A dozen cousins—men he barely knew—flanked him, including Aristonymus, ruler of Methymna on Lesbos; Simmias of Ephesus, a relation of their mother's; and sullen-eyed Thymondas, a Rhodian mercenary captain who Memnon suspected of being Mentor's bastard.

Mentor himself stood at the base of the dais, transfixed by the sight of white-veiled Barsine drifting through the crowd; on the periphery of his vision, Memnon saw the Great King hunch forward on his throne, licking his lips, a lecherous gleam in his eye. The Rhodian dug his nails into his palms, squelching the urge to leap up on the dais and throttle the dissolute little toad.

The wedding party stopped at the proscribed distance and made their obeisance to the King before two Magi guided them up to stand opposite of Mentor. Barsine stepped forward. Memnon, alone, could discern her nervousness; to the rest, she exuded a haunting sense of calm as the Magi, attended by slaves bearing lustral vases, purified bride and bridegroom with wands of myrtle and chanted prayers.

The two priests concluded their rituals and withdrew. The third Magus, ancient and bent, shuffled up, leaned on his staff, and raised a leathery hand in benediction. The voice that issued from his shriveled breast, however, still contained strength. "Who speaks for this bridegroom, Mentor, son of Timocrates?"

Memnon stepped forward. His chest tightened as he answered. "I do. I am Memnon, son of Timocrates, his brother."

The old Magus continued. "Who speaks for this bride, Barsine, daughter of Artabazus?"

"I do," Artabazus replied. "I am Artabazus, son of Pharnabazus, her father."

"In the presence of this assembly," the old priest said, his hawkish face shifting to stare at Memnon, "that has met together in Sardis on the twentieth day of Tashritu, in the Seventeenth Year of His Majesty's Accession, say whether you have agreed to accept this maiden, Barsine, daughter of Artabazus, in marriage for this bridegroom, in accordance with the will of blessed Ahuramazda and the laws of our Reverend and Exalted Majesty."

She is his prize, his spoil of war. "I have agreed," Memnon said, clamping his jaw shut.

The Magus fixed Artabazus with his rheumy gaze. "Have you and your family, with righteous mind and truthful thoughts, words, and deeds, agreed to give, forever, this bride in marriage to Mentor, son of Timocrates?"

Artabazus, his eyes moist, nodded. "I have agreed."

Hobbling forward, the old Magus reached out, grasped Barsine's hand, and placed it in Mentor's scarred fist. "Then I say these words to you, bride and bridegroom! Impress them upon your minds: May you two enjoy a life of goodness by following the will of blessed Ahuramazda and the laws of our Reverend and Exalted Majesty. May each of you clothe the other in righteousness. Then assuredly there will be a happy life for you." The old priest bowed to the Great King.

Ochus stood and descended from his dais. He placed his hand on theirs. "May the merciful God bless your union and keep you long happy, long healthy, and long fertile. Rejoice!" With that, the crowd of guests erupted. Horns blasted a triumphal song, competing with applause and shouts of health, virility, or long life. Both families surged together, Persian mingling with Greek; Artabazus embraced his daughter and her new husband, and thanked the King for his blessing.

"Had I known your garden hid such exquisite beauty, my old friend," Ochus replied, clapping Artabazus on the back, "I would have pardoned you long ago!" The King's eye lingered on Barsine as his courtiers coaxed him away.

With gracious ease, Memnon chatted with the swirling tide of well-wishers, allowing their flux and flow to draw him from the bridal couple. Over their heads, he spotted Barsine as she glanced about for him; Mentor, too—no doubt craving a word with his brother before retiring to the nuptial chamber. Memnon, though, let the crowd force him to the periphery of the celebration.

Here, Khafre found him, standing beneath the spreading boughs of an immense plane tree, watching as Mentor escorted his bride back up the processional staircase. Khafre leaned against the tree bole.

"That could not have been easy," he said.

"What do you mean?"

The Egyptian edged closer. "I know of few men who could have given their heart's desire to another and still maintained their poise. I cannot imagine the effort it required."

"Don't be absurd," Memnon said. He scuffed at a tree root with his sandaled foot. "She's my brother's wife."

"And so?" Khafre smiled and shook his head. "You have forgotten a lesson from years ago. Though a slave no longer, I yet possess eyes and ears. If they are kept open and the mouth shut . . ."

"Wondrous things may be learned," Memnon said, closing his eyes. "A plague on sharp-eyed Egyptians, who are the most cunning of men. Who else knows? Has my perfidy become fodder for the rumormongers and the fools?"

"I may be sharp-eyed," Khafre said, bristling, "but I am no tittle-tattle. Knowledge of your plight goes no further than from me to you."

Memnon sighed. "Forgive me, Khafre. I didn't mean to impugn your discretion. How did you discover . . . ?"

"I know my friends, and I know when my friends are in agony. What can I do?"

"There's nothing for it," Memnon said, shrugging. "But, you can drink with me. Drink with me until there is no more wine left in Sardis." The Rhodian motioned for one of the servants to bring them a jug. "I want this evening to be a blurred memory."

IT WASN'T THE MORNING SUN FILTERING THROUGH THE LEAVES OF THE plane tree that woke Memnon, nor the ripping snores of his fellow revelers. It was the none-too-gentle prodding of a sandaled foot in his ribs. He pried his eyes open and cursed as he rolled from his belly onto his back, his limbs stiff and unresponsive.

Mentor stood above him. "Rise, brother," the elder Rhodian said. He wore a plain soldier's kilt under an open black robe, his silver-furred chest bare.

"What goes?" Memnon croaked. He hawked and spat, clearing his throat.

"Come, get up. We need to talk."

Memnon struggled into a sitting position. His breastplate was gone and his tunic clung to him, still damp from some foolish escapade involving serving girls and the garden fountain. Memnon recalled nothing with clarity. Around him, some of the other revelers stirred. He knew a few of the faces; most, Memnon could not place. Amid the roots of the plane tree, Khafre cursed the sun's rays in his native Egyptian; Aristonymus, draped across one of the few divans they were able to procure, belched and swatted at a fly that bedeviled his ear. Pharnabazus lay wrapped in the embrace of two serving girls, while Thymondas sat with his back to the garden wall, his head tilted forward with his chin resting on his breast. He muttered drill commands in his sleep.

"You arranged quite a *symposium* last night," Mentor said, glancing at the sprawling bodies. "Though I doubt Spithridates approved of you corrupting his house girls or using his azalea bed for a piss bucket. A pity I had to miss out on the merriment."

Memnon experienced a flash of alarm. "Where's Barsine?"

"She's already up and about," Mentor said. "Good cousin Simmias offered to escort her, Deidamia, and the children down into the markets so they could experience the wonders of Sardis firsthand. I sent a pair of guards along, to be safe." An odd expression crossed Mentor's face. "She is . . . unlike other women I've known."

"You mean educated?"

Mentor grinned, reached down and hauled his brother to his feet. "I see exile didn't cure you of your sharp tongue. Perhaps a task will prove more therapeutic."

Memnon steadied himself on his brother's shoulder; he staggered over to the fountain, knelt on the curb, and splashed handfuls of water in his face. "What task?"

Mentor shook his head, indicating the men scattered about the garden. "Walk with me, brother." Memnon followed him to the garden wall. A flight of steps led to the parapet.

In the bright morning sun, the whole of the Hermus Valley stretched out below them. The upper slopes of Mount Tmolus were terraced with vineyards and orchards; its lower slopes with crooked streets and mudbrick houses. The Pactolus split Sardis in two, flowing through the heart of the agora and into the business district. Here, potters turned the river's red mud into the terracotta tiles Sardis was known for, and merchants arranged shipping overland or by water to the Ionian coast and the Aegean. Ironically, many of the potters' own houses had roofs of mud and thatch.

Memnon inhaled the pleasant north breeze. "Do you fear prying ears?" he said.

"One can never be too cautious," Mentor said. "The King's gone to Zeleia, to hunt, and he's taken most of the Persian lords with him. Artabazus, too. I'll have to leave out today to join them unless I want those parasites he calls satraps to defame my good works. The lot of them would argue how best to pour piss from a boot and not a one would think to look for instructions on the heel."

"I'm surprised a king with Ochus's reputation tolerates that sort of infighting," Memnon said.

"Tolerates it? That gold-shod jackass encourages it! He believes if his courtiers spend their days conspiring against one another, they'll be too busy to conspire against him. It was the same in the days of Artabazus's father, I'm told."

"Xenophon wrote a great deal concerning old Pharnabazus and the rivalries of the Persian satraps, though how accurate his portrayal is I cannot say. What about this task you mentioned?"

Mentor leaned against the battlements and peered out through an embrasure. "We're beset by our own Agesilaus, it seems. Philip's close to sewing up Thrace and then he'll move against the Chersonese. I wonder, will he content himself with the European shore?"

Memnon shook his head. "Why should he when he can have the Asian Greek lands, as well? He will cross the Hellespont, brother. Make no mistake. And he's no Agesilaus. He's not going to march here and there until he tires, or until we pay his enemies to have him brought home. Philip's coming for land, for gold and for blood."

"Then we must be prepared," Mentor said. "Cousin Aristonymus has pledged his city to our cause; to him I'm giving the task of subduing the rest of Lesbos. Thymondas I'm sending to Taenarum, in the Peloponnese, with enough gold to hire every disaffected Greek between there and Thermopylae."

Though likely his by-blow nephew, Memnon had not spent enough time in Thymondas's company to gauge his character. A dishonest man with that amount of bullion could wreck untold havoc on Mentor's plans. "You trust him?"

Mentor nodded. "I've also instructed him to get word to Patron at Syracuse. That Phocaean bastard's been out there diddling Carthaginian whores long enough. Time he came back and partook of some real work."

Memnon smoothed his beard; his eyes were fixed on something beyond the distant horizon as his mind worked through problems of logistics and supply. "You're going to need more than mercenaries if you hope to give Philip pause," he said.

"I've lobbied the King for permission to bring a fleet from Cyprus into the Aegean. So far, though, I've been blocked by Spithridates and Rhosaces—those meddlesome sons of bitches!" Mentor spat over the parapet, his darkened face screwed up in a rictus of disgust. "Zeus, protect me from their incompetence! They're the reason I need you up north, in the Troad. Cut out those little kinglets my fellow satraps have so graciously allowed to prosper, the ones most liable to side with Philip. That way, the Macedonian can't seize piecemeal what he could never hope to win as a whole. The Troad must be brought to heel!"

Memnon looked away north, his eyes narrowed to slits as a plan of action coalesced in his mind. "I know just where to start."

16

THE GALLEY PITCHED LIKE A DRUNKARD, ROLLING IN THE SWELLS OFF the northern tip of Lesbos. Methymna lay astern; across the straits, seven miles away, a gray veil of rain obscured Assos and the Asian shore. In the whistling wind, icy and sharp, the *auletes* dispensed with his flute and kept the oarsmen in rhythm by marking cadence on a hide drum. Memnon watched their exertions from the comparative shelter of the deckhouse.

Though the arrival of winter with its frequent storms and contrary winds beached most ships, the sailors of Methymna routinely made the short run to Assos and back—a journey of less than an hour in fair weather now trebled by a foul squall howling down from the north. "Thetis will guide us," the captain had said, blowing a kiss at an image of the sea goddess carved into his sternpost. Memnon prayed he was right. A mischance at sea would wreck his delicate plans . . .

"You've done it," Aristonymus said, brandishing a letter brought to Methymna by a fast courier ship. Memnon broke off his contemplation of a map he had made of the Troad and glanced up. "The eunuch has taken an interest in you. He sends his compliments and invites you to join him in Assos next month to celebrate the Lenaea."

Memnon stroked his bearded jaw. "He's taken the bait, to be sure, but what piques his interest more, I wonder? That I am a fellow devotee of philosophy or a former rebel and soldier?"

"Does it matter?" Aristonymus said, frowning. "You belabor this whole affair with your plots and your secrecy. Dionysus rules the Lenaea. The eunuch will conduct the god's worship from the theater. He'll be exposed, affable, and fuddled with drink. All you'd need is one courageous fool with a knife . . ."

"If control of Assos was my only concern, cousin, then perhaps you would be right. But, knifing the eunuch during a chorus of Lysistrata *won't win us Atarneus, Sigeum, Troy, Abydus, or the dozen other towns under his thumb. Murdering Hermeias will gain us nothing but civil discord and outright war—the very things Mentor wishes to avoid."*

Aristonymus grumbled. "It would be easier."

"The easy route," Memnon replied, "is not always the most prudent."

The Rhodian braced himself against the deckhouse door as the galley pitched forward, lunging into a trough between the swells. The seas washed over the bow, drenching the rowers. They redoubled their efforts; the captain's trust in the goddess seemed well placed when, as the ship crested the wave, Memnon observed the first glimmers of Assos through the mist.

Homer called it 'steep Pedasos,' though what man, Titan, or god carved a city out of the rocky crags overlooking the Bay of Adramyttium was unknown even in the Poet's day. Walled on three sides, its fourth guarded by the sea, Assos was a place of shelves and terraces, of narrow streets connected by stairs beyond number and public buildings of gleaming marble. At the pinnacle of its fortified acropolis, some thousand feet above the harbor, the temple of Athena Polias kept unending vigil.

Within the hour, Memnon's galley wallowed into the calmer waters of the mole-protected harbor. Triremes were drawn up on shore and protected for the winter by timber sheds; smaller craft rode out the weather on the water, moored to stone bollards lining the mole.

The Rhodian emerged from the deckhouse as the galley docked. Beneath a black wool cloak, heavily embroidered in gold thread, the Rhodian wore a *chiton* of similar material cinched by a thick leather belt. A sheath hung from his left hip, a long knife with a silver pommel. Memnon waited as two sailors wrestled the boarding plank into place. A third fetched the Rhodian's travel chest and deposited it on the mole.

"My thanks, Captain," Memnon said, glancing over his shoulder at the shipmaster standing atop the deckhouse.

The captain grinned. "I told you the goddess would watch over us." He turned and raised his hands to the carved sternpost. "Thrice-blessed mother of Achilles, gold-wreathed mistress of the Nereids . . ."

Memnon disembarked as the crew joined their captain's *paean* to Thetis.

Despite the weather a knot of men made their way down the mole to where Memnon stood. Some might have had business with the pious shipmaster, such as small cargoes from Lesbos to claim or letters to deposit for the return trip, but Memnon could tell that the fellow leading the group, a servant dogging his steps, was there for him. The man's cloak billowed out behind him, revealing the polished bronze breastplate and leather kilt of a soldier. He stopped at a respectful distance and raised a hand in greeting.

"You are the Rhodian called Memnon?"

"I am."

"Very good! I am Kritias, a captain of the *Basileus*'s Guard. My lord has instructed me to escort you to his palace." The officer motioned for his servant to take Memnon's chest. "Follow me, sir." He abruptly turned and marched back the way he had come, scattering those men who had been in his wake.

With courtesy, if not actual friendliness, Kritias led Memnon up from the harbor and through the lower slopes of Assos. Though years had passed since his last visit, a brief stop on his way north from Phoenicia to Macedonia, he could discern little in the way of change. Even in the throes of winter the city buzzed with life, like a beehive tipped on its side by a careless gardener. Citizens and foreign residents scurried on their errands, pausing at stair-heads and on street corners to share the latest news—from Philip's victory in Thrace to Athens's decision to dispatch its most popular general, Chares, to the aid of Diopeithes in the Chersonese. Memnon shook his head. *Chares.* With that fool in the region instances of piracy in the Aegean would soar but he expected little else would be done.

Memnon trailed Kritias across the agora—its crowded public spaces constructed on the Doric order rather than the Ionic—and up another flight of steps. Once atop this next terrace, the Rhodian paused and looked away to the west. An offshore wind ruffled his hair and cloak. From his vantage point, halfway up the hillside between the harbor and Athena's temple, Memnon could see down to the twin turrets of the Lekton Gate; beyond them, he caught sight of the necropolis, a monumental park thick with sculptures and *steles*—his father's among them.

Are you proud of us, Father? Are you proud of your sons?

Ahead of him, Kritias stopped and turned. "Sir? What is it you see?"

Memnon stirred at the sound of his voice. "A memory, nothing more," he said, motioning the captain to continue on to the palace.

In truth, Assos had no residential buildings deserving of the term 'palatial.' Most of the houses in its terraced neighborhoods were squat and unlovely, built of mudbrick and clay covered in thick lime stucco. Some had touches of color—yellow and red-striped awnings above the door or a window box overgrown with herbs—but the rest formed an indistinguishable warren with boundaries dictated by the demands of the landscape.

Hermeias's palace was only called such because its occupant styled himself a king; it lacked extravagance because he also styled himself a philosopher, molded in Plato's image. His palace sat at the center of the terrace, surrounded by offices of the court functionaries who governed the city in the king's absence. Save for a columned portico guarded by bronze-clad pikemen, it looked identical to every other block of houses.

"I must ask you to surrender your knife, sir," Kritias said as they neared the portico. Memnon did so willingly. "It will be kept safe and returned to you once you leave. My duty also requires that I search you for hidden weapons. I mean no disrespect. If you will permit me?" Again Memnon acquiesced; indeed, he expected no less. Despite his philosophical pretensions, Hermeias's rise to power involved the murder of his predecessor, Eubulus—a very anti-Platonic solution to the removal of a tyrant with Persian sympathies. Memnon held his arms away from his body as Kritias ran practiced hands up his flanks in search of hidden blades.

"Does Hermeias fear for his life?"

"Our *Basileus* is a cautious man," Kritias replied, "and no matter how benevolent the ruler, there are always those envious of his position and desperate enough to contemplate murder to achieve their ends. For my part, I would not want the example of the Athenian tyrannicide to be repeated in fair Assos."

Not again, you mean, Memnon thought.

Finding nothing amiss, the captain nodded and gestured for the door wardens to allow the Rhodian entry. Memnon was ushered into a stone-tiled vestibule, where a courteous slave took his cloak, and thence into a long, narrow room full of natural and artificial light. Shelves lined the walls, partitioned into niches holding countless scrolls. Clerks bustled between the shelves checking and double-checking scroll tags. Some they removed from their niches and carried to a table for a trio of scribes to fair-copy.

At the far end of the room, a dark-haired man sat behind a desk of polished wood, a crackling fire on the hearth behind him. He raised a sheet of parchment up to the light and read aloud in a clear voice: " 'Consider further what a disgrace it would be to allow Asia to be more successful than Europe, non-Greeks more prosperous than Greeks, to let the dynasty of Cyrus, a foundling, win the title of Great King, while that of Herakles, a son of Zeus, is given a humbler style. None of this can be permitted. It needs to be altered to the exact opposite'."

"I pray I am as eloquent in my dotage as Isocrates is in his," Memnon said by way of greeting, his face a smiling mask of politesse.

Hermeias, the Troad's eunuch king, glanced over the edge of the parchment, a twinkle in his eyes. "You recognize the piece from that small excerpt?"

"Isocrates' *Address to Philip*, of course," Memnon said. "The call of an old sophist for the unification of Hellas and the destruction of Persia. I read it years ago. A remarkable bit of writing."

"It is, indeed." Hermeias put the parchment aside. He stood and came out from behind his desk. "Ah, Memnon! It has been too long!" He embraced the Rhodian as though they were lifelong friends.

Gelded in his youth, it was plain Hermeias had mastered his appetites at an early age, avoiding the habit of other eunuchs who let a love of food replace the pleasures of the flesh. He kept himself trim, and thus had aged far more gracefully than other men, even those who shared his condition. Gray frosted his close-cropped black hair, and an old scar cut diagonally across his face, beginning above his left eye, crossing the bridge of his nose, and continuing down his right cheek—a sword cut gained in battle against the Carians, dispelling the myth that geldings lacked martial fire.

Nor did Hermeias's dress lean toward the kind of extravagance one might expect from a eunuch. He wore a simple Ionic *chiton*, cream-colored, stitched with a border of plain black thread. The signet ring on his right index finger was the only touch of gold on his person; its sardonyx seal bore the carved image of Athena, in her guise as the goddess of wisdom, with an owl perched on her upraised palm.

"I'm amazed you remembered me at all," Memnon said.

"Who could forget the youngest—and I daresay the brightest—of good Timocrates' sons?"

"You are too kind," Memnon replied, sloughing off the needless flattery couched in a lie. In the old days, Hermeias would not have known Memnon if the Rhodian passed him on the street. Mentor and Artabazus, alone, had dealings with the eunuch's former master, Eubulus, an Ephesian banker turned tyrant—and by extension with the eunuch himself, who was Eubulus's pet sophist and favorite Ganymede.

"Come," Hermeias said. "Sit and drink with me. No doubt crossing the straits in midwinter has left your nerves ill at ease. I will have mulled wine brought to us." He turned to his clerks and scribes and waved them out. "That is enough for today. Have Sthenelos fetch us a good Chian, or is Thasian more to your liking, Memnon? No, no, make it Chian."

"You have your former master's palate for fine wine," Memnon said.

For a split-second, Hermeias's mask of courtesy slipped, giving the Rhodian a glimpse of the naked rage and ambition lurking beneath. The eunuch mastered these emotions as swiftly as they appeared. "My one indulgence," he said, his smile returning. The men sat on couches and made small talk as a servant arrived with two steaming mugs of wine. Their conversation resumed after the servant left.

"Your invitation to join you for the Lenaea was wholly unexpected," Memnon said. "I didn't think an independent and energetic ruler such as yourself would want to associate with the brother of a Persian officer. By rights, our very positions should put us at odds."

Hermeias cocked his head to the side. "It would be true, perhaps, if we chose only to approach it from the narrow perspective of possible competitors. But, for all our differences, we—you, your brother, and I—share one inalienable trait: we are Greek. It would be a sad world, indeed, if fellow Greeks could not put aside their differences long enough to participate in the very festivals which bind us as a people."

"Well spoken," Memnon said, raising his mug in salute. "It's that same sentiment that allows the warring factions of Hellas to unite in celebration of the games at Olympia."

"Exactly!" Hermeias leaned closer, adopting the mien of a conspirator. "I will be honest with you, Memnon. I also wished to speak with you because your brother's unique position in the Great King's hierarchy intrigues me. I find the subject of Persian politics to be endlessly fascinating! Perhaps you will share some of your anecdotes with me during the festival?"

Memnon apprehended something in the eunuch's studied enthusiasm, an implied understanding that their shared Hellenic ancestry trumped any perceived allegiance to a barbarian king. Without realizing it, Hermeias tipped his hand. Memnon's smile widened and he inclined his head, a gracious guest to his host. "It would be my pleasure."

"Excellent!" The eunuch clapped and his steward entered. "You must be exhausted. I have taken the liberty of having accommodations made ready for you here, at the palace. Sthenelos will show you to your rooms. I must attend to state business tonight, which unfortunately means leaving you to dine alone. Do you still have friends in Assos?"

Memnon drained his wine. "None I can recollect, but think nothing of it, good Hermeias. I would beg a favor of you, though. I have an errand I must run—one I have put off for far too long—and I should require a lantern to light my way."

Both men stood. "That is an odd request," Hermeias said. "What errand could draw you away so soon after your arrival, I wonder?"

"A family matter," Memnon replied. "I must attend my father's grave."

The eunuch clicked his tongue against his teeth and nodded. "Of course. Assos does homage to all of its honored dead, without fail, but the reverence of a community cannot replace that of a son. Sthenelos, see our guest has whatever he needs. I will personally instruct Kritias to look for your return after dark. And now to business." With a smile and a nod, Hermeias swept from the room.

Memnon's own smile faded; his eyes hardened as he watched the eunuch's departure. *Our business is only just beginning . . .*

BEYOND THE LEKTON GATE, THE DEAD WAITED IN DEEPENING SHADOW. Statues decorated the tombs of the great and mighty—nude athletes frozen for all time in poses of victory, armored soldiers bidding their wives and mothers farewell, sailors watching the horizon from the prows of ships long since claimed by Lord Poseidon. Smaller monuments marked the graves of lesser men and of women, hung with grave wreaths or sprays of flowers woven with locks of mourners' hair, their offering bowls empty and overturned. Their painted *steles* revealed something of the deceased's personality. One depicted a man with his sons, and another, a woman at her dressing table combing her hair. A child played with his favorite ball for eternity while an elderly couple enjoyed their small stone garden. The dead waited, but they did not fret over their fates.

In the smoky yellow light of the lantern Memnon made his way to his father's grave. Timocrates' *stele* captured his spirit perfectly. He stood on a plinth, declaiming to a sea of upturned faces. Though not the most elaborate monument in the necropolis, it was of exceptionally higher quality, wrought of Parian marble by the hands of the Athenian master Praxiteles.

Under the watchful eyes of sentries atop the Lekton Gate, Memnon knelt and placed the lantern on the ground beside him. He carried a basket prepared by Sthenelos for the occasion with everything he would need to pay homage to his father's shade—a flask of oil and one of wine, a honey-cake, a new offering bowl, and a fresh wreath. He lifted the old wreath off the grave and put it aside, replacing it with the new, and did the same with the old chipped offering bowl. A cold wind fanned the flames of his lantern.

"Forgive me, Father, for my absence," he said. "Long have I been away, toiling in lands not my own for causes unworthy of my efforts. Soon, perhaps, I can return you to your beloved Rhodes, where men would doubtless raise their voices in admiration of your deeds." Memnon placed the honey-cake in the offering bowl. Next, he uncorked the oil flask and used its contents to anoint the *stele*. "May you be blessed in Hades' realm, and if down there the good have merit, then may you be raised up to sit beside Hades' dread and beautiful Queen."

Finally, Memnon picked up the wine flask. "Do not think ill of me, Father, for straying so far from the path you had envisioned for me. Though I never became an Alcibiades or a Pericles, I am something those men never could be—a son of Timocrates. That honor is enough for me. May Zeus Savior and Helios watch over you." He poured his libation into the dead grass at the base of the *stele*.

Sighing, Memnon gathered up the old bowl and wreath and placed them in the basket. As he rose to his feet, however, a flash of movement out beyond the ring of his light caught his eye, an impression of silvery-gold hair. Memnon's breath caught in his throat. *Did Hermeias send a spy?* He raised his lantern higher.

The light flickered on a man-high *stele* of yellowish marble.

"Zeus!" the Rhodian said, chuckling. "Now I'm jumping at shadows." He gathered up the basket, waving to the sentries as he retraced his steps through the Lekton Gate and into the city. No doubt word of his every move had already made its way to Hermeias's ears.

Memnon reached the palace near the end of the first watch, three hours after dusk, and was shown to his rooms by one of the eunuch's household slaves. Tidy and well kept, the accommodations followed the philosopher-king's bias against excess—a sitting room with divans and a table, and a bedroom with a low mattress, bolsters, and thick furs. His travel chest sat in the corner, untouched.

In the sitting room, a fire roared on the hearth. Platters of food awaited sampling on the heavy oak table and a pitcher of mulled wine stood ready. Memnon, though, ignored these temptations. Nudging a divan closer to the hearth, he sat and removed the old grave wreath from the basket.

Memnon studied it by the light of the fire, his eyes narrowing. Its flowers were dry and crackling, bound together by a fillet of fine gray wool. He turned the wreath over in his hands, knowing exactly what he would find. On the underside, someone had stitched another scrap of wool over the first to form a pocket. It was recent work, and hastily done. Memnon plucked out the threads. From between the two pieces of fabric a tiny scrap of parchment fluttered to the floor. The Rhodian tossed the wreath into the fire, bent to retrieve the parchment. He could see it bore three words written in a strong hand:

All is ready.

Memnon exhaled. "You're a good man, Omares," he whispered. The Rhodian touched an end of the parchment to the fire and watched as it burned, then ground the ashes between his thumb and forefinger . . .

"By the dog of Hades, Memnon!" Aristonymus threw his hands up in exasperation. "How can you remove the eunuch if not by assassination? True, it will call for tense times and loss of life, but such things must be part and parcel of the Troad's reunification."

Memnon tapped his map of the region. "No. I reject your hypothesis. I believe I can return the Troad to the Persian fold without bloodshed. It's going to require a bit more planning, a dash of creativity . . . and earning the eunuch's trust."

Aristonymus laughed. "Would you listen to yourself? You sound like a madman! If you think Hermeias's trust is such an easy commodity to earn then you've obviously taken leave of your senses and should be bundled off to Sardis, and back to your brother, without delay!"

"I'm perfectly sane, cousin," Memnon replied, smiling. "Perfectly sane and perfectly sure that I can not only earn Hermeias's trust, but that I can earn it in the span of a single hour."

Aristonymus's laughter failed. He stared at the Rhodian's smiling face, bereft of humor, and his eyes narrowed. Something about his kinsman's vast reserve of confidence gave him pause. Was he privy to some mystery no other man could see? "An hour, you say? How?"

Memnon's gaze returned to his map. "There is a man in Assos I've known since the days of Artabazus's rebellion. He was one of Mentor's officers and as good a man in a pinch as any I've met. In turn, this man knows dozens of others in the city who are in desperate straits, men of the former regime who have been persecuted and driven to the depths of poverty by the eunuch's reign. I'm certain he can find the perfect pawn for this game we play."

"What is the perfect pawn?"

"A man," Memnon said, "who is both courageous and a fool."

THE NEXT DAY, THE DAY OF THE LENAEA, DAWNED CLOUDY AND COLD. Memnon rose early to break his fast with Hermeias in the eunuch's study, their conversation constantly interrupted by ministers clamoring for their king's attention. It struck Memnon as odd that a self-professed philosopher-king did not give more thought to the everyday problems of his rule, but Hermeias breezed through his affairs in a manner the Rhodian could only describe as informed neglect. If one of his ministers said he needed a *talent* of silver for some ridiculous purpose, the eunuch trusted the man at his word. Those who embraced the teachings of Socrates and Plato he considered beyond reproach, while the eunuch treated better men who espoused the causes of rival sophists as enemies of the state.

"For all that I admire Isocrates," Hermeias said as they left the palace and made their way to the theater, "I would never give him leave to dwell in lands under my control. Can you imagine the mischief he would cause if he decided to unleash his literary arsenal on autocrats and tyrants?"

"A wise decision," Memnon murmured. He and the eunuch walked side by side, trailed by courtiers and hangers-on, flanked by Kritias and the *Basileus*'s Guard. Not even an early morning rainstorm could dampen the enthusiasm of the crowd streaming into the theater. There was a carnival atmosphere despite the lowering sky, a cacophony of voices glad for the opportunity to pay homage to the god Dionysus. This year, a great part of that homage would be a comedic contest—five plays in the Attic mode enacted by some of the finest players in all of Hellas, including Thettalos of Athens and Nikos of Olynthus. One could hear musicians tuning their instruments in the orchestra as the throng, with their cushions and awnings and bags of food, found places to sit.

Five thousand souls packed into the tiered seats, citizens and foreign guests mostly, leavened with a handful of courtesans who flouted social customs by being seen with their favorites in public. The whole erupted in a thunderous ovation as Hermeias entered. He acknowledged them with a wave and took his place, his guards discreetly out of the way. Next came a parade of the gods, Dionysus in the lead; priests made sacrifices and read the omens, declaring it a blessed day.

As this was going on Memnon scanned the audience. Once or twice he thought he caught sight of Omares or his sons, though he could not be certain; regardless, he did nothing to draw attention to them. The faces around him were smiling and gay as the first play, a bawdy piece called *Lesbia* by Eupolis, got underway. *Which one?* Memnon wondered, staring at those nearest him. *Which one is my pawn?*

"Nikos of Olynthus is an excellent Phaon, is he not?" Hermeias said, his lips barely moving. He gave the impression of rapt attention. "A rare find, though Eupolis bores me to tears."

"Indeed," Memnon replied. "I prefer tragedy to comedy on the stage."

"As do I. Since we are both bored, perhaps you would share an anecdote," the eunuch said. "Tell me how your brother earned the Great King's gratitude."

And so, in a voice barely rising above a whisper, Memnon related to Hermeias the story of Mentor's conquest of Egypt. He had little need to embroider the tale, though he did add details of intrigue and slaughter that perhaps Khafre had been remiss in mentioning to him. In all, he made it last through Eupolis and well into Aristophanes' *Frogs*.

"Extraordinary," Hermeias said at the conclusion of Memnon's tale. "He virtually rules western Asia, you say?"

"Not virtually. He *is* the commander of the Great King's western armies and a Satrap of Satraps. We—Artabazus and I—were only pardoned by Ochus because Mentor wished it," Memnon said. "Now, Mentor wishes to pardon other Greeks who once opposed the Persians and quietly move them into positions of authority."

"To what end?"

Memnon watched the actors for a moment, listening as their lines gave way to the chorus's final song. "Ochus is an old man. When he dies, Mentor's afraid the Great King's heirs will renege on their sire's patronage. He seeks to guarantee himself a position in future regimes, be it through bribery, marriage, or threat of arms."

Hermeias looked pensive, his scarred face grave. Memnon knew, though, that he had snared the eunuch with that last bit of fiction. An ally of Philip's could not ask for a gift greater than news—reliable news, at that—of an exploitable rift in the Persian high command. It was as irresistible to him as an unbarred door to a thief. "A bold man, your brother," he said. "Bold and not without foresight. No doubt many men along the Asian shore are eager to deal with him, and I know of at least one in Europe who would welcome a strong Greek ally on this side of the Hellespont."

Memnon glanced sidelong at the eunuch, frowning as though such an idea never occurred to him. "Philip, you mean?"

Hermeias's silence spoke more plainly than any explanation.

On stage, the *exodos* unfolded and the actor playing Aeschylus, now free of Hades' realm by the comic misdeeds of Dionysus and his servant, delivered his final lines. "And remember," the fellow said, puffing himself up, "let not that villainous fellow—that liar, that clown!—sit upon my throne, not—"

Memnon's pawn chose that moment to strike.

From the corner of his eye, the Rhodian saw a man approaching from his left, over the eunuch's shoulder. He looked no different than the other theatergoers, cloak-wrapped, his features ruddy from the chill air and from drink, driven by necessity to seek the privy. He pulled a dog-skin cap down over his balding pate. As he passed close to Hermeias, though, Memnon saw a spasm of hate contort the man's face. Iron flashed.

"Death to the tyrant!" the assassin roared.

Memnon was in motion as the words left the man's lips, dragging the startled Hermeias out of his attacker's path. Gracelessly, the eunuch tumbled to the stone floor. "Guards! Protect your king!" The actors and the crowd recoiled; a woman screamed.

The assassin lashed out, his blade gashing the Rhodian's left biceps; before he could draw back and strike again, Memnon caught his knife-hand and twisted it, feeling bones break under his fingers. The weapon clattered to their feet. The man bellowed in agony and made to claw at Memnon's eyes, but the Rhodian ducked his head and thrust the fellow away, pushing him into the path of the onrushing guards.

Kritias reached him even as the failed assassin turned to flee. The captain's spear took him high, staving in his breastbone and punching through his body. The man crashed to the ground, writhing, spewing bright blood and curses as he died in sight of the gods.

More guards spilled into the theater, blocking exits and holding the milling crowd at bay while the sponsors and a few of the actors tried to restore calm. Memnon helped the eunuch to his feet. "Are you injured?"

"N-No . . . I am unhurt." Hermeias held his arms aloft so the crowd could see him. "I am unhurt!" His scarred face was ashen, though, as he came forward and studied the dead man's visage.

"Who was he?"

"One of Eubulus's old partisans, I imagine, though I thought I had rid myself of the last of their kind." The tyrant looked over at Memnon, who was wringing blood from his lacerated arm; a rush of concern replaced his pallor. "Come, my dear friend. That cut needs a doctor's care. Kritias! Clear a path!"

Memnon lingered a moment over the corpse, wondering at his pawn's name and if his kin were in the theater. Was he a truly martyr, or just a desperate cutthroat eager for gold and renown? No matter his motives, the courageous fool had done his duty.

I have Hermeias's trust.

SPRING CAME EARLY TO THE TROAD. TWO MONTHS AFTER THE LENAEA, ships put to sea from Assos harbor, fat merchantmen shadowed by lean triremes, bound for Athens, for Pella, for Syracuse. Some would even brave the Persian-held waters off Cyprus for a chance to trade Greek wool and bronze for Egyptian linen and gold. For Memnon, though, the advent of spring heralded an end to his business with Hermeias.

"It's done," the Rhodian said, bounding into the eunuch's sun-drenched study without waiting to be announced. "Mentor has agreed to meet you."

Hermeias put his stylus down and leaned back in his chair, stroking his chin with ink-stained fingers. "When?"

"Midmonth, at my estate near Adramyttium. He's troubled by the rumblings of open war between Athens and Philip, and is eager to secure allies of his own."

"Why does he not come here?"

"For the same reasons you do not go to Sardis," Memnon said, smiling.

"You're both afraid of treachery from the other. Adramyttium is a neutral place. My estate is out of the way, secluded, so you both can let your guard down and talk like men. His terms are not unlike those of a parley. Ten men apiece—though he'll only have nine, as I will be his tenth—and the setting will be a fine Attic *symposium*, as befits gentlemen of your respective ranks. I will send ahead and have everything ready."

Hermeias looked askance at the Rhodian. "I had no idea you owned an estate near Adramyttium."

"It was a gift from Artabazus, for when I become too old and gray to follow where Glory leads," Memnon replied, not bothering to mention that he had only seen the estate once, and from afar. "But what's this? I hear reluctance in your voice now. Have you changed your mind about the meeting?"

"No," Hermeias said, concern knitting his brow. "Of course not. I am . . . since the incident at the theater I am leery of entering a place not under my complete control. I am sure, though, that all is as you say."

"I can vouch for the setting," Memnon said. He sat on a divan near the eunuch's desk, any consternation over the unraveling of his plans well hidden. "As for the rest, you will have ten handpicked guards plus me as a hostage. Even if it were Mentor's intent to seize you, for whatever reason, he wouldn't lift so much as a finger so long as I'm under your power." The Rhodian grinned. "I'm excellent insurance, if nothing else."

Hermeias rose and paced the study. "You are no hostage, my friend, and you are much more than mere insurance. I trust your judgment on these matters." The eunuch smiled suddenly. "A *symposium*, eh? Perhaps I should pare my guards down to seven and invite a trio of learned friends? Trustworthy men, of course."

"A fine idea," Memnon said, relief flooding his limbs.

And so it was decided. In the second week of Mounichion, the Troad's eunuch king left Assos by ship in the company of a contingent of his Guard, three sophists from Aristotle's old school at Mytilene on Lesbos, and

Memnon. Bearing east, their galley hugged the coast of the Bay of Adramyttium and reached the town that lent its name to the Bay on the morning of the second day.

Adramyttium was a small hamlet, rustic compared to Assos, its beaches and roadsteads dotted with fishing boats. Homes of old timber and dun-colored brick topped a low hill, along with ruined walls that spoke of a time of greater prosperity. Gulls hovered over fishermen's shacks, alighting on drying racks or canting beams, ever watchful for a free meal. Naked children made a game of scaring them off.

The galley beached and the party disembarked. Memnon had arranged their transportation weeks in advance—a carriage for Hermeias and his sophists, a wagon for their luggage, and horses for the rest. The Rhodian assigned one guardsman to drive the carriage; another, the wagon. Kritias and the other four were unaccustomed to traveling on horseback, so it took Memnon the better part of the morning to get them where they could sit astride the shaggy ponies without falling off. Finally, near noon, under a cloudless blue sky, the cortege set out for the estate.

Hermeias looked uneasy. "How far is it, again?"

"Less than an hour to the south of town," Memnon replied. He rode beside the carriage, unarmed and unarmored, looking like a country squire out for a leisurely ride. His calm manner assuaged the eunuch's nerves so that before a mile had passed the carriage was alive with dueling dialectics.

They arrived at the estate without fanfare, clattering over a small wooden bridge and passing between a pair of stone pillars. A grove of oaks shaded the main house. As he rode closer, Memnon could not keep a smile off his face. During his sojourn at Assos, Artabazus's workmen had kept themselves busy transforming the old house with its peeling whitewash into a stonewalled villa with windows covered by fretted screens and a roof of red Pactolus tile. Silver chimes tinkled in the warm breeze.

The carriage drew up out front and the guardsmen dismounted. Kritias, his hand on his sword hilt, studied the portico, with its red-daubed columns and bronze-studded doors flanked by young potted poplars. Memnon knew the guard captain felt the same sensation he did—the tangible force of invisible scrutiny. The Rhodian, though, knew its source.

"Be at ease," Memnon said, clapping Kritias on the shoulder as he bounded onto the portico.

Hermeias clambered down from the carriage. "Are we the first to arrive, I wonder?" he said. "Still, though I had hoped your brother would meet us, by arriving ahead of him we have an excellent opportunity to survey the lay of the land, as they say. I am eager—"

"Mentor's not here," Memnon said, his manner suddenly brusque. When he turned to face the eunuch, the composure he'd maintained since arriving at Assos was gone, replaced by cold rage. "Nor does he plan on coming. He wants you brought to him at Sardis. In chains, if need be."

Hermeias recoiled, stricken. "What? What are you saying?"

"You men!" Memnon gestured to the milling guardsmen. "If you value your lives, do not move! You've been easy prey, Hermeias. Far easier than I would have believed for a man of your reputation. You should be flattered that your enemies hold you in such high regard."

"Black-hearted bastard!" Kritias snarled. He jerked his sword free and took a step toward Memnon. "Protect the—"

An arrow loosed from high among the oak leaves struck Kritias in the back of the neck, shattering his vertebrae. The guard captain pitched forward, dead before he hit the ground. His sword skittered across the portico. Memnon stooped and retrieved the weapon. To the other guardsmen, who looked on the verge of action, he said, "Move and you die! Understood?"

Behind Memnon, the villa doors crashed opened and a dozen soldiers emerged, spear-bearing *kardakes* in scaled Median jackets and peaked helmets, commanded by Omares, Artabazus's old partisan, his hair and beard as long as a Spartan's and shot through with gray. Under his direction, the *kardakes* divested the eunuch's men of their weapons and herded them into a knot. A handful of green-and-brown-clad archers dropped from the oak trees; from the rear of the house more soldiers came and led the horses away. All the while, Hermeias spluttered and cursed.

"You foul betrayer!" the eunuch screeched. He might have leapt at Memnon had his fellow sophists not restrained him. "I trusted you! I trusted you and this is how you repay my hospitality?"

Memnon's smile lacked any vestige of humor. "You trusted me because of what I could offer you, not out of some poetic gesture of guest-friendship. You wanted access to my brother. For all your insufferable posturing about the merits of philosophy, you are no different from a common tyrant. At least Eubulus was honest."

"Strike me down, then!" The eunuch shrugged off his companions and stepped closer to Memnon. "Strike me down if you style yourself a tyrannicide, and avenge your dear Eubulus! I will die for my philosophy, dog!"

"Indeed, and you likely will, but not today. Nor should you delude yourself into thinking this has anything to do with your former master, though one could argue that you authored your own doom with his murder. With Eubulus alive, Artabazus would have retreated to Assos instead of seeking asylum at Philip's court." Memnon descended from the portico. He towered over the eunuch as he grasped his right hand, tugging his signet ring off. "Bind them," he said to Omares.

Quickly, Hermeias and his sophists had their hands lashed together with leather cords. The unlucky philosophers were separated from their patron and put with the guardsmen—who, at a gesture from Memnon, were led to the rear of the villa while a pair of *kardakes* removed Kritias's body. "See he receives a proper burial," Memnon said. "For all his misplaced loyalty, he was a good man." In a moment, Memnon and Omares were alone with Hermeias.

The Rhodian sat on the portico steps and stared at the sardonyx signet.

"An interesting place, Philip's court," he continued. "That's where I happened across your old crony, Demokedes. Honestly, I thought it nothing more than innocent coincidence until Philip installed your own son-in-law as young Alexander's tutor. That's when I decided you had become too much of a liability and would need to be removed. But how . . . how to prize you from this comfortable little nook you've created for yourself without sparking rebellion in all the cities that pay you homage?"

Hermeias gave a triumphant bark. "The sting of rebellion will be my legacy to you! My people will never stand for Persian autocracy! When they hear of your foul treachery they will rise up! My people will avenge me!"

"Don't waste your melodrama on me, eunuch. Wait until you have an audience who might appreciate it," Memnon said. The signet ring glittered in his fist. "These people you so fervently believe in . . . they are staunch partisans? Followers of the king's law?"

"To the death!"

Memnon laughed, tossing the ring in the air and catching it. "Omares, fetch me something to write on! The king of the Troad is about to draft a letter to his loyal, law-abiding followers!"

17

EDICTS CIRCULATED THROUGH THE AGORAS AND COUNCIL HALLS of the Troad; in steep Assos; in Atarneus, with its impregnable walls; in Antandrus, on the slopes of Mount Ida; in hallowed Troy and the towns of the Skamandros Valley; in Sigeum, on its windswept headland; and in Abydus, on the Straits. With exceptional gravity, heralds read aloud the wishes of their king:

> *Hermeias to the councils and people of the Troad: greetings. To the bearer of this letter we have given the authority to rule as governor in our stead. He shall be entitled to receive the same obedience in religious and military matters as is offered to us. He shall have access to the councils and the people, to the tax rolls and the treasury. The joint officials currently in office shall take care of him if he has need of anything. Obey him as you obey us. Farewell.*

Those who doubted the edict's veracity had but to glance at the impression in the wax seal to have those doubts allayed. Clearly they could see the image of Athena in her guise as the goddess of wisdom, an owl perched on her upraised palm.

It was Hermeias's seal . . .

ON MIDSUMMER'S DAY, MEMNON RETURNED TO SARDIS. HE RODE AT THE head of a column of soldiers, mounted *kardakes* whose long spears bore fluttering pennons of purple and gold. Wagons trundled behind them and in their wake shuffled a line of dusty prisoners chained together at the neck. Word of the Rhodian's arrival fired the city's curiosity; commoners lined the road to the fortress, jostling for a chance to view the procession as it passed. Courtiers and functionaries watched from the battlements as Memnon's troops rode through the fortress gates, whips cracking over the bowed backs of the prisoners.

Mentor, attended by Spithridates and Rhosaces, awaited him at the head of the monumental staircase leading to the palace's columned portico. A thousand eyes watched as Memnon dismounted, his blue linen cloak settling around his armored shoulders. A thousand ears heard the scuff of his cavalry sandals as he ascended the stairs, shadowed by two soldiers carrying a bronze-bound chest. The Rhodian stopped at a respectful distance and made his obeisance to the satraps, straightened and, in a clear and commanding voice, said, "Brother, I bring you tokens from the people of the Troad!" At his gesture, the two soldiers brought the chest forward, placed it at Mentor's feet, and retreated. Memnon knelt; he unfastened the hasps and threw the lid back, revealing a pair of terracotta jars. "Earth and water, symbols of their submission!"

The pronouncement caused a furor among the courtiers, a buzz of disbelief. "All of the Troad?" Rhosaces of Ionia said, giving voice to the crowd's skepticism that anyone could bring the region to heel in so short a time. Younger than his brother Spithridates, Rhosaces had a lean face dominated by a hooked beak of a nose and a bristling black beard.

"All of it!" Memnon's nostrils flared. "And since I knew there would be those among you who would doubt my accomplishment, I've brought a witness!" Another gesture produced a rattle of chains as Omares led one of the prisoners up the stairs, thrusting him onto his belly at the satraps' feet. Dirty and disheveled, clad in the remnants of royal finery, the prisoner struggled against the pressure of Omares' foot on his back.

"Who is this creature?" Spithridates said, his nose wrinkling.

"Surely you recognize him, this man who once made you a gift of three *talents* of unrefined gold from Mount Ida to insure his ships would be welcome in your brother's Ionian ports?" That was a rumor learned from his cousin, Aristonymus; for it to cause the Persian brothers to exchange troubled glances only confirmed Memnon's suspicions that neither man could be trusted. With a flourish, he said, "Here is the eunuch, Hermeias, who once ruled the Troad, stripped of his office and his dignity! I present him to you, my brother, as proof of my success!"

"Foul traitors!" The eunuch spat at Mentor's sandals. "May you drown in the cursed Styx!"

A slow smile spread across Mentor's face. "Proof, indeed. You've done well, Memnon. I accept the Troad's submission! Take this wretch away. We will speak soon, Hermeias—soon and to agonizing lengths."

Omares removed his foot from the eunuch's back and manhandled him to his feet. Chains clashed as two of Mentor's men seized the prisoner. Hermeias, though, wrenched himself free of their grasp; he drew himself up to his full height. "I will walk to my doom!" he said. *Here's the audience he hoped for,* Memnon thought, *the chance to carve his own epitaph.* He did not disappoint. "Tell my friends I have done nothing base, or unworthy of our master's teachings!"

"Ever the philosopher," Memnon murmured as the eunuch strode off like an honored guest rather than a prisoner under escort. Mentor, though, immediately dismissed the captive from his mind; the elder Rhodian grinned at Omares, who returned the gesture.

"You old dog!" Mentor said. "I knew he'd embroil you in this!"

"It was my pleasure, sir."

" 'Sir,' is it? Zeus Savior and Helios! Aren't you the proper one, now? What have you done to him, Memnon?"

"It must be the immensity of your august presence," he replied.

With the formalities at an end the onlookers drifted away, returning to whatever business brought them to the palace in the first place. Some were petitioners seeking a moment of the satraps' time; others simply attended court day after day in hopes of securing their lords' favor. Memnon saw visitors from the Royal Court at Babylon, envoys from the Aegean cities, Phoenicians and mainland Greeks, all haggling with the chamberlains for Mentor's attention. *Little wonder he's looking even thinner and as pale as a shroud,* Memnon thought as he signaled for his officers at the base of the stairs to dismiss the *kardakes.* A groom led his and Omares' horses off to the stables.

"Come." The elder Rhodian turned and made his way across the broad portico to the Apadana. Heavy doors stood wide-open all around, allowing cool incense-laden air to flow without obstruction between the myriad columns. "How many men did this venture cost me?"

It took a moment for Memnon's eyes to adjust to the gloom after the brilliant sunshine on the portico. "None," he replied, his words amplified by the cavernous chamber. "We didn't lose a man."

Upon overhearing this, Spithridates, who had preceded them with Rhosaces, stopped and spun around. "Impossible! You cannot pacify a region of that size without casualties!"

"I am no liar, my friend," Memnon said, a dangerous edge to his voice. "And you'd do well to remember that. We suffered no casualties."

Mentor frowned. "How not?"

"I used a weapon they weren't expecting." From beneath his armor, Memnon drew out a silver chain; Hermeias's signet ring dangled from it. He held it aloft for the others to see. "A weapon borrowed from our own Great King's arsenal. You see, I sent letters to the city councils and officials."

"Letters?" Spithridates sneered. "Preposterous!" Beside him, Rhosaces laughed aloud.

"Don't scoff, my lords," Omares said. "It was the damnedest bit of sleight of hand I've ever seen."

Mentor silenced them with a look. "You sent . . . letters?"

"Yes. Letters of abdication, sealed with the eunuch's own emblem. Hermeias's partisans decided he'd gone off on some half-baked philosophical crusade, but they acceded to his wishes and confirmed the letter-bearers, all allied Greeks of my own choosing, as governors of their respective *poleis*. All that remained was to root out the malcontents."

Mentor's rumbling laughter degenerated into a fit of coughing. He held up his hand, forestalling his brother's concern. "Zeus Savior!" he wheezed, catching his breath. "Thank the benevolent gods you're on our side!"

Both Persians, though, sniffed in disdain. "No matter how cunning," Spithridates said, "artifice is a poor substitute for valor." With that the satraps turned and retreated deeper into the Apadana, their retinues cleaving to them like toddlers to their mother's skirts.

"Brother," Memnon said in a low voice. "If it's in your power to strip them of their rank and send them from you, do so. They mean you harm. I can feel it."

"Me? I'm but a stumbling block to their ambitions, an annoyance at best. It's you they should fear." Mentor draped an arm around his brother's shoulder. "Still, if it is harm they're hatching, I trust you will avenge me with more than a letter. Come on, Omares! We need wine! Wine to celebrate both Memnon's triumph and your sudden rise to respectability!"

IT WAS NEAR DUSK BEFORE MEMNON COULD SLIP AWAY FROM HIS BROTHER'S impromptu drinking party, leaving the elder Rhodian and Omares deep in their cups, singing off-key hymns to Dionysus. Nor were they alone in their revelry. Guests from the Asian Greek lands happily joined in, along with a handful of adventurous Persians who saw great wisdom in their ancestors' admonition to debate serious matters first drunk, then sober. Mentor, however, sent their debate spiraling into oblivion by insisting they switch to undiluted wine.

Sounds of their merriment faded as Memnon retreated into the heart of the palace. He had missed seeing Khafre and Pharnabazus; a chamberlain reported they were both at Ephesus—Khafre to replenish his store of medicines and Pharnabazus as Mentor's liaison to the shiploads of mercenaries Thymondas had sent over from the Greek mainland—and were due to return soon. The rest of the family had gone with Artabazus to the Great King's court at Babylon.

Memnon's rooms, in a wing of the palace reserved for royal kin, once belonged to Croesus's beloved son, Atys, slain hunting wild boars in Mysia "to punish his father's *hybris*," according to Herodotus. Polished bronze lamps illuminated a wall-sized painting depicting the young man's death: his body sprawled in the heather, encircled by his weeping comrades, with his gory head cradled in Croesus's lap. The old king's tragedy became the room's theme. Antique iron boar-spears hung above the cold hearth and inlays of yellowed tusk-ivory decorated the woodwork—chairs, table, and bed.

Slaves had delivered Memnon's belongings from the wagons; servants had put everything in its place, hanging his weapons and shield near the door and erecting two stands for armor. One held his bronze breastplate and greaves, the other his lighter linen cuirass. His helmet, with its tall crest of blue-dyed horsehair, rested on the shoulders of his *lineothorax*. His traveling chest of cypress-wood, its patina worn with age and scarred from indelicate handling, lay at the foot of the bed, while a wicker-and-leather scroll basket, filled with volumes appropriated from Hermeias's library, sat atop the table. Memnon caught this up by its carrying strap and headed back out the door.

The women's quarters lay at the end of a long hallway, behind a door guarded by silver-haired *kardakes*, veterans who had served Artabazus's cause in their youth. They smiled and clapped Memnon on the shoulder as he passed into the antechamber. Inside, the Chief Eunuch of the harem held court. He was a balding and fussy little man, his potbelly straining against the multicolored linen of his robes. A lesser eunuch fanned him while a pair of Barsine's maids—who should have been attending to their mistress—massaged warm, herb-laced oil onto his swollen ankles.

Memnon glared at him as he crossed the antechamber to Barsine's door.

"Wait!" the Chief Eunuch squealed, rising and scattering the maids. "The mistress is taking her rest!"

"Then lower your voice so you don't disturb her," Memnon replied. Unperturbed, the Rhodian entered Barsine's rooms, closing the door in the Chief Eunuch's face. Lamps of silver filigree revealed a suite spacious enough for a large family. Rugs cushioned a floor of patterned marble, muffling Memnon's footfalls as he traversed a central hallway that ended in a small fountain court still aglow with the last light of day. He peered into sitting rooms and changing rooms, rooms for bathing and rooms for sleeping, all empty. As he neared the courtyard, its cool shadows scented with lilies and jasmine, he heard faint sounds of whimpering.

Outside, Barsine slept on a divan near the softly trickling fountain. Her fingers knotted in a shawl draped across her upper arms. Memnon placed the basket on the ground and knelt by her side. Loose, her dark hair pillowed her head. Delicate brows were drawn together, troubled, her features as pale as alabaster. Morpheus, god of dreams, had her in his clutches.

"No," she muttered in Persian, barely audible. "Wait . . . come back."

Her fingers convulsed.

Memnon placed his hand over hers. "Barsine," he said, softly so as not to startle her into wakefulness. A dreamer had to return gradually or else run the risk of being separated from their *daimon*. "Barsine."

"No!" She gasped; her eyes, moist with tears, fluttered open as her hands locked on Memnon's. Barsine glanced around, frantic. "Where is he?"

"Who? There's no one else here."

"Memnon?" She flung her arms around his neck. He could feel tremors running through her. "Memnon! Thank the gods!"

"It was just a nightmare," he said, stroking her hair. "You're safe now."

"It . . . It seemed so real. I was trapped in a labyrinth of the kind Daedalus had crafted for his patron, King Minos of Crete," she said.

"Were you being chased by the Minotaur?"

"No." She released him and pushed her hair from her eyes, wiping away the tears with the heel of her hand. "I was the pursuer. A man ran from me, though not from fear. He taunted me, pausing to let me get close before sprinting off, again. He had something I needed to retrieve, something whose loss left me aching with sorrow, though I have no clear memory of what it was. I ran faster and faster still, my heart pounding against my ribs like a blacksmith's hammer. The gap between us narrowed with each step. But, as I came within arm's reach, I woke." Barsine settled back on the divan, hugging her shawl to her chest. She smiled. "Listen to me. Rambling on like mad Cassandra. I am pleased you have returned from the Troad unscathed."

"And I am glad you've emerged from the realm of Morpheus unharmed," Memnon said, returning her smile. "This dream-figure, did you recognize him?"

She shook her head. "I saw his face but for a moment, and that moment was enough."

"That hideous, eh? Perhaps you did see the Minotaur."

"No," she replied, "he was that heartbreakingly beautiful. It was as if

I looked upon the model for Praxiteles' *Apollo.* His hair and beard were a silvery-gold and he seemed to glow with a divine light . . . what is it, Memnon?" Color drained from the Rhodian's face; for a moment, the old scar on his right shoulder pulsed and burned. "Memnon?"

"I think I've seen the very man you describe," he said, "though not in a dream."

She bolted upright. "When? Here in Sardis?"

Memnon rocked back on his heels. "Years ago. In the Macestus Valley, before we were forced from Dascylium." And Barsine listened, enraptured, as Memnon told the tale. Twilight deepened. Stars flickered in the heavens. Over the trickle of the fountain, night creatures chirped and trilled. Light spilled out into the courtyard; inside, Barsine's maids went about their nightly duties while the Chief Eunuch spied on the two figures near the fountain . . .

Memnon exhaled. "I have never spoken of that night to another, not to Mentor, not even to Khafre. Perhaps he was but a figment of my imagination, an illusion borne of trauma."

"If that is true, how does he come to my dream?" Barsine said. She sat with her knees drawn up under her, her fingers worrying the fringe of her shawl. "What if he is a messenger of the gods?" Suddenly, Barsine began to cry. She cradled her face in her hands, her shoulders wracked by spasms.

"Come, now," Memnon said. "There's no need for tears. You're safe." He rose and sat alongside her, pulling her into an embrace. Her anguish made him regret sharing the story with her. "Everything's fine, Barsine."

"You do not understand," she sobbed. "If . . . if he is a messenger, what message did he bear for me? He did not speak save to urge me on, to taunt me. He stole something from me . . . something precious . . ." She looked up, her eyes shining with tears. "I am with child, Memnon. Is this an omen that I will not bear the infant to full term?"

Memnon blinked, taken aback. "You're . . . with child?" Barsine's head bobbed in assent. The Rhodian's mind whirled. Though not unexpected in and of itself, the revelation coupled with Barsine's dream left Memnon virtually dumb with shock. "Does Mentor know?"

She wiped her eyes again. "I only became sure of it myself a few days ago. I will tell him soon, though I doubt the need if my dream rings true and the gods plan to steal this child from me." Barsine's rubbed her palms across her belly, offering a silent benediction.

"No, you must tell him," Memnon said. He smiled, and then laughed. "He would never admit it, but my brother's hope is to have a large family, large enough to rival your father's. You must tell him, Barsine, and soon."

"But my dream . . . ?"

"I can't explain the similarities, but not every dream is an omen of things to come. Some are simply dreams." He rose and gently helped her to her feet. "I can promise you this, though. Man or god, anyone seeking to harm that child will answer to the sons of Timocrates! By Zeus Savior and Helios, I swear it!"

MENTOR REACTED TO THE NEWS OF BARSINE'S PREGNANCY WITH UNACCUStomed solemnity. He summoned priests, both Persian and Greek, to take the omens and offer sacrifices to Hera and Anahita. He brought a Lydian wise-woman into the palace to propitiate the local spirits with chants and clouds of sweet incense. At Memnon's urging, Mentor appointed Khafre to be Barsine's chief physician; after the Egyptian announced that she and the baby were both in good health, Mentor dispatched couriers east, along the Royal Road. In a fortnight, it was common knowledge in the streets of Babylon that a Pharnacid princess was with child.

All the while preparations for war continued apace. Through Thymondas's efforts, mercenaries filtered in from mainland Greece, first to Pharnabazus at Ephesus and thence into camps in the Hermus Valley. Summer waned.

Before the first frosts of autumn, word reached Sardis of the death of the Carian satrap, Idrieus. Seizing the opportunity to rid himself of the threat of petty dynasts, Mentor—backed by five thousand mercenary hoplites and a thousand mounted *kardakes*—descended on Halicarnassus, capturing Idrieus's younger brother and self-styled heir, Pixodarus, at unawares. In the aftermath, he confirmed their older sister, Ada, as satrap and left a Persian garrison behind to insure her loyalty.

Mentor returned to Sardis to find his pregnant wife bedridden. "Khafre's orders," Memnon explained. "Something about an imbalance in her humors and her body's desire to expel the child too early."

"Is she in any danger?"

Memnon shrugged. "Who's to say? Giving birth is deadly business, brother, even under the best of circumstances. But, if anyone can lessen the danger, I trust it to be Khafre."

Memnon visited her daily, bringing scrolls to read to keep her spirits up; as the affairs of state allowed, Mentor would drop in on her, and the three of them would spend hours locked in conversation until Khafre or weariness drove them away.

Autumn drew to a close and winter's cold north wind whistled over the bare rocks of the Tmolus range. It was on a day of pale sunshine, though, that a messenger came west along the Royal Road—a messenger from Babylon.

Memnon found his brother in the silent Apadana, wrapped in his cloak and sitting next to a crackling brazier. His chin on his fist, he tapped a roll of parchment against his thigh as he stared into the brazier's smoldering depths. "We've buggered ourselves," he said as Memnon drew near. "The bastard begins to think the impossible is commonplace where we're concerned."

"What is it?"

"Ochus's newest edict." Mentor held the parchment up; Memnon could tell he fought hard the urge to hurl it onto the coals. "Artabazus has finally convinced him of the threat Philip represents. To counter him, the King wants the Aegean islands returned to the Persian fold. He wants sixty ships brought north from Cyprus, and he wants them in place *before* sailing season begins!"

"A winter campaign I can understand, but a winter campaign at sea? Is he mad?"

"No, just an old fool! I guarantee you it was Bagoas who put this idea in his head! That eunuch bastard has hated me since I saved him from his own stupidity in Egypt and this is his way of settling the score! I would stake my life on it!"

"It seems that's his intent," Memnon said. "What will you do?"

"My duty, of course! I'll bring his ships into the Aegean, Bagoas and the north wind be damned!"

Memnon shook his head. "Send me."

"You would seize all the glory for yourself?" Mentor growled.

"Glory? You're an idiot if you think glory's my concern! No, brother. You're many things—a peerless tactician, a brilliant strategist—but you're no idiot and you're no sailor. You never were. How often have you lectured me to choose the proper tool for the proper task? For this task, I am that tool. Besides," Memnon said, his voice softening, "you should be here for the birth of your child, in case there are any complications."

Mentor squinted at his younger brother. He scratched at the back of his neck, rubbed his bare scalp as he mulled over Memnon's logic. "Damn you and your slick sophistry!"

"Then it's settled?"

Mentor sank back in his chair. "Aye, it's settled. Leave quickly, before this mild weather breaks. A messenger should reach Salamis well before you, so your arrival won't be unexpected. Take command of two trireme squadrons—thirty from the Cypriots and thirty from the Tyrians—and return north. I'll see that you have the required documents as well as sufficient funds before you leave."

"And the campaign?"

"If you survive the voyage north," Mentor said, his eyes narrowing, "wage the campaign as you see fit." Memnon nodded and made to turn away, but his brother's hand on his forearm stopped him. It was obvious by Mentor's expression that relinquishing the responsibility for such a dangerous task pained him; still, he forced a smile. "Don't do anything reckless, Memnon. I'd hate for my children to grow up without their favorite Rhodian uncle."

Memnon returned the grip on his forearm. "Don't worry, brother. I'll be a paragon of caution."

"Hard to port!"

From the fighting deck of his Tyrian flagship *Astarte*, Memnon shouted orders to his crew. He clutched the railing as the trireme slewed about, brushing alongside an enemy ship whose oars splintered under a glancing blow of *Astarte*'s bronze ram. Men screamed; grapnels crunched into the wood of the crippled vessel, while sailors brandishing axes struggled to hew the ropes tethering both ships together. Archers exchanged volleys, the higher deck of the Tyrian giving Memnon's Persians a slight advantage. Javelineers hurled their darts. From behind his shield, Memnon shouted for his rowers to drop their oars and seize the grapnel lines. Sailors scurried to do his bidding. They ignored the withering barrage of arrows and pulled in unison, with all their might.

Slowly, the two hulls met with a sinister *choonk*.

"Marines!" Memnon bellowed. Greek and Phoenician soldiers in bronze breastplates and open-faced helmets, armed with axes and boarding pikes, boiled over *Astarte*'s outrigger. Enemy archers redoubled their effort, filling the air with the whistle and hiss of greased iron-heads. Arrows ripped through the close ranks of the marines, killing many outright, in mid-leap, their bodies falling to foul the deck of the enemy ship below.

From his position high in the stern of *Astarte*, Memnon caught sight of the enemy captain, a bearded man of Chios in bronze and leather armed with a heavy-bladed saber. He exhorted his archers, offering them a *drachma* for every one of Memnon's men they killed.

The Rhodian cursed. He wrenched a javelin from the deck near his feet, twisted, and slung the weapon with uncanny accuracy. It struck the Chian captain in the collarbone, transfixing his body at a downward angle. The man staggered, spewing blood into his beard; a pair of Persian arrows finished him off. He went over the side, vanishing beneath the reddening waters of Chios Harbor . . .

SMOKE FROM BURNING HULKS DRIFTED OVER THE CITY, OBSCURING THE face of the late-morning sun. A carpet of flotsam clogged the bloodstained waters of the harbor: splintered oars, deck planking, tholepins, scraps of charred rigging, bilge buckets—and the arrow-riddled corpses of Chian sailors and marines. A rower's bench bobbed in the wrack like a child's cork, the body draped across it long since bled dry. A great wailing arose from women onshore as triangular fins churned the water into a bloody froth.

In a little more than an hour, Memnon's fleet had sent the cream of the Chian navy to the bottom of the harbor in an attack so swift that most of the enemy captains were unable even to cut their mooring cables. Tyrian and Cypriot rams holed them while still tied to the docks, smashing broadside or astern then backing water and moving to the next. Those that got underway had their oarsmen and tiller crews targeted by archers or were set ablaze by marines wielding crocks of flaming pitch. A single ship had run their blockade and made it to open sea.

Memnon, surveying the ruin from the deck of *Astarte*, felt little remorse for the Chians. He had given the island a chance to surrender under the same terms embraced by the rulers of neighboring Cos and Rhodes. The democrats on Chios, though, had refused, banking on the hollow promises of that Athenian rabble-rouser Chares, who swore his own fleet would aid them in their rebellion against the Great King's minions.

"Where's your savior now?" Memnon said, turning to face the deputation of city officials who had come to beg his mercy. "Are those Chares' ships we sent to the harbor bottom? Are those the bodies of Chares' men the sharks are defiling? Where is he, gentlemen? Don't you know? Well, let me enlighten you—Chares is sitting warm and dry in Mytilene because it offends his Athenian sensibilities to put to sea before spring is properly underway!"

"Everything you say is true, my lord," their spokesman said with a grave humility Memnon found suspect. "We were fools to have believed the words of a man such as he. We understand that now and beg your—and the Great King's—forgiveness."

"You must think me a fool as well."

"What?" the spokesman stammered. "No, my lord! No!"

"You must," Memnon said, his eyes narrowing. "Why else would you ask me now to grant Chios the same terms as those offered to Rhodes and to Cos? You Chians had your chance for a peaceful settlement but you refused! Why should I show you leniency?"

"We . . . we were led astray, my lord! We—"

Memnon silenced him. He walked to *Astarte*'s railing, lost in thought. Absently, he watched as Autophradates, who commanded his Cypriot squadron, deployed marines along Chios's long mole in anticipation of the city's occupation. Their weapons and armor glittered in the pale spring sun.

"Rhodes and Cos both capitulated without bloodshed," Memnon said. In each instance, too, the act of leniency had cost him nothing but brought about great dividends. Cos provided him with sailors and stores to replenish those lost on the voyage from Cyprus. Rhodes opened their shipyards to him and had even given him a hero's welcome worthy of one of the island's long-lost sons.

The old oligarch Philolaus, Memnon wrote to Barsine in the days after the subjugation of Rhodes, *did not long survive his coup, they told me. Queen Artemisia, widow of his Carian benefactor Mausolus, put him to death in the very same year as our flight to Macedonia. That I did not learn of this sooner speaks to my profound dislike of the island and my long-standing refusal to set foot on it; still, I've buried my animosity. It is high time Mentor and I returned our father's bones to the soil for which he died . . .*

In the end, he treated both states fairly, expelling their Carian garrisons and instituting moderate pro-Persian oligarchies in place of harsh governors. But, with staunchly democratic Chios eager to avoid the Persian yoke by war or wiles, leniency would likely come at great cost and offer little in return.

"There will be no terms," Memnon said suddenly, turning to face the startled envoys. His eyes were cold and hard as he indicated the troops onshore. "Chios surrenders unconditionally or I order its destruction."

The men of the deputation—stolid democrats, merchants, and members of the old aristocracy—exchanged glances. One by one, they nodded to their spokesman. It required no great intellect to divine their plot. They would agree to anything Memnon demanded now; later, when his back was turned, they would renege and plead to Athens for aid. "Chios surrenders, my lord," the spokesman said.

Memnon smiled. They would not find him an easy mark. "I accept Chios's surrender," he said. "And to insure your complete cooperation and continued goodwill, I require hostages. The eldest sons of all the island's leading men should do . . ."

Chios paid a heavy price for its folly. Not only were the heirs of its greatest families—from toddlers to men in their fifties—herded onto a ship and sent to Ephesus, thence overland to Sardis and beyond, but many of the island's most outspoken democrats faced execution or exile. Memnon established an oligarchy backed by a garrison and levied a crushing tax designed to make other enclaves of wealth and prosperity think again before challenging his will. He sailed away confidant he had emasculated any plans Chios might have had to rise against him.

News was slow in reaching the fleet in the Aegean, but Memnon received the very best news at Erythrae on the Ionian coast at the beginning of summer, borne by Pharnabazus: two months prior, in early Elaphebolion, Barsine had given birth to a healthy little girl.

"And how's the mother?"

Pharnabazus smiled. "She had fully recovered by the time you stormed Chios. And you should know . . . she now swears by Khafre and refuses to let him leave her service, and woe to any who try to take him from her!"

"Staying put will be good for him," Memnon said. "Our Egyptian's getting too old to go traipsing around the Mediterranean. Have they decided on a name for the baby?"

Pharnabazus beamed. "Apame, after our grandmother."

They shared a meal of fish stew and bread in Memnon's cramped quarters onboard *Astarte*, eating from wooden bowls over a table cluttered with maps and correspondence, many of them from cousin Aristonymus. Pharnabazus raised an eyebrow. "What goes?"

"Chares has moved against Methymna. Athenian ships blockade the harbor while Athenian allies attack Methymna's landward wall. If I handle Chares, Aristonymus assures me he can break the allied siege." Memnon licked stew from his fingers and shuffled through the letters and missives. "However, *this* concerns me more. It's from the governor of Abydus, on the Hellespont." He handed Pharnabazus a brief note.

Damastes to Memnon, greetings. Philip has reached Propontis. A Macedonian army has invested Perinthos, whose leaders have issued a call for aid. Byzantion has answered, sending fresh troops and supplies by sea to the embattled city; the Athenians of the Chersonese have responded by expelling their Macedonian garrisons. Of Chares and the Athenian navy there has been no sign.

"They need only look as far as Lesbos to find their wayward admiral," Pharnabazus said. "Are we to fight Chares on one front and be allies with him on another?"

Memnon gave a dark chuckle. "In a manner of speaking, yes. We split the fleet at Lesbos. You and Autophradates take the Cypriots and sail west around the island, through the Straits and into Propontis. Once there, keep to the Asian shore until Mentor or the Great King orders otherwise. I'll take the Tyrians and sail east, into the Bay of Adramyttium, and break Chares' blockade."

"Just like that?" Pharnabazus looked askance at his uncle.

"Just like that. Do you see a flaw?"

"Only the one father has drilled into me since birth: never underestimate your enemy. Are you sure you do not underestimate Chares?"

Memnon smiled. "I've already taken Chares' measure. He has a silver tongue and a surfeit of bravery. But, in and of itself, bravery means nothing. Tartarus overflows with the shades of brave men. No, Pharnabazus, I don't underestimate him at all. The gods granted Chares many gifts, yet they withheld the most important—the *daimon* of a true leader. Without it, he is a figure of great splendor but of little substance."

"You can tell who has this gift, this *daimon*?"

"Can you not?" Memnon said. "Examine the traits of those men you admire most and you'll begin to see it, weaving through their deeds like threads on a loom. It transcends bravery or thirst for glory. A man in possession of it elevates not only himself but also those around him; he inspires them to be greater than they ever thought possible. If you must fight, Pharnabazus, it's best to fight a man who owns nothing of this *daimon*. A man like Chares."

Pharnabazus leaned forward, his forehead wrinkled in thought. "What if you are given no choice? What if it is your misfortune to be arrayed against a man whom the gods had graced with this gift, and others to boot? How would you fight him?"

"Honestly," Memnon said, smoothing his beard with his thumb and forefinger. "I don't know. I've never fought a man in possession of it. Perhaps I would refuse to engage him head-on, let him expend himself in bits and pieces, or maybe devise a way to assault his followers' morale. The trick, I think, is in knowing where your own gifts lie."

" 'Know thyself'," Pharnabazus said, nodding as Memnon's words brought clarity to that oft-heard phrase.

"Exactly."

From Erythrae, Memnon's fleet would have sailed north against the Athenians at Lesbos had a messenger not come from Sardis, one of Mentor's *kardakes*, hollow-eyed and gaunt from lack of sleep. The day was bright, the winds favorable, and the threat of a delay spoiled Memnon's fine humor.

"What goes, man?" he said as a sailor escorted the messenger to the stern-deck of *Astarte*. "You'd better have a message from Zeus himself ordering Atlas to cede to my shoulders the weight of the world!"

"Sir! You must return with all haste to Sardis!"

Memnon's eyes narrowed. "Why? Does Mentor have need of me?"

"No, sir! Lord Mentor has fallen!"

FROM ERYTHRAE, A RIDER COULD REACH SARDIS IN A LITTLE OVER FIVE DAYS. Memnon and Pharnabazus made it in three, leaving a string of dead and broken horses in their wake. Along the road, at Old Clazomenae and ghost-haunted Smyrna, Memnon asked for news. Had there been a battle? Had the lords of Sardis marched to war? But, no one knew; to their knowledge, spring in the Hermus Valley had passed in peace and plenty.

Memnon and Pharnabazus reached Sardis at dusk on the third day. The palace of Croesus was ablaze with light; courtiers and commoners loitered at the base of the stairs leading to the portico and the Apadana, awaiting some announcement from the palace. Sullen-faced guards kept the curious at bay. Murmurs arose from the onlookers as the two road-weary horsemen pushed through their ranks. "That's Memnon," they said, "he'll know" or "it must be grave news." The Rhodian ignored them, spurred his horse up the stairs and clattered across the portico. He and Pharnabazus dismounted and tossed their reins to the startled guards.

A chamberlain met them in the Apadana. "Thank Mithras! Hurry! This way!" This functionary, a beardless eunuch, led them across the great hall to the suite of rooms Barsine had used during her wedding. He kept plucking at Memnon's sleeve, exhorting him to hurry.

Memnon, though, caught the eunuch by the arm and hauled him up short. "What's happened, damn you? Is my brother dead?"

The chamberlain quailed. "No, my lord! No! Hurry!" The Rhodian thrust him aside and stormed into the suite. Nobles and men of high rank, priests and envoys from Mentor's subject cities clogged the antechamber. Spithridates and Rhosaces held court in one corner, surrounded by their confederates—transplanted Iranians who longed to see a return to the old order. They all turned as Memnon entered. Was that satisfaction glittering in their serpentine eyes? *No matter*, Memnon thought. He would find out what happened and exterminate any member of their little clique who might have had a hand in it. Beside him, his nephew's features echoed the same clarity of purpose.

A familiar face met them at the door to the inner chamber.

"Khafre!" Memnon said. "What happened? I was told Mentor had fallen?"

Khafre shook his head. The Egyptian looked ragged, unkempt, like a man who had begged off sleeping or eating for days and now propelled his limbs to action through sheer force of will. "A sickness, Memnon. It came upon him suddenly—a high fever and shortness of breath. I undertook his healing, and he seemed to recover by day and relapse by night, which indicated among other things the presence of a foul spirit. I bade him breathe the fumes of frankincense, cassia, and myrrh."

"Did this help?"

"At first," Khafre said. "But the pestilence settled in his chest and attacked his lungs. No doubt its virulence was compounded by the lingering effects of the many wounds he has suffered through the years."

"You can still heal him, though, can't you?"

The Egyptian passed a hand over his brow, rubbing the silver bristles growing on his scalp. "It is beyond my art, Memnon. I have tried everything, but this evil will not relinquish its hold on his lungs. It drowns him in his own fluids."

Stricken, Memnon sagged against the wall. "Surely there is something yet that we can do?"

"He is in Lord Osiris's hands now." Tears rimmed the Egyptian's eyes; he would have sobbed had he not clenched his teeth against it. "I am sorry," Khafre hissed. Memnon embraced him.

"You've done my family great service," he said with surprising calm. "And you've nothing to apologize for. We . . . I am forever in your debt, Khafre. Thank you." He turned to Pharnabazus. "Look after him, nephew, and send these vultures away. If they refuse, summon the *kardakes* and have them herded out at spear-point. I must see to my brother."

Pharnabazus, his own eyes moist, nodded. The Egyptian leaned against him, allowing the younger man to escort him to a small sitting room off the antechamber. Memnon turned and entered the inner room.

It was as he remembered from the wedding but with a few alterations: the walls were now hung with rich fabrics and in one corner stood an exquisite bronze lamp stand wrought in the shape of a tree with gold and silver leaves. Curtains were drawn, hiding the balcony from view. Linen sheers undulated with the faint night breeze. From beyond, Memnon could hear the Pactolus chuckling over the rocks.

Mentor lay on a bed of carved and polished wood, pillows raising his head high in an effort to ease his discomfort. The elder Rhodian's face was bloodless and glazed with sweat. His jaw hung slack; his breath rasped and bubbled.

Barsine sat at his bedside, a bowl of cool water in her lap. She removed a compress from his forehead, dampened it and wrung it out. Her hands trembled as she smoothed the cloth back into place. She turned slightly at the sound of Memnon's approach, the strain of the last week evident in her wrinkled brow, her sunken cheeks. Relief flooded her red-rimmed eyes as saw Memnon's face.

"I have prayed to the blessed gods for your return," she said, setting the bowl aside and rising. Memnon caught her hands.

"I came as soon as I received word. How is he?"

"Khafre says—" She paused, exhaling against the torrent of emotion that threatened to rob her of speech, "he says he is at Hades' threshold, but still he clings to life. He's been asking for you."

Going to his bedside, Memnon leaned over and kissed the crown of his brother's feverish head. This close, he could not miss the fact that Mentor's every breath came at great effort, the muscles and tendons of his neck standing out like cords. Slowly, his eyelids peeled back. His chest wracked like a forge bellows as he fought to take in enough air to speak. "You're . . . here . . ." he gasped. Tears seeped from Mentor's bloodshot eyes.

Memnon sat by his side and clasped his hand, finding it cool and clammy. He yet wore the gold ring of his office. "Yes, brother. I'm here. I've brought you a gift, as well: the islands of the Aegean. They're unified under you, Mentor. Under you! So, you see, you must fight this pestilence—"

Mentor worked his jaw, muscles clenching and unclenching. "It's . . . time . . ."

"No, no." Memnon's voice cracked. "All you need is rest. You'll get your strength back. Until then, I'll look after things for you. I won't let those dogs spoil your good works!"

Mentor swallowed with difficulty, gasping and coughing. "Barsine . . ."

She came back to his side and caressed his sweat-drenched cheek. "Please, husband. Save your breath." He beckoned her closer. Barsine leaned over him, her ear near his lips. For several moments she hovered in this position, her eyes closed, tears streaming down her cheeks as she nodded. Memnon could not hear what he said, but Mentor's words wrenched a sob from Barsine's breast. At last she turned and buried her face in Memnon's shoulder. The younger Rhodian comforted her.

Mentor's tear-streaked face showed no reproof, no recrimination that his wife sought solace in his brother's embrace. Instead, his eyes registered a grim sense of fulfillment, as though he had made amends for a long-perceived wrong. He tightened his grip on Memnon's hand, though his strength was fading fast. "I . . . speak . . . for you," he said in a hoarse whisper. His eyes fluttered and closed. "I . . . speak . . ."

Mentor's breathing grew shallower and more labored, rattling in his chest as his spirit ebbed. His grip on Memnon's hand loosened.

"What did he say?"

Barsine raised her head. "He absolved me of my duty, and he told me there is no shame, no dishonor in love. He said," her voice caught in her throat as she turned back to her husband, "my father gave me to the wrong son of Timocrates."

I speak for you. Memnon's jaw clenched as he apprehended his brother's last words to him, his last gift. For it was a gift as much as a duty—as Mentor's heir, Memnon was bound by obligation to protect Barsine, to see to her future disposition whether it meant sending her back to her father or finding her a suitable husband. On that matter, Mentor's wishes left little doubt. *I speak for you.*

Tears blurred Memnon's vision; he fought to maintain his composure. He raised his brother's hand to his lips. "It will be as you desire," he said, kissing the heavy gold ring. Barsine mimicked the gesture; she sobbed, her head falling onto Memnon's shoulder.

They sat at his bedside in silent vigil until near midnight, when Mentor gave a small shudder and breathed his last. In the custom of her people Barsine raised her voice in lamentation, a keening wail taken up and amplified by the Persian men and women of the palace. Eunuchs cried aloud and beat their breasts. *Kardakes* clashed spear-shaft against shield-face. The Greeks—mercenary, merchant, or envoy—stood still, their relative silence in sharp contrast to the Persians ritual clamor. "He is dead, then," they said, and whispered among themselves about what the coming days would hold.

And at his brother's side, against all notion of Greek propriety, Memnon closed his eyes and wept.

Interlude IV

"Mentor's funeral lasted three days and nights," Barsine said, brushing away tears with her fingertips. "Culminating in a great pyre that lit the night sky like a beacon for all to see. Come dawn, solemn priests quenched the last of the embers with wine and gathered the charred bones, wrapping them in cloth of gold and placing them in an urn of the finest Egyptian alabaster." With a grimace, she rose from her chair. Ariston followed suit and offered his arm for her to lean upon as she slowly shuffled to the bed. To move even that short a distance left her winded. She was weakening; soon, Harmouthes would bring her a *pharmakon* to ease her breathing. She coughed as she crawled into bed, her voice growing harsh and raspy. "We brought him north with us and buried him at Assos, beside his father."

A chill permeated the room. Ariston went to the hearth and stirred the embers. "Memnon never returned them to Rhodes?"

Barsine shook her head. "That, I think, was his greatest regret." She pulled the coverlet up.

"And what is yours?" Ariston asked.

"My greatest regret?" Gray sunlight, diffused through winter's clouds, gave little color to Barsine's face; her features hardened. "Not dying with him."

As Ariston tended the fire, Harmouthes entered bearing a steaming mug, cloth-wrapped so as not to scald his fingers. Barsine gave him a sad smile. "You expend too much energy in keeping this old woman alive."

"It gives my declining years purpose, mistress," Harmouthes said. "Without you to look after I would doubtless pass my days engaged in mischief and skullduggery. You would not wish that, would you?"

Barsine accepted the mug from him, staring at it as if it were an obstacle keeping her from a long-held goal. She raised it to her lips, stopped; with a sharp nod she set the mug aside. "Bring me plain, cold wine, instead," she said, "with no water, herbs, or medicines."

The Egyptian frowned. He retrieved the mug. "As you wish, mistress. But you must drink this, first."

"No, Harmouthes, no more concoctions. Wine only."

"What are you saying?"

Barsine took the mug from him again, placed it on the table by her bed, and clasped his hands in hers. "My old friend," she said gently. "You have been my rudder, my steersman through storms both great and small, but we both know my time grows short. Soon, I will depart on a journey on which you cannot follow. I am ready, Harmouthes. I am weary of this world. I want to finish my tale and, on reaching its end, linger not one heartbeat longer than necessary. Surely you understand?"

Harmouthes shoulders sagged. He bent and kissed her hands. "I do. It will be as you ask. Wine only."

Barsine sank back onto her pillows. "Thank you, Harmouthes."

Ariston finished stoking the fire, watched as the Egyptian gathered up his mug and withdrew. He could feel the old man's grief. After he closed the door, Ariston brought a chair to the side of Barsine's bed. "I am sorry for him," he said. "I don't know if I could stand aside and let someone I love simply fade away."

"You would do it," Barsine replied, her eyes moist, "if the person you loved had no hope of recovery." She cleared her throat. "Where were we?"

"Traveling north with Mentor's bones . . ."

"Of course. After the funeral, we settled at Memnon's estate near Adramyttium and, following Mentor's wishes, we were married before the year ended. Though my father blessed and approved of the union, Mentor's death hit him hard, as hard as the death of one of his own sons; he divided his attention between the court at Susa and the satrapy of Armenia, the demesne of his cousin, Artashata. He returned to the West only once that I recall, a year later, when I gave birth to Apame's sister, Artonis—named after my own mother." Barsine smiled suddenly. "Memnon doted on both daughter and niece, and he taught them how to ride almost from the day they took their first steps. Despite my father's absence, family and friends surrounded us. Patron and Omares both dwelt in Assos; Pharnabazus married a Greek girl and had an estate nearby, while Cophen and Ariobarzanes visited us often, bringing news of Father or letters from Deidamia. For four years we lived in peace, until—"

Ariston frowned. "Excuse me, Lady, but could you elaborate on your marriage? Four years, even peaceful years, do not merely pass in the blink of an eye. Perhaps there are anecdotes you could share?"

"No," she said.

Ariston bristled at her flat refusal. "You threaten to do this history a grave disservice. To write with authority on a subject I must know all that I can. You've given me much insight into what manner of man was Memnon—in war, in intrigue, and in planning. You've even given brief glimpses of him in peace, but I should like to know more in order to do his memory justice."

"And it is on account of my own memory that I must refuse," Barsine replied.

"Why? Is that epoch of your life so distasteful that you've expunged it from your mind? If it's not, then I don't understand your reticence. I would have thought you eager for the world to know everything about your husband."

Barsine's eyes narrowed; her lips curled in disgust at the young Rhodian's attempt at manipulation. "You spoke of love, earlier, but have you ever been in love, Ariston? Not mere infatuation or salacious longing, but the kind of love that leaves you unable to breathe in your beloved's presence, the kind of love a poet seeks to capture in words or a sculptor in marble? Have you ever stayed awake all night watching your beloved sleep, thanking the gods for your good fortune even as you curse them for making him a man you must share with the world?"

Ariston felt his face redden. "No, madam, I have not."

"Only after the gods bless you with the experience will you begin to understand my reticence, as you name it." Her hand rested lightly on the silver chest at her side. "Suffice it to say I spent my life preparing for those four perfect years, even as I have spent the balance of my life trying to recapture them. Age is ever our enemy, Ariston, and I have few memories that have not paled with time or become diluted by pain and loss and the bitterness of dreams unfulfilled. I have shared much with you, and I will share more, but those four years are not for posterity." Barsine sighed. "They are mine alone."

Ariston swallowed his annoyance and nodded. "I apologize, Lady. We will move on, then. You were about to tell me what happened to ruin this idyll."

Barsine said nothing for a moment, her brows drawing together as she gathered her thoughts. "Do you believe that all things share an interrelation, that the loom of the Fates weaves all of our diverse threads into connected strands? Cut one and it affects others of the same strand?"

"It is certainly possible," Ariston said.

"Mentor's death—and I do not call it 'untimely' as has become the fashion of so many; his death was determined by the gods and came at the preordained time, as will yours and mine—his death touched more lives than just mine and Memnon's. After us, the person most affected was the eunuch Bagoas."

Ariston leaned forward, chewing his lip. "His is a name I would have least associated with feeling anything where Mentor was concerned."

"Oh, no," Barsine said. "Mentor was the one man Bagoas feared above all, and his position in life, his very presence, served to hinder the eunuch's ambitions. Bagoas saw Mentor's passing as a sign of favor from the gods, a validation of his naked thirst for power."

"He was a eunuch. How far could he hope to rise?"

Barsine shuddered. "He sought the pinnacle. Gelded or not, Bagoas was one of the most bloodthirsty and cunning men I have ever had the misfortune of knowing. Even before Mentor's death he plotted the destruction of every possible rival for Ochus's affections. The Blessed One, alone, knows how many innocent souls he sent to the headsman, their families too, on trumped-up charges and outright lies. But he knew, as you have surmised, that Persia's nobility would never countenance being governed by a eunuch, so he was forced to find a pliant member of the royal family and elevate him to the throne. Most believe he aided an already sickly Ochus into the grave, and his sons too, sparing only the youngest—a stripling named Oarses. That poor young fool ruled as Bagoas's puppet for over a year before he exhibited a little too much self-reliance and died because of it.

"By this time, Persia was in a sorry state. Nations, like Nature, abhor a vacuum, so in the absence of power the Egyptians sought their independence—thus ruining Mentor's good works—and Macedonia made tentative, and unopposed, raids onto Asian soil. Nevertheless, because of his penchant for poisoning those who displeased him, Bagoas was hard-pressed to find a member of the royal house willing to take the throne. In Armenia, my father convinced Artashata to accept it."

"Why not Artabazus himself?" Ariston said. "Surely none could find fault with his blood."

"Not with his blood, no, but many did not trust him because of his past. Also, he was well into his seventh decade. My father believed the rigors of kingship would have been too much for a man of his age. Twenty-five years Father's junior, Artashata's pedigree was equally impeccable—his grandfather and my great-grandfather, Artaxerxes the Second, were brothers—and he had served the rightful king all his life, even earning great renown in combat against the barbaric Kadousioi on the shores of the Sea of Ravens. Still, he was a mild man, almost gentle, and it was with some reluctance that he donned the peaked tiara and became Darius, the third to bear that storied name. His first act as Great King, before marching to Egypt, was to listen to my father's counsel and have his murderous benefactor drink from his own poisoned cup.

"His second act, again guided by my father, was to invest Memnon with the powers of a Persian general and order him to repel the Macedonians . . ."

The Hellespont
Year 1 of the 111th Olympiad
(336 BCE)

A PALL OF DUST HAZED THE BLUE SUMMER SKY, THROWN UP BY THE shuffling feet of seven thousand Macedonian infantrymen. Memnon could see the flash and glitter of tall *sarissas*, of bronze helmets and breastplates, as individual phalanx battalions took up positions on the far bank of the Skamandros River. "Look at them, Ephialtes," he said to the dour-faced Athenian standing at his left hand. "Are they not magnificent?" Ephialtes, a giant of a man in an ill-fitting cuirass, hawked and spat, the only answer he deigned to give. Memnon grinned at Pharnabazus, who stood to his right. "Ah, the sting of defeat yet troubles him. Tell me, Ephialtes, did the Macedonians look this magnificent at Chaeronea?" That battle, two years prior on the Cephissus River in Boeotia, cemented Philip's supremacy over the Greeks and made Athens tributary to Macedonia—a situation the proud sons of Athena longed to rectify.

"Damn you," Ephialtes rumbled, "do we attack or not?"

"Impatience is what cost Athens the field that day. Philip, you see, cannot be goaded. He will not move one moment before he's absolutely ready, and if he can provoke his enemies into impulsively attacking, so much the better. But, that's not Philip we're facing. That's Parmenion. Cut of the same pattern, perhaps, but from cloth of far lesser quality. Still, he won't make a move until we do."

Memnon's soldiers seemed in no great hurry to launch an attack against the Macedonians, either. They held the southern bank of the Skamandros, on a slight rise overlooking the sluggish flow of the river. Five thousand men stood at Memnon's back, his personal guard of *kardakes* stiffened by a mixture of Greek mercenaries, Arcadians mostly—men trained for war in the iron schools of the Peloponnese and paid for by Persia's new Great King, Darius. To Memnon's pride they stood their ground, patient and unconcerned.

Ephialtes gestured at them. "What is the point of having this army if you're not going to use it? Zeus Savior, Memnon! You've marched us out here for five days now! For five days we've formed ranks, stared at those whoreson Macedonians for an hour or more, and instead of charging you sound retreat and back we go into camp! Have you no spine, man?"

"Have you no respect, dog?" Pharnabazus stepped toward Ephialtes, the slender Persian's anger unfazed by the Athenian's size. Memnon, though, caught his arm, a slight smile on his face.

"It's not a question of spine, Ephialtes, nor of spleen, nerve, or backbone. It's one of wits. You've noticed, I'm sure, that Parmenion follows my lead as though he were under my command: we march out; he marches out. We form ranks; he forms ranks. We stand; he stands. We withdraw; he withdraws. He waits because that is what Philip has inculcated in him—the idea that your enemy *will* become impatient and he *will* make a mistake. Pharnabazus, tell our erstwhile Athenian what would happen if we charged the Macedonians now."

Sneering, Pharnabazus crouched and drew his knife, sketching out the battlefield in the sandy loam. "I see no cavalry, so Parmenion's center would hold us at bay—his *sarissas* are five feet longer than our spears—while both his flanks executed a split to the right and left. This would thin his flanking battalions by half, from twenty men deep to ten, but it would give him the extension he would need to overlap and encircle us. Then . . ."

The tip of the Persian's knife obliterated their position.

Ephialtes grumbled. "So what do we do? Play this game with them until winter sets in and we all go home?"

"The Macedonians don't break off their campaigns on account of the seasons, Ephialtes, and neither do we." The Rhodian's other officers joined them: Omares, Patron, and Damastes, the former governor of Abydus.

"What's the word, Memnon?" Patron asked. Since his return from Syracuse, Patron had renounced the sea, becoming a land commander and even working at developing his skill as a horseman. *Saw too many good lads lost to Poseidon's fury,* he told Memnon once, while deep in his cups, *unburied and cursed to never know peace. By Hades! I want my bones put under good, solid earth when I die!* "Do we attack?"

Memnon pursed his lips. "We've seen them. They've seen us. Parmenion doesn't expect me to make a move until he does, and he won't. He remembers the holy terror we caused when we crossed Mount Ida in the spring and caught his man, Attalus, by surprise at Cyzicus. That debacle cost him three thousand good soldiers. He likes his odds if he can wait us out and lets us make the first move. Let's crush his hopes again, shall we? To your posts, gentlemen," he said. "Prepare to sound the withdrawal."

A quarter of an hour later the *salpinx* blared. Slowly, like some great lumbering beast, Memnon's forces hung a fresh curtain of dust in the air as they pulled back from the riverbank. From the Macedonian side could be heard jeers and catcalls. *Sarissas* rattled and laughter erupted as a few of Parmenion's highlanders raised the hems of their linen tunics and shook their genitals at the backsides of the retreating Greeks. "Come over," they called, "and we'll give you a proper fucking!"

Last off the field, Memnon simply waved to the Macedonians and strolled after his column.

While the Macedonian camp lay less than a mile from the Skamandros,

Memnon pitched and fortified his own some five miles up the river valley; now, a well-worn road led between camp and potential battlefield. The first two miles passed in less than an hour.

His men were in good spirits, as they should be, for they were well paid, well fed, and well commanded. After defeating the Macedonian invaders at Pitane on the Gulf of Elaea, then at Cyzicus, and finally at Percote, they had driven them back almost into the Hellespont's turbulent waters. All that remained to Parmenion were Abydus, Cape Rhoeteum, and the Dardanian Plain.

"Soon, not even that," Memnon said. He marched among his men, listening to their stories as he spun fables of his own. The only long face belonged to the Athenian.

"At least we could have camped closer," Ephialtes muttered, "then we wouldn't have so far to march every gods-forsaken day!"

"It's beautiful weather, my friend, and marching is good for the soul. Truly, what else do you have to do?" Memnon clapped the Athenian on the shoulder.

"Killing Macedonians would be preferable to slogging through this heat and dust."

"Patience, Ephialtes."

Halfway into the third mile a flurry of activity behind them brought Memnon up short. He turned as a mounted scout, a native of the Skamandros Valley, reined in and vaulted from his saddlecloth.

"My lord!" he said in an accent so thick as to be almost unintelligible. "The Macks! They didn't wait around! Gone back to their camp, they have! And they put out no patrols!"

"Sentries?"

"Aye, but they ain't paying much heed!"

Memnon thanked the man and walked away. He studied the makeshift road, looking back the way they had come. It was late afternoon, the sun bright and hot in the western sky. They should have plenty of time . . .

A sharp whistle brought his aides running. Memnon sent a command to Pharnabazus at the head of the column. He didn't use the trumpeters in case the sound of their clamor echoed over hill and hollow. A single word, the command easily remembered by even the most lack-witted ground-pounder: *exeligmos*. The aides ran to do his bidding and in moments the army shuffled to a halt. Memnon heard his command bawled down the line, from officers to veteran rankers to individual infantrymen; he watched as his five thousand men executed a countermarch with practiced precision.

At the command "*Exeligmos!*" the ten soldiers leading each thousand-man company stepped right, faced to the rear, and marched between the files, back the way they had come. The second soldiers followed, and the third, until finally the troopers in the one-hundredth position, the *ouragoi*, had but to turn in place and dress ranks with their mates. An aide brought Memnon his shield and helmet as his officers hurried to take their posts at the new head of the column.

Ephialtes glanced about, a bemused look on his face. "What goes?"

"It's time," Memnon said, slipping his arm into his shield's leather sleeve. "Now, we kill some Macedonians."

MEMNON'S SUDDEN REAPPEARANCE CAUGHT THE GLUM MACEDONIANS unprepared. Annoyed at being denied battle once again, most had stripped off their armor and were tending their cook fires, baking bread for their evening meal or slugging back their daily ration of wine. The last thing they expected was to see a battle line of Greeks fording the Skamandros, charging full-tilt toward the ditch and earthworks protecting their camp.

Trumpets blared on both sides. Five thousand Greek throats raised the *alala*, the undulating war cry that vented fear and bolstered courage; from Macedonian throats came curses and shouts of alarm. Parmenion and his officers scrambled to whip their men into some semblance of a phalanx. The Macedonians jostled one another, tripping over their equipment; some snatched their *sarissas* and met the Greeks half-naked, others paused to throw on chest armor or a helmet.

It availed them nothing.

With Memnon in the lead, the Greeks breached Parmenion's defenses. The Rhodian leapt the ditch and scrambled up the earthworks, his shield held high to deflect *sarissa* blades or sword strokes. He reached the top and, with an underhand thrust, sheathed his spear in an attacker's unarmored vitals. The man went down screaming, clutching the blood-slick shaft. Memnon clambered over the crest of the earthworks and planted a foot in his victim's groin, tearing the weapon free. Another Macedonian naked but for greaves and a Thracian helmet howled as he charged into the breach. Memnon swung his shield edge-on. Oak and bronze met flesh and bronze with a sickening crunch; the man dropped, helmet and skull staved in. The Rhodian shifted his weight. A third attacker, coming on the heels of the second, received the gory blade of Memnon's spear on the point of his bearded chin. His head snapped back in a spray of blood and shattered teeth as the iron sliced through the roof of his mouth, into his brain. Memnon kicked the corpse free of his spear.

Greeks poured over the earthworks on three sides of the camp. Damastes' company struck from the right; Omares' from the left. Memnon's company, flanked by Pharnabazus's and Patron's, drove through the Macedonian center, making for the command tent and Parmenion. Here, the fighting was fiercest. A wild mob of highlanders, men of Parmenion's own county, raised a hedge of *sarissas* to protect their general and kinsman. Iron ripped through bronze and flesh, each true strike marked by a rooster-tail of bright blood. The ground underfoot, churned and saturated with bodily fluids, became reeking mud that clung to a man's sandals.

The Greek advance might have faltered there had Ephialtes, bareheaded and bloody, not carved a breach in the enemy line. Memnon watched as the huge soldier hoisted a wounded Macedonian over his head and hurled the unfortunate onto the *sarissas* of his comrades, adding another and another until their combined weight snapped pike-shafts, opening a hole. Ephialtes, snatching up a sword in each hand and bellowing like a madman, plunged into this rupture. Memnon sent a dozen hoplites after him to give the Athenian cover.

With his camp overrun and defensive line shattered Parmenion had little choice but to call for a general retreat if he hoped to salvage anything of his army. A *salpinx* wailed, its final note trailing off in a mournful echo. Memnon recognized the signal. Through his own trumpeters, he ordered the Greeks to cease their slaughter. By the hundreds, the Macedonians disengaged and ran; those unable, through wounds or the ravages of heat, threw away their weapons and begged for mercy.

Ephialtes struck down one would-be prisoner and had his sword upraised over another as Memnon caught his arm. The Athenian, eyes glassy and wild, snarled and tried to shake free; Memnon backhanded him across the cheek.

"Get hold of yourself, damn you!" Memnon roared. "Get hold or I will kill you where you stand!" Ephialtes blinked. Blood drooled down his face, and his chest heaved with his exertions. Lowering his sword, he looked around not unlike a man waking from a deep sleep. "Go," Memnon said, gently this time, "take some rest. You've earned it." The Athenian nodded, stumbled toward the earthworks.

All around, shattered by heat, thirst, and exhaustion, Greeks sprawled amid the dead and wounded Macedonians, gasping for breath through the narrow slits of their Corinthian helmets. Others scoured the bodies for allied wounded, ignoring Macedonian pleas for succor.

"No, brothers!" Memnon called to them, wrenching off his helmet and handing it to an aide. "Help them, as well!" Water bearers circulated among friend and foe, alike.

The Rhodian found Pharnabazus sitting outside Parmenion's tent, bruised and blood-spattered, but otherwise unharmed.

"This one is going to keep the old bastard up nights, Uncle," he said, smiling. "I imagine he is cursing himself for letting you leave Thrace alive."

"Ah," Memnon said, "but the true test for us will come later. Parmenion is a mere preamble, a rehearsal for the carnage that is Philip."

"Surely Philip will not be so foolish as to continue his plans for an invasion, not after we have sent his famed general back to Europe with a bloodied nose?"

Memnon smiled. He held out his hand and helped Pharnabazus to his feet. "That, too, is but a preamble. Come, we've much left to do besides taking care of the wounded and the dead. We will camp here, tonight. Anything of any use we'll take back with us tomorrow. Send out the scouts. I want to know precisely where Parmenion is. I'll have Patron set sentries and guards for the prisoners—how ironic would it be if we fell victim to our own ruse, eh?"

Memnon's men worked well into the night securing the Macedonian camp. Men fed from captured stores while bonfires of *sarissa* shafts provided enough light for Greek armorers to harvest every scrap of bronze and iron. Sweeter smelling cressets flared around the surgeons' tents on the edge of camp, nearest the Skamandros. Cleaned up, though still armored, Memnon went among the pallets of wounded, talking to men of both sides. His own soldiers he hailed by name, asking after their wounds and listening as they recounted their deeds that day; among the Macedonians, he introduced himself and tried to allay their fears, asking their names and their fathers' names in return. Many of them recognized him from his exile at Pella.

Memnon saw one familiar face in particular among the Macedonian wounded. The Rhodian crouched. "Koinos, isn't it?" he asked. The red-bearded man nodded. Blood welled from a cut in his side; another in his scalp left his hair matted and filthy. "It's been many years since the road to Mieza, but I've not forgotten your patience with my nephew. Is there anything I can do for you, my friend?"

"My lord," Koinos croaked, tears in his eyes. He rose on his elbow. "I beg your mercy. Kill me and have done, for I'd rather be dead than any man's thrall."

Memnon, though, summoned one of his Greek surgeons. "Get this man cleaned up. You need fear neither death nor slavery, Koinos," he said. "I give you my word. You and your men will be my guests until terms can be arranged with Parmenion. Failing that, I will send you back to Pella myself. All of you."

Koinos sighed his thanks and sank back onto his pallet.

Damastes and Omares were among the wounded, as well. For Damastes, the surgeons held out little hope. His helmet had been split open by an axe-wielding highlander, the skull beneath shattered. Memnon sat at his side, clasping his limp hand and whispering reassurances in his ear. Omares' prognosis was much better, though the *sarissa* wound to his left thigh would keep him bedridden for a month or more.

"I'll send you off to Assos," Memnon said, smiling. "Let a few courtesans nurse you back to health."

"Praise Zeus! Better make it two months," Omares replied. His grin became a grimace. A surgeon worked over his leg, stitching and cauterizing. "Wish your Egyptian was here. This one has a ham-handed touch."

"Ah, Barsine won't let Khafre out of her sight." In truth, he wished Khafre were here, too. Perhaps he could do something for poor Damastes. But, he'd sent the Egyptian to Ephesus with Barsine and the children to keep them well out of harm's way. Memnon smiled. "You told me once that each of your wounds reminded you of something. What will this one remind you of?"

Sweat glistened on Omares' scarred forehead. "That I'm slower than I used to be."

An hour later, Pharnabazus found him still at Omares side. The older man slept fitfully; Memnon studied the dancing flame of a lamp. The Persian's light touch on his shoulder roused him. "A messenger delivered this." Pharnabazus held a scrap of parchment, torn from a corner of a map, rolled up, and tied with a leather thong.

Memnon slipped it out and unrolled it, holding it closer to the light. There was no mistaking the blocky Greek letters . . . or the location the map fragment depicted.

"What is it?"

"A message from Parmenion," Memnon replied. "He wants to talk."

NEAR SIGEUM, ON THE WINDSWEPT DARDANIAN PLAIN, A TUMULUS OF rock and scrub brush overlooked the choppy waters of the Aegean Sea. The sandy strand below had known the tread of giants, for here, in the old days, Agamemnon, king of Mycenae and of the Achaeans, beached his fleet and unleashed the fury of the Greeks on the citadel of Troy. That ancient city, now little more than a sleepy village, lay four miles inland, across the Skamandros and near its confluence with the Simois River.

Memnon approached the tumulus from the south, riding alone along the ridge that formed a natural bastion between the plain and the coast. No guards shadowed him; he had even forbid Pharnabazus from following.

"It could be a trap, Uncle! You cannot trust him!"

A beaten man could, indeed, be desperate enough to attempt an ambush, but Memnon did not have that sense about this meeting. Parmenion wanted something—something specific. So Memnon rode alone, his interest, and his instincts, piqued.

From the base of the tumulus a goat trail wound up to its flat summit.

Memnon dismounted, wary. The Rhodian wore his full panoply—a muscled cuirass of silver-inlaid bronze, a kilt of studded leather, bronze greaves etched with images of snarling Gorgon heads, and sandals of thick ox hide. The gold-chased sheath of his cavalry saber hung from a plain leather baldric, and the bronze face of his bowl-shaped shield bore a Persian eagle device, cobalt-etched and lapis-inlaid. Memnon's Corinthian helmet, its tall horsehair crest dyed Egyptian-blue, sat cocked atop his forehead.

He tied his horse's reins to a bush and ascended the trail, his hand on his sword hilt, ears straining to catch any sound that might betray an ambush. Above the booming wind and the distant crash and hiss of breakers, though, the Rhodian heard nothing out of the ordinary.

Reaching the summit of the mound he found Parmenion, fully armed and armored, awaiting him. The Macedonian's cuirass was of dull bronze, etched not for decoration but from use, as were his plain greaves. His sword hung at his left hip, and he leaned on a short cavalryman's spear. Sunlight gleamed from its honed iron blade. Neither man moved or spoke.

Wind whistled through the rocks, ruffling Memnon's helmet crest. "Do we talk," he shouted at length, "or do we settle this like Hector and Achilles?"

Parmenion drove his spear butt-first into the thin soil, stripped off his sword and placed it on the ground. Memnon did the same, leaning his shield against a rock with his helmet and saber. Both men straightened and walked to the center of the tumulus.

"I didn't think you'd come," Parmenion said. He looked haggard in the bright sunlight; a man pushed to the edge of exhaustion then asked to take one step beyond. "I didn't think you'd trust me."

Memnon smiled. "I don't. But, we were friends, once, and I came to show you that I bear you no ill will."

"You have some of my men."

"And they will be well cared for, I promise you. My surgeons have treated your wounded same as mine."

"What of my dead?"

"We burned them," Memnon said. "I will have their bones sent to your camp. The men I hold prisoner, however, I cannot return to you until Macedonia leaves Asian soil. I have no wish to fight these same soldiers next month, or a year from now."

"Philip won't like that," Parmenion said.

Memnon's nostrils flared. "Then let Philip come and ask me for their release himself."

"He'll come soon enough," Parmenion said, baring yellowed teeth in a snarl of defiance. "Why do you prostitute yourself for a foreign despot when a king of Philip's caliber would be honored to have you in his confidence? Do you not see that your slavish manner is not in your people's best interest?"

"On this ground." Memnon scuffed at the soil. "You serve the foreign despot, not I! My people are not Macedonian, they are Asian Greeks and I serve them admirably!"

"Persia is unworthy of your best efforts, Rhodian, and you know it! Join us! You'll lose nothing, but think of what you'll gain! Imagine it, Memnon! A kingdom of your own stretching from the Straits in the east to the Halys River in the west, and from the Cilician coast in the south to the shores of the Euxine in the north—all the lands and cities therein yours to rule as you see fit."

"Under Philip's aegis, of course. By Macedonia's leave."

"Of course."

"And you say I'll lose nothing, Parmenion? What about my honor? I've sworn to defend my liege and master, the Great King, His Majesty Darius the Third. How could Philip trust me with a battalion, much less an entire kingdom, if I were to betray Darius to him? What would keep me from betraying Philip to some other warlord in exchange for even more land?"

Parmenion scowled. "It's not a slight to your honor to betray a barbarian. Indeed, Philip believes such perfidy should be rewarded."

"I'm sure he does," Memnon said. "Unless the perfidy is directed against him. How magnanimous would he be then, I wonder?"

"You're intractable, Rhodian." Parmenion shook his head.

"My father used to say much the same thing."

"That's your answer? You would die for this Darius, for this man you barely know?"

"I would."

"Why?"

Memnon, though, only smiled. He made to turn away, but stopped. "One last thing. It pleases me to let you keep your bridgehead at Abydus. Stray too far inland, though, and I will drown you in the Straits. Have we an understanding?"

Parmenion gave a short bark of laughter. "It pleases you to have an army at your door?"

"Army?" Memnon said. "A lofty name for a few bruised and beaten battalions. Yes, it pleases me. When Philip tires of scrapping with the dogs of Hellas and wishes a real fight, tell him I will be here, waiting."

"The years have made you arrogant, Rhodian," Parmenion said.

"Not arrogant," Memnon replied, walking off. "Honest."

TRUE TO HIS WORD, MEMNON RETURNED THE BONES OF THE MACEDONIAN dead to Parmenion at Abydus, along with the names of men captured and a list of the wounded. He rebuffed any attempt to ransom the prisoners, though, much to Ephialtes' chagrin.

"We could make a fortune off them, Memnon!"

"*We* would make nothing," the Rhodian said. He sat in an old folding campaign chair of sweat-stained wood and yellowed ivory, reading a dispatch from his man in Lampsacus, warning him of a growing pro-Macedonian faction in that city. "Such monies would go into the Great King's coffers and *we* would be left facing men we'd beaten before, men doubly inspired to regain both their honor and their family's wealth."

Ephialtes leaned closer. "The Great King wouldn't have to know . . ."

"I would know." Memnon dismissed the Athenian with a wave. Behind him, Pharnabazus watched the hulking Greek depart, a look of disgust on his face.

"You were right, Uncle. His people own nothing of their former glory. They have become a city of panderers and demagogues."

"But they might yet have their uses," Memnon replied, returning his attention to the dispatch.

The days grew long and tedious, the monotony broken by small skirmishes, clashes between patrols and foragers. Parmenion lacked the strength to stage a full-scale assault, and in the high summer heat, inactivity wore on his soldiers' nerves; to subvert them, Memnon sent the Macedonians a gift—a shipload of Thasian wine.

"That should keep them occupied long enough for me to slip away to Ephesus," the Rhodian said. "I leave you in charge, Pharnabazus. Send word to me should anything change."

Traveling by horseback and ship, Memnon arrived unannounced at his estate in the hills overlooking Ephesus a week later, knocking at the front door like a common visitor.

The older man who opened the door was one of his household *kardakes*, Phraates by name, a brawny old lion clad in a simple blue tunic, a sheathed sword at his side. Memnon smiled and caught his arm before he could exclaim. "Greetings, my friend," the Rhodian said, his voice low. "Quickly, fetch your mistress! Do not tell her what it's about!"

Phraates grinned. "Mistress!" he bellowed, vanishing into the heart of the house. "Come quickly! There is a man at the door with news!"

Moments later, Memnon heard Barsine's voice: "What news?" No music could have been sweeter, not even if made by Aphrodite's fingers plucking the enchanted lyre of Orpheus. Memnon sighed.

"Hurry, mistress!"

News was ever slow in reaching Ephesus from the Troad, despite the surfeit of ships that called on the port or the caravans from the interior that came to meet them. In a city of commerce and enterprise information was the most precious commodity. Thus, Barsine discarded dignity and sped to the door, her eagerness tempered with dread—not all news was of a pleasant nature. "Have you word of my husband?" She rounded the corner, her eyes wide with anticipation.

"Indeed I do," Memnon replied.

With a shout of joy Barsine sprang into his arms. "Oh, you cruel man! You cruel and heartless man!" The Rhodian caught her and spun her around. Both laughed like children, decency and decorum sloughing away as they kissed and laughed some more. Old Phraates wiped a tear from his eye and went to spread the good word: the master of the house had returned.

That night, fireflies danced through the garden, their glow competing with the lights of Ephesus burning in the valley below Mount Coressus and with the stars blazing overhead. Sounds of merriment drifted from the house as Khafre regaled the household with the story of Queen Nitocris's cats, each comedic turn accompanied by the squealing laughter of the girls, Apame and Artonis.

Memnon cocked his head, smiling at the sound. On the bench beside him, Barsine stirred. "They love Khafre's tales," she murmured.

"He has that magical touch," Memnon said. "In Egypt, I expected at every turn to encounter talking cats because of his stories. It disappointed me when they did nothing but yowl and demand attention."

Barsine traced the line of his jaw with her fingertips. "When will it be safe to return north? The girls miss their horse trails so."

"Hopefully soon." Memnon caught her hand and kissed each fingertip.

"Have you missed Adramyttium?"

Barsine rested her head on his shoulder. "I have missed the quiet. Ephesus has its . . . charms, but it has too much bustle and its politicians declaim too loudly for my tastes. I fear your Penelope has become a country girl."

He kissed her forehead. "As soon as the Macedonians pull back across the Straits we'll return to Adramyttium. I've missed the quiet, too."

"Will they? Pull back, I mean?"

Memnon sighed and did not answer.

"You do not believe they will, do you?" Barsine read his thoughts. "Even though you have broken their spirit, shattered their army? What purpose could it serve them to remain?"

"A temporary setback to Philip's plan is the only triumph I can claim," Memnon said. "He'll mend their hurt by bringing a new army. I've purposefully left open a route to Asia in hopes it will draw him in. Once that happens, our best option will be to crush Philip decisively, on ground of my own choosing."

"Be careful, my love," she replied.

Memnon ran his fingers through her hair; gently, scarred hands cupped Barsine's face and drew her close. "Say it again," he whispered, his lips brushing hers.

She laced her arms around his neck, caressing the muscles of his back and shoulders. "My love."

She gasped as Memnon swept her up and carried her deeper into the garden, where none but the fireflies and the stars could witness their lovemaking.

Summer in Ephesus lacked the tedium, the monotony of the Troad. Memnon filled his days with the business of war, from reviewing Thymondas's mercenary recruits to haggling with bronzesmiths over the price of shield facings, greaves, and helmets. His nights belonged to his family, to his niece and daughter, and especially to Barsine.

On such a night, a month after his return, a fist hammering at the front door shattered the evening calm; a familiar voice yelled Memnon's name above the staccato pounding.

"Merciful Zeus!" the Rhodian said, rising from bed and pulling on a tunic. "What is Pharnabazus doing here?" Barsine reached for her robe. Her hands shook, and a sudden feeling of despair knotted her stomach. She followed Memnon out into the courtyard. Khafre, too, joined them, as well as Phraates and his fellow *kardakes*.

Two of the soldiers helped Pharnabazus as he staggered into the courtyard. The Persian looked disheveled, caked in the dust of his hurried flight south. Memnon caught him as he tried to stand.

"Uncle!" he gasped.

"Barsine! Fetch water! Khafre, check him for wounds!" Carefully, Memnon eased his nephew down near the fountain at the center of the courtyard. Unbidden, Phraates brought a lamp closer as Khafre knelt and ran his hands over Pharnabazus.

"I . . . I am not wounded, Uncle!"

Barsine brought a pitcher and filled a clay cup. Water sloshed as Pharnabazus snatched it from her and gulped it down, spluttering and choking. "Not so fast, brother," she said. A second cup blunted his thirst.

"What goes, Pharnabazus?" Memnon asked, his face a mask of concern.

"It's Philip!"

"Has he crossed into Asia?"

The Persian shook his head. "He's dead, Memnon! Assassinated by a man from his own guard!" Stunned silence followed. "I rode as fast as I could to bring you the news."

Memnon exchanged glances with Barsine; Khafre clutched a scarab amulet hanging around his neck, his lips moving in silent prayer. The *kardakes* in earshot blinked, unsure if they should credit what they had just heard. Philip? Dead?

"A man of his own guard did it, you say?" The Rhodian rocked back on his heels. "Who paid him, I wonder?"

"It was Pausanias," Pharnabazus said. "Do you remember him? An Orestid; he was one of Philip's former lovers."

"I remember him," Memnon said, though he could scarce believe that the man had nursed a grudge against Philip for nine years. What had caused him to exact vengeance now? Memnon noted the confused expressions on Barsine and Khafre's faces. "Pausanias insulted the King's new lover," he explained, "causing the lad to get himself killed against the Illyrians—this would have been the year I returned from Sidon. The lad's kin, with the King's blessing, got their revenge on Pausanias by getting him drunk and handing him over to the stable hands. As a gesture of reconciliation, Philip promoted him to his guard. Pausanias obviously never forgave the slight. How did it happen?"

"As I heard it, Philip was preparing to enter the theater at Aigai, part of the celebration of his daughter's marriage to the king of Epirus. Philip planned to go in alone, to show his Greek guests he had nothing to fear from his own people. Pausanias approached, made to embrace the King, and put a dagger through his heart, instead. He tried to escape, but soldiers of Alexander's entourage killed him before he could get far."

"Or before he could be questioned."

Pharnabazus raised an eyebrow.

"Come, nine years is a bit long to nurse a grudge, don't you think?" Memnon said. "Someone had to put Pausanias up to it. If not Alexander, then likely it was Olympias. The queen has ever hated her husband."

"No matter. Alexander rules Macedonia now," Pharnabazus said.

"We'll send word to Artabazus, to the Great King, and continue with our own preparations."

"Preparations for what? Philip's dead, so too his crusade against Persia. Parmenion has withdrawn from Asia, leaving his deputy, Calas, in charge of the few troops that remain. We should sweep them into the Straits and celebrate our victory, Uncle." Pharnabazus smiled through the dust.

Memnon stood. Seeing the grim look on his face, Barsine felt the knot in her stomach tighten. "Nothing's changed," he said. "Alexander will come in Philip's stead, with Philip's generals and Philip's army. We've earned a respite, perhaps, but that's all. Only celebrate when your enemies are dead, Pharnabazus. *All* your enemies."

No sooner had Philip been laid to rest than the first ripples of discontent began, spreading outward from the cultural epicenter of Athens. Even as the Greeks did homage to Alexander, they whispered against him. "A mere Margites," sneered the orator, Demosthenes, recalling the Homeric buffoon who lacked the intellect to count beyond ten. Alexander ignored them; he went about securing his borders in preparation for his march to Asia.

A year of Demosthenes' rhetoric stoked mere discontent into fiery, full-blown defiance. Thebes struck the first blow. Supported by Athenian weapons and money, and with promises of aid from Sparta, the Thebans threw off the Macedonian yoke, laid siege to the garrison inside the fortified acropolis, the Cadmeia, and slaughtered those citizens whose sympathies were with the King. News of the uprising reached Alexander in Illyria, where he campaigned against the tribes of the Apsus Valley. Though only twenty-one, Alexander responded with the ferocity of a seasoned monarch.

He razed Thebes.

Perhaps Alexander meant it as a warning to the Greeks, or perhaps to illustrate the lengths to which he would go to punish those who flouted his will. Regardless, a city that had stood for centuries, a city celebrated in song and poetry, ceased to exist after only a few days of fighting. Six thousand men were massacred; their women and children sold into slavery. Twenty thousand Thebans, Memnon heard later, had glutted slave markets as far away as Egypt.

"Yet," Memnon said, "he proclaims it's his intent to bring freedom to the Greeks of Asia and avenge Persia's past invasions of Hellas." Along with the sons of Artabazus—Pharnabazus, Cophen, Ariobarzanes, and young Hydarnes—Memnon rode across the ridges of Mount Ida and into the valley of the Aisopus River at the head of three thousand cavalry, mounted *kardakes* and mercenaries. Omares with five thousand Greek mercenary infantry followed in their wake. They were bound for Zeleia at the behest of the western satraps, to attend an assembly of war.

"Alexander is a hypocrite!" Pharnabazus snarled. "Mark my words, brothers—he will kill more Hellenes on his own than any Persian in history!"

"We should send an embassy to Pella," Cophen said. The twenty-three-year-old half-Persian chewed his lip, his dark brows furrowed in thought. Unlike his brothers, Cophen was clean-shaven, a Greek affectation frowned upon among the Persians. "Perhaps there's a diplomatic solution we've overlooked."

"An embassy?" Ariobarzanes twisted in the saddle, staring at his brother with a mix of shock and contempt. Though only nineteen, Ariobarzanes towered over the others—he had Deidamia's height, Artabazus's sharp features, and Mentor's thick shoulders and corded muscle. Even lanky Hydarnes, two years Ariobarzanes' junior, derided Cophen's comment, snorting under his breath.

Pharnabazus shook his head. "The time for talk is past, Cophen. We go to fight, and if you have not got the stomach for it, you had best tell us now."

"I'm no coward!" Cophen snapped.

"No?"

"No," Memnon said sharply. "But he is in a delicate situation."

Relief flooded Cophen's face. Beside him, Ariobarzanes frowned. "How so?"

The Rhodian glanced back. "He's Alexander's guest-friend."

"A silly boys' pact," Pharnabazus said.

"It is nothing of the sort," Memnon replied, his tone chiding. "He is a prince of Pharnacid blood who pledged friendship to the son of a Macedonian king. They were too young, perhaps, but it was rightly done. Though now, Cophen, you're also a soldier of the Great King, and the Great King has ordered us to stop Alexander. To do otherwise is to betray your oath to Darius. So, which do you break? Your word to Alexander, sworn before the gods, to always act in friendship, or your word to the Great King, also sworn before the gods, to serve him to the best of your ability? A delicate situation, to be sure."

"I do not envy you," Hydarnes muttered.

"Who would the rest of you choose were you in my place?"

"The Great King," Ariobarzanes said without delay. "He is our kinsman, our blood."

"I would never have befriended that little peacock in the first place, but I agree with Ari," Pharnabazus said. "What's more, Alexander owed it to you, too, to not act in an unfriendly manner. In my mind, he broke the bond the moment he declared war on your kinsman."

"Hydarnes?" Memnon looked back at him. "Speak up. What say you on this matter?"

The teen blushed at being singled out. "I would hold my oath to the Great King above my friendship with Alexander," he replied. "If for no reason beyond Father and Mother's sake. We are beholden to them to act in a forthright manner. Should we not, their lives would be forfeit."

Memnon nodded.

Cophen listened, his head cocked to one side, absorbing his brothers' opinions. "What about you, Uncle?"

Memnon did not answer immediately. His brow furrowed as he turned the question over in his mind, examining it from every angle. His silence stretched into minutes.

"Uncle?"

"I would fight," Memnon replied, at length. "And here's my reasoning: you've befriended Alexander, not the whole of Macedonia. Therefore, you're under no compulsion to avoid battle against the followers of Alexander, only against Alexander in person. It is simple, really. Keep clear of his path and fight with all your heart. That way, you will have kept both your oaths—to your friend and to your King."

The brothers nodded in unison.

"My thanks," Cophen said. "You've made clear my obligations. I will fight."

Pharnabazus wiped his brow in mock seriousness. "I, for one, am relieved, brothers. We should tell the men. It will ease their concerns . . ."

Laughter erupted; even Memnon grinned, shaking his head at the eldest of Artabazus's sons. Cophen took their ribbing in stride. "None of us will fight if we don't pick up the pace." He spurred his horse to a canter.

Memnon's forces reached the shaded vale of Zeleia late the next day. The small hamlet had changed little since Artabazus ruled the region. A few more buildings, perhaps, but still rustic by comparison with the towns of the Aegean coast. More impressive was the second city that ringed Zeleia, a city of tents and pavilions crawling up the sides of the valley from both banks of the Aisopus. Cook fires and forges spewed smoke into the cloud-laced sky; shouts in half a dozen tongues competed with the clamor of ironworkers and the bellow of oxen. Battalions of levies drilled in open fields, farmers given spears and told how to march by a cadre of grizzled old soldiers. Squads of cavalry, Hyrkanians in fur-trimmed helmets or turbaned Medes, cantered past on reconnaissance duty.

"How many men do you estimate the satraps have gathered?" Pharnabazus asked.

"Thirty or forty thousand," Memnon replied. "But only a fraction of them are soldiers. The rest are an armed rabble."

Memnon signaled a halt as a mounted Persian officer in a jacket of brilliant green, shimmering with gold embroidery, met them on the road. He reined in and raised a manicured hand in greeting. "Memnon of Rhodes? Lord Arsites bids you welcome. I am Niphates and I have been instructed to show you to your camp site."

"Greetings, Niphates," Memnon said, bowing at the waist.

"Lord Arsites also bid me remind you that the council of war begins the third hour after dawn tomorrow."

"I would speak with him tonight."

"Alas, that is not possible," Niphates said. "Lord Arsites is closeted with his brother satraps, and they have commanded that no one disturb them. They will speak with you tomorrow, sir."

"Which satraps, good Niphates?" Memnon felt the initial sting of exclusion turn to suspicion.

"The lords Spithridates and Rhosaces," Niphates said. "Arsamenes of Cilicia, Mithrobarzanes of Cappadocia, and Rheomithres of Greater Phrygia. If you will follow me, sir?"

Memnon gestured for him to lead the way and followed with his troops.

"A rogue's gallery," Pharnabazus muttered, in Greek. "And we arrived just in time, I think."

"I don't believe they would have summoned us at all," Memnon said, "if not for your father's influence with the Great King."

"Will this council be a waste of time, you think? If they have already decided on a plan of action . . ."

Memnon shrugged. "I doubt it. They will drink tonight and dicker tomorrow, each man jockeying for the most advantageous position. For myself, I will say and do what is best for the kingdom, no matter how uncomfortable it makes our hosts. We're all fighting for the common good, after all."

Pharnabazus nodded to their guide. "Let us hope they realize that, as well."

Niphates escorted them to a dusty field close to a mile down river from Zeleia. Crude tents already clogged a portion of the field. Tribal levies, Memnon reckoned, noting their rough homespun tunics and leather leggings, men of the river valleys and hollows of the Phrygian interior. Curious eyes watched as glittering ranks of Greek infantry filed onto the field. Memnon ignored the implied insult that came from billeting his men at the ass-end of the army and bid Niphates farewell.

"Send my compliments to Lord Arsites," he said, smiling as the smug Persian trotted off. When Memnon turned back to the sons of Artabazus, his eyes were as cold and hard as flint. "Ari, find who commands these levies and ask them to join me. Pharnabazus, we will share our food with them, our wine. Instruct the men to fan out and get to know our neighbors. I want them to be our allies by dawn."

He would show these satraps how well he could play their political games.

By the second hour after dawn, Memnon's officers had the Phrygian levies on the drill field, inculcating in them the necessary skills to fight a Macedonian phalanx. They were light troops—javelineers and slingers mixed with a few hundred archers. Omares made new battalions out of them, assigning animal totems they would recognize from their homeland: fox, lion, and bear. While he taught them flank and cover, augmenting the Phrygians' already prodigious skill at hit-and-run, their headman, Bocchus, stood off to one side, grinning in approval.

Leaving orders for a day of merciless exercise, Memnon and Pharnabazus took their horses and cantered up the Aisopus to Zeleia. Both men cut striking figures, grim-faced and armored in glittering bronze with gold and silver ornaments. Beneath his armor, Memnon wore the plain *chiton* and leather kilt of a Greek soldier; Pharnabazus opted for the richly worked tunic and trousers of a Persian lord.

The castle of Zeleia, with its tall turrets and ancient stables, bustled with activity as servants scurried to do their lord's bidding. Arsites had commandeered every inch of space, evicting the town's ruler and his family so he might have extra room for courtiers, kinsmen, soothsayers, and musicians. Graciously, he offered shelter his brother satraps Arsamenes and Mithrobarzanes who did not have palaces nearby, their personal entourages adding to the swirling chaos.

Niphates met them in the crowded castle yard. "I trust you slept well, sir?"

Memnon and Pharnabazus dismounted and passed their reins to a pair of grooms. "Exceptionally well, good Niphates," Memnon replied through a mask of politesse. A hint of mockery clung to the Persian as he gestured for them to follow.

Their path took them through the heart of the castle and out onto a stone-paved terrace overlooking the Aisopus River. At its center, slender columns carved of local hardwood supported a loggia, its roof tiled in slate and terracotta. In true Median fashion, gardeners had positioned pots of fragrant shrubs and flowers around the loggia; divans awaited their repose while servants and wine stewards stood close at hand, ready to answer the satraps' needs. Under the loggia, a map table awaited their perusal.

Memnon spotted the gaunt form of Spithridates reclining on a divan, his eyes serpentine and his beard peppered with gray; his brother Rhosaces and other high-ranking officials, perhaps a dozen men altogether, clustered around him, laughing and chatting amiably.

"Is this a council of war or a garden party?" Pharnabazus muttered.

Niphates announced them. "My lords, Memnon the Rhodian and Pharnabazus, son of Artabazus."

Heads swiveled.

"My lords," Memnon said. He and Pharnabazus sketched slight bows, a minor obeisance reserved for perceived equals. After a pause conversation resumed; Memnon and his nephew exchanged glances. They were to be ignored, it seemed. But two men detached themselves from the rest and approached Memnon. One was tall and well muscled, perhaps thirty, with jet-black hair and beard. His companion was older by twenty years, at least, with the expansive girth of a man accustomed to rich foods and wines. His flushed face, all wattles and jowls beneath an unruly beard, bore scars of debauchery rather than battle.

"You are the brother of Mentor?" the younger man asked.

"I am."

"It saddened me to hear of his passing. I am Arsamenes. This is my uncle, Mithrobarzanes."

"Rhodian," the fat Persian burbled.

"My lords." Memnon indicated Pharnabazus. "This is—"

"He needs no further introduction, Rhodian. We all know *whose* son he is." A third satrap drifted over. Arsites of Hellespontine Phrygia, a slightly built man with a thick mane of dark hair and a narrow hatchet-face, curled his lips into a sneer of disgust. To his credit, Pharnabazus refused to rise to the baiting. "I have heard that your officers were putting the Phrygian levies through their paces this morning," Arsites said. Over his shoulder, he called to another satrap. "Have you heard this, Rheomithres? The Rhodian hopes to make your hillmen into better fighters."

"They are sneak-thieves and curs," the satrap Rheomithres replied. He was a barrel-chested Persian with a light olive complexion; his russet hair and beard, both painstakingly curled, betrayed his Armenian ancestry. "It would be a better use of your time if you could teach my dogs to dance."

Memnon accepted a goblet of wine from the steward. "I disagree. Under the proper leadership your Phrygians would make excellent light troops."

"And whose is the proper leadership? Yours?"

"Or yours, if you would but take the time."

Rheomithres bristled. "My time is none of your concern, Rhodian! Neither are my Phrygians!"

Spithridates rose from his divan. "We have not assembled here to discuss your wretched Phrygians!" he said. Shadowed by his brother, the Iranian crossed to the map table. Memnon and the others followed. "Philip's whelp seeks to make a name for himself outside of his illustrious father's shadow. The Great King has charged us with stopping him."

"He is a boy, this Alexander?" Arsamenes asked. He and Mithrobarzanes, both hailing from deeper inside Asia, had heard very little about Macedonia's young king, save rumor and innuendo gleaned from Greek traders. "A lad of twenty?"

"If that."

"He is twenty-two," Memnon said. "But do not judge him based solely on his age. He learned warfare at the foot of one of its greatest practitioners—his father—and he's inherited a veritable machine of destruction in the form of the Macedonian army. His soldiers revere him. What's more, he has the backing of Philip's men, Parmenion and Antipatros among them. No, my lords, the whelp is just as dangerous as the sire. Perhaps more so."

"Where is he, and do we know the disposition of his forces?"

Memnon looked to Pharnabazus, who stepped up to the map table. "At last report, our spies put the Macedonians near Cardia in the Chersonese. That was several days ago. I would wager he has reached Sestos by now and is crossing the Straits to Abydus as we speak. The bulk of his army is infantry—six phalanx battalions, the Foot Companions, supported by various light and missile troops—but his true striking power is in his cavalry, the elite Companions and the famed horsemen of Thessaly. All told, Alexander commands close to forty thousand men."

"What forces are at our disposal?" Memnon asked Spithridates. The satrap studied the map.

"We are rich in cavalry drawn from regions where men are born on horseback: regiments from Media, Bactria, Hyrkania, and Paphlagonia. Add your own allied Greek cavalry and we have over ten thousand horsemen. We have gathered another ten thousand infantry, mostly levies and your own mercenaries."

Concern crossed Memnon's face. "Twenty thousand men? Can we expect more from the Great King?"

"We must rely on what we have."

"Then we must hope Alexander splits his forces or leaves enough behind to guard his lines of communication. It would be best if we could avoid a face-to-face battle—"

"You would have us play the coward?" Arsites snapped. "Advise us to run and hide, and hope the boy grows bored and decides to move on?"

Memnon kept his calm. "Nothing of the sort. I suggest we strike Alexander where he is most vulnerable—his supply line. We know Philip beggared Macedonia with his constant warring and political machinations, leaving Alexander with scarcely two *drachmas* to rub together. Thus, the young King is wagering his future on finding all the forage and supplies his army will need in our rich granaries and fields. We must deny him access."

"What *are* you suggesting, Rhodian?" Spithridates asked.

"That we withdraw our forces ahead of him and lay waste to the countryside," Memnon said, staring at the Persian lords in turn. He gestured to the map. "Destroy anything he might be able to use: livestock, crops, wells. Foul the rivers and the lakes. Gut those towns where he might seek succor. Burn every leaf, every branch, and even the grass underfoot. Deny him the luxury of forage, gentlemen, and I promise you he will be forced to return to Thrace before the month is out. That's when we strike. Bring up the fleet from Cyprus to contest his passage back to European soil. Then, we can crush Alexander in one combined action, on land and sea."

Arsamenes of Cilicia nodded, clearly impressed with Memnon's thinking, while the faces of his fellow satraps registered a gamut of reactions—from disbelief to anger to moral outrage.

"All well for you to propose the destruction of our lands," Arsites said, "when your own estates are elsewhere!"

"I will burn every scrap of land I own if it means Alexander's defeat," Memnon said.

Arsites, though, shook his head. "No! I will not consent to such desolation, not in my lands! You, brothers, may vote to override me and bring poverty and horror to this district, but I will have no part in it!"

"Nor will I," Spithridates said. "And to even suggest it is an affront to the gods."

"Were I you, my lords, I would worry less about offering offense to the gods and more about failing the Great King. His Majesty wants Alexander stopped," Memnon said, "and we do not have the luxury of squeamishness."

"We must stop him, yes, but at what cost? You would have us destroy the very lands we fight to preserve! It is madness!" Rheomithres said. "Listen, brothers! We must give our cavalry free rein! Allow them to do as they have done for centuries—strike and retire, strike and retire! Let them harry the Macedonians back to the Straits!"

Spithridates absently knuckled his beard. "No," he said. "This calls for a decisive stroke."

"You think we should meet the boy head-on?" Rhosaces folded his arms over his chest. The brothers exchanged looks.

"This bald-faced challenge to His Majesty's suzerainty demands nothing less. We must meet Alexander face to face; albeit on ground of our own choosing—ground that will negate their numbers."

"You mean to engage the cream of Macedonia's army," Memnon said, a measure of disbelief in his voice, "with tribal levies and inexperienced soldiers?"

"No." Spithridates' eyes narrowed. "I mean to engage it with the cream of Asia's cavalry. Our horsemen outnumber theirs, Rhodian. If we make this a fight between cavalry corps, how can we not grind this whelp's pony-mounted hillmen into dust?"

"Do you understand the threat you're facing?" Memnon replied. "I have seen the Macedonian army in action, gentlemen, in Thrace. It doesn't fight as you think it should. Have you ever stopped to wonder why Philip outfitted his phalanx with the sixteen-foot *sarissa*, surely the most unwieldy weapon ever devised? No? Because of its ability to hold an enemy at bay. It is the anvil to his cavalry's hammer. Philip trained these elements to fight in unison, not as separate arms. The phalanx holds a foe immobile while wedges of Companions slice through their ranks. In battle after battle I've seen it used to the same grisly effect. Our levies, our cavalry, will not fare any better!" Memnon slapped the map table with the flat of his palm, emphasizing his words. Words lost on the Persians. He read defiance in their sneers, their flared nostrils. They would listen to no other options.

Memnon shook his head in resignation. "As you wish, my lords. If open confrontation is the course you choose, my best advice would be to select ground that can be held against infantry and cavalry, a place where the cohesion of their phalanx would be in jeopardy."

The satraps stared at the map, the Troad and Hellespontine Phrygia delineated on papyrus in fine black ink, major towns and roads marked in red. Where? Where could they face the Macedonians and have the advantage of position?

"A riverbank," Pharnabazus said suddenly, breaking their silence. He gestured to a spot on the map a day's travel from Zeleia. "This is the plain of Adrasteia—horse country, well-watered by streams and small rivers flowing from Mount Ida to Propontis. Most are wide and shallow, though swift, but this one, the Granicus, has an eastern bank that rises to the height of a man over the riverbed."

"I know this place," Arsites said, nodding to Pharnabazus. "It is perhaps eighty feet across, thigh-deep in places, with a bed of mud, clay, and loose rock. The western bank has little or no elevation."

"And," Pharnabazus added, "it is on the road to Dascylium. Alexander will have to attack if he hopes to dislodge us, thus breaking Philip's cardinal rule of warfare—make your enemy come to you."

"Praise Mithras!" Rhosaces thumped Pharnabazus on the back. "The son of Artabazus has hit upon something! An excellent plan!"

"What say the rest of you?" Spithridates said. One by one, the satraps voiced their assent. Finally, the Iranian lord raised an eyebrow at Memnon. "Rhodian?"

Memnon glanced from man to man then back to the map, chewing his lip. "I strenuously urge you to reconsider this," he said. "Nevertheless, Pharnabazus is right. It's perfect ground for the confrontation you desire." He placed a hand on his nephew's shoulder.

Spithridates nodded; he leaned over the table, his weight resting on his balled fists. "Granicus it is, then. And it must be decisive, brothers. Decisive. I do not doubt that the Great King will be generous to the man who brings him the head of Philip's son!"

SUNSET TURNED THE RUSHING WATERS OF THE GRANICUS RIVER TO BLOOD. Memnon crouched on the high bank and contemplated an approaching rider. The horseman, a Persian by his dress, forded the river and guided his mount up the treacherous eastern bank. Watching his struggle, Memnon knew Pharnabazus had been right. This river, properly held, would be the rampart upon which Alexander's soldiers shattered themselves.

"But it must be properly held," the Rhodian muttered, rising. And therein lay the problem: the satraps had no conception of what was needed to properly hold the Granicus against Alexander. "Put infantry and missile troops in the center," Memnon had told Spithridates that very day, as they surveyed the ground from horseback. "Put strong contingents of cavalry on both flanks and another to the rear of the infantry, in reserve. Let Alexander exhaust himself on our spears, then rake in from the flanks and finish him!"

The satrap, though, had disagreed with him. Honor demanded he meet Alexander's threat of cavalry with his own. "We will line the bank with horsemen," Spithridates said, nodding as he imagined ranks of armored riders glittering in the sun, heir horses pawing the ground in anticipation, the breeze snapping their bright pennons. "The infantry can have our leavings."

In the end, Memnon saw his counsel tossed aside yet again. In the order of battle he would anchor the Persian left with the horsemen of the Troad; beside him would be Arsamenes and the half-wild Cilician cavalry. Arsites would come next at the head of the riders of Paphlagonia, a country on the southern coast of the Euxine Sea, their war-gear of the finest manufacture, from iron-rich Sinope. Spithridates would hold the next position with the Hyrkanians of the Caicus Valley—the same Hyrkanians who had helped defeat Artabazus nearly two decades ago—and the white-cloaked Lydian lancers; Rhosaces would be on his brother's flank with a hodge-podge of Ionians, mercenaries for the most part, and in Memnon's reckoning the weakest of the cavalry contingents. Mithrobarzanes and Rheomithres would anchor the right with the Bactrian and Median troops, respectively—more military settlers brought west in the early days of the empire, and who maintained their cultural identities despite the passage of two centuries.

Omares, at Memnon's recommendation, would command the infantry in reserve, on a hillock some four hundred yards to the rear. All told, ten thousand horsemen would comprise the Persian front, which would stretch in an unbroken line for over a mile.

Memnon prayed it would be enough.

The Rhodian walked to where the Persian horseman waited, attended by one of the *kardakes* who held the reins of his mount. The disheveled and mud-spattered soldier was a scout. In the gloom Memnon could not tell whose man he was.

"What did you find?" he asked.

The scout saluted. "The Macedonians are near. They will be here tomorrow, by midmorning at the earliest."

"Could you get close enough to discern their forces?"

The man shook his head. "They had a screen of light horse well forward of their main column."

"Very good." Memnon gestured to the *kardakes*. "Escort him to Lord Spithridates, and see that he gets food and wine. Draw them from my own stores."

The scout bowed at the waist. "Thank you, my lord."

Memnon waved him away and turned to look at the Granicus one last time. The ruddy glow of dusk deepened as the sun sank below the distant shoulders of Mount Ida. Stars flared to life overhead, their light made more sublime by the proximity of the sons of Ares: Metus and Pallor—Fear and Terror. Few would sleep, even among the veterans. Nor was Memnon immune. Tonight, he would dine with his nephews and his officers, followed by a tour of the camp so he could speak quietly with his men, and finally he would retire to his tent with ink and papyrus to write letters to Barsine and the girls in Ephesus. In the small hours before dawn he would pray to the gods of peace . . .

For once the sun rose he would again belong to the Lord of War.

"ZEUS!" HYDARNES MUTTERED, PATTING THE NECK OF HIS RESTIVE horse. The seventeen-year-old son of Artabazus watched the far bank of the Granicus with a mixture of fear and awe as rank after glittering rank of Macedonians took up positions there. Churning clouds of dust drifted downstream on the faint breeze. "How many of them are there?"

Memnon nudged his horse closer to his nephew. Though Hydarnes' youth troubled him, it was not his place to deny the boy a chance to prove himself, not when he was here at his father's urging. All Memnon could do is keep him near, shield him to the best of his ability. "It doesn't matter. All you need worry about is the one man in front of you. Focus on that one man, Hydarnes. After you kill him, focus on another, then another. Understand?"

Hydarnes swallowed and nodded.

"Look," Pharnabazus said, gesturing with his spear. Like Memnon, and indeed all of the first rank, he had traded his javelins for a heavy eight-foot spear, a hoplite's weapon, counterweighted with an iron butt-spike. "There goes Parmenion. I guess the little peacock plans to attack after all."

Easily, Memnon spotted the old Macedonian general, surrounded by his officers as he galloped into position on the enemy left. He would face Rheomithres and Mithrobarzanes on the Persian right. "Probably his last attempt to preach caution to Alexander," Memnon said.

"Alexander is not Philip," Cophen, who was in formation behind Pharnabazus, said, his voice as severe as his features. "Caution is not a fixture of his personality."

"Nor is anonymity." Memnon shaded his eyes against the late afternoon glare. "Look, there."

The Macedonian right wing faced their position, wedges of Companion cavalry flanked by light infantry on their right and battalions of the *sarissa*-wielding phalanx on their left. A cheer burst from thousands of throats as Alexander, astride the massive Thessalian stallion Boukephalos, took his place at the head of the Companions. Though broad-shouldered and muscular, the young King lacked Philip's height. He wore armor similar to that of his men—a bronze breastplate and greaves—along with an open-faced Boeotian helmet topped by a red horsehair crest and a pair of tall white kestrel feathers. *He stands out, even without Philip's height.*

The cheering faded; the two armies stood in silence.

There would be no grand speeches, no boastful promises. The men at Memnon's back, like the men at Alexander's, were professionals, grim students of the War God's murderous academy, their skills honed not from useless dialectic but from the blood and suffering of martial necessity.

Horses stamped and whinnied.

Alexander, Memnon decided, stared right at him; the Rhodian stared back, eyes narrowed. He wanted to ride over and ask the young man why . . . what hurt had the world done to him to make him desire its subjugation? Why was he hiding behind this fiction of Greek vengeance? More than that, though, Memnon wanted to know what happened to the inquisitive child who had sat with Artabazus and questioned him at length about Persia's inner workings. But Memnon knew there would be no answers. There would be only blood.

Blood and suffering.

Between them, the Granicus swirled and bubbled.

Memnon exhaled. Up and down the line leather creaked, bronze clattered as men shifted in the mounting tension. Beside him, Pharnabazus cracked his knuckles, one by one. Ariobarzanes rattled his sword in its sheath for the hundredth time. In the second rank, Cophen muttered a prayer. And Hydarnes—seventeen-year-old Hydarnes, whose sweat-drenched face was as smooth as Alexander's own—panted in terror and tried to keep his breakfast down. *Was I any different at Lake Manyas?*

Across the river Alexander raised his hand, dropped it. Behind him a Macedonian *salpinx* wailed. A vanguard of three cavalry squadrons—two of light horse and one of Companions—began their advance, followed by a battalion of the phalanx. They raised a din, shouting curses and war cries against the Persians holding the far bank against them. Reaching the Granicus, the cavalry plunged into the river, leaving the phalanx to struggle in their wake.

"Do your best!" Memnon said to his nephews and his men in earshot, recalling his brother's words to him on the cusp of battle at Lake Manyas. "Fight with heart and with honor, and leave the rest to the Fates!" He raised his spear to the heavens and shouted, "For Zeus Savior and Victory!"

"Zeus Savior and Victory!" his men thundered.

From the rear of Memnon's formation a trumpet sounded; the first volley of javelins lofted into the sky. He glanced up as the missiles arched over their heads. They seemed to hang motionless in the air for the span of a heartbeat before weight and gravity brought them slicing down into the Macedonian ranks. A second volley followed, and a third.

Chaos erupted in the riverbed.

Horses screamed and thrashed, toppling their riders into the foaming waters of the Granicus. Men lost their footing and were dragged along by the current. The light horse faltered; the Companions, protected by heavier armor, weathered the storm of javelins and surged up the treacherous bank, into the teeth of Memnon's cavalry.

"For the King!" the Rhodian bellowed, rising on his thighs and thrusting his spear into a snarling Macedonian face. Blades licked out down the line; javelins flew thick and fast, cast from the middle ranks to rip pointblank into enemy flesh. Again and again Memnon stabbed down into that seething mass of men, some on foot, others on horseback, thwarting their attempts to ascend the bank. It was butchers' work. Iron grated on bronze, on bone. A miasma of churned mud, sweat, and damp leather could not mask the coppery stench of mingled human and equine blood rising off the Granicus.

No one could maneuver, so tightly were the horsemen of both armies compacted. It was thrust and draw, thrust and draw, all while trying to stay mounted. Javelins hissed over Memnon's shoulders; to his left, he watched a *sarissa* blade gut the horse of one of his *kardakes*, sending man and beast toppling down the bank. The mortally wounded animal crushed enemy soldiers under its flailing hooves, while the rider regained his footing and sowed havoc with his short spear until the weighted butt of an infantryman's pike shattered his skull.

On either side of him, Pharnabazus and Ariobarzanes fought with maniacal fury, their spears ripping into the morass of flesh until their arms ached from sheer homicidal exertion; Cophen slung his javelins with the accuracy of a man spearing fish in a net. Hydarnes, too, kept pace, drawing and casting the ash-and-iron missiles with manic urgency.

"Hold the line!" Memnon called. "Check your interval!" Over the din of slaughter—the screams of rage and fear, the crack of javelins and spears on shields, the splash of blood-fouled water—came a new round of trumpet calls, orders played on a Macedonian *salpinx*. Memnon glanced out over the field, expecting to see a fresh wave of troops bearing down on his position. Rather, amid shouts and invocations to the War God, he watched as Alexander wheeled the Companion cavalry half-right and charged the

Persian center at the oblique. Rhosaces' inferior cavalry would receive the brunt of the Macedonian's main assault.

The vanguard was a feint, Memnon realized, his respect for the young king growing. *He attacked our left knowing Spithridates or that fool Arsites would draw from the center to reinforce the flank. We played right into his hands!*

But Memnon had no time to dwell on Alexander's tactics. As the Companions charged the Persian center, the balance of the Macedonian line also rushed to attack. Now, his cavalry had to contend with archers and javelineers from Alexander's right flank, men of Crete and the Agrianians who could clear swaths of the bank to afford their allied horsemen a bridgehead.

Memnon ground his teeth in fury. If he could hold them here, perhaps Alexander would overextend himself . . .

The Rhodian's horse shied from the gory *sarissa* blades; onto that sliver of ground a Macedonian clawed his way up from below, a heavy shield on his left arm. Javelins caromed off its oak-and-bronze bowl. One of his mates thrust a broken *sarissa* into his hand, and the valiant soldier stayed in a crouch, sweeping the weapon low and wide as he inched forward, hoping to hamstring a horse, to break a foreleg. Two more shielded men clambered up behind him.

"Stop them before they form a wedge!" The Rhodian raked his spurs back along his horse's flanks. The terrified animal started, hooves stamping. Memnon leaned out and put his weight, and the weight of his skittish horse, into a murderous thrust of his spear. It deflected off the first Macedonian's shield to skewer his left-hand companion in the neck, snapping shaft and vertebrae. Blood spewed.

Bellowing, the lead Macedonian brought his *sarissa* up in a wild slash at Memnon's head. The Rhodian saw it coming. He twisted, throwing his broken spear-shaft into the path of the blade. Wood cracked and splintered. The impact, which would have split his skull, helmet and all, numbed

Memnon's arm to the shoulder. His attacker stumbled, shield dipping mere inches. Inches were all Memnon's men needed. Iron flashed. Two javelins punctured the Macedonian's torso and sent him cartwheeling back onto the pikes of his fellows.

A single man remained.

"Spear!" Memnon roared, dropping the remnants of his shattered weapon. From the second rank, someone—Hydarnes, maybe—pressed a javelin into his palm. Whirling, Memnon flung the dart with such ferocity that it punched through the bronze cheek-piece of the Macedonian's helmet, ripping through flesh, bone, and brain until its point burst out behind his opposite ear. The corpse vanished in the wrack. Weaponless again, Memnon tore his saber from its sheath.

The archers on the far bank found their range, sending a hail of arrows into Memnon's soldiery. From closer quarters, *sarissas* and javelins were emptying saddles as the Macedonians attacked with renewed vigor, maiming horses and destroying the cohesion of Memnon's front ranks. Inexorably, the Companions and the men of the phalanx forced their way onto the bank. He would have to give ground.

Memnon held his sword aloft. "By ranks, fall back and reform! Fall—"

The Rhodian recoiled. An arrow glanced off his helmet even as the breeze from a wickedly barbed Agrianian javelin fanned his beard, missing him by a hairsbreadth. He heard it crunch through the armor and flesh of the man behind him. Recovering, he called out: "Trumpeter! Fall back and reform! Sound the order!" The horn skirled; slowly, the Persians began disengaging.

Memnon glanced to either side. Pharnabazus and Ariobarzanes, though slashed and bloodied, held their positions along with the remainder of the first rank—they would screen the withdrawal, giving the rear time to pull back a hundred yards and reform. He spotted Cophen's red-spattered face farther down, wielding a dead man's spear and filling his space in the line. Memnon looked for Hydarnes . . .

That son of Artabazus he found slumped against his horse's neck, the barbed iron-head of an Agrianian javelin buried in his chest. Gore-encrusted hands clutched at the shaft. Hydarnes looked up; his eyes held the most piteous expression, like a child in shock, unsure of what had just happened. "U-Uncle?" he managed, ropes of blood drooling from his mouth.

Before Memnon could react, though, a wall of Macedonians swarmed up the bank, *sarissas* and sword blades flashing, their charge preceded by a storm of arrows and javelins. Memnon's horse screamed and crumpled as a pike ripped through its neck. The Rhodian toppled backward. He struck the ground hard, his saber jarred from his grip. His attacker wrenched his *sarissa* free and clambered over the thrashing horse, his pike raised for a killing blow. Whatever exultation the Macedonian might have felt was short-lived as Ariobarzanes rammed his spear through the fellow's side.

"Move, Uncle! Move!" he heard Ari scream. Memnon clawed for his saber; he stood and staggered out of the fighting. Behind the clashing lines, he cast about for Hydarnes. The youth lay on his side in the trampled grass a dozen feet away, unmoving, his horse nowhere in sight.

"No!" Memnon rushed to his side. "Hydarnes!" Kneeling, he gently rolled the boy onto his back. Hydarnes' mouth hung open; lifeless eyes stared at the sky. Memnon's shoulders slumped. He leaned down and kissed his nephew's forehead. "I give you into Zeus's care," he whispered. "Go to the gods as a man." But, Memnon had little time to mourn. Alexander's charge had smashed the center of the Persian line; the flanks were breaking and the Macedonians threatened to overrun their position.

Memnon stood. A gesture brought a pair of *kardakes* to him. He recognized both men, despite their patina of blood and grime. "Mardius, Azanes, take my nephew's body and fall back to Omares' position. We will make our stand with the infantry." He looked about for a horse.

"Take mine, sir," Azanes said, dismounting. "I will find another in the rear."

Memnon nodded. "My thanks, Azanes." He studied Hydarnes' face, so pale and youthful in death, as Azanes handed the body up to Mardius. He wondered how he was going to tell Deidamia that he'd gotten one of her sons killed. For an instant, he prayed it would only be one . . .

The Rhodian vaulted onto Azanes' horse and gathered up the reins. Time to extricate the others. "Trumpeter!" he called. "Sound retreat!"

THE INFANTRY, FIVE THOUSAND GREEK HOPLITES, WAITED ON A HILLOCK a quarter of a mile from the Granicus. Omares knew the tale of the battle before Memnon arrived, having heard it from the Persian cavalry streaming past him in flight. Alexander was driving home his advantage but the sheer press of enemy horsemen slowed his advance. Dusk would fall before he could engage the infantry.

"I heard most of the satraps are dead," Omares said by way of greeting as Memnon and the sons of Artabazus cantered up. They had thrown the Macedonians back once more, hurling them back into the Granicus; in the brief lull, they had made good their escape.

"From whom?"

"Their men, as they hightailed it past us. Mithrobarzanes, Rhosaces, Spithridates . . . they all left their positions and rode against Alexander. The boy slaughtered them. Arsites and Rheomithres each scampered away with a handful of men. I don't know about Arsamenes. It seems the chivalry of Persia is leaving their loyal infantry in the dust without the slightest hint of regret."

"We've come to stand with you," Memnon said.

Omares glanced over his shoulder to where Mardius and Azanes stood vigil over Hydarnes' body. With his own hand he had drawn out the killing dart. He had composed the boy's limbs and washed the blood from his face with water from his own canteen before draping his cloak over the corpse. Still there was no kindness he could do that would begin to repay the debt he owed Artabazus. Save one. Omares turned back to Memnon as Cophen and Ari went to their brother's side, cries of anguish wrenched from their breasts. Pharnabazus remained on his horse, head bowed. "You can't stay with us, Rhodian," Omares said.

Memnon shook his head. "No, my friend. I won't leave. I led you and your men into this and I'll lead you all out or I'll spill my blood next to yours."

"A fine sentiment," Omares replied, "but useless. If you die here, the Great King will appoint some Iranian bugger to wage his war for him. He'll bungle it and a lot of good men will die needlessly. You're the only one in my reckoning who has the wherewithal to stop Alexander. This battle's lost. It's on you to win the war."

"He is right, Uncle," Pharnabazus said, looking up. "Darius will realize his mistake in not putting you in supreme command, and he will move swiftly to rectify the matter. Only through your generalship do we have any hope of recovering the Hellespont. But to lead us, you must live . . ."

Memnon said nothing; he chewed his lip, staring at the body of Hydarnes.

"You've got to withdraw, Memnon!" Omares said. "If for no other reason than to get these boys to safety, for Artabazus' sake! We will stay behind and cover your retreat!"

"Swear to me, Omares! Swear to me you'll throw down your weapons and sue for terms once we're off the field! There's no call for you and your men to martyr yourselves!"

Omares nodded. "Once you're away, I'll kiss the whelp's arse if that's what's required of me! First, though, we'll form ranks and give them a show. You and the boys get moving, sir."

Memnon gave a sad smile. "Sir, is it?"

"Aye, it must be your august presence." He gripped Memnon's hand. "If anything should happen here . . ."

"I won't let you go unavenged. You have my word."

Omares exhaled and nodded. "You'd best get going. What about the lad's body?"

"Pharnabazus?"

"We will take him with us," the Persian said. "Father . . . Father would not want us to abandon him to the Macedonians."

The Rhodian motioned for his men to mount up. Mardius and Azanes gently lifted Hydarnes' body and draped it over the back of a spare horse, handing the reins to Ari. Memnon vaulted into the saddle. Bridle fittings rattled as he spun back to Omares. "Remember, no martyrs!"

"Farewell." The old soldier smiled, slapping the horse's rump as Memnon turned and followed his column south, away from the circling vultures.

MEMNON LED THE SURVIVORS OF THE GRANICUS ALONG THE RIDGES OF Mount Ida, through valleys thick with pine. A carpet of fallen needles muffled the dull *clop* of their bone-weary horses. Despite exhaustion, despite wounds, Memnon drove them on through the long night, riding up and down the column to give his men encouragement, to make sure none were left behind. Finally, the Rhodian called a halt near dawn to allow stragglers from other cavalry brigades to catch up with them. He greeted the Hyrkanians, Medes, Bactrians, and Lydians personally, eager to piece together from them the fate of the Persian satraps.

"They very nearly killed him," he told Pharnabazus, groaning as he settled onto the ground beside him. The Persian handed Memnon a chunk of barley bread and a cup of wine. "I think luck was all that saved the bastard."

"Alexander?"

Memnon drained the cup, refilled it with water. "Satraps attacked him with their personal guards. Mithrobarzanes died first, I'm told, on

Alexander's lance. Rhosaces struck next, shearing off part of Alexander's helmet, but before he could land the killing blow the young king spun and impaled him. Spithridates came on his brother's heels; Alexander didn't see him. They said he was on the verge of splitting Alexander's skull when one of the Royal Bodyguard took Spithridates' sword-arm off at the shoulder."

"One cannot fault their lack of valor," Pharnabazus replied.

"No, only their lack of vision."

Pharnabazus stirred the embers of their small fire. Ari and Cophen slept, as did most of the men, sprawled out on the ground without cloak or wrap, still in their bloodstained armor. Some, like Memnon and Pharnabazus, sat and talked quietly. Others sat alone, lost in thought. "What are we going to do, Uncle?"

"Regroup. Alexander will secure Dascylium then make for Sardis, most likely. Then Ephesus." The Rhodian's face darkened. He had sent Barsine and the children there before leaving for Zeleia. "That's where I'll take the men. You I'm sending east to Susa, perhaps as early as tomorrow. Take Ari with you and deliver news of all you have seen to the Great King . . . and to your father. Tell His Majesty that, barring orders to desist, I will make ready to retaliate against Alexander."

"Retaliate? How?"

But Memnon would say nothing more. The Rhodian stared at the crackling embers, idly sketching a battle plan in the dirt with the tip of a stick. His brows drew together . . .

FEAR GRIPPED EPHESUS IN A VISE. MEMNON SENSED IT AS HE AND HIS MEN rode through the valley of the river Cayster and around the foot of Mount Pion. As fast as they had traveled, news from the Granicus traveled faster still, arriving as if borne on the wings of crows. Alexander was coming, but would he bring freedom or despair? Many of the town's leaders, pro-Persian oligarchs, had not waited to find out; they packed their belongings into ships and bolted, making for the islands or mainland Hellas.

By midday, Memnon reached his estate on the outskirts of Ephesus, where he dismissed his soldiers and sent Cophen to make preparations for Hydarnes' funeral. News of Memnon's arrival preceded him and a knot of men in fine Median robes met him at the gate, a deputation of the town's remaining leaders. They twittered about his horse like a flock of finches, peppering him with questions.

"Is it true, General? Is Alexander planning to destroy Asia?"

"Should we flee, too?"

"What should we do, my lord?"

Memnon raised his hand, demanding silence. "Alexander is a man, and a young man at that. He could no more destroy Asia than you could or I. But he is coming to Ephesus, gentlemen. We must make ready to repel him. Please, I have traveled a long distance. Right now, I want only to see my wife and family."

"But you say we should fight?" one man said, standing defiant. "Even after what he did to your mercenaries?"

Memnon frowned. "He did nothing to them. They surrendered—"

"You . . . you don't know?" Defiance fled, replaced by uncertainty. The others shrunk away from him.

"Know what? Speak up, man!"

"A-Alexander refused to accept their terms, General! He . . . he allowed his men to slaughter them even after some had thrown down their weapons!"

Memnon swayed in the saddle. Red rage gripped the Rhodian as he imagined Omares being struck down, his call for terms ignored. *I abandoned them.* Guilt and grief mingled, adding their weight to the unimaginable responsibility already on Memnon's shoulders. He ground his teeth until he tasted blood. "Is this true?" he hissed.

The men of the deputation nodded. "S-Some survived, but he has e-enslaved them and refuses r-ransom."

"They are to be examples, as Thebes was an example."

"If this is the war Alexander wishes to wage, need you ask what you should do?" Memnon snarled, gesturing for his *kardakes* to open the gate. "My thanks, gentlemen." He gave a curt nod and spurred his horse to a canter, leaving the officials frightened and bewildered.

Barsine met him on the portico of the house, greeting him with a goblet of wine and a damp cloth, the expression on her face as grave as his own. Memnon dismounted and walked slowly up the steps. Sunlight dappled her blue linen gown. He stopped a step below her, eyes level with her shoulders, and sighed. His forehead creased; he had to tell her about Hydarnes.

"Barsine, I—"

"No, my love," she said. "Say nothing until you have had a chance to rest and marshal your thoughts. Whatever ill news you bear will not spoil by keeping." She bid him drink the chilled wine, a strong Thasian, while she wiped dust from his face with the cloth. "I have ordered a bath prepared, then a light meal and a few quiet hours of sleep." She kissed the wrinkles on his forehead.

"What I have to tell you can't be put aside," he said, his hands going around her waist. "It's Hydarnes . . ." Memnon stared hard at the hollow of her throat, unwilling to raise his eyes to meet hers. He choked off a grief-filled sob. "He . . ."

Tears glistened on Barsine's cheeks as she leaned closer to him. She stroked his hair and neck. "Oh, Memnon," she whispered.

"I . . . I should have left him at Zeleia," Memnon said. "He was too young . . . too young."

"Come, my love. Come and rest." Barsine took Memnon's hand and led him through the house to a bathing chamber, its deep stone tub filled with steaming water. She dismissed the servants and tended him herself.

Mechanically, Memnon stripped off his armor, his tunic—stiff with dried blood—his sandals, and eased himself into the tub. He groaned as the water stung every gash and bruise on his body. As Barsine washed and trimmed his hair and beard, his eyes never left her face. He blinked slowly, exhaustion overtaking his taxed muscles. She cleaned his cuts, assuring herself that none needed stitching or bandaging, and massaged the kinks from his shoulders and neck. By the end of the bath, Memnon needed her help just to rise.

Barsine dried him with towels smelling of an extract of mint, and then led him to the next room, where servants had prepared a soft divan. Beside it were low tables of bread, olives, cheese, and wine. Near the ceiling, a fringed *punkah* circulated the cool air, its cord pulled by unseen hands.

Memnon stretched out on the divan, asleep before Barsine had a chance to fill a bowl of wine for him.

The Rhodian awoke some hours later, opening his eyes to stare at the ceiling. Fingers of light and shadow danced from the flame of a clay lamp. He felt warmth and weight on his arm; Memnon looked down to see Barsine's head pillowed on his forearm, her hands twined around the muscular limb. She sat on the floor at his side, her body leaning against the divan as she dozed. With his free hand, Memnon stroked her hair. Touching the silk at the nape of her neck sent a shudder of desire through his frame.

Barsine's eyes fluttered open. "Are you hungry?" she murmured.

Memnon shook his head. Gently, he drew her on top of him, kissing her with an intensity that left both breathless. Barsine straddled his hips, feeling heat radiating from his body, feeling her own moist response. She rose up, pulling her gown over her head. Memnon's fingers traced meaningless designs over the skin of her thighs, her hips; he ran his hands up her sides to cup her breasts. Sinking down, Barsine moaned as Memnon slipped inside her.

Their shadows writhed in the thin golden light; the hungry press of lips muffled their cries of passion. Soon, their sweat-beaded bodies lay intertwined on the divan, Barsine's head resting on Memnon's chest as she listened to the pulse of his heart.

For a long time neither spoke. Finally, Barsine sighed. "How . . . how did my brother die?"

"A javelin," Memnon replied. Quietly, he told her about the battle and its aftermath. She looked up, troubled, when he spoke of Omares' fate.

"May the Great God preserve us," she said.

Memnon stirred. "Have you seen Cophen?"

She snuggled closer, shaking her head. "I have not left your side. Khafre came in while you were sleeping. He has gone to look after the wounded. Lie still."

"There's too much to do."

"Can it not wait till morning?"

Memnon ceased moving, one arm pillowing his head, the other draped across Barsine's back. She could sense the tension flowing back into him, his muscles knotting and unknotting—no doubt a side effect of his mind growing restless and active.

"What is wrong?" she asked, rising up on her elbows.

He exhaled. "I have to send you away, Barsine. You and the children," he said, his voice low and hoarse. "Asia's no longer safe, not so long as the Macedonians remain unchecked. Even cities not on Alexander's route won't be spared from conflict. Democrats will rise up against the oligarchs . . . it will be the chaos of Rhodes all over again."

Barsine sat up. "Where will you send us?"

"To the Great King . . . to your father. I'm sending Cophen with you. Alexander is his friend, and he doesn't have the stomach to do what's necessary against him."

"What do you mean?" She reached down and picked up her robe, shaking it out before she stood and slipped it over her head. "Is this to be a unique war?"

Memnon sat up, too. He ran his fingers through his hair, rolled his shoulders, and cracked his neck. Exhaustion yet lined his face. "Unique? Only in its brutality. Alexander has proven his capacity for barbarity, shown the quality of his mercy at Thebes and at the Granicus. He seeks to cow Asia as he cowed Hellas. I mean to show him his error. I'll make him waste himself in siege after useless siege, force him to spend his most precious asset—his men. Then, after he's watched his companions shatter themselves on Asia's walls, I will take the fight back to his home. I will burn Macedonia to ashes if that's what it takes to get him out of our lands." Memnon took her hand, kissed it. "But I can't wage this kind of war if I know you and the children are near."

"Send us to Damascus or to Egypt, instead. I am sure Khafre would take excellent care of us in Egypt," Barsine said. Tears sprang to her eyes. She knelt. "Please, my love! Do not send us so far from your side!"

"I must," he replied. His heart wrenched in his chest. "Only in the shadow of the Great King will you be beyond the reach of my enemies, Macedonian and Persian. I must be free to move and to act without constrains of worry."

Barsine sobbed. Memnon gathered her up in his arms, holding her gently as she cried into his shoulder. "W-When?"

Memnon closed his eyes, tears streaking into his beard. "Soon."

THEIR SEPARATION CAME SOONER THAN MEMNON EXPECTED. THREE WEEKS after the debacle at the Granicus, in early Skirophorion, news came from Sardis. The commander of the citadel, one of Spithridates' cousins, betrayed the city to Alexander. His perfidy meant there would be no long siege, no pitched battle on the Hermus plain, no loss of Macedonian life.

"Alexander has his father's gift for intrigue," Memnon said, frowning. He and Khafre stood over a table set up in the courtyard of the estate, studying a map of Ionia and Caria. "His clemency toward Sardis will invigorate our opposition."

"How long before news of this reversal becomes common knowledge?" Khafre asked.

"We have hours, a day at the most." Memnon glanced up as Cophen entered the courtyard, followed by Thymondas, Azanes, and Mardius. "Well?"

Cophen nodded. "A ship is waiting, Uncle. We can leave as soon as Barsine and the children are ready."

"Good. You'll leave within the hour. Take them south, Cophen, to the Gulf of Issus. Disembark and travel overland to the Royal Road; your path should be unhindered all the way to Susa. Mardius, you and Azanes will accompany them. Take fifty *kardakes*, men you trust. Khafre?"

The Egyptian exhaled. "I will go, as well, though I still maintain my services would be of better use nearer to the battlefield."

"I feel better knowing you will make the journey with them, Khafre," Memnon said, gripping the Egyptian's shoulder. "Thymondas, you and I will lead the troops out before the good citizens of Ephesus realize we're gone. Take a thousand hoplites and reinforce Miletus. I'll take the balance with me to Halicarnassus." He straightened. "Gentlemen, time is of the essence. Go."

Men hustled about their business; soldiers and servants pitched in to ready horses and wagons, officers spread the word of their imminent withdrawal by word of mouth, exhorting their charges to be ready. Amid this buzz of activity Memnon remained still, dissecting the map again and again to be certain his tactics were sound. *Draw him in. Make him waste—*

Cloth rustled. He turned.

"So it is true? Sardis has fallen?" Barsine stepped out into the sunlight. In her black gown, her long hair hidden in the folds of a charcoal shawl, she looked as severe as Hades-bound Persephone.

"It's true," Memnon said. "Alexander is fifty miles distant. We're ill prepared to face him, so we're pulling out of Ephesus. You and the girls will leave for Susa within the hour."

"Where will you go?"

"Halicarnassus, to await the Great King's decision."

Barsine nodded. "We . . . we will be ready." She turned and vanished into the house, leaving Memnon alone in the courtyard.

The Rhodian sighed and turned back to the map. *Make him waste his men's lives . . .*

To avoid sparking a panic, Memnon staggered their departures from the estate to the harbor. The Rhodian sent Khafre and his family first, in a wagon with only a few meager belongings; Cophen followed. Azanes, Mardius, and their *kardakes* split up and took back-routes, looking to the curious like reinforced patrols. Memnon came last.

The ship, *Hesione*, had a wide deck and two banks of oars to give it added power on days of unfavorable winds. "Keep an eye on the captain," Memnon said to Khafre before he embarked. "And post your own lookout once you're past Rhodes. That stretch of the Lycian coast is thick with pirates."

"I will school them personally, Memnon," the Egyptian said. "My friend, may Lord Osiris watch over you and shower you with his blessings."

"And you, Khafre." Memnon bid farewell to Azanes and Mardius, acknowledging each of their men as they filed aboard. Finally, Cophen came with the children.

"Ah, my Little Dove and my Little Sparrow," Memnon said, kneeling. Both girls rushed to him and flung their arms around his neck. He kissed their cheeks, one then the other. "Obey your mother, and carry my love to your grandmother."

"Will we see you again, Father?" Apame said, tears falling from her thick lashes.

"Of course you will, Little Sparrow! I'll bring your horses to you in Susa next year and we can ride to Babylon, to see the Hanging Gardens."

Artonis sobbed. "Promise?"

Memnon smiled and kissed her, again. "I promise. Now, go with Uncle Cophen." Reluctantly, the girls disengaged themselves from Memnon and followed Cophen across the gangplank. The Rhodian stood, smiling despite the suppressed emotion trembling his lips, waving them on as if they were off on an afternoon's adventure rather than a journey of many months.

He felt Barsine's hand slip into his, turned.

"Is this truly for the best?"

"It is," he replied. "You'll be safe in Susa, I promise you. You'll be with family, with your father and Deidamia, and you'll want for nothing."

"That is not true," she raised his hand to her lips. "I will want for you."

Memnon gathered her in his arms. "I love you."

"My Odysseus," she whispered through her tears. "My love, come for us! No matter what you must endure, no matter the cost, come for us, Memnon! And soon! Promise me!"

"You have my word," he said, releasing her. "It's time." Memnon escorted her to the head of the gangplank, handed her down to Cophen. "Take care of yourself, lad, and watch over my most precious treasures."

Cophen smiled. "Like they were my own, Uncle."

With leaden steps, Memnon returned to the quay. Once clear, sailors drew the plank onboard, cast off the mooring ropes, and prodded *Hesione* away with punting poles. The captain bellowed for the rowers to "man the ash"; oars emerged from the ports, creaking as an *auletes* set the rhythm by piping a tune on his flute. The ship backed water. It spun away from the quay, putting its bow to the sea.

A sudden commotion in the stern caught the Rhodian's eye. Barsine appeared at the railing. Wind tugged at strands of hair that escaped from beneath her shawl. She raised her fingers to her lips . . .

Memnon stood and watched, burning her image into his memory, until *Hesione* vanished around the headland. "Watch over them, Lord Poseidon. I beg of you," he whispered. With a sigh, Memnon turned and left the harbor.

LONG SHADOWS STRIPED THE WALLS OF THE HOUSE BY THE TIME MEMNON returned to the estate. On the portico, golden light filtered through the oak leaves that gave the place its name. A profound sense of emptiness struck him as he crossed the threshold; even the paving stones missed the sound of children playing, the soft tread of Barsine's slippered feet.

Voices drew him to the courtyard, where he found Thymondas hunched over the map table. Nor was he alone. To Memnon's surprise, Pharnabazus stood across from him. Though filthy from weeks of near-constant riding, the Persian flashed a triumphant smile upon seeing Memnon.

"I pray you bring good news," the Rhodian said, his mood black.

Pharnabazus grabbed his arm. "His Majesty has made his decision, Uncle. Letters have gone out to every satrap and garrison left in the West."

"And?"

"On Father's advice, the Great King has appointed you supreme commander of the Asian war, on land and sea! He bids you exterminate this Macedonian threat in whatever manner that you deem most expedient, no matter where it takes you. He asks only that you send Alexander to Susa in chains, if the opportunity arises."

Thymondas grunted. "This changes things."

"It gives us a much needed edge." The Rhodian exhaled. He felt the fetters of subservience drop from his limbs. *This will be my war, my Egypt.* "Thymondas, you and I will leave before dawn. Pharnabazus, you'll bring the fleet up from Egypt and Cyprus."

"How many vessels?"

"All of them!" Memnon snarled. "It's time we taught Alexander a lesson!"

Interlude V

Barsine's condition worsened with each passing hour. Was it the emotion involved in reliving the past? Or perhaps it was the advanced nature of her illness coupled with her refusal of the old Egyptian's concoction? Whatever the culprit, Ariston could only watch in despair as her breathing grew shallow and labored, as sweat slicked her feverish forehead. She lay on her side; Harmouthes sat behind her, patting her back as one would a child's in hopes of loosening the humors clogging her lungs.

"Last . . . last time!" Barsine hissed through clenched teeth, bloody spittle flecking the coverlet. "L-Last time I s-saw him!"

"Mistress, please!" Harmouthes said, wiping her lips with the sleeve of his robe. "Let me prepare you a draft! I beg of you!"

"No!" Spasms wracked her body; a fit of coughing not even her silver chest could abate. Her hands knotted around it. "Almost . . . time!" she croaked. "H-Halicarnassus! Tell him . . . !"

Ariston leaned forward. "I know about Halicarnassus, madam. After Ephesus, which Alexander took without a struggle, he marched south to Miletus, reduced it, and set his sights on Halicarnassus. It's an impressive city. I have been there, seen the ruins of the siege. Some of the old soldiers lived nearby and were eager to tell the tale."

"Macedonians?" Harmouthes asked. Ariston nodded. "Then you know but a fraction of the truth, young sir. The flatterers of Alexander have scoured the official records clean of anything derogatory toward their king. His former soldiers have scoured it even from their memories. I am sure they told you that Halicarnassus was an unequivocal Macedonian victory."

"To be fair," Ariston said, "Alexander *did* take the city."

Harmouthes glanced at Barsine. Though she wanted to speak, her fight for each breath left her with little to expend on words. Tears glistened in her eyes. Harmouthes sighed, stroked her damp brow. "Alexander did not take the city, Ariston. Memnon gave it to him . . ."

Halicarnassus
Year 3 of the 111th Olympiad
(Late 334 BCE)

Halicarnassus is a rock.

That thought ran through Memnon's mind as he walked the high battlements at sunrise, stopping now and again to peer through an embrasure at the deep ditch ringing the landward side of the city. A remarkably defensible location, besides its dry moat Halicarnassus boasted forty-foot walls with towers at close intervals, three fortified gates, a walled acropolis, and two citadels—Salmacis in the west and Arconessus in the east—guarding the mouth of the harbor. Springs and cisterns provided ample fresh water, and so long as his fleet controlled this part of the Aegean Memnon could re-supply the place at will. *Not just a rock*, the Rhodian thought as he ascended a series of steps to the highest point of the city—the wall above the acropolis, *but an atoll poised to wreck the Macedonian advance.*

Spread out below him, the city resembled a theater. Its harbor-side agora was the *orchestra* (the "dancing floor," as his men called it), and in a semicircle above rose successive tiers of stone, mudbrick, and plaster—houses, shops, and factories that were shaded by myrtle, boxwood, and scrubby oak. Its beauty, its simplicity, rivaled that of Assos save for one piece of architectural folly. On the terrace above the agora squatted a monolith that, in Memnon's eyes, represented nothing but raw and unapologetic *hybris*: the unfinished tomb of Mausolus, the Mausoleum.

Massive even from the height of the acropolis, the Mausoleum had a podium base of white marble topped by an expansive colonnade and a step pyramid. At its apex one hundred sixty-five feet above the ground a statue group of Mausolus and his queen-sister, Artemisia, riding in a four-horse chariot gleamed in the morning sun. Scaffolds marked where a quartet of sculptors and an army of apprentices carried out their work despite the threat of war. Already, he could hear the ring of hammers, the creak of ropes.

Memnon shook his head. He had no reservations about pillaging that eyesore of its marble and brick—the dead tyrant's memory be damned!—should he need it for the city's defenses. He'd rip up the very paving stones and fling them over the walls himself if it came down to it.

The Rhodian passed into the shadowed heart of a tower, its cool air spiced with the tang of smoke, sweat, and oiled leather, and took a flight of stairs down to the level of the acropolis. Outside on the grassy sward soldiers assigned to the tower busied themselves sharpening and greasing the heads of stockpiled arrows. Nearby, in the shade of an old boxwood tree, a troop of slingers filed grooves in their lead bullets, etching slogans in the soft metal—'take that!' or 'regards.'

One fellow, a jolly-faced killer from Cos, separated his bullets into piles, each lot bearing the name of one of the twelve gods of Olympus. "Who should get the extras, sir," he called out as Memnon passed. "Zeus or Poseidon?"

The Rhodian grinned. "Ares." Their chuckles followed him down to the next terrace of the acropolis, where a knot of officers awaited him on the steps of the temple of Zeus Polias. Pharnabazus and Thymondas stood together, talking in low voices; Ephialtes sat on the steps, slicing sections from an apple with his belt knife. Memnon's fleet commander, Autophradates, a slender Mede with heavy-lidded eyes and sleek black hair, waited with two men the Rhodian barely knew. The first, Orontobates, was a freebooter from Susa who had finagled his way into becoming satrap of Caria; an unassuming man of average height, his serpentine eyes reminded Memnon of Artaxerxes Ochus. The second man, Amyntas, son of Antiochus, was a renegade Macedonian with the pale skin and russet hair of a Lynkestid. If he could be believed, his family's ties to Philip's assassin, Pausanias, sparked a blood feud with Alexander. Already, the young king had executed two of Amyntas's brothers.

"Gentlemen," Memnon said. "All is prepared?"

In unison, the assembled officers nodded assent. "The bulk of the fleet awaits your orders on Cos," Autophradates said. "Per your wishes, one squadron is moored in the harbor and another is north, across the peninsula, in the Bay of Mendelia."

"All of the city's magazines and stocks are overflowing," Pharnabazus said. "We have enough supplies in place to withstand a siege of many months, should the fleet be needed elsewhere."

"And the men," Memnon said, "are they ready to fight?"

"More than ready," Ephialtes grunted.

"Morale," Thymondas added, "is as high as I've seen. Some of the citizens, though, grumble and complain that we are heavy-handed tyrants and should be supplanted."

"Orontobates?"

"I will root them out, General," the Persian said, glaring at Thymondas.

"See that you do." Memnon turned and looked out over the city. He gestured to the tomb of Mausolus. "There is a certain irony at work here. The bastard buried under that monstrosity was responsible, in a round about way, for my father's murder. Now I'm defending his city from Alexander." He turned to Orontobates. "How well did you know the commander of Sardis?"

"Mithrenes?" The satrap shrugged. "Not well."

"So you're not one of those malcontents who would betray your rightful king for a whore's wages?"

"Do not be absurd!" Orontobates bristled, his face darkening in anger. "Who are you to question my loyalty to the Great King?"

"Your lord and master, by the grace of His Majesty, and your executioner should I sense the slightest air of perfidy about you!" Memnon stared at his other officers, especially Orontobates and Amyntas. "The same warning applies to every man under my command, so bear witness: play me false and I swear—by the shade of my murdered father and by the foul waters of the river Styx!—you will not live to enjoy it! Understood?" With no dissent forthcoming, the Rhodian gave a curt nod. "Dismissed. Pharnabazus, Thymondas, I would speak with you."

The other four headed off to their commands—Orontobates to Arconessus, Ephialtes to Salmacis, Autophradates to the harbor, and Amyntas to the main gate. When they were alone, Memnon turned to his nephews. "Any word from Patron?"

"Nothing yet," Pharnabazus replied. Memnon frowned. He had sent the Phocaean to Crete, to meet with emissaries of the Spartan king, Agis; the Rhodian knew he would need the red-cloaked warriors of Sparta if he hoped to invade Macedonia. But could he trust them? That was the gist of Patron's mission, to gauge Spartan disgust with Alexander's rule of greater Hellas and to see if they were amenable to an alliance.

"I want to know the moment he returns. This—"

A noise interrupted the Rhodian. The sentry on the tower above raised an alarm by striking with the butt of his spear a bronze shield hanging from a tripod. Other sentries along the circuit of the wall took up the alarm, until harsh clanging resounded over the city. Sparta would have to wait . . .

"To your posts," Memnon said, his lips curled into a mirthless grin. "Our guests are arriving."

DUST. IN THE DRY HEAT OF BOEDROMION, THIRTY THOUSAND MEN, THEIR animals and machines, kicked up billowing clouds of it, a choking yellow haze that hung over Alexander's army like a shroud. Little detail could be discerned save the flash and glitter of their weapons as the column wound its way through the hills east of Halicarnassus.

Memnon watched their progress from the acropolis tower. A constant stream of aides and messengers reported to him or hurried off on their assigned tasks. From Ephialtes came word that scouts had been spotted surveying the land outside the eastern gate—called the Mylasa Gate after the town twenty-five miles inland that Halicarnassus had supplanted as capital of Caria. Memnon ordered Thymondas to bring up two peltast battalions, over a thousand light troops, to reinforce the Mylasa Gate and the adjacent wall connecting it to Arconessus. He sent Pharnabazus to marshal platoons of heavier troops, hoplites and *kardakes*, in the agora, making them ready to move to wherever the fiercest fighting would be.

The sun traversed the brilliant blue sky. By midday excitement had abated; wary, soldiers stood at ease, their weapons never more than a hands breadth away. Memnon walked the wall from the acropolis to the Mylasa Gate. He stopped often, talking with the men of the different tower garrisons, the archers and slingers and crewmen of the dart-throwing *katapeltoi*. He had a polyglot of Greeks and barbarians under his command—veterans of the Granicus alongside green recruits of the Carian hills, proud patriots fighting for their homeland standing elbow to elbow with mercenaries lusting for plunder. Memnon welcomed renegades of every stripe: Thebans burning to redress the destruction of their *polis*, Macedonians who could not stomach the rule of a half-Epirote bastard, Athenians whose wounded pride would not accept submission. Though divided by ideology and culture, the soldiers defending Halicarnassus shared one thing in common: a belief that Memnon the Rhodian would deliver them from the son of Philip.

A belief Memnon was loath to discourage.

Reaching the Mylasa Gate, he found Thymondas leaning against the battlement, watching the Macedonians through the veil of dust, a half-mile distant and tugging his beard in thought. Ephialtes joined them from Salmacis on the other side of the city, the Athenian's bull-like shoulders clad in bronze, the head of Medusa in raised relief on the chest-plate of his armor.

"What are they doing?" Memnon asked.

Thymondas shrugged. "Well, they've reconnoitered the walls. Mostly the engineers have kept their distance, but one of the bastards tried to get close to the ditch. He scuttled off before the archers had a chance to drill him. Otherwise, they look to be erecting camp."

"No heralds? No offers to parley?"

Ephialtes grimaced and spat. "Why would the little shit-stain waste his breath? Hades' teeth! Lure him within arm's reach and I'll plant my spear in his bunghole—though I'd likely have to kill that boyfriend of his just to make room!"

Memnon fixed the Athenian with a look that could scorch iron. "You're here to fight Alexander, not to malign him." The Rhodian remained silent for a time, watching Alexander's men through squinted eyes. Finally, he turned to Mentor's son. "Do you know what the greatest enemy of both besieger and besieged is, Thymondas? Complacency . . . the boredom of repetition. When you perform a task enough times you become numb to its dangers. Alexander thinks we will wait behind our walls for him to launch the opening salvo."

"Will we?" Thymondas said.

"No. I think we'll remind him how dangerous this business of war can be." Memnon clapped his by-blow nephew on the shoulder and descended from the Mylasa Gate. He dispatched runners to the agora, to the fortresses of Arconessus and Salmacis, to the acropolis, and to the main gate with orders to stand ready. Something was about to happen . . .

Memnon assembled a mixed force—a thousand light troops, slingers and archers, around a core of five hundred hoplites; two hundred mounted *kardakes* would guard their flanks. To the cavalrymen, Memnon ordered that torches be distributed. "Get in, wreck havoc, get out," the Rhodian said, striding up and down the column. "Burn what you can, even if it's just a pile of brambles. Men, horses, stores, tents—everything is fair game. Keep hammering at them until you hear the long note of the trumpet. After that, disengage and get back to the city. Understood?" Soldiers rattled their weapons in approval.

The setting sun flooded Halicarnassus with ruddy light. Memnon looked up to the battlements atop the Mylasa Gate. "Thymondas! Any change?"

"None!" The son of Mentor leaned over where Memnon could see him. "The dust is settling. They've kindled their cook fires."

"Good." Memnon drew his sword. "Open the gates!"

Ropes snapped and hinges creaked as mule teams dragged the portal open. As with the two other gates of the city, the Mylasa Gate had sixteen-foot doors of ironbound oak, studded with bronze roundels and daubed black. Simultaneously, men atop the battlements lowered the wooden bridge that spanned the dry moat. Speed was of the essence. Chains rattled on stone. Voices yelled warning as gravity caught the bridge and brought it crashing down; before it could settle into place, Memnon and his troops surged out and across.

A half-mile separated the walls of Halicarnassus from Alexander's camp. With the sun at their backs, the Persians came into missile range before the Macedonian pickets raised the alarm. Memnon heard their shouts, heard the blare of a *salpinx*.

"Fan out!" he bellowed. "Fan out!" His horsemen spurred their mounts to a gallop, torches crackling, fanned by the breeze. Sling bullets hummed. Archers drew and loosed, targeting the pickets who stubbornly held their ground and died on it. Memnon saw a lead bullet take a trumpeter in the throat, silencing his *salpinx* in a foaming rush of blood.

His cavalry converged on the outskirts of the camp, tossed their torches into tents, into stands of *sarissas.* Flames erupted. Black smoke belched into the air, masking the fading light and adding to the chaos. Memnon sent his hoplites forward; archers softened their advance with volley after volley. The slingers used a more surgical approach by targeting individuals: men stumbling from tents, half-armored soldiers lunging for their weapons, officers roaring orders.

Memnon hung back from the fighting. He focused his attention on the heart of the camp, on where the inevitable counterattack would originate. Soon, Alexander would realize the limit of this sortie and mobilize his entire corps. His officers would rein in their men, their iron discipline would reassert itself, and they would seek to push the Persians back. Better yet, the Companions would try to cut off their retreat, reach the Mylasa Gate before it could be closed. Memnon could not allow it. His men had one more minute before he ordered their withdrawal.

A stack of fodder blazed to his left. Through the rolling smoke Memnon saw enemy cavalry massing. "Back to the city! Trumpeter, sound the retreat!" The order echoed above the din, its long last note trailing off.

His men didn't tarry. With a parting shot, a last spear thrust, they disengaged and turned for home. Nor was it a disorganized retreat with troops running pell-mell for Halicarnassus. They acted like men aware they were in sight of their fellows—brothers, friends, and lovers watched from the walls and their scrutiny lent the soldiers on the plain an insurmountable valor.

Macedonians pounded after them, mounted and on foot, howling with rage. Twice, their proximity forced Memnon to turn and hold them at bay. His archers slaughtered their horses, his slingers went after their infantry, and his hoplites waited in close formation to skewer any who penetrated that cordon of bloodshed.

As they neared the Mylasa Gate, archers on the battlements rained death on their pursuers. Horses screamed, their dusty flanks gashed by iron-barbed shafts. Soldiers skidded to a halt and sought cover behind their shields as their prey made good their escape.

Persian horsemen clattered over the bridge, followed by the light troops. Hoplites brought up the rear. Inside, raucous cheers and shouts of victory could be heard. Memnon was the last man to cross back into Halicarnassus. He stopped in the middle of the bridge, turned. Out of range of Persian arrows a lone Macedonian horseman watched him. There was no mistaking the intensity of his gaze, or the red horsehair crest and white kestrel feathers adorning his helmet. Alexander's men trudged past him, their eyes averted, faces downcast with the shame of being outfoxed. They had failed their king and knew it.

Memnon could hear the soldiers of Halicarnassus chanting his name. The Rhodian sketched an exaggerated bow to his enemy, filling the gesture with every ounce of scorn and mockery he could summon. It said to the young king: "You are but a boy playing at war; I am a soldier." And with a calculated shake of his head, Memnon crossed beneath the Mylasa Gate to the adulation of his men.

Now we'll see how well Alexander's learned his father's lesson on the folly of judgment-clouding anger.

By midnight Memnon knew the cost of that first sortie. Eighteen of his men were slain, another thirty-eight wounded. Of the wounded, twelve would likely never recover; the rest received only minor injuries. The Rhodian ordered the names of the dead be inscribed on a marble *stele* and enshrined in the temple of Zeus Polias.

"How many men did Alexander lose, you think?" Pharnabazus asked. The Persian brought Memnon the latest reports from sentries stationed at the Mylasa Gate—great bonfires blazed on the edge of the Macedonian camp, now bristling with pickets, a sign of their heightened vigilance.

"Twice our casualties, perhaps more," Memnon replied. He stripped off his armor and sat on the edge of his narrow cot, in a room he commandeered at the rear of Zeus's temple atop the acropolis. A faint breeze stirred the papyrus scraps on his makeshift desk.

"When do we go again? The men are ready for another—"

The Rhodian held up a hand, forestalling his nephew's exuberance. "Patience, Pharnabazus. Now we wait, gauge Alexander's response. Go take your rest. Tomorrow is going to be another long day." Grudgingly, Pharnabazus agreed. He left Memnon stretched out on his cot.

An hour later, the Rhodian exhaled and sat up. He could not sleep. The scar on his right shoulder ached and the pain triggered memories of a golden mist, of a young-old voice: *a messenger, some call me.* Nor could he keep himself from brooding over his separation from Barsine. Never had they faced such a long parting; in the quiet dark he could not rest for the questions that thundered through his mind: *Where is she? Is she safe? How are the girls?* Memnon longed for the gift of flight, for the winged sandals of Hermes, so that he might be at Alexander's throat by day at Barsine's side by night.

Memnon rose and went to his desk—a lofty term for five old planks spiked to an uneven trestle. A sheet of papyrus spread out before him, its frayed corners weighted down with lead bullets. On it, he was in the process of recreating from memory the map Parmenion used on his campaigns in Thrace and Macedonia. Near it sat a stylus and a waxed writing board full of notes on what an invasion of Macedonia would entail—what spies would he need and where, what allies could he rely on, how much bullion would be required to buy off Alexander's Greek troops . . .

He picked up the writing board, read its contents again, and dropped it back onto the desk. Tonight, not even the minutiae of strategic planning offered Memnon solace. He needed air. Perhaps a turn along the walls would clear his mind. Barefoot and wearing only a *zoma*, the short kilt soldiers wore under their armor, Memnon settled a cloak about his shoulders and caught up his sheathed sword.

From the rear of Zeus's temple, Memnon crossed to the stairs and ascended to the battlements of the acropolis walls. Here, a sea breeze tugged at his cloak. To the east, acrid smoke yet rose from the Macedonian funeral pyres; staring at the greasy orange glow, the Rhodian wondered at Alexander's state of mind. Had he succeeded in goading the young king? Would he make a potentially deadly mistake out of anger? Memnon's instincts told him he would not. Alexander was Philip's son through and through; he would act when the time was right—likely launching his assault in a day or two. *Pity*, Memnon thought, *I had such hopes for his temper.*

Memnon walked the battlements under cold and distant stars. In his mind's eye he watched the Macedonian attack unfold, a spectral tragedy conjured from dust and starlight—a ghostly *Iliad* bereft of immortal heroes. In the chirp of crickets he could hear the snap of enemy bowstrings and the crash of siege engines as they provided cover for the sappers struggling to fill sections of the dry moat. In his own heartbeat he heard the echo of rams battering at the walls' foundations. He heard his own voice, faint, calling a rain of death down on the besiegers' heads.

Shouts and screams, the clash of iron, the crunch of bone mixed with strains of the *paean* to Ares drifted on the night breeze; already, Memnon could feel the War God's presence at his shoulder, as familiar as that of a brother or a trusted companion. The sensation raised gooseflesh on his arms as he continued walking.

Reaching a part of the wall where the towers were farthest apart, where the contour of the terrain provided respite from the glow of distant fires, Memnon stopped. He frowned as a noise intruded on his thoughts. No aural phantom this, but the very real clink of metal on stone, followed by the hiss of an exhaled warning. The Rhodian dropped to a crouch. Half a dozen paces ahead of him, a figure clad in dark clothing and moving with exaggerated care crept up the stairs from the base of the wall, a rope trailing from his waist. Another figure followed.

"Keep down so the sentries don't see you," a voice whispered. "You positive you know what you're doing?"

Memnon saw the first man give a sharp jerk of his head. "Make sure you get your part done. You and the others seize control of the gate and get it open. Don't want the Macks to think I'm setting them up."

Memnon ground his teeth in rage. Traitorous bastards! Through his anger, Memnon felt a sense of relief that these weren't his men. They were locals, citizens of Halicarnassus most likely. No matter. Greek or Carian . . . their perfidy stopped here.

Memnon sprang, exploding from the shadows in a swirl of cloth. The man with the rope tied about his midsection saw him first. His eyes widened; he might have bellowed a warning had Memnon's callused fist not cracked against his jaw, knocking his head into the cold stone of the embrasure. The blow felled him like a sapling in a squall.

His companion turned, hand clawing for the knife at his belt. Memnon gave him no opportunity to use it. In one fluid motion, the fingers of the Rhodian's right hand wrapped around the hilt of his sword; he jerked it clear of the sheath, driving the weapon's pommel into the would-be traitor's nose with a satisfying crunch. The fellow howled, his hands flying to his face. Blood from a shattered nose spurted between his fingers. None too gently, Memnon shoved him against the battlement and leveled the point of his sword at him.

"Guards!" Memnon roared. "Traitors at the wall!"

The rope went slack; he heard the desperate footfalls of men retreating into the night. The first soldiers to reach him recognized the sharp crack of their commander's voice. "There were others! Search the base of the wall and the surrounding houses! Find them! Bind these fools with their own rope! Go!"

A soldier brought a lantern. By its thin light, Memnon paced while his men trussed up the two Carians like suckling pigs. The one with the broken nose wept and blubbered about his innocence, "A v-victim of ill f-fortune!" he said.

"Ill fortune?" Memnon replied. "Stupidity breeds ill fortune!"

"But, my lord! I—"

At a gesture from Memnon, a soldier stepped in and planted his sandaled foot in the man's belly. The *whoof* of air silenced his protestations, if not his sobs.

Amid the chaos Pharnabazus arrived from the acropolis with another squad. The Persian had been awoken from a deep sleep; his hair hung in disarray about his shoulders and he wore wrinkled trousers and an open robe. He clutched a naked saber in his fist. "Uncle! What goes?"

"We have traitors in our midst, Pharnabazus!" Memnon said. "Citizens who'd rather side with our enemy! Deploy your men and double the guard at every gate and on every tower! I want you to organize walking patrols atop the wall and along its base! Arrest any civilian who approaches wall or gate, no exceptions!"

"What about these two?"

Memnon looked down at his captives, one still unconscious, the other trying not to choke on his own blood. "Take them to the harbor and have Autophradates hold them in the belly of his ship. I want them questioned. If they tell me everything I want to know, perhaps they'll have a brighter future than will their cronies who escaped. Those men are to be executed on the spot."

"As you wish." Pharnabazus's squad hoisted the captives and made for the harbor, leaving Memnon alone again atop the wall.

No, not alone, he thought, feeling the familiar fury of the War God at his side. *Never alone.*

First light brought marked changes to the streets of Halicarnassus. On Memnon's orders, soldiers rounded up the eldest sons of the town's most prominent citizens, the heirs of merchant princes and tradesmen of renown, of orators and politicians. From young men in their thirties to babes in their mother's arms, they were dragged from their houses, from their beds, herded to the harbor and packed aboard ships bound for Cos. Their aggrieved fathers came to the acropolis demanding answers.

Memnon met them on the steps of the temple of Zeus Polias. Haggard from little sleep, nevertheless the Rhodian cut a magnificent figure in full armor, his cloak billowing in the warm breeze that presaged another cruelly hot day. Orontobates, in the robes of his satrapal office, stood in attendance as did Ephialtes and Amyntas, both men glittering in panoplies of war. Still, the voices of three dozen men rose in anger.

"Why have you done this?"

"Where have you taken our sons?"

"There are men among you who think it wise to take an interest in my business," Memnon said, "who think it best to welcome Alexander into the city with open arms . . . by opening my gates to him! As you have inserted yourselves where you are neither needed nor wanted, I have decided to return the favor! Your sons are now my property!" A hush fell over the assembled men. Memnon had not used the word 'guest' or even 'hostage,' rather a word whose connotations meant 'slavery.' They stared at the Rhodian, aghast. "They will be well cared for, but their continued existence depends wholly on your behavior! Should one man here cross me—just one!—then all of your sons will suffer for it!" Memnon let that promise sink in.

"When . . . when will they be returned to us?" asked Scopas, one of the sculptors working on the Mausoleum, whose eldest son was also his chief apprentice.

"When I am sufficiently convinced you and your comrades no longer harbor Macedonian sympathies," Memnon said. "Now, gentlemen, if you will excuse me I have business to attend to."

From the back of the group he heard a shrill voice. "This is outrageous! I . . ."

The protestor, though, was not allowed to continue—his fellows silenced him with curses, punches, and kicks.

Memnon acknowledged their effort. "You learn swiftly. That bodes well for your children's future. Good day, gentlemen."

As they left, their anger replaced by fear, Memnon turned to Orontobates. "I leave it to you to assign men to watch them. Report the slightest instance of grumbling."

The satrap nodded. "Will you rest and take some refreshment before you continue?"

"Perhaps later. I have business with the fleet that cannot wait," the Rhodian replied. "Send word if there's any change."

Descending from the acropolis, Memnon made his way through the dusty streets to the harbor. A skiff waited to row him out to Autophradates' flagship *Ganymeda*, a Cypriote trireme built on a Phoenician-style hull. The sailors going about their morning duties were a mixed complement of Greeks and Phoenicians, even a pair of whip-lean Egyptians, men chosen for their skill at seafaring from among the thousands of souls who comprised the Persian armada. A rope ladder was lowered as the skiff bumped *Ganymeda*'s hull; Memnon ascended and met Autophradates at the railing.

"Have our prisoners given you anything of use?" Memnon asked.

The Persian shook his head. "They gave us the names of other sympathizers. Otherwise, nothing we were not already aware of. I believe their use is at an end."

Grimly, Memnon gestured for Autophradates to lead the way. Into the belly of the ship they went, past the superstructure that secured the benches of the topmost rowers to the hull and into the bilges beneath the lowest bank of oars, a trio of leather-armored marines following in their wake. What light filtered down through the forest of wooden support beams gave the salt-heavy air of the bilges a grayish cast. The two men, naked with their hands cruelly bound, lay on their bellies in the rising bilge water. When their heads drooped, a fourth marine prodded them with the curve of a boathook.

"Get them up," Autophradates barked. "On their knees." The marines wrestled the shivering Carians upright, looping lengths of knotted rope about their necks to keep them from sagging. Both men bore the welts and bruises of a judicious beating on top of the injuries inflicted by Memnon.

"So these are the dogs who sought to betray me," Memnon said. Hard-eyed, he stared at each man like they were offal he needed scraped from his sandals. "Tell me, what makes you think Alexander would be a more clement ruler than the Great King? Has he promised you freedom? Autonomy? Has he declared you exempt from the burden of tribute? I think not, on all counts. Why, then? Speak up!"

"W-We . . . thought . . ."

Memnon lashed out, cracking the back of his hand across the would-be traitor's cheek. "You thought? What did you think? Speak up, damn you!"

"Gold!" the other fellow, the one whose nose Memnon broke the night before, stammered. "W-We thought Alexander w-would give us g-gold!"

"Greed," Memnon said, his nostrils flaring. He shook his head. "Base and petty greed. A political motive I could at least respect; even vengeance is permissible in the eyes of the gods. Not so greed." He turned to Autophradates. "They seek gold. Have you any?" The Persian produced a pair of coins, golden *darics* from the royal mint at Persepolis in the heart of the empire, each worth a month's wages to a Greek. He handed them to Memnon, who held one of the coins up before the first captive's eyes. "Good yellow gold. Open your mouth."

The Carian blinked rapidly, sweat popping from his brow. He glanced at his companion and saw his own fear reflected.

"Open your mouth!" Memnon roared. The man flinched; trembling, his jaw inched open. Savagely, Memnon rammed the coin between his teeth. "For the ferryman, you son of a bitch!"

At Memnon's gesture, the marine at the would-be traitor's back put his knee into the fellow's spine for leverage, and jerked taut the rope. Corded muscle bulged along the marine's arms. His victim thrashed, his bound hands clawing at nothing. Gold gleamed amid splintered teeth as he sought to draw breath; his eyes pleaded with Memnon, but the Rhodian's features remained impassive, unmoved by the death throes of a man who would have betrayed him to his enemy. The marine gave a final wrench of his shoulders and was rewarded by the wet snap of vertebrae. He dropped the dead man into the bilge water at Memnon's feet. Nodding, the Rhodian's attention shifted to the remaining man.

"M-Mercy! I b-beg you!"

Memnon raised his hand; the coin flashed in a stray shaft of light. There would be no mercy . . .

"Throw their bodies overboard," Memnon said as the last Carian's corpse crumpled beside that of his companion. "Send soldiers to arrest their confederates. We'll execute them in the agora. I've made my case with the aristocracy; now, I want the common people of Halicarnassus to understand I will brook no betrayal."

"I will see to it myself," Autophradates said. Leaving the marines to dispose of the bodies, Memnon and the Persian retraced their steps from the bilges. On deck, a sea breeze alleviated the rising heat. Autophradates, staring at the rising terraces of Halicarnassus, scratched his short beard, his forehead creasing. Memnon had known him long enough to recognize a look of worry.

"What is it?"

"Have you apprehended Alexander's strategy? He is cutting us off from our naval harbors on the mainland—Assos, Ephesus, Miletus, and now Halicarnassus. If this city falls we will lose our ability to operate along the Aegean coast for any length of time."

"Then we will find new harbors, my friend."

"Where? The islands?"

Memnon heard a splash from the stern, then another; in low voices, the marines wagered on which body would lure the sharks first. "Macedonia," he said finally. Autophradates fell silent. Memnon reckoned the Persian doubted what he had just heard. "No, your ears are not playing tricks on you."

"A daring plan," Autophradates said. "How—"

Memnon stifled his curiosity with a raised hand. "In due time. Can I confide something in you, and trust that it will go no further?"

"Of course," the Persian replied. "I swear to you, on pain of death, that what you say to me will never leave my lips."

Memnon nodded and inclined his head toward the city. "Halicarnassus isn't going to fall. No, it's going to be sold to Alexander. I've placed a high price on those walls and the only coin I'll accept is Macedonian blood. When the boy has met my fee, when I can't wring another bloody drop from him, I will give him Halicarnassus in return—and willingly. For too long I've fought on Alexander's terms. It's time for him to fight on mine."

"My lord," Autophradates said, his voice rising little above a whisper, "the Great King was right to put his trust in you."

"We'll see." Before he clambered down into the skiff for his return to shore, Memnon leaned in close to the Persian admiral. "It is the easiest thing under heaven to form a plan. Only when you execute it will you begin to see where you've gone wrong. In the end, I fear this war will boil down to luck—mine versus Alexander's."

"I pray yours will be the stronger."

"So do I, Autophradates," Memnon said, climbing down the ladder. "So do I."

THAT NIGHT, HALICARNASSUS SLEPT UNEASILY BEHIND WALLS OF STONE and fear, its aristocracy haunted by the fate of their children, its commoners by the fate of the six men hanged in the agora. Their corpses yet dangled from gibbets as reminders of Lord Memnon's resolve to defend the empire at all costs. The moneylender in his mansion, the blacksmith in his foundry, the cripple in his hovel, all looked out their doors this sleepless night, beheld the shining pyramid atop the Mausoleum, and wished for a return to the halcyon days of King Mausolus and his Queen. They were trapped, the citizens of Halicarnassus, between the hammer of Macedonia and the anvil of Persia. Trapped, and unable to fight back . . .

UNEASY DESCRIBED MEMNON'S SLEEP, AS WELL, HIS DREAMS HAUNTED BY the young-old man with hair of silver and gold. The memory of his voice sent tendrils of pain lancing through the Rhodian's scarred shoulder. *The* Moirai, *the Fates, ration human existence.* Memnon thrashed, sweat beading his forehead. *They have rationed your existence, son of Rhodes. I have seen the weave of your life, its warp and weft; I have seen its colors and its textures.* The Rhodian's hands clawed at the material of his cloak, which he used as a blanket. *And I have seen its end. The blade of Atropos, Memnon . . . the blade drifts closer with the passage of mortal years. Would you like to know the hour of your death? Come . . . let me show you."* A phantom touch on Memnon's shoulder wrenched a gasp from him. "No!"

The Rhodian bolted upright. Pharnabazus stumbled back from the edge of his cot, alarmed by the rage in his uncle's voice. A clay lamp burned on Memnon's desk; in its dim light, Pharnabazus marked well the trembling of Memnon's limbs, his rapid breathing, and the sweat plastering his hair to his forehead.

"What . . . what is it, Pharnabazus?"

"There's something afoot, Uncle. I believe Alexander's preparing his men to attack this morning."

Memnon nodded, ran his hand through his hair. "Fine. I'll meet you on the battlements."

"Are you all right, Uncle?"

"I'm tired, Pharnabazus. Nothing more." Rising, Memnon clapped the Persian on the shoulder. "Go ahead. I'll be along in a moment."

Concern etched Pharnabazus's brow, but he did as Memnon asked; after a moment, the Rhodian stood alone in his small room. His armor hung from a wooden rack in the corner. In the sheen of bronze, Memnon imagined he saw the distorted reflection of a young-old face. *Would you like to know the hour of your death?*

"No," he whispered. "No."

MEMNON, BUCKLING THE LAST STRAP OF HIS BREASTPLATE, ASCENDED THE acropolis wall as the rising sun set fire to the eastern horizon. Sparrows whirled in the sky above, their voices competing with the plaintive cries of gulls hovering over the forest of masts in the harbor. Though cloaked still in gray shadow, he could tell the valleys surrounding Halicarnassus seethed with men—half-glimpsed figures of bronze and iron like the shades of dead warriors before the cold throne of Hades. The Rhodian could hear their voices, the clatter of their harness. He could hear the windlasses creaking on Alexander's siege machines, the rattle of iron bolts and stone missiles.

"They are coming," Pharnabazus said.

Memnon nodded, glanced up and down the battlements. "Rouse the tower garrisons, but quietly. Let Alexander make the first move, not react to our alarms. Send word to Thymondas and Amyntas to bring their archers to the parapet. Have runners dispatched to Salmacis and Arconessus. We have little time, Pharnabazus. Go!"

Memnon would send no heralds across the no-man's land between Halicarnassus's walls and Alexander's battle lines to seek indulgences, to buy time, or to offer diplomatic solutions; no embassies from the city would be allowed past the gates. He knew Alexander's intentions as clearly as the young king knew his. Neither would insult the other with wasted parleys and empty rhetoric.

Which part of the wall will he attack first? Memnon scanned his own defenses, wondering what weaknesses Alexander had detected. Would he assault the gates? Would he use logs to form makeshift bridges in order to bring ram crews to bear on the stout timbers of the Mylasa Gate? Or would he fill in sections of the dry moat, paving the way for the rolling towers he used at Miletus? In truth, he reckoned it made no difference to the men freshly roused from sleep and filing into position atop the parapet. The archers and slingers, spearmen and javelineers would engage the Macedonian regardless of where he chose to launch his attack.

"Don't wait for my order," Memnon said as he walked among his men. "Loose as soon as you have a clear target. Keep pressure on them, but don't get reckless. Remember—they have archers, as well."

"What say the gods, my lord?" one of his *kardakes* asked, a pale young man who gripped his bow white-knuckle tight.

"What say the gods?" Memnon replied, grasping the young man's upper arm. "They say we are thrice-blessed and today will be a day of slaughter and red ruin for the Macedonians! Make ready!" His words cheered those men in earshot; confidence spread from man to man, from tower to tower. Soldiers shrugged off their fear and trepidation. They waited with arrows nocked, sling bullets pouched, javelins selected. Memnon drew his sword.

The sun crested the hills, flooding the vale of Halicarnassus with light.

Alexander's point of assault became evident by the thousands of Macedonians massing just out of bowshot northeast of the acropolis, at a spot between the city's main gate, the monumental Tripylon (so called for its three protective towers), and the Horn, the northernmost extremity of Halicarnassus. At the Horn, the wall turned sharply south and began its descent down the hillside to the Mylasa Gate and the harbor fortress of Arconessus. The Macedonians carried baskets of fill dirt—meaning Alexander intended to bring his towers to bear—and shield-bearers moved among them to provide cover as best they could.

Behind the mass of troops the Rhodian spotted Alexander's siege train—another legacy of Philip's. Dozens of *katapeltoi* were trained on the wall near the Horn, each machine capable of discharging a six-foot dart of wood and iron or a stone the size of a large stew pot. Beyond them, four siege towers waited. These were fifty-foot-high frames of timber covered with planking and hide and mounted on reinforced wagon wheels. Memnon had seen such monstrosities before. Each had three levels—the lowest sported a suspended battering ram; the second and third levels were slitted for archers. With the amount of manpower he could draw upon, Memnon reckoned it would take Alexander no more than two days to fill in enough of the moat; then, the towers could be rolled into position. The Rhodian resolved to make it a costly two days.

From the Macedonian lines a *salpinx* wailed. In response, the *katapeltoi* bucked as engineers discharged them. Seconds later Memnon heard the *choonk* of horizontal torsion bars, like giant bow-staves, striking the wooden frames. Soldiers ducked down behind the battlements as several darts hissed overhead; others struck below the parapet, splintering against the dressed stone of the wall. A cheer erupted as the archers stood and loosed a volley at the Macedonians advancing on the dry moat. A hail of iron-heads scythed through the front ranks, cracking on shields and piercing flesh.

And so the battle began.

It quickly became a duel between archers, with clouds of arrows darkening the sky from both directions. The Macedonians fought to clear the battlements and give their comrades time to work on the ditch. Arrows and darts raked the walls. Rocks flung by the siege engines were too soft to damage the granite of Halicarnassus's defenses, but on impact the stones shattered into razored shards capable of punching through a shield's bronze facing and tough oak chassis. A sharp crack, an explosion of dust, bodies falling, and runnels of blood marked each strike. Horrific screams rippled from the wounded.

Memnon directed his men's rage. From the Tripylon's three sturdy towers and from the Horn, he ordered his archers to rain shafts down on the center of the Macedonian line; to his slingers he gave the more nerve-wracking task of targeting the enemy archers. They worked in pairs, ranging up and down the battlements in search of their prey. Taking turns, one acted as lookout while the other, exposing his body to Macedonian missiles, stood and loosed. More times than not their lead bullets found their mark. On occasion, though, the Rhodian saw his soldiers' daring repaid in blood. One pair, seconds after killing a man, were literally ripped apart when a *katapeltes* stone struck the embrasure next to them. Debris from the same stone tore a jagged gash across a nearby archer's eyes. He rose, clutching his mangled face, and stumbled into the path of a whistling dart. The oversized arrow transfixed his body, knocking him from the parapet and into the growing ruin of stone, wood, and flesh inside the wall.

Each death caused redoubled effort among the living. Memnon and a squad of hoplites, better protected by their heavier armor, braved the hail of stone and iron to drag the wounded to safety and replenish empty quivers.

"Keep up the pressure!" Memnon roared. "Don't let the bastards draw breath!"

By midday, Pharnabazus brought news of similar attacks against the Mylasa Gate and its twin in the western wall of the city, called the Myndus Gate, though neither as ferocious as the one at the Horn.

"The others are feints," Memnon said. "Meant to draw men from the center to reinforce our flanks. It's a tactic Alexander has some fondness for."

"He used it at the Granicus."

"To good effect," Memnon said. Rock dust plastered his face, his hair, mixing with sweat and blood from the injured to create a ghastly mask. The Persian handed him a skin of water. He sucked the warm liquid down, and then held the stream over his head, sluicing away the accumulated grime. "We need to double the casualties we're inflicting on him."

"What do you suggest?"

"Send word to Autophradates. Have him ransack the fleet, the harbor, the warehouses, any place he can think to look, and bring me every drop of bitumen he can find in Halicarnassus. While he's doing that, you loot the potters' workshops for clay jugs."

Pharnabazus grinned. "Incendiaries?"

"Crude, but effective," Memnon said. Pharnabazus nodded and rushed off. The Rhodian returned to the thick of the assault, calling for the archers to keep low while water-bearers passed out their skins.

The day wore on. Bowstrings and staves snapped from relentless use. Arrows ran low; while runners fetched more from the fleet, archers had only to stoop and seize spent shafts off the bloody parapet—yours or theirs, it did not matter. Iron warheads knew nothing of loyalty.

At the base of the wall, Macedonian bodies tumbled into the moat . . . that portion no longer dry thanks to the fluids pouring from their pierced and riven corpses. Twice, Memnon spotted Alexander himself in the wrack, surrounded by a guard of shield-bearers, exhorting his men to greater effort. The Rhodian felt a grudging sense of admiration for the young king, as one man who leads by example to another.

By the time Pharnabazus returned the sun was beginning its descent into the West. "The incendiaries are ready, Uncle," the Persian said. "Over two hundred jars, each filled with a mix of bitumen and lamp oil. And so you know, when we did not take the bait Alexander ordered his men back from the Mylasa and Myndus Gates. Feints, as you said."

"Our casualties?"

"Minimal," Pharnabazus replied. "As were his."

Memnon scowled. "Let's see if we cannot compel him to pull back from the Horn, as well. Bring up the incendiaries." The Rhodian started to turn away.

"There is more news, Uncle. Patron has returned from Crete, and he's brought a guest."

Memnon's head snapped around. "Patron's returned? Thank Poseidon! Where is he? Who is this guest he's brought?"

"A Spartan, Uncle. Who he is, I do not know," Pharnabazus said. "But, they both await you in Zeus's temple."

Memnon's brow creased. *A Spartan?* "Take over here. Hold off on the incendiaries until I return."

DESPITE THE TUMULT OF THE SIEGE A PALL OF SILENCE CLUNG TO THE TEMPLE of Zeus Polias. Memnon paused on the threshold of the open doors and waited for his eyes to adjust, the clotted shadows providing a welcome respite from the searing heat of battle. Bronze braziers spewed sweet-smelling incense into the cool air; fluted columns lined the central hall, the *cella*, where the stern visage of Zeus looked down on worshipers from his marble throne. The Thunderer, Lord of Dark Clouds, clement in his own fashion but implacable when aroused, Memnon mouthed a silent prayer that the Lord of Olympus might grant them victory. No doubt Alexander had asked the same boon for his own people. When Greek fought Greek, whom would the gods love more?

From within, Memnon could hear voices—one familiar, the other clipped and raspy. The Rhodian moved to his left, passed between the columns, and spotted Patron and his guest at the rear of the temple, near a side door that opened on the peristyle ringing the building. Though still as lean as from his days piloting *Circe*, the passage of time had scarred Patron, adding deep creases to his face and gray to his hair and beard. His plain blue *chiton*, worn cinched at the waist with a belt of old leather, stood in marked contrast to the finery of his companion.

The Spartan at Patron's side cut an impressive figure—tall and well muscled with a full beard and long, immaculately groomed hair, both chestnut-colored. He sported a cuirass of fine bronze, etched and silver-inlaid, and greaves embossed with the faces of Nymphs. In spite of the heat, he wore the scarlet cloak of a Peer, a member of that ever-dwindling class comprised of full Spartan citizens.

"You speak of superiority," Patron was saying. "But under Spartan standards would Alexander not be the superior man by virtue of his being a king?"

"Superior to other Macedonians, perhaps, but not to Spartans. In the company of lions, does a king of mice crow about his exalted position?"

"Only if the mouse has the wherewithal to align himself with the eagles," Memnon said.

The two men turned.

"Zeus Savior, lad!" Patron said, grinning. "You look like a man whose been scrapping in the dust with a pack of dogs!" The Spartan nodded approvingly.

Memnon glanced down at himself. A rime of dried blood, sweat, and dust caked his limbs and armor. He grinned back. "Not all of us get the plum missions, Patron. How *were* the whores of Crete?"

"They send their regards," he replied. Patron gestured to the Spartan. "This is Callicratides, envoy of King Agis of Sparta."

"Greetings, noble Callicratides."

"Rhodian. Patron speaks highly of you. So much so that I felt compelled to meet you in person, to take your measure back to Agis."

"Just so you know," Memnon said, winking. "Phocaeans are inveterate liars, Callicratides, worse than Cretans. Still, what's mine is yours, for the duration of your stay. Before you depart for home, though, I would like to draft a letter to King Agis, something that defines my position in the plainest possible terms. I ask from you the added burden of delivering it into his hands for me."

"Of course," Callicratides said.

Through the open side door came the distant echo of a *salpinx*. Memnon frowned, cocking his head to the side. "That sounds like the call to withdraw. Surely Alexander's not had his fill for one day?"

"How goes the fight?" Patron asked.

"Well enough. For all Alexander's faults, he is tenacious and he has an inventive streak in him. Though we're enemies we must respect his ability to lead men, to inspire them. Already his Macedonians would march to the gates of Tartarus and spit in Cerberus's eyes just to please their king."

"Respect?" Callicratides snarled. "Faugh! The gods have marked the slayer well, and in the end the black Fates always destroy the lucky but too lawless man! Philip, at least, was a worthy adversary who knew his place!"

"You mangle Aeschylus's words but at least you're familiar with them, my good Spartan," Memnon said, recognizing sentiments from that poet's

Oresteia. "It's exactly because Alexander doesn't know his place that he has the potential of being a far more terrifying adversary than Philip could have ever dreamed of being. There's little need to fear the man who recognizes his boundaries, Callicratides. Myself, I fear the man who doesn't."

The Spartan pursed his lips, his eyes narrowing in thought. "I will relay your words to Agis. No doubt he will find interest in them." Callicratides extended his hand. Memnon took it.

"Deeds speak louder than words," the Rhodian said. "A favor, Patron? Tonight—say perhaps near midnight—bring noble Callicratides to the acropolis walls. Our talk has inspired me to undertake an experiment. I want to see if Alexander truly recognizes no boundaries."

"How?" Patron asked.

Memnon smiled, devoid of humor. "With incendiaries."

STARS GLITTERED IN THE NIGHT SKY OVER HALICARNASSUS, THEIR SPLENDOR rivaled by the fires burning in the Macedonian camp. Exhaustion gripped both armies; yet, movement could be discerned as pickets on the ground mirrored sentries walking their routes atop the walls. Music drifted up from the harbor, from a wine shop where the fleet's *auletes* staged an impromptu Dionysia.

The sound of dueling flutes reached even to the Horn. Here, in blazing torchlight, Memnon's men kept a close eye on the nearly filled section of the moat, insuring the Macedonians didn't attempt to finish the job under cover of darkness. Alexander's men, too, watched the Horn, alert for any sign that the Persians might disrupt their day's progress.

Memnon crouched behind an embrasure some distance from the Horn, near where he had captured the would-be traitors two nights previous. Thymondas and Amyntas crouched with him. Bareheaded, their faces daubed with soot, all three men wore cuirasses of leather rather than bronze. Lampblack dulled the sheen of their weapons; strips of cloth muffled their sheaths and baldrics. Dozens of ropes creaked as similarly camouflaged men on both sides of them lowered ladders and woven baskets full of straw-packed clay jars to their comrades outside the wall. Another three hundred raiders waited on the parapet for the Rhodian's signal.

"You're clear about your orders?" Memnon asked the renegade Amyntas. The Macedonian nodded.

"My men and I will make a hole in their sentry line near the siege train. We'll cover Thymondas and his lads while they put those jars to good use."

"Thymondas?"

The son of Mentor leaned forward. "We get in, spread the bitumen around, and get out. Nothing fancy. Once my men are clear, I'll give the order for it to be lit." He spat thrice, a gesture to ward off evil.

"When Alexander sends soldiers to snuff the fires," Memnon said, "we'll strike from the shadows. Kill as many as you can, but when they begin fighting back—and they will—disengage and make for the Tripylon. Pharnabazus will be at the gate and he'll sound the call to arms. His archers will cover our withdrawal."

Amyntas grinned, white teeth glimmering against blackened skin. "Bastards won't know their arse from a knot hole after we've finished with them."

"Gloat when you've brought your men back safely, not before," Memnon chided. He gestured to the ropes. "Let's go."

Amyntas wasted no time. He scampered down the knotted line like a seasoned mountaineer. Thymondas and Memnon followed. Behind them came waves of black-clad fighters, Cretan archers and javelin-wielding *kardakes*, Ionian peltasts and a score of Amyntas's fellow renegades. They reached the ground and low-crawled to the dry moat, where they quickly vanished down the ladders. Even in the pitch-black bowels of the ditch each man knew his place, his rally-point. Thymondas's soldiers formed up on the left flank, Memnon's on the right. Amyntas's squad of renegades kept to the center. Weapons clattered; Memnon hoped the muffled cursing from stubbed toes or gouged thighs would not give away their position, spoil their plan. He stood still, listening.

Silence. No cries of alarm carried on the still air; no horns or thudding hooves sounded. With an unseen nod, Memnon touched Amyntas's shoulder. The Macedonian hissed an order; his renegades repositioned the ladders and ascended to the far bank of the moat, fading into the night in the direction of Alexander's picket lines.

Memnon waited. Seconds stretched on, a lifetime encompassed in each pulsing heartbeat. Hearing nothing, he gave Thymondas a low whistle. One hundred twenty Ionians followed him up the ladders, every second man carrying a jug of bitumen in the crook of his arm—a quarter of their arsenal of incendiaries.

After giving the Ionians time to disperse for their targets, Memnon led the final one hundred sixty men, the Cretans and *kardakes*, up and out of the ditch. The Rhodian had studied this terrain for a month, incorporating its every rise and fold into the defense of the city. He guided his men straight ahead, to where a dry streambed between two low hills, both thick with lonely olive trees and shrubs of wild myrtle, served to mask their movements from prying eyes. Loose soil and scree crunched underfoot, each step an explosion of sound to Memnon's attenuated hearing.

A half-mile from the walls, the whitish scar of the streambed curled around the shoulder of the hill. Memnon paused; using hand gestures, he deployed his men in a loose skirmish line, led them out of the streambed and to the crest of the slight rise. Vegetation provided added cover. Memnon could see the fires of Alexander's camp. They were behind the siege engines, now, and even with the towers. He motioned for his men to halt.

Pickets guarded the perimeter of the siege works, but the Rhodian couldn't discern if they were his men or Alexander's. *Did I make a mistake in trusting Amyntas?* Then he saw it. Movement. Faster than he could credit, shadows rose behind the five nearest pickets, figures that grappled and bore them to the ground. As each soldier fell, another man emerged from the undergrowth and assumed the picket's station, leaning on his spear with feigned nonchalance. Soon after, an owl hooted twice, paused, then twice more—Amyntas's signal for all clear.

Memnon heard the rustle of cloth off to his right; he saw the dark shapes of Thymondas and his men making for the breach in the Macedonian picket line. The Ionians kept low, those with jars of bitumen ahead of those without. Wisely, Mentor's son kept his raiders from rushing forward in a mass—that many men blundering about the siege train would surely have raised an alarm. Instead, he assigned himself and four others the task of spreading the flammable liquid, two jars at a time. The rest of the Ionians waited in the shadows, ready to exchange full jars for those their comrades emptied. Soon, the acrid stench of bitumen reached Memnon's nostrils.

A half-hour passed before the deed was done. The Ionians vanished in the darkness, followed by Amyntas and his false pickets. A remaining soldier—surely Thymondas—used a torch snatched from one sentry post to light a trail of bitumen, and then he too disappeared.

Memnon watched as a rivulet of fire raced along the ground, spreading, igniting pools of oil. It reached one of the *katapeltes* first; tongues of flame licked the machine's oil-soaked wooden chassis, gnawing at torsion cables made from twisted sinew and human hair. With a roar the fire blazed to life, consuming the engine like a corpse on a pyre. It spread to other siege machines, the conflagration following a river of bitumen from engine to ammunition cache, all the way to the base of the nearest siege tower.

From the picket line, a *salpinx* cut through the din of the rising inferno. The alarm spread to the Macedonian camp; Memnon could hear the shouts and cries of engineers roused from sleep. Seeing their beloved creations devoured by flames, they rushed out naked, bearing cloaks and water skins as tools to snuff out the blaze. An officer among them recognized the stench of burning oil.

"Dirt!" he bellowed, pointing at a mound of loose soil as more men stumbled up. "Throw dirt on it!"

"Him," Memnon whispered to the archer at his side, a swarthy Cretan with thick black brows. The man nodded, kissed his bow, and nocked a wickedly barbed arrow. All along the line bow-staves creaked. Memnon raised his hand, dropped it.

The thrum of bowstrings brought to mind the sound of ripping linen.

A hail of death dropped out of the night sky. Engineers, who seconds before cared only about saving their livelihoods now fought for their lives, clutching at arrows that punched through flesh, their cries of alarm turning to screams of agony. The fallen writhed or lay still.

Though unable to follow its flight with the naked eye, Memnon saw the end result as the Cretan's iron-head found its mark in the officer's cervical spine. His body sprawled over the mound of dirt.

"Hit them again!"

Memnon's archers sent a second and third volley into the chaos; his *kardakes* went after the remaining pickets, and any man foolish enough to try and fight the flames. Off to the right, Amyntas and his renegades cried out to the Macedonians in their shared tongue, begging for them to come to their aid. Those who did were slaughtered in a storm of Ionian javelins.

The siege tower blazed, fully engulfed. By its light, Memnon spotted a wedge of Companion cavalry circling to the left; a second wedge on their heels. No doubt more were advancing from the right, along with Alexander's own archers and a horde of *Pezhetairoi*. It was time to make for the safety of the Tripylon.

"Break off!" he called. "Break off!" One of the Cretans blew a short blast on his horn. Their withdrawal required speed rather than secrecy; making made no pretense at stealth, the Cretans stood and pelted down the hill to join the Ionians. Thymondas bellowed orders, sorted out the shuffling troops; then, as a single entity spearheaded by the renegades, they set off at a run toward the glimmering walls of Halicarnassus. Memnon and his *kardakes* brought up the rear.

After a moment of uncertainty, Alexander's Companion cavalry picked up the raiders' trail and pounded after them, their shouts and whoops drawing the attention of the men streaming out of camp to help douse the fires. "There!" Memnon heard a Macedonian scream, followed by the pounding of hooves as horsemen changed course.

"Aim for their mounts!" the Rhodian panted. Now!" The rearguard paused at the bottom of a shallow depression, whirled with their javelins cocked over their right shoulders, and slung the ash and iron darts pointblank into the fire-etched silhouettes bearing down on them. Horses and men screamed, all toppling as the javelins slammed into them. Flailing hooves snarled the legs of other riders to create a writhing wall of flesh. Memnon did not loiter to watch the unfolding chaos. He and his *kardakes* were off and running before the remaining horsemen could circle around them.

A quarter of a mile away the walls of the city blazed with light, its torches and iron cressets beckoning to the men on the ground. Trumpets rang from the battlements. Another two hundred yards and they would be in range of Pharnabazus's archers, who could hold the Macedonians at bay while the raiders escaped through the Tripylon Gate. Less than two hundred yards, now. Memnon cuffed sweat from his eyes . . .

Hooves thundered. Unseen until the last moment, a wedge of Companion cavalry smashed into the right flank of the rearguard, splitting it into two groups. Bones snapped as horses trampled the *kardakes*; the soldier two paces in front of Memnon screamed when a spear ripped through his leather armor, gutting him and filling the dusty air with the stench of blood and bowel. The Macedonian's exultant cry became a death rattle as the Rhodian jammed the blade of his javelin through his neck and rolled him off the back of his horse.

Off balance, Memnon collapsed with the dying Macedonian and scuttled away from the crushing hooves of a second rider. Cursing, the fellow stabbed down at him; the Rhodian took the butt-spike of his spear deep in the hip, gritting his teeth against the pain as metal scraped on bone.

"Son of a bitch!" Memnon caught up a fallen javelin and raked it across the horse's belly. The screaming animal bolted; its rider lost his grip and fell, his armored spine crashing into the dust.

Memnon was on him before he could recover. The Rhodian planted the iron tip of his javelin against the bronze cuirass protecting the rider's chest. Metal squealed as his weight drove it through armor, flesh, and bone. The Macedonian convulsed and spewed blood. Gasping, Memnon staggered to his feet.

The Companions, now clear of the rearguard, wheeled and made ready for another pass. Before their horses could find their rhythm, though, Memnon heard the ripping sound of Cretan bowstrings. Scores of arrows lashed from the darkness to pierce flesh and armor. The Rhodian seized the opportunity his archers afforded. "Get the wounded!" he yelled. "Get to the gate!" He limped along, his hip and leg trembling with pain. Blood sheeted down his thigh. *Would you like to know the hour of your death?* He heard the voice, clenched his teeth against the wave of white-hot agony. "No!" Memnon stumbled; he fell to one knee, a golden mist playing at the edges of his vision. "No!"

Suddenly, Thymondas was there. The younger man caught Memnon by the arm and hauled him to his feet. "Hurry, Uncle!" he said. "We're almost there!" The Rhodian felt his strength return as the voice in his head receded. *No, not yet.*

The final hundred yards passed in a blur; soon, the Tripylon Gate loomed above them. Its three cyclopean towers rose sixty feet above their heads, twenty feet higher than the surrounding battlements, their crenellated tops bristling with Persian archers. They drew back on their bowstrings, the smoky air thrumming as they sent flight after flight of iron-heads into the pursuing Macedonians.

Though the Tripylon sported three towers and two bronze-and-oak gates, it had but a single wooden bridge that could be lowered over the dry moat from the center tower. Memnon grinned at the welcome rattle of chains—even as he the shouts of warning reached him from above. The Rhodian glanced over his shoulder to see a battalion of Macedonian infantry, the *Pezhetairoi*, emerge from the ruddy gloom, their shields canted as they advanced on the gate, oblivious to the hail of arrows.

Memnon snarled, shook himself free of Thymondas. "Archers!" he roared. The Cretans heard him, wheeled. The *kardakes* and Ionians, too, ceased their withdrawal and turned, interposing themselves between the Macedonians and the yawning gates of Halicarnassus. "Kill the bastards!"

The Macedonians could not defend against arrows shot from the walls and those loosed at close range on the ground—their shields were smaller than the traditional bowl-shaped *aspides* of the southern Greeks; shifting from high guard to low left them exposed, and vice versa.

They were like wheat for the sickle.

At close range, Cretan arrows hit with the slaughterhouse sound of a cleaver striking flesh, sinking up to their black fletching in enemy chests, bellies, and throats. Men thrashed and toppled, blood pouring from pierced organs. The front rank of Macedonians disintegrated; the second, too. The third, from what Memnon could see of their eyes, resigned themselves to death and pressed on. These were born soldiers, men who marched into battle with an *obol* already under their tongues, ready to pay their passage into Hades' realm. They died well, but they died nonetheless.

The Cretans emptied their quivers before Memnon gave the order to resume their withdrawal. As they neared the Tripylon, Ephialtes led a platoon of hoplites over the bridge and formed a protective phalanx to cover the last few yards. Firelight gleamed from their hedge of spears, from their overlapped shields and the crests of their bronze helmets. Ephialtes bellowed an order and their formation split to allow the raiders through, then turned and followed them back into the city.

With Thymondas's aid, Memnon limped through the gate tunnel and out into the packed street. Men cheered, pressing forward to clap the exhausted and bloody raiders on the back. The wounded were hustled off to the field hospital at the foot of the acropolis; the dead were lifted with reverence and borne away to houses where they could be washed and prepared for the pyre.

"How many did we lose?"

Thymondas could only shrug. "I'll find out after I've seen you to the surgeons."

"They almost had me," Memnon whispered. Word of his injury had spread; concerned soldiers shouted prayers at him while their officers pushed through the milling troops to be by his side, to offer their aid. Thymondas clung to him like an overprotective guardian. Pharnabazus appeared, Amyntas and Ephialtes, too. Patron and the Spartan, Callicratides, cleared well-wishers from the Rhodian's path.

"Did you learn anything, Memnon?" the Spartan asked.

"That Alexander's army isn't invulnerable," he replied, gasping for breath. He coughed, spat dust and blood. "Tell your king, Callicratides . . . tell Agis that if he wants to ally with me against Alexander, if he wants to partake in the reduction of Macedonia, then meet me in Euboea in the spring!" The men who heard this cheered, and the cheers multiplied until it seemed the very stones of Halicarnassus vibrated with praise.

"I will tell him," Callicratides said over the din. Memnon gave a curt nod and motioned Thymondas along. To himself the Spartan added, "And I will pray, perhaps in vain, that the black Fates take no notice of you, Memnon of Rhodes."

Morning sunlight filtered through smoke rising from the still-smoldering siege engines. Flames had destroyed one of the towers and badly damaged another before the inferno could be brought under control. The charred *katapeltoi* were silent, the engineers either dead or too exhausted from wounds and exertion to set about making repairs. Closer to the city, the Macedonians tried time and again to recover the corpses of the slain *Pezhetairoi* only to be driven back by massed volleys from the walls. "Let them rot," the Persian archers snarled, drawing and loosing with vindictive fervor.

Memnon expected some manner of response from Alexander, a renewal of the assault on the Horn, his men's fury lashed to a fever pitch by their repeated failures. He expected redoubled fighting, redoubled bloodshed. What he didn't expect Alexander to do, though, was send a herald.

Pharnabazus fetched Memnon from the surgeon's tent, turning a deaf ear to the doctor, a bearded Chian with a huge beak of a nose, who had swathed the Rhodian's hip in herb-steeped compresses, bound it with strips of linen, and now vocally demanded he stay in bed. Memnon dismissed him with thanks and hobbled from the tent under his own power. The Rhodian was pale; his lips thin and hard as he limped up the stairs to the battlements, stifling a gasp of pain with each step. Pharnabazus looked no better. The Persian had not slept, and Memnon could see evidence of exhaustion in his haggard face, his glassy eyes. Adrenalin and willpower were all that kept both men mobile.

"Has he asked for anything?" Memnon said.

Pharnabazus shook his head. "He stands just out of bowshot and calls your name. I have forbid the men from taking potshots at him until after you have heard what he has to say. Ephialtes thinks we should reward the archer who can skewer him first."

"Ephialtes is a fool," the Rhodian spat.

"You will get no argument from me on that score."

Atop the wall, the sight of Memnon upright and walking, albeit with a limp, bolstered his men's morale. They cheered as he joined his commanders at the Horn. Amyntas and Ephialtes muttered together, laughing at some jest they deigned not share with Orontobates. The satrap stood apart, his face set in the scowl that was fast becoming his signature expression.

"What goes?" Memnon snapped.

"He refuses to say," Orontobates said, gesturing to the figure of the herald. "He will speak only to you."

Memnon walked past his men and stood alone.

The herald, an older Macedonian wearing a simple tunic, stood under a flag of truce on the far side of the slain *Pezhetairoi*. Grim-faced, he bellowed, "Memnon the Rhodian, son of Timocrates! Come forth!"

"Speak," Memnon shouted. "I am here."

"My lord, Alexander, son of Philip, King of the Macedonians, and Captain-General of the Greeks, would speak with you. He gives you the honor of choosing the time and place, saying only that you come alone and unarmed and he will do likewise."

"I smell a trap." Memnon heard Ephialtes grunt. He ignored the Athenian, pondered Alexander's offer.

"What say you, my lord?" the herald shouted.

"My compliments to your king. Tell Alexander I will meet with him in one hour on the crest of that hill, there." Memnon pointed to the hill his men had skirted during last night's raid. An old olive tree grew from its low summit. The herald turned, surveyed the site, and nodded.

"So be it. Yonder hilltop in one hour." The herald turned and retraced his steps to the Macedonian camp.

Pharnabazus walked over to where Memnon stood. "What do you think Alexander wants?"

"We'll find out soon enough." The Rhodian shrugged. Sweat beaded his forehead; he shifted his frame, putting all of his weight on his uninjured side.

"This is madness, Uncle!" Pharnabazus hissed, pitching his voice low so the others couldn't eavesdrop. "You cannot sit a horse right now, and there is little chance you can walk to that hill without aid!"

"So what?" Memnon said. "We call the herald back and have him ask Alexander to meet me elsewhere? Perhaps he'd like to sit under the battlements and enjoy our archers' scrutiny? He's no fool, Pharnabazus, and neither am I. So do me a favor, nephew—save your opinion for another day and find me a chariot!"

MEMNON BREATHED THE HOT, DUSTY AIR KICKED UP BY THE HOOVES OF HIS chestnut gelding as the chariot, an antique rig of tarnished bronze and worm-eaten wood, rattled over the rough ground. Already, he could see the stallion Boukephalos cropping the sparse grass near the base of the hill. At the crest, under the boughs of the olive tree, Alexander's armor glinted in the sun.

The Rhodian slewed to a halt and gingerly dismounted, his hip a swollen mass of raw and lacerated flesh, hot against his leather kilt. He tethered the gelding to a myrtle shrub; limping, he ascended the rise to the crest of the hill.

Unarmed, possessing not even a belt knife, Memnon nonetheless wore his full panoply—ox-hide sandals, greaves, kilt of bronze-studded leather, and his silver-inlaid cuirass. He removed his helmet and carried it in the crook of his left arm. In a pinch he could use it as a bludgeon, though he did not expect treachery from Alexander. Such behavior ran contrary to the young king's nature.

Reaching the summit, he sensed the power of Alexander's unrelenting gaze. The king watched him; in return, he studied his adversary, whom he had not seen since that summer at Mieza. Alexander had grown over the years, though not by much. He stood a full head shorter than the Rhodian but the muscular lines of his physique made up for his less-than-impressive height. Clean-shaven and with thick hair like dark gold hanging to his shoulders, Alexander's features were finer than those of his father, his skin flushed by sun and wind. In his eyes, Memnon could discern that mysterious *daimon* he had often warned Pharnabazus about, the spirit of a true leader.

"You're wounded," Alexander said suddenly, lines creasing his high forehead. He took two quick steps to Memnon's side and offered him an arm to lean upon. The king wore a *lineothorax* crusted with gold ornaments and reinforced with plates of iron, the center boss protecting his chest wrought in the snarling visage of a lion.

"It's nothing," Memnon said. "A scratch only."

"I can fetch my physician, should you require him. He's a good man, an Acarnanian called Philip." Alexander ushered him to the shade of the olive tree, where Memnon leaned against the wiry bole, relieving the pressure on his hip.

"As I said, it's barely a scratch." Memnon's eyes narrowed as he stared at Alexander. He could still perceive the inquisitive boy underneath the trappings of war, a discovery he found oddly comforting. "You're looking well, Alexander. The mantle of kingship agrees with you, it seems."

"It is a responsibility I savor," Alexander replied. He returned Memnon's frank stare. "You've done well for yourself, also. Most commanders who suffer a resounding defeat such as what befell you at the Granicus are put aside rather than elevated. Darius must put great stock in your skills."

Memnon smiled, though the gesture didn't extend to his eyes. Those remained slitted and cold. "The Granicus wasn't my battle; its failure belongs solely on the shoulders of the satraps. Men you conveniently killed, as I recall, thus relieving the Great King of the burden of their executions—a burden he would have likely handed to me. I don't thank you for it, though. I lost too many good men. Friends and kin."

Alexander's face clouded. "It's true that a son of Artabazus died that day?"

"It's true," Memnon said, exhaling. "Hydarnes. You probably don't remember him. He was only a toddler during our stay at your father's court." The Rhodian's voice hardened. "One of your Agrianians slew him."

The young king nodded. "Cophen spoke frequently of his brothers, which intrigued me. I have only one, a half-brother, Arrhidaeus, and he is a simpleton through no fault of his own. A defect of his birth, or so my mother claims. I am sorry for the loss of your nephew, Memnon, and to Artabazus for the loss of his son. War is a harsh master, as you well know. Is Cophen with you in Halicarnassus?"

However genuine, Alexander's condolences left the Rhodian apathetic toward the young king and immune to his mystery. "No," he said. "I sent him back to his father. The dichotomy of friendship to you and duty to the Great King caused him much consternation. Removing him from the path of possible temptation seemed the wisest course."

"A pity. I would've liked to have seen him again."

Memnon's patience ebbed. "Did you call this meeting simply to reminisce, Alexander, or do you plan to use our meager shared history as a way of convincing me to transfer my allegiance?"

"Parmenion assured me such an effort would be in vain," the young king said, coldness creeping into his voice. "You've made your decision and

I respect your sense of loyalty, misguided though it may be. No, Rhodian, I'm here because I wished to ask a favor of you, man to man: allow my troops the chance to recover their slain brothers and cousins from the shadow of the city walls. In return, I'll have the dead you left in the field last night brought to the gates."

"You ask for a truce?"

"Do not read too much into this, Memnon." Alexander's eyes flashed. "Call it a truce if you like, but understand it is a pause only, an exchange between friends."

Memnon straightened, ignoring the agony of his hip. "I will grant your request because it's the right thing to do, not because of some imagined bond we share. We've never been friends, Alexander. You're the son of a man who offered my family safe haven, nothing more. Is the balance of today enough of a pause to recover the dead and see to their funerals?"

"It's more than enough time." Alexander's thin nostrils flared; Memnon sensed a wave of anger flowing off him. The young king was not accustomed to having his friendship rebuffed, and the idea of if stung his pride worse than the loss of his siege machines. Though his face remained impassive, inwardly Memnon cackled with glee.

"So be it. Farewell, King of Macedon." Memnon inclined his head.

"Rhodian," Alexander said, rage bringing a touch of pallor to his cheeks. "When my men breach the walls of Halicarnassus—and they will breach them!—I will treat you no different from any of my enemies. Do you understand?"

"*If* your men breach the walls," Memnon said, turning away. "I would expect nothing less."

UNDER THE WATCHFUL EYES OF MEMNON'S ARCHERS, THE MACEDONIANS gathered the bodies of their slain *Pezhetairoi*; afterward, they carted the Persian dead to the Tripylon and left them, twenty-two in all. Memnon ordered the gate opened and the cart brought inside—though not before his men searched it thoroughly, making sure the dead were their own and not enemy soldiers masquerading as such. Treachery might not have been in Alexander's arsenal but it was surely in Parmenion's; the Rhodian was no Priam, to be gulled by a wily Odysseus.

Though a truce existed, preparations for the resumption of fighting never slackened. Outside the wall crews cleared away the wreckage of charred siege machinery, repairing damaged *katapeltoi*, and restocking ammunition caches. Inside the wall, workmen demolished buildings behind the site chosen by the Macedonian king for his breach; then they used the rubble to reinforce existing defenses. Soldiers looked to their weapons, restringing bows and honing blades, casting lead into fresh sling bullets, and replacing dented shield faces with new bronze. Night fell, and funeral pyres blazed in both camps.

"Prepare yourself," Memnon said to Pharnabazus. His nephew had brought him a platter of roasted fowl, bread, and cheese, with a jug of strong Thasian wine to wash it down, and lingered about until the surgeon finished changing the dressings on his hip. Now Memnon lay on a divan, his weight on his good side. "Tomorrow marks the beginning of the real siege."

"Worse than the other battles we have endured, Uncle?" the Persian said. "I find that difficult to believe."

Memnon sniffed the wine, his eyes closed. "It will be," he replied, "the most horrific battle you've ever seen."

The Rhodian's prediction came true. At dawn Alexander's wrath exploded against the walls of Halicarnassus; his anger and frustration funneled down to his men, and they fought like animals, eager to prove their quality to the young king. The *katapeltoi* were brought closer, inside Persian missile range, where they could send heavier stones against the battlements, stones that smashed embrasures and the men behind them. Arrows streaked through the sky in both directions, wounding as many men as they killed. Screams and curses drifted in the dust-thickened air.

On the ground, soldiers filled the moat at a breakneck pace, reinforcing the top layers of earth with split logs snaked down from the hills; already sappers, engineers whose specialty lay in assaulting wall foundations, could cross the moat under their huge hide shields and begin work. The sounds of picks and hammers echoed through the heavy masonry. To counter, Memnon ordered incendiaries lit and dropped from the parapet. The pottery jars shattered, raining burning bitumen down on the sappers' heads. Their shrieks replaced the staccato rap of tools.

By dusk, when a *salpinx* called an end to the day's fighting, the battlements of the Horn resembled a slaughterhouse—bodies riven or split asunder, spackled with blood, naked bone gleaming through torn armor and flesh. Pharnabazus, his face hidden beneath a ghoulish veneer of dust and gore, swayed on his feet and might have fallen had Memnon not been there to offer him a shoulder to lean upon. "Merciful gods," the Persian whispered, his voice raw from the constant effort needed to shout orders over the din. "Why . . . Why was this so different from the first day?"

"Because their resolve has changed," the Rhodian said. He limped with Pharnabazus over to a pile of broken stone and sat. "In that first clash, Alexander sought to learn our limits. How far could he push us before we pushed back? Now, he doesn't care how far he pushes. All that matters is the wall—ripping it down if you're Macedonian, preserving it if you're Persian. You're accustomed to field battles, infantry and cavalry, where there's ebb and flow, movement and countermovement, charge and retreat. Not so in a siege. The wall is immobile until it falls, and so are we." He gestured out over the fifteen-foot-wide battlements, the dead mercifully cloaked in the shadows of twilight. "We stand. No charge, no retreat. We face the fury of their missiles, and we either live or we die, as the Fates will it. But we do not move. If we do, Alexander will gain a foothold before we're ready for him."

"In the name of all the gods," Pharnabazus said, his face grim in the deepening darkness. "When will we be ready for him?"

But Memnon did not answer.

The siege progressed in earnest. Day after bloody day Alexander chipped at the city's defenses. His men completed the road over the moat, making it wide enough to allow the two undamaged towers to be rolled up against the wall simultaneously. The third tower stood a hundred yards to the rear; all three wooden Titans bristled with archers, their massed volleys sweeping Persians from the Horn's battlements. Protected by the hulking structures, the two battering rams—iron-tipped logs suspended from chains—crashed against the wall, a relentless rhythm driven by sheer muscle.

Memnon strode the battlements, his pain consumed by white-hot anger. His men fed off him. His rage stoked theirs, provoking acts of breathless valor. Men broke cover to hurl incendiaries at the arrow slits in the siege tower walls, splashing the men inside with combustibles even as they were cut down by enemy missiles; in their wake, Persian archers sent tow bolts, arrows wrapped with a length of smoldering twine, through the slits. Flames exploded from the heart of the tower, doing more damage to the soldiers inside than to the green wood around them. Cheering defenders drowned out the Macedonians' screams.

Later in the day, a detachment of marines from the fleet, protected by hoplite shields, rushed the towers, casting grapnels at their tops. The iron hooks dug into the wood. Men hauled on the ropes. Timbers creaked and snapped. Before the tower could be overturned, though, an axe-wielding Macedonian severed the ropes; his triumph was short-lived—Persian arrows sent him plummeting to his death.

Still, the rams hammered the walls, and they did not stop until the *salpinx* sounded their recall. Under a hail of darts and shafts, Alexander's soldiers drew the siege machines back from Halicarnassus, across the earthworks bridging the moat, and into their nightly positions closer to the camp.

That evening, Memnon used the respite to convene his officers. They met on the acropolis, on a terrace overlooking the unfinished Mausoleum. A loggia of carved and painted cedar provided a sliver of shade against the setting sun. Each man came straight from the walls. Still caked in the grime of battle, they shucked their armor at the edge of the terrace. Servants met them with basins of cool water and scented towels, with fresh tunics and deep cups of fragrant wine, and escorted them to a ring of divans.

Memnon wasn't the only wounded man among them. Amyntas, his forehead and one eye swathed in bandages, groaned as he sat; Orontobates, too. The satrap had lost a finger and hamstrung himself leaping out of the path of a *katapeltes* stone. Pharnabazus nursed bruised ribs from where rock shards dented his cuirass, and even Ephialtes, with his Heraklean vitality, drank his wine in exhausted silence. Autophradates, alone, bore not the slightest scratch, his post on the water being farthest from combat. Thymondas and Patron arrived last, both men caked in sweat and dust. Patron limped from an arrow wound in his thigh, while Thymondas still bled from a wicked gash in his shoulder. A dart had missed impaling him by a matter of inches. He sat and pressed a wad of linen to the laceration.

"So?" Memnon said. The others looked up.

Patron shook his head. "Another day, maybe two, and that wall is coming down."

"Can we reinforce it?"

"Perhaps," Patron said, "but what's the use? Once the core of the wall is down we could put all the rubble in Halicarnassus into that breach and it wouldn't be enough to stop the rams."

"We need to burn those gods-be-damned towers," Ephialtes muttered.

"How?" Pharnabazus said. "Alexander's on guard against another night sortie."

"Do it during the day," the Athenian said.

Amyntas coughed and spat. "Hera's tits, man! They've got us outnumbered. We go scotching off outside the walls in broad daylight and they'll hand us our own arses, well-buggered at that."

"Get rid of the gods-be-damned towers!" Ephialtes lapsed into silence.

"What are our casualties, Thymondas?"

The soldier winced as he applied pressure to his shoulder. "We've lost close to four hundred men in the last few days. Twice that number in wounded and a goodly part of those will never fight again. Those stone throwers . . . a pox on their inventors! And a pox on the man who had the idea of launching a single rock any halfway agile man could dodge, causing it to impact against an embrasure where it splits into a dozen pieces, each one a crude spearhead!" Wood creaked as Thymondas leaned back on the divan. "It's the most dishonorable manner of fighting I've ever seen!"

"It's only dishonorable because we didn't think of it first," Patron said. He studied Memnon as he sat in silence, his brow creased in thought. "Well, lad?"

The Rhodian stirred. "Autophradates, send to Cos and have the balance of the fleet brought over."

"They will be here before noon," the admiral assured him.

Memnon nodded. "We'll start by evacuating the wounded. Orontobates, I'm leaving you with a thousand men to garrison Salmacis and Arconessus, and a flotilla of ships to secure the harbor."

Orontobates glanced around in confusion. "Leaving?" he said. "What do you mean?"

"Is Halicarnassus not the seat of your satrapy? When I leave, someone will need to stay behind to maintain a Persian presence. Who better than the satrap himself?" Memnon shifted his gaze to the other officers. All save Ephialtes and Amyntas apprehended his meaning, and their faces displayed varied levels of relief. The two remaining Greeks, however, glowered.

"You're just going to give it to him?" Ephialtes snarled. "Give Alexander the city?"

Amyntas stood and paced. "I didn't spill my blood here so you could cut and run when things heat up!"

Memnon checked his temper. He looked from one man to the other, from Athenian to Macedonian; both had reason to hate Alexander, but they were motivated by pride—Ephialtes to redress the insult to Athenian supremacy, and Amyntas to advance his own petty ambitions. Neither could see what lay beyond the tips of their own noses. "When King Xerxes marched on Hellas nearly a century-and-a-half ago," Memnon said slowly, "was the outcome of the war decided in the pass of Thermopylae? No, gentlemen, it wasn't. But Hellas needed Thermopylae in order to prepare themselves for the victories at Salamis and Plataea. Halicarnassus is no Thermopylae, but it has served its purpose. Nor am I just *giving* the city to Alexander, as you put it. He's purchased it with his most precious commodity—the blood of his men. But, what has he purchased my friends? Not a harbor, because we will maintain control of that. Not the harbor forts, because Orontobates will hold those in the name of the Great King. What has Alexander been fighting for control of?" Memnon gestured to the Mausoleum. "That? A gaudy pile of stone housing the corpse of a dead tyrant?"

Ephialtes' scowl faded; the Athenian chuckled. He swallowed the last of his wine, held out his cup for a servant to refill. "Where will we go?"

"Pella," Memnon replied. "By way of Euboea."

The words galvanized his officers. Thymondas gave a low whistle. Ephialtes nearly choked on a fresh swallow of wine. Amyntas stopped pacing. By the look on his face, one could tell he was attempting to make sense of what the Rhodian had said. "Why to Pella?" Orontobates asked.

"Taking the war back to Macedonia is the easiest way to drive Alexander from Asia—and that is my mandate from the Great King. It was never my intention to defeat Alexander at Halicarnassus, only to take his measure. That's done. Now we move on to the real target."

"The regent Antipatros and his son, Kassandros, command the Home

Guard," Amyntas said, chewing on his lip. "Antipatros is a staunch King's Man, but Kassandros hates Alexander . . ."

"And he'll hate me after we trounce his father," Memnon said. Amyntas looked skeptical. Obviously, the renegade held Macedonia's regent in high regard. *No matter*, Memnon thought. He'd beaten Parmenion; he would beat Antipatros. "But, we're getting ahead of ourselves, my friends. Before we can invade Macedonia we must first extricate ourselves from Halicarnassus . . . and give Alexander a final lesson."

"Have you a plan, Uncle?" Pharnabazus said. Of all the officers, he and Patron showed the least surprise at Memnon's dynamism—no doubt they were inured to it by virtue of their long association.

Memnon smiled. "I do," he said. "And it involves those gods-be-damned siege towers."

THE SUN ROSE THROUGH A PALL OF DUST. FROM THE TRIPYLON'S CENTRAL bastion, Memnon and his nephews watched as Alexander's men plodded out to the towers, putting their shoulders to the wheels and moving the massive structures back to their fighting positions. Sappers filed after them, followed by battalions of archers and shield-bearers, Agrianian javelineers and armored Foot Companions. Even from this distance Memnon could sense an air of indifference about them.

"Remember what I told you, Thymondas?" the Rhodian said, turning. "On that first day?"

"Beware complacency."

"Indeed. Complacency is the insidious enemy of siege warfare. It's like a disease, striking without regard to allegiance or loyalty." Memnon led the way as the trio descended down to the level of the parapet. All stood in readiness—every man knew his place, what was expected of him. In the shadow of the Tripylon Gate, Amyntas and a thousand lightly armored Greeks bearing torches and incendiaries awaited Memnon's signal.

"Your targets are the siege towers," Memnon had told the Macedonian renegade. "Archers will cover you from the walls, but it's still going to be like walking into a threshing machine. You'll have to rely on speed, nimbleness, and prayer."

"We'll burn those bastards down!"

A second wave would come on their heels. Ephialtes with another thousand Greeks—the heavy infantry, hoplites in full panoply bearing nine-foot spears and broad shields—would pour out, form a phalanx, and strike Alexander's flankers while their attention rested on the burning towers.

"Your sole purpose is to kill," he said to the hulking Athenian the night before. Upon hearing this, Ephialtes' face had lit up like a man in love.

Finally, when the chaos reached its crescendo, Memnon himself would lead out the final wave: two thousand *kardakes* in close formation. If all went as planned they would split the Macedonian ranks like a hammer and wedge.

If, Memnon thought, leaning against an embrasure and watching the towers roll closer. *How can such a small word encompass so many possibilities?* Yet battle plans were tenuous by their very nature; even if his men failed to split the enemy apart, at least they would spill a great deal of precious Macedonian blood in the attempt. Memnon straightened. His hip burned, but adrenalin masked the pain of it.

"To your posts," he said to Pharnabazus and Thymondas. "It's almost time." Thymondas would command the archers on the wall of the Horn, Pharnabazus at the Tripylon Gate. Of his remaining officers, Orontobates was overseeing the restocking of the harbor fortresses while Patron and Autophradates loaded the wounded, and any excess equipment, on the ships.

No trumpets heralded the commencement of the day's fighting. As the towers lumbered into range the archers on the wall loosed their arrows—a drizzle at first, then a rain, and finally a hail. Iron-heads struck the timbers and hidebound planking of the towers with a dull crack, punctuated by cries as the occasional shaft threaded a chink in the wood and nailed flesh. Sling bullets whirred and clacked, ricocheting off bronze or wood, shattering into lead fragments that peppered the attackers on the ground.

Sporadic at first, Macedonian archers matched volley for volley once the towers found their marks and the wheels were spiked down. The men inside those infernal machines turned their attention to the rams, and within minutes the walls of Halicarnassus resounded with their thunderous crashes. Each paired impact sent vibrations running through the parapet.

Finally, the *katapeltoi* engaged the walls, their stones and darts aimed for positions on the flanks of the siege towers in an effort to negate the Persians ability to shoot down on the men behind them. By midmorning, all of Alexander's assets were about the task of reducing the ramparts of the city.

Only then did Memnon give the signal for the assault to begin.

A horn blasted, the trumpeter holding it for a long note. Atop the Tripylon, Pharnabazus ordered the bridge lowered; the gates crashed open and Amyntas, howling like a madman, led his men out, their fiery brands held aloft.

Arrows sheeted from the battlements. Disdaining cover, Thymondas's archers stood and loosed with reckless abandon. Most were Cretans, men who crawled from their mothers' wombs bow in hand and who could shoot eight iron-heads in the span of a minute. On this day, their skill rivaled that of the Archer, Apollo. Even the Persians, themselves no slouches with the bow, kept the Cretans' furious pace, creating a storm of slaughter among the Macedonians.

Though Memnon could not gauge their progress from the ground, he gave Amyntas to the count of one hundred before he loosed the hoplites. Ephialtes, with the fearsome visage of snake-haired Medusa in bas-relief on the chest of his cuirass, held his spear aloft, bellowing, "Kill the sons of bitches!" Then, in two columns, he and his men marched at the double through the Tripylon Gate and into battle.

Skeins of smoke drifted from the siege towers; embattled soldiers plied the *salpinx*, its desperate howl echoed and redoubled by those battalions in Ephialtes' path. It was a cry for help.

Memnon turned from the sounds of fighting and walked among his *kardakes*. Many of them were survivors of the Granicus, hard-bitten men who burned to avenge that slight on their honor. In their ranks, though, stood silver-haired veterans of Lake Manyas, soldiers who remembered Artabazus's rule and who were with the old satrap and his family at Dascylium. In their eyes it was Memnon who sprang from Zeus's loins, not that upstart, Alexander.

"Do you hear those horns?" Memnon began, his voice carrying despite the din of battle that poured through the still-open gates. "Do you? Have you ever heard such wild and off-key bellowing? Fear fills their lungs and they blow their horns from want of succor! Those horns will bring Alexander to us!" Spears clashed on shields; Memnon's sword flashed in the sun. "Let's go forth and greet him in a manner he won't soon forget! Forward by column! At the double!"

An *aulos* flute marked cadence as the Persian soldiers hustled out the Tripylon Gate. It clanged shut behind them, only to be opened when Pharnabazus heard the signal to withdraw. Beyond the walls, Memnon could see better the havoc his men wrought. The base of one siege tower burned; the other two smoldered, needing only the application of an incendiary to burst into open flames. Amyntas's men tangled with Alexander's light troops while the archers on the walls dueled with their Macedonian counterparts. Already, Ephialtes' phalanx scythed through the unprepared battalions of Foot Companions, driving them back, their advance angling left to engage the siege engines, as well.

Memnon guided his *kardakes* into the gap between Ephialtes and Amyntas. Dust and smoke cloaked the field, choking friend and foe, alike. In the chaos, whole companies intent on rescuing the siege towers passed in front of the Persian spearmen. The *kardakes* struck mercilessly, splitting their ranks wide open and scattering men in all directions.

The battle raged throughout the day. The fires died out, quenched in part by the blood of the slain. For hours, the Persians had the upper hand as their archers kept the Macedonian cavalry from entering the fray; nor could Alexander bring reinforcements from the other gates—the young king feared catastrophic sorties from those points, should he turn his back on them. He had to contain the assault with the troops at hand.

Ephialtes took the Persian left as far as the line of *katapeltoi*. The Athenian's hoplites slaughtered the engineers, wrecking several of the machines before they were hit with a Macedonian counterattack. Alexander's veterans, men of Philip's era, cursed their younger brethren as whelps and cowards even as they engaged the Greeks—phalanx against phalanx, *sarissa* against spear. The longer Macedonian pikes proved their worth once again, driving the hoplites back toward the Tripylon.

The Rhodian felt the timbre of the battle change. His left compacted; the soldiers his *kardakes* faced, a mix of Thracian peltasts and Macedonian hill-fighters, fought with redoubled fury as the veterans spiked into the Persian ranks.

A screaming Thracian leapt on Memnon's shield, dragging it down as a second man, a blood-spattered Macedonian, came at him with axe and knife. He didn't even take two steps before a *kardakes* over Memnon's shoulder rammed his spear straight into the Macedonian's sternum. Bone shivered and cracked. The Thracian, realizing his ploy had failed, looked up as the Rhodian's blade sheared through his skull.

The tide of the battle definitely turned. They were being forced back, Memnon reckoned, and with mounting casualties. *We can do no more.* Content with the enemy blood soaking the ground, Memnon called for his trumpeter to sound withdrawal . . .

TWILIGHT'S MANTLE LAY OVER HALICARNASSUS. STARS BLAZED, COLD AND aloof, their patterns shaped by the deeds of gods and men. By their thin light Memnon took measure of the dead. Of the four thousand men who fought in the assault, fifteen hundred still lay on the field. Another thousand bore wounds, a third of those serious. A quarter of the seven hundred Cretans atop the walls would never return to their sea-girt island. The balance of them displayed with pride the marks of arrow, stone, and fire.

Ephialtes died fighting Alexander's veterans—Philip's men—those very soldiers who had shamed his *polis* on the field at Chaeronea. By all accounts, the hulking Athenian took a few of them with him on the long road to Tartarus.

Amyntas, too, was slain—his head hacked off by a pair of rival clansmen who recognized him. Memnon could do nothing to recover his body or even to prevent it from being dishonored. Such was a renegade's fate, and Amyntas well knew it. Ephialtes at least would be buried with the rest of the Persian dead, for that was Alexander's way. Not so Amyntas. Memnon said a prayer for the Macedonian's shade.

"What now, my lord?" a soldier asked, his face unrecognizable beneath a mask of blood. Memnon clapped him on the shoulder and walked on, through the heart of the agora as it quickly filled with troops. The wounded had gone to the ships; seeing the whole of the fleet anchored off Halicarnassus, the rest of the garrison milled about, waiting for orders. They sensed a change.

Pharnabazus and Patron wrangled a couple of blocks into the agora's center, creating a makeshift plinth. The Rhodian ascended to it. At a gesture, his trumpeter sounded assembly. Men pressed closer, listening. His words would be relayed to every corner of the agora.

For a moment, Memnon said nothing. He looked out over the sea of upturned faces, some bandaged and bloody, all covered in the dust of a city not their own. In every visage, he read a tale of bone-crushing weariness, grief, and pain. What did they read in his?

"There was a time," he began, "when I could spool off a speech faster than an Athenian demagogue. My father was an orator, you see, and men claimed I inherited his gift. Perhaps, perhaps not. For myself, I make no such boast. If I speak well it's because of you, my brothers; your deeds have given me a foundation on which to construct a flimsy tower of words. By all the gods, you make me proud! All of you!" They responded in kind, cheering the Rhodian on until he raised a hand for silence.

He continued. "This city came under my custody bearing a price for its walls, a price quoted in blood! Not ours, my friends, but Alexander's! He's met that price, and then some! Now, we must relinquish Halicarnassus to him!" Cries of "no!" and "stay and fight!" erupted from the assembly. Memnon raised his hands again, shouted over them. "He's bought it, friends! Paid for it with his most precious possession—Macedonian blood! And he can have it! Aye, he can! For you and I, my brothers, have greater things to accomplish! What's this one city compared to the whole of the Aegean?"

The agora exploded in wild screams. Sword hilts and spear shafts clashed on shields, on armor. Soldiers chanted Memnon's name until the stones threatened to crack. Let the whelp have Halicarnassus! They would seize the Aegean, perhaps Hellas itself! It took another blast of the trumpet to bring them under control.

"We're done here, brothers!" Memnon said. "When Alexander rises tomorrow we'll be long gone, and his men will be able to see for themselves what their comrades died for." The Rhodian pointed off to his right, to the massive Mausoleum. Laughter rippled through the crowd. Slowly, they broke up and filed down to the harbor, placated; they would board the ships secure in the knowledge that their own sacrifices at Halicarnassus were for a greater good.

Pharnabazus helped his uncle down from the plinth. The wound in the Rhodian's hip reopened during the day, leaving his bandages sodden with blood, and the pain a deeper throb than ever before. "The gift is there," the Persian said. "No matter how much you deny it."

Memnon sighed, looked up at the stars. It was the time of night he missed Barsine most. "Will the gift ever be for peace, I wonder?"

Interlude VI

"Halicarnassus was a Macedonian victory only in the strictest sense," Harmouthes said. "Alexander occupied the city, yes. But at a terrible price." The Egyptian looked at Barsine. She slept restlessly. Her eyes flared open every little while as she fought to breathe. Her struggles ebbed, growing less frantic.

Ariston pursed his lips. "Is she . . . ?"

"She is in Lord Osiris's hands now. We can do nothing more."

"I'm sorry, Harmouthes."

The Egyptian gave the young man a sharp look. "I will not mourn her yet," he said. "She fights the summons into the West. She may yet save herself."

Ariston sighed. "What became of Memnon's plan to transfer the war to Euboea?"

Harmouthes rose from Barsine's bedside and went to the window, cracking it a little so he could inhale the cold night air. Stars shone through jagged rips in the clouds. "He pursued it after Halicarnassus, but uprisings against him on Chios and Lesbos threatened to delay his plans. No one knew how long the fickle Spartans would wait for him, so he spent the winter retaking those islands, reinstalling their garrisons and delivering crushing retributions; fighting when he should have been healing." Harmouthes pulled the window shut and returned to his bedside vigil. He stroked Barsine's brow; she murmured in her sleep. "Chios proved as effortless as before, as did four of the five cities of Lesbos, thanks to his cousin, Aristonymus." The Egyptian sighed. "Mytilene, though . . ."

Mytilene
Year 3 of the 111th Olympiad
(Early 333 BCE)

THE STINK OF DEATH SHROUDED MYTILENE.

Under an iron gray sky, fires smoldered in spite of the drizzling rain—fires set in the night by bands of Greek mercenaries who had infiltrated the city on Memnon's orders, creeping ashore from the southernmost of Mytilene's two Persian-blockaded harbors to end the month-long stalemate. Even now, two hours after sunrise, screams echoed through the streets, the clash of arms audible even to the pinnacle of the city's walled acropolis. Behind their ramparts the rulers of Mytilene—wealthy patriarchs from the best democratic families—listened helplessly as their *polis* died around them.

Thymondas, who had led the night assault, waited on the quay as Memnon came ashore. The younger man's face was soot-blackened and streaked with blood, his armor dented from the fury of the fighting. Still, he grinned triumphantly, extending his hand to help Memnon out of the skiff.

"So?" the Rhodian said, taking his nephew's proffered hand. Gaunt, dark circles ringing his eyes, and in no condition to fight, Memnon nevertheless came clad for battle in cuirass and kilt, his blue cloak wrapped tightly about his shoulders. The Rhodian leaned heavily on the shaft of his spear, his limbs weak. His face felt clammy and hot. Five months since Halicarnassus and the wound in his hip had yet to properly heal, leaving him prone to fevers; it suppurated constantly, an endless stream of blood-laced pus his surgeon appeared unable to explain, much less to stem. Once Mytilene was pacified he would cave to his nephew's wishes and send east for Khafre. "Did all go as planned?"

"We captured half their fleet in dry-dock, the ones who didn't skin out a month back when we first showed up," Thymondas said. Together, they walked off the quay and into the shelter of a harbor-side *emporion*; its columned arcade showed signs of recent bloodshed—spent arrows and discarded javelins, splintered shields and riven helmets. Corpses sprawled in puddles of mud and gore, limbs skewed, bodies slashed by blades or pierced by missiles. The Rhodian found himself unable to discern attacker from defender in the jumble of bodies. Death, pale Thanatos, stripped a man of his individuality as surely as it stripped him of his future. *Why do dead men look alike*, he wondered, *same glassy-eyed expression, same rictus of shock?*

"Where's the worst of the fighting been?"

Thymondas gestured out the rear of the *emporion*. "They nearly had us in the agora, but we were able to put Cretans on the roofs of a couple of adjacent houses. Still they only gave ground after we set fire to half the block. They're retreating toward the acropolis, though I doubt the bastards behind those walls will open a gate and let them in."

As in most Aegean cities, Mytilene's life revolved around its harbors, the northern and southern, on either side of a wide promontory extending out into the sea. On the western extremity of this spit of land the acropolis stood on a flat hillock—a fortress complete with towers and battlements and bronze-bound gates. Memnon could barely see its ramparts through the veil of rain, but he knew its layout, its strengths, and its weaknesses. He had paid well to learn its weaknesses . . .

Memnon's vision blurred. Angrily, he cuffed sweat from his eyes. Heat emanated from his brow even as chills wracked his body. His hip throbbed.

"Have . . . Have they made any . . . overtures for peace?"

Thymondas frowned and shook his head. "We've had nothing from them but curses and blows. You should sit, rest a moment. Memnon?"

The Rhodian swayed on his feet, his face pale. "S-Send a herald," Memnon said. He blinked, rubbed his eyes, again. "Tell . . . Tell them the terms will be f-fair for their . . . for their s-surrender . . ."

"Memnon!"

Suddenly, the Rhodian staggered, clutching at Thymondas's arm before he crashed to the ground. A roaring filled his ears, like the howling winds he'd experienced in Egypt, so loud that it drowned out his nephew's voice. Thymondas's face hovered in and out of his vision; Memnon wanted to speak, to tell him everything would be all right, but his tongue felt like a hank of dried leather in his mouth. All he could do was close his eyes. *Sleep*, he thought. *Merciful sleep . . .*

And in the back of his mind, he heard a distant voice: *You are almost ready to make the journey, child of Rhodes. Your time approaches.*

Memnon woke to the watery reflection of winter sunlight, a liquid silver glow playing across smoke-stained ceiling beams. Pillows cushioned his head and a thick coverlet draped his body. His skin was moist, febrile; his hip burned, but he could feel nothing below his upper thigh. The air reeked of garlic and medicinal herbs, wood smoke and too-sweet incense. Memnon blinked.

The Rhodian lay in a whitewashed room, afternoon's light—and cold salt air—streaming through a trio of shuttered windows. He could hear seagulls, muted voices, and the ringing of metal on metal. A brazier smoldered near his bed, and in one corner sat a jumble of equipment and armor, his traveling chest among it. *Where am I?*

Voices reached him from an adjacent room, along with the clatter of crockery.

"The leg must go, sir! Already it's likely too late!"

"That will kill him, you fool!" Memnon recognized Patron. "Do you even know what is causing his fever? Is it not your responsibility to clean his wound and change his dressings? I say this infection is your fault, you unclean son of a bitch!"

"His humors are unbalanced, sir!" the other voice, his Chian surgeon, lashed back.

"You and your gods-be-damned humors! Get out of my sight before I hack your cursed leg off! Useless wretch!"

Memnon coughed and lay back, closing his eyes . . .

The river swirled through a marshy wasteland, its oily waters reflecting the sun that hung motionless in the gray-white sky, frozen in a state of perpetual eclipse. Heat and pale light emanated from its blackened disk. Memnon walked closer. Nothing stirred the desiccated air, yet he could hear the keening moan of a breeze curling through the skeletal groves.

"I know this place," Memnon said, his speech flat and distorted.

The reply, coming from behind him, was in a voice as mellifluous as his was grotesque. "Of course you do, son of Timocrates."

Wracked with pain, Memnon gave a long and drawn-out sigh. His breath rattled in his chest. "I know you now," he said softly. "*Psychopompos*."

The figure behind him was one of unearthly beauty, but familiar. Clad in a short Doric tunic, with a silvery-gray khlamys *thrown over his shoulder, he had hair of gold and silver, a young-old face, and lambent eyes the Rhodian could not suffer himself to meet.*

He smiled, a gesture of sublime kindness. "This is the river Styx, the frontier of Hades' realm."

"I'm dead, then?" A weight crushed Memnon to his knees, a burden of despair and of fear and of grief for those left behind.

"Not quite. Soon, though."

The Rhodian stared at the hateful waters of the Styx. "Why am I here if I'm not dead?"

"Curiosity?" he said. "Fear of the unknown? It is the great dichotomy of your people. You love discovering what is around the next bend even as you fear taking that first step toward it. Death is but a part of that journey."

"You told me once that I should endeavor to make my mark upon the world, that the gods look unkindly on those who waste their gifts . . ."

"Fear not, Memnon of Rhodes. The gods are pleased."

"What about Barsine?" Memnon said. Hot tears spilled down his cheeks. "I gave her my word that I would come for her! Please, I can't die! Not now!"

"That is not your decision, child. Atropos wields her blade without concern for the demands of love, or for the wishes of man or god. Your thread is at an end, son of Timocrates. Go back and set your affairs in order. I will come for you soon, to guide you on your journey . . ."

Memnon blinked back the tears blurring his vision. Slowly he sat up. Gritting his teeth against the pain, the Rhodian threw the coverlet back and swung his legs over the edge of the bed. Cool air raised gooseflesh on his body.

"Don't be a fool." Patron stood in the doorway, looking older and more careworn than Memnon ever remembered. Sunlight highlighted the scars lacing his chest and arms. "Stay in bed and put those covers back on. Things are bad enough without you taking the lung sickness, as well."

"How long have I been . . . ?"

"Three days," Patron said. "The Mytileneans surrendered last evening, after we threatened them with the fate of Thebes. Pharnabazus and Thymondas have things well under control. You should rest."

"Help . . . me up, old friend," the Rhodian gasped. "To the . . . window."

With Patron's aid, Memnon rose and shuffled to the window. He nudged open a shutter and took in the day. A chill breeze blew in off the sea, but the sun sparkled on the water of the Southern Harbor and thin skeins of cloud drifted high in the faded blue sky. Below, along the quay, his men were busy salvaging the debris of war. Spent arrows were re-fletched, their iron-heads sharpened and greased, while spearheads were socketed onto new ash shafts. It reminded him of another city, another harbor . . .

"Rhodes seems so far away," Memnon whispered. "I wonder what ever happened to Thalia. You remember her?"

"Your Cyrenean friend?" Patron chuckled. "She was easy on the eyes. I'm sure she lived a fine life, Memnon. They say Aphrodite looks after her own, and she was every inch a suppliant of the goddess. Yes, I'd wager she did just fine."

"I pray she did." Memnon lapsed into silence, his body sagging. "Help me . . . back . . ."

Concern etched Patron's brow as he eased Memnon into bed and drew the covers over him. The Rhodian's fever-ravaged body weighed next to nothing; he looked like he'd been bled dry, so pale was he. Cracked lips mumbled thanks. "You should rest now, my friend," Patron said. "The spring campaign will begin before we know it. You need to be hearty and hale in order to bring destruction to the Macedonians."

Memnon nodded. He caught Patron's hand. "Should . . . Should something happen to me, I want control of the fleet to pass to Pharnabazus, until such a time as the Great King decides otherwise." The Rhodian pulled the older man closer. "Keep him on course for Euboea! Antipatros will doubtless send troops and money to dissuade him, even ships, if he can find them. The lad will need your guidance more than I ever did, especially if he's able to lure Alexander back to Pella."

"You'll both have my counsel, whether you want it or not," Patron said, smiling. "Is there anything you need?"

Memnon gestured to the equipment in the corner. "That chest," he said, breathing heavy. "Inside it there's a small silver casket, a coin box. Could you empty it and bring it to me? And my writing kit?"

"Then you'll rest?"

I will come soon, to guide you on your journey. Memnon sighed. "Then I will rest."

Patron found the items easily enough. The silver casket, inlaid with mother-of-pearl, held a small fortune in golden *darics*; he upended its contents into a leather bag. The writing kit was a gift from Khafre—an Egyptian *mestha*, a flat palm-wood box decorated with scenes of scribes serving the Lord of the Nile. Inside, it held papyrus, reed pens, and flasks of ink.

Memnon levered himself upright in bed as Patron brought these things to him. "Your nephews will be back this evening with Aristonymus. They'll want to see you, so make sure you're well rested." Patron leaned down, kissed Memnon's forehead. "You are as a brother to me, my friend." And then he was gone.

Memnon fought off a wave of despair. His hands trembled as he withdrew a sheet of papyrus, tacked it to the smooth surface of the *mestha*, and took up his reed pen. His brows knitted. Carefully, he wetted the pen in the ink and began:

Memnon to his love, Barsine, greetings . . .

By the time he ended his letter, the light was failing and Memnon barely had strength left to roll up the papyrus and place it in the silver casket, along with the ring of Hermeias. *Pharnabazus will see they reach her.* Shutting the lid, he sank back onto his pillow. *Zeus Savior, watch over them. Keep them safe and whole, and let them live good lives. Give them wisdom, Lord of Olympus.*

A golden glow brighter than the meager radiance of sunset played at the edges of his vision. *Rhodian*, said a familiar voice. *I have come.*

"I want to live," he said softly, closing his eyes.

You have, and you lived well. But now the thread is cut, child. It is time.

Memnon felt a ghostly hand on his shoulder, comforting and peaceful. Pain fled, replaced by exhaustion. He exhaled, and very quietly Memnon of Rhodes surrendered to the encroaching darkness . . .

Epilogue

Dawn broke over Ephesus, the sun rising into a cornflower blue sky. The warmth streaming through the window promised a mild day. From his bedside perch, Harmouthes rubbed his eyes and sighed. "Memnon never regained consciousness. He died the next day, toward evening, surrounded by his nephews and his friends. I have heard wild tales regarding the manner of his passing—everything from a poisoning plot cooked up by rival satraps to an assassin sent by Alexander's courtiers. It was fever, stemming from an infection of the wound he received at Halicarnassus. Nothing more.

"I consider his death to be the strongest evidence of Alexander's improbable luck. Without Memnon to divert the war to Macedonia, the Great King lost heart. Alexander could not be stopped. Darius fled from him at Issus, and again at Gaugamela; Egypt welcomed him as a god, Babylon as a liberator. The whole of Persia was his for the taking. But, there was one thing he could not conquer, one thing his prodigious luck could not overcome." His eyes moved to Barsine; the Egyptian touched his mistress's precious silver casket. "Alexander found this in her belongings some years later, in snowy Maracanda on the frontiers of Farthest Asia, and he had the temerity to open it." Harmouthes lifted the lid. Inside the casket, Ariston caught sight of a signet ring—Athena enthroned—along with a smallish leather bag and a roll of papyrus. Harmouthes removed this last and handed it to him. Age darkened the papyrus and it looked worn from the countless hundreds of miles it had traveled, never far from the Lady's heart. Carefully, the young Rhodian unrolled it.

It was Memnon's final letter.

Memnon to his love, Barsine, greetings. By the time this letter reaches you, the snows will have melted; field and forest will have received new raiment, discarding winter's grays and browns for the rich greens of springtime. And I know that as you read this, word will have already reached Susa of my death.

Do not despair, my love! There is nothing for it. Those cruel sisters, the Fates give and they take with little regard for fairness, weaving each life in patterns of their own inscrutable design. The same words you spoke to me at Ephesus on our last day together I speak now to you: no matter what, you must endure! Do and say what you must to survive, to ensure your own safety and that of our daughters. Kiss them for me, and give them my love. You must carry on, fair Penelope! Carry on where I have failed.

There is much I would say to you, dear wife. So much to tell, but too little time in which to tell it. You have given my life balance and purpose; your love has given me the strength to carry on when nothing else could have stirred me. In war, your memory has given me peace. I wish only that I could have kept my promise to you, to greet you and the children in Susa and fetch you back to Adramyttium, to live in peace by the sea. Know that I would give up everything to hear the sound of your voice once more, for one last glimpse of you, for a last touch, a final kiss. Time and distance are ever our enemies . . .

I love you with all my heart, Barsine, and I will never be far. You need only remember the summer nights at Adramyttium, the call of cicadas and the twinkling of fireflies, and I will be there. Farewell.

Scrawled at the bottom of the papyrus was a fragment Ariston recognized as being from Euripides:

Weep for those entering the world
Since such misfortune awaits them,
But raise joyful song over the dead
Whose sufferings are now at an end.

Ariston looked up, his eyes moist. With care he re-rolled the letter and returned it to the casket, closing the lid again with unaccustomed reverence.

"Afterward," Harmouthes continued, "Alexander put her aside—properly, for that was his way—sent her back to Nearer Asia and married instead the daughter of a Sogdian swineherd, an illiterate virgin, I am told."

"Why?"

The Egyptian rubbed his bald scalp. "Because for all his gifts, Alexander could not suffer being second in anyone's heart, and surely not a distant second. She loved Memnon, and Memnon alone."

Sunlight slipped through the window and crept across the bed. Golden radiance touched Barsine's face and suffused her pallid flesh with life. *She looks peaceful,* Ariston thought, *beautiful, even.* Lines of age and worry smoothed away; still, he could discern no movement. Her chest neither rose nor fell.

The Egyptian trembled; he reached out, placed his palm over her heart, and held it there. Nothing. The old man exhaled. "She has gone to him," he said. And crumpling beneath the weight of his grief, Harmouthes hid his face in age-spotted hands and wept.

ARISTON, SON OF THRASYLLUS, RETURNED TO RHODES, AFTER A BRIEF VISIT to Assos, in the spring, and settled on his father's estate at Lindos, on the southeastern shore of the island, to write his *Historiai Rhodos*. With him traveled an old Egyptian. Curiously, the men bore four ossuaries, which they laid to rest in a Persian-style garden at the crest of a hill overlooking the wine-dark waters of the Mediterranean Sea.

With his father, his brother, and with the woman he loved, Memnon, son of Timocrates, had returned to Rhodes . . .

END

Historical Note

CONJECTURE IS THE LIFEBLOOD OF THE HISTORICAL NOVEL, ESPECIALLY one dealing with a figure of antiquity. In the broad narrative of human existence Memnon of Rhodes appears as a mere footnote in the life of King Alexander III of Macedonia. As such, there has been only small interest from scholars, a cursory examination into the life of this Greek-born Persian aristocrat, which has raised more questions than it has provided answers.

Memnon's life is riddled with lacunae. We do not know, for instance, the names of his parents, or their social standing on the island of Rhodes. In extant sources he is never named by his patronymic, only by 'the Rhodian' or 'of Rhodes.' Timocrates of Rhodes is mentioned in Xenophon's *Hellenica* [III.5.1] and in the anonymous (but enlightening) *Hellenica Oxyrhynchia* [7.5] and I have preserved his deeds as they were recorded—plus one more: I made him Memnon's father due in large part to his association with the satrap Pharnabazus. Similarly, the name of Memnon's sister, the wife of Artabazus, is lost to the ages. The episodes of his youth, including the death of his father and the circumstances of his flight from Rhodes, are entirely fictional.

There is some evidence that Memnon had a wife prior to his marriage to Barsine. Arrian, in the first book, section fifteen, of his *Campaigns of*

Alexander, describes Memnon and his sons fighting in the van at the Granicus. But, because of a paucity of information I have chosen to overlook this previous wife and the children arising from the union. Instead, he fights at the Granicus with the sons of Artabazus.

In all the sources, much is made of Artabazus's age and of the size of his family. According to Quintus Curtius Rufus, he was ninety-five years old in 330 BCE and had fathered twenty-four children—two by a Persian wife and another twenty-two ostensibly by Memnon's sister (for no mention is made of other wives). Modern scholars like to dispute his age, saying ninety-five must surely be a mistranslation and fifty-five is probably closer to the mark. Still, I have chosen to follow Curtius Rufus's lead in making Artabazus older.

One of the most tantalizing gaps in Memnon's life is his exile to the court of Philip II of Macedonia. He vanishes from the historical record for a decade, which raises innumerable questions as to his dealings and movements during that period. How well did he come to know Alexander and the young men who would become Macedonia's generals? Did he fight in Philip's numerous border campaigns? Did he journey to Egypt and fight at his brother's side? By his character we can extrapolate he was not idle, but exactly *what* he did is open to interpretation. As with Memnon's youth, I have taken spectacular liberties, inventing associations and events for the sake of story. Hopefully, such highly fictitious scenes won't be too difficult for readers to accept.

Bibliography

Authors' names in **bold** indicate an ancient source.

Adkins, Lesley and Roy A. Adkins. *Handbook to Life in Ancient Greece*. Oxford: Oxford University Press, 1997.

Arrian. *The Campaigns of Alexander*. Trans. Aubrey de Sèlincourt, intro. and notes J.R. Hamilton. New York: Penguin Books, 1971.

Athanassakis, Apostolos N. *The Homeric Hymns*. Baltimore: The Johns Hopkins University Press, 1976.

Bunson, Margaret. *A Dictionary of Ancient Egypt*. Oxford: Oxford University Press, 1991.

Cartledge, Paul. *Alexander the Great*. New York: The Overlook Press, 2004.

Casson, Lionel. *The Ancient Mariners*. New York: The Macmillan Company, 1959.

Cook, J.M. *The Persian Empire*. New York: Barnes and Noble Books, 1983.

Davidson, James. *Courtesans and Fishcakes*. New York: HarperCollins

Publishers, 1997.

Diodorus Siculus. *Library of History*, vols. XVI and XVII. Trans. C. Bradford Welles. Cambridge: Harvard University Press (Loeb Classical Library), 1939.

Durando, Furio. *Greece: A Guide to the Archaeological Sites*. New York: Barnes and Noble Books, 2004.

Flacelière, Robert. *Life in Ancient Greece at the Time of Pericles*. Trans. Peter Green. London: Phoenix Press, 2002.

Fuller, J.F.C. *The Generalship of Alexander the Great*. Hertfordshire: Wordsworth Editions Limited, 1998.

Grant, Michael. *A Guide to the Ancient World*. New York: Barnes and Noble Books, 1997.

Graves, Robert. *The Greek Myths*, vols. 1 and 2. New York: Penguin Books, 1984.

Hammond, N.G.L. *The Genius of Alexander the Great*. Chapel Hill, NC: University of North Carolina Press, 1998.

Hanson, Victor Davis. *The Wars of the Ancient Greeks*. London: Cassell, 1999.

Hendricks, Rhoda A. *Classical Gods and Heroes*. New York: William Morrow, 1978.

Herodotus. *The Histories*. Trans. Aubrey de Sèlincourt. New York: Penguin Books, 1996.

Homer. *The Iliad*. Trans. Samuel Butler. New York: Barnes and Noble Books, 1995.

———. *The Odyssey*. Trans. Samuel Butler. New York: Pocket Books, 1997.

Houtzager, Guus. *The Complete Encyclopedia of Greek Mythology*. Edison, NJ: Chartwell Books, 2004.

Lane Fox, Robin. *Alexander the Great*. New York: Penguin Books, 1986.

McCoy, W.J. "Memnon of Rhodes at the Granicus." *American Journal of Philology*, vol. 110, 1989, pp. 413–433.

Plutarch. *The Age of Alexander*. Trans. Ian Scott-Kilvert. New York: Penguin Books, 1973.

Polyaenus. *Stratagems of War*, vols. 1 and 2. Ed. and trans. P. Krentz and I.L. Wheeler. Chicago: Ares Publishing, Inc., 1994.

Quintus Curtius Rufus. *The History of Alexander*. Trans. John Yardley, intro. and notes Waldemar Heckel. New York: Penguin Books, 1984.

Renault, Mary. *The Nature of Alexander*. New York: Pantheon Books, 1976.

Rhodes, P.J. *The Greek City States: A Source Book*. Norman, OK: University of Oklahoma Press, 1986.

Sacks, David. *A Dictionary of the Ancient Greek World*. Oxford: Oxford University Press, 1995.

Saunders, A.N.W. *Greek Political Oratory*. New York: Penguin Books, 1970.

Shaw, Ian, Ed. *The Oxford History of Ancient Egypt*. Oxford: Oxford University Press, 2000.

de Souza, Philip, Waldemar Heckel, and Lloyd Llewellyn-Jones. *The Greeks at War*. Oxford: Osprey Publishing, 2004.

Strabo. *Geography*, vols. 1–8. Trans. Horace Leonard Jones. Cambridge: Harvard University Press (Loeb Classical Library), 1969.

Tarn, W.W. *Hellenistic Civilization*. New York: New American Library, 1975.

Thucydides. *History of the Peloponnesian War*. Trans. Rex Warner, intro. and notes M.I. Finley. New York: Penguin Books, 1972.

Warry, John. *Warfare in the Classical World*. New York: Barnes and Noble Books, 2000.

Worley, Leslie J. *Hippeis: The Cavalry of Ancient Greece.* Boulder, CO: Westview Press, 1994.

Xenophon. *Anabasis.* Trans. Rex Warner, intro. and notes George Cawkwell. New York: Penguin Books, 1972.

———. *Hellenica.* Trans. Rex Warner, intro. and notes George Cawkwell. New York: Penguin Books, 1979.

———. *Minor Works.* Trans. E.C. Marchant and G.W. Bowersock. Cambridge: Harvard University Press (Loeb Classical Library), 1925.

Zimmerman, J.E. *Dictionary of Classical Mythology.* New York: Bantam Books, 1971.

Appendix I: A Chronology of Events

All dates are BCE (Before Common Era).

c. 375 Memnon is born on the island of Rhodes.

371 Epaminondas and the Thebans defeat the Spartans at the Battle of Leuctra, ending Spartan supremacy in Greece.

370 Death of King Amyntas III of Macedonia, father of Philip. His eldest son, Perdiccas III, succeeds him.

369 Young Philip held hostage at Thebes to insure good relations with Macedonia.

367 Birth of Pharnabazus by the Persian wife of Artabazus. In Macedonia, Ptolemy (Alexander's companion and the future king of Egypt) is born.

364 Barsine is born to the Persian wife of Artabazus. Her mother dies in childbirth.

362 Epaminondas is slain fighting the Spartans at Mantinea.

360 Artabazus marries Deidamia, the daughter of his lifelong friend Timocrates of Rhodes; Timocrates' eldest son, Mentor, enters the satrap's service that same year. Death of King Agesilaus of Sparta. In Macedonia, Philotas son of Parmenion is born.

359 In Macedonia, King Perdiccas III is slain in battle; his younger brother, Philip, ascends the throne as King Philip II; late in the year, Kassandros son of Antipatros is born.

358 Death of King Artaxerxes II. His son, Ochus, becomes King Artaxerxes III. He orders his western satraps to disband their private armies; orders Artabazus to present himself before the throne at Susa. Artabazus refuses, goes into open rebellion. In the Aegean, Mausolus of Caria sparks the Social War by convincing Cos, Chios, and Byzantion to leave the Athenian Confederation. The Athenians respond by dispatching a fleet of sixty triremes under Chares and Chabrias.

357 Rhodes joins the rebellion against Athens; Timocrates of Rhodes is slain in factional fighting. His son, Memnon, joins Artabazus's rebellion at Assos. The Athenian fleet is destroyed off Embata by the combined forces of Cos and Chios. Chabrias is slain and Chares limps away to Imbros. In Asia, Mithridates of Dascylium is ordered to subdue Artabazus. Philip of Macedon marries Olympias, a princess of Epiros.

356 Artabazus rescues Chares and the Athenians from Imbros; he hires them to form the core of his mercenary army. The satrap also secures the services of a band of Boeotian mercenaries led by Pammenes. In Macedonia, Alexander is born to Philip and Olympias. At Assos, Thymondas is born to Mentor's Rhodian mistress.

355 Battle of Lake Manyas; Mithridates is defeated and Dascylium returns to Artabazus's control. Carian troops occupy Cos and Rhodes. Tithraustes, Ochus's right-hand man, is sent west against Artabazus; Ochus also dispatches a letter to Athens demanding Chares' recall and that peace be established with the rebellious islands.

354 The Social War ends. Late in the year, the eunuch Hermeias leads a coup against his master, Eubulus of Assos. Hermeias then becomes tyrant of much of the Troad. In Macedonia, Philip loses an eye at the siege of Methone, a town on the border of Macedonia and Thessaly.

353 Mentor flees to Egypt; Artabazus and Memnon, with their families, seek asylum at the court of Philip of Macedon. Philip is twice defeated in Thessaly by Onomarchus.

352 Philip returns to Thessaly, defeats and kills Onomarchus at the Battle of Crocus Field. In Asia, Mausolus of Caria dies; his sister-wife, Queen Artemisia II, succeeds him. She begins construction of the Mausoleum (one of the Seven Wonders of the World).

351 At Athens, Demosthenes advocates an anti-Macedonian stance in his *First Philippic*.

350 Pharaoh Nectanebo of Egypt sends Mentor with four thousand mercenaries to the aid of King Tennes of Sidon against the Persian satraps Belesys of Syria and Mazaeus of Cilicia. Mentor sends for Memnon to be his lieutenant.

348 Philip seizes Olynthus in the Chalcidice and razes it.

347 Death of the philosopher Plato. Aristotle leaves Athens and settles at Assos and near Mytilene on Lesbos. His friend Hermeias becomes his patron.

346 Ochus marches on Phoenicia. Mentor discovers Tennes' planned betrayal and turns the tables on him, offering Ochus Sidon, Phoenicia, *and* Egypt in exchange for his service. Philip and Athens make peace (the Peace of Philocrates). The aging philosopher Isocrates pens his *Address to Philip*.

345 Memnon is sent back to Macedon. Barsine is betrothed to Mentor, pending the outcome of the Egyptian campaign.

344 Demosthenes delivers his *Second Philippic*. Alexander tames Boukephalos. Memnon joins Parmenion in Thrace as a mercenary.

343 Aristotle becomes Alexander's tutor at Mieza. Mentor is successful in Egypt; Ochus makes him Supreme Commander of the West. Artabazus and Memnon are recalled to Persia. Barsine marries Mentor at Sardis.

342 Memnon captures Hermeias and takes control of the Troad through trickery. The eunuch is sent to Susa to be executed.

341 Philip conquers Thrace. At Athens, Demosthenes delivers his *Third Philippic.*

340 Death of Mentor of Rhodes. Memnon becomes lord of the Troad; he marries Barsine at Adramyttium. Philip besieges Perinthus and Byzantion. Late in the year Athens declares war on Philip.

338 King Artaxerxes III Ochus is assassinated by his vizier, the eunuch Bagoas, who then elevates Ochus's youngest son, Oarses, to the throne. In Greece, Philip and Alexander crush a combined Greek army at Chaeronea. Egypt goes into rebellion once more.

336 Bagoas kills Oarses, then is himself dispatched by Artashata, the satrap of Armenia, who ascends the throne as Darius III. Philip sends an advance force across the Hellespont into Asia. Later in the year, Philip II of Macedon is assassinated by an ex-lover while attending the wedding of his daughter Cleopatra to King Alexandros of Epiros (Olympias's brother). Alexander is proclaimed King of Macedon.

335 Destruction of Thebes. Darius tasks Memnon with stopping the Macedonians; he defeats Parmenion, forcing him back to his bridgehead at Abydus on the Straits. Aristotle returns to Athens and starts a philosophical school, the Lyceum.

334 Alexander crosses into Asia. The Persians marshal at Zeleia; ignoring Memnon's advice, the Persian satraps meet Alexander at the river Granicus and are defeated. Memnon is then given supreme command over the Persian army and navy. He sends envoys to the Spartans to form an alliance with the intent of invading Macedonia as a way of drawing Alexander away from Asia. Siege of Halicarnassus; Memnon wounded during a sortie. Persians withdraw into the Aegean.

333 Memnon dies suddenly, from a fever brought on by his wound, at the siege of Mytilene, on the island of Lesbos. Upon hearing news of his death, Darius musters his forces and meets Alexander at Issus. The Persians are defeated. Barsine, along with numerous members of the royal family, is captured at Damascus.

Appendix II: On Currency

THE USE OF STANDARDIZED METAL COINAGE BEGAN IN THE MID–seventh century BCE in Asia Minor, in the region known as Lydia (modern Turkey). These first coins were flattened pebbles of electrum, a naturally occurring alloy of silver and gold, bearing the stamp of the issuing authority—generally a stylized lion representing the Lydian king—on one side and a punch mark on the other. The Greeks of the Aegean coast of Asia Minor were quick to adopt this new currency and by 575 BCE the use of coins had spread throughout the Greek world.

Later coins were minted of pure gold or silver, stamped on both sides, and often displayed patriotic or religious designs. Each *polis* (city-state) reserved the right to issue its own currency, thus making trade between *poleis* a complicated affair due to variations in their standard weights (differing sometimes by as little as a fraction of a gram). Finally, around 449 BCE, Athens issued a decree to its allies and client states barring them from using anything but Athenian coinage, weights, and measures. For simplicity's sake, *Memnon* makes use of the Athenian system, formally known as the Euboic-Attic standard.

Because of the scarcity of gold on the Greek mainland most coins were of silver—a commodity Athens had a plentiful supply of thanks to the nearby mines of Laurium. The smallest silver coin was the ***obol.*** Six *obols* equaled one ***drachma***; one hundred *drachmas* equaled a ***mina***, and sixty *minas* (or six thousand *drachmas*) equaled one ***talent***, about fifty-eight pounds of silver. The two larger denominations existed only as units of accounting or for assessing the worth of bulk goods; no *mina* or *talent* coins were ever produced. Mints, called *argyrokopeion*, turned out a variety of coins including the ***didrachm***, or two-*drachma* piece, also known as the ***stater***, and the ***tetradrachm***, or four-*drachma* piece. By the fourth century BCE, the Athenians were also producing bronze or copper coins, called ***chalkoi***, to represent the smallest denominations. Twelve *chalkoi* equaled a single *obol.* One other coin favored by the Greeks was the Persian ***daric***—a type of gold coin first minted circa 512 BCE by King Darius I. Renowned for its purity, the *daric* was easily worth twenty Greek *drachmas.*

Though direct comparisons are impossible, in a modern context the 'minimum wage' for an unskilled laborer in Memnon's era was one-and-a-half *drachmas* a day (nine *obols*). A pint-and-a-half of the lowest-quality wine could be had for one *obol*; the same measure of fine wine, perhaps from Chios, cost as much as fourteen *drachmas.* A full set of hoplite armor would set a man back two to three hundred *drachmas.* Horses cost anywhere from five hundred to six thousand *drachmas*; contrast this price to that of Alexander's Boukephalos, for which Philip was rumored to have paid the astronomical sum of eighteen thousand *drachmas* (three *talents*), a substantial fortune by anyone's reckoning.

Appendix III: On the Greek Calendar

It's especially difficult to define an event from antiquity by our modern calendar due to the great discrepancy in the way the ancients recorded time. The Greeks, for example, had no one system for marking the passage of months and years. Each *polis* kept at least two calendars—its original lunar calendar and a civil calendar in sync with the solar year—and different regions often started their calendar years at different times. In Attica, Athens and its environs, the New Year began in the modern month of July, while Macedonians began their year in October. The Ionian Greeks of Asia Minor had their own system of reckoning time, no doubt influenced by their long association with Persia and the East; I imagine Memnon himself would have been most familiar with the Ionian calendar. Yet, for simplicity, I have opted to use the Athenian system in *Memnon*, as it is the best known.

The Greek year was comprised of twelve months, each with an alternating number of days, either twenty-nine or thirty. Because of its lunar origins, magistrates and city fathers found it necessary to insert extra days—known as intercalation—in order to reconcile their civic calendars with the solar year. The names of the months, and their approximate modern equivalents, were as follows:

Hekatombaion (June/July)
Metageitnion (July/August)
Boedromion (August/September)
Pyanopsion (September/October)
Maimakterion (October/November)
Poseideon (November/December)
Gamelion (December/January)
Anthesterion (January/February)
Elaphebolion (February/March)
Mounichion (March/April)
Thargelion (April/May)
Skirophorion (May/June)

By Memnon's time, Greek historians were using the quadrennial Olympic Games, held in honor of Zeus at Olympia in the western Peloponnese, as a benchmark for dating events unfolding in the wide Hellenic world. Each four-year cycle between Games was known as an "Olympiad," and they were numbered from the first—held in 776 BCE.

As the premiere Pan-Hellenic festival, the Games were of incalculable importance to all Greeks, not just athletes. To Olympia came the most influential men in the known world, statesmen and generals, poets and artists. By religious decree all hatreds and animosities were put aside for the duration of the Games, so that even states engaged in an active conflict (such as Athens and Sparta during the Peloponnesian War) could compete side by side and in relative peace. It made sense to historians, then, that they should mark the passage of time from the inaugural Olympic festival, making it Year One of the First Olympiad.

But, by the late fourth century BCE, after the conquests of Alexander the Great brought Egypt and the East under Greek control, the superior systems of the Egyptians and Babylonians were adapted for use with the Macedonian/Greek calendar, and reckoning by Olympiads fell into disuse.

Don't miss Scott Oden's first novel from Medallion Press now available in paperback format:

MEN OF BRONZE

scott oden

★ Publishers Weekly Starred Review!

"Oden's masterful story of bloody battles, political intrigues, betrayal and romance offers a gripping portrait of the collapse of an empire."
— *Publishers Weekly*

"Sing, O Goddess, of the ruin of Egypt . . ."

It is 526 B.C. and the empire of the Pharaohs is dying, crushed by the weight of its own antiquity. Decay riddles its cities, infects its aristocracy, and weakens its armies. While across the expanse of Sinai, like jackals drawn to carrion, the forces of the King of Persia watch . . . and wait.

Leading the fight to preserve the soul of Egypt is Hasdrabal Barca, Pharaoh's deadliest killer. Possessed of a rage few men can fathom and fewer can withstand, Barca struggles each day to preserve the last sliver of his humanity. But, when one of Egypt's most celebrated generals, a Greek mercenary called Phanes, defects to the Persians, it triggers a savage war that will tax Barca's skills, and his humanity, to the limit. From the political wasteland of Palestine, to the searing deserts east of the Nile, to the streets of ancient Memphis, Barca and Phanes play a desperate game of cat-and-mouse — a game culminating in the bloodiest battle of Egypt's history.

Caught in the midst of this violence is Jauharah, a slave in the House of Life. She is Arabian, dark-haired and proud — a healer with gifts her blood, her station, and her gender overshadow. Though her hands tend to Barca's countless wounds, it is her spirit that heals and changes him. Once a fearsome demigod of war, Hasdrabal Barca becomes human again. A man now motivated as much by love as anger.

Nevertheless honor and duty have bound Barca to the fate of Egypt. A final conflict remains, a reckoning set to unfold in the dusty hills east of Pelusium. There, over the dead of two nations, Hasdrabal Barca will face the same choice as the heroes of old: Death and eternal fame . . .

Or obscurity and long life . . .

ISBN#1932815856
ISBN#9781932815856
Gold Imprint
US $6.99 / CDN $9.99
Historical Fiction
Available Now
www.scottoden.com